THE RISEN PRINCE

THE DEMONIC COMPENDIUM BOOK 1

DAVID VIERGUTZ

Building a relationship with my readers is the very best thing about writing. I send newsletters with details on new releases, writer-life, deals and other bits of news related to my books. And if you sign up to my mailing list I'll send you something I think you'll like, my terrifying novella, *Peel*.

Details can be found at the back of this book.

Lands of
The Demonic Compendium

CHAPTER ONE

SHAW WAS LOOKING FOR SOMETHING. Something that did not want to be found. Something that could lose itself. Something harmless on the outside, yet of terrible and awesome power within.

Shaw was looking for a book.

He hated even the notion that such an object had this much of a hold on him. Since the Book had brought him back, he owed it a debt and this deal was signed and sealed in blood. The Book offered him his life in exchange for a task not yet revealed to him and if the Book could bring him back, maybe it could bring his wife back as well.

He stared east across the Valor, its mighty flow raging south until it broke against the Bone Bottom Crags many leagues away. The Valor was much like the Book; cold and absolute in the middle, yet peaceful at its borders.

"Where are you?" Shaw mouthed. A light throb on his left forearm indicated a snide remark from the demon imprisoned within it was imminent. Shaw pulled back his sleeve to examine it.

Perhaps it is at the bottom of the river. Why not swim for it? A shrill, disembodied voice replied in his head. Shaw shifted his gaze away from the froth and rolling waves to the cracks of the shallow dock and into the river below.

"Perhaps it's still in the Far East…that last King's Guardsman thought so," he spoke aloud.

He told you what you wanted to hear; we cannot rely on the word of a dying man.

"But we can rely on the word of a living demon?" Shaw questioned, somewhat taken aback by his own retort; *was this demon considered alive?*

He examined the three rubies embedded in his arm. Inside the center ruby, a magpie with too many eyes stared back at him.

The gems pulsed again, this time painfully.

You imprisoned me. But I am the one you say cannot be trusted. The magpie hopped back and in a swirl of red dust disappeared. The gems resumed their usual amber glow.

His own face stared back at him. He breathed deep and rolled down his sleeve. Turning on his heels he walked back towards town, leaving the Valor raging and frothing behind him. The shallow dock was a testament to his quest, empty and bare. He opened up his stride and pulled his hooded tunic over his head, disguising himself. On the Fringe, swarming with refugees, thieves, outlaws, beggars, and the discarded, hiding one's own face was expected. His footsteps fell heavily on cobblestone as he left the dock and pushed through the crowded side street. The roar of the river faded as the sound of trade and commerce steadily rose. When he arrived at the center of town, the early morning sun was already blocked by the market banners. The center-facing huts stared down at him suspiciously. The Fringe was aptly named for the way of life here. Most lived on the edge of poverty and others preyed on that same poverty, all of which was centered on the market.

The market was unusually crowded, and the traders were

out en masse. Some yelled above others, holding fish and weaponry and clothing. Others carefully guarded their wares, eyeing customers as the buildings did, suspiciously. Shaw flashed a half-hearted smile under his hood. A large scar, running the length of his face to the bottom of his neck, ached in response. It was a painful reminder of bestowing trust where it was not earned. He moved towards the western side of the market, used a handful of silver coins to purchase a small, deer-skin water-bag and sat in the archway of a crumbling church; one of many on the Fringe. Shaw contemplated the surge of people in the market and remembered a Great Barge was to arrive today from the Far East, carrying refugees, trade-spice and other goods. He was not interested in these things, what he needed was information…

He felt a small tug on the bottom of his tunic. He looked down upon a small boy, skinny and dirt-ridden. Unfortunately, the Fringe was not well-known for taking care of its own. It was a hub for trade and travel, but the poorest of poor also make home here, with alleys, ruins and a host of surrounding trees to retreat to.

"Silver for a poem?" the boy said, looking up, his hopeful, toothy grin peeking through his overgrown head of hair. Shaw smiled back, tossed a silver coin from his pocket and waved at the boy to continue.

The boy stood up proudly and took in a chest full of air. "A King sat high, poised and proud…"

"…Another, boy…" Shaw interrupted.

"Shipwreck, shipwreck on the Valor…"

"…Another…"

The boy furrowed his brow, "I know of one other, kind sir, it's a new one I've just heard."

"Go on with it, and if I have heard it I'll surely retrieve my silver".

"Written in fire, bound in blood…" the boy whispered.

Shaw's eyes widened in surprise.

"A demon's word, buried in mud. A beggar's hand grasping tight, two royal children, got up to fight. One of royal blood remains, the other gone, throne of shame." The boy continued, picking up speed.

Shaw stood up, sliding his hand across the gems in his arm.

Wake up, he thought.

"A common name, they once held. A mighty blade of demon weld."

Demon, awaken, he bellowed in his head, never taking his eyes off the small boy who seemed in a trance, lost in his own words.

*I love when you take charge, t*he bird squawked. The magpie appeared in the center of the three gems, beak open, head tilted slightly as if confused.

Listen.

"On the Line, one did tread, men in boots, bound in thread," the boy continued, taking a gingerly step towards him.

"Black spires black spires raise the night, TWO DEAD BOYS GOT UP TO FIGHT," the boy screamed.

"Compendium lost, you can't find. Before dark on land, becomes dark of mind."

The boy backpedaled a step as the poem came to an end, turned around in a flash of ragged clothing, and leapt into a full sprint. He ducked below a horse drawn cart of exotic looking fruits and continued to pick up speed. Maniacal laughter bounced between the walls of the buildings lining the street as Shaw picked up the pursuit. The boy dodged and weaved through the herd of people shuffling towards the center of town. Shaw was quick, but this boy was quicker. Shaw vaulted another hand cart and continued on, the boy on the edge of his view, his small black-haired head bobbing up and down as he ran. Slowly, the boy's head became a distant speck. Shaw was tall and limber but he was no match for the boy's stamina. Sweat poured from his brow with the rising temperature. He slowed down and removed his outer tunic, leaving a thinner green one in place, also equipped with a hood.

Aging well I see, Shaw, the magpie quipped, its sharp tones piercing the sounds of his own heartbeat in his ears.

"Shut-up, the boy knows about the Compendium," he thought.

That was the Compendium, taunting you. It knows you are looking for it.

Shaw drank deeply from the waterskin. It was cold and refreshing and helped his dry throat.

"I'll find it. It has the answers we need."

We have bigger concerns, the bird squawked.

The gems throbbed and he pulled up his sleeve. The magpie was no longer in the center gem but was now squeezed into the ruby farthest up his arm. It pressed its head tightly against the surface, and its eyes bulged in their sockets. The other two gems lay dark and dormant.

He caught his breath and plopped down in the shadow of a stone archway. Blood-red lettering defaced the stone, catching his eye. "The King, our redemption from filth" it read. Even in the Fringe, where a cutthroat is welcomed and a beggar shunned, there was still disdain for the King. He was to blame for the rapid decay of the Kingdom after all. He took a moment and heaved himself to his feet, dusting off his tunic. He shifted his belt, keeping mental note of where the boy disappeared from view. It would not likely be useful information. The boy was just a boy, and the Compendium had easily overpowered his will.

"Demon, have you heard that poem before?"

I have not, he mused. *If it was written in the Book, it is unlikely anyone has heard or read it before. It appears differently to its readers.*

He sighed. "We must find somewhere we won't be bothered."

The ruined church north of the shallow dock is frequently empty, the magpie replied.

Shaw moved purposefully, cutting through the north half of the market to the main road dividing the eastern and western halves of the Fringe. The eastern half featured the shallow dock and the Valor waterfront, the western half was comprised of homes and slums. The life of the town was focused on the market which clogged the crossroads for travelers from mid-morning until sunset. Without the market, the Fringe would be a place where the unwanted would go to die. Here, he felt at home.

He passed through one of the many alleys, stepping over someone sleeping in the dirt and turned the corner of the building. The spire of the church came into view and rose above the huts as he walked, a decaying bell drooped to one side in the tower held by a frayed rope. He came upon the entryway of the church and stepped over two boards half-heartedly blocking the door. Inside the church, only a few pews remained and those that did were discolored from mold and moisture. He walked between the rows of remaining pews, imagining that at one point people of faith must have gathered here to worship their god. He bowed instinctively before the lectern and stepped up, aiming for the priest door leading to the spire. Light poured in from broken-out windows and highlighted various holes in the floor. At one point beautiful portraits of stained glass would have filled the vacant slots. Now, the hot afternoon sun bled into the church, illuminating the decay.

Why did you do that? the magpie asked softly.

"I don't know, it seemed appropriate," Shaw said.

Who, or what, are you bowing to?

"A god, if there is one."

There is no god, and if there were, would he approve of your actions... Arbiter? The magpie hissed.

"Shut-up."

-consorting with demons, rising from the dead, sabotage, revenge....murder...and just to be clear, there are three gods...

"ENOUGH!" he bellowed aloud. Enraged by the demon's mocking, questioning tone, his fists were clenched tight, pale and shaking. The small rubble about his feet had begun to vibrate and the light within the church began to dim. He realized his throat burned as his anger began to manifest.

Easy now, the magpie chuckled.

He pulled in his breath with purpose and unclenched his hands. Shortly after his anger dissipated, he was able to relax his body. He glanced beyond the lectern and forced himself to ignore the demon's temporary win and made for the narrow stone stairs leading to the choir loft. He climbed the winding stairs and stepped out onto the platform where another set of pews sat crumbling in the corner. The platform, however, remained clear. He had frequently rested here in the past. He stepped to the center of the platform and crouched. He held up a finger in the light, focused in on it, and pressed a small amount of energy from the well within him. The gems pulsed as he focused intently on his fingertip, willing the energy, feeling its warmth travel down his arm. The room shivered around him, then faded in on itself. The energy flowed more freely now, like the gates of a dam opening. He countered with his own inner strength and held the flood back. The gems pulsed again as he pressed his finger to the last gem where the magpie was waiting to open its beak. It filled the rim of the gem with twisting darkness until only a black window remained.

He backed his finger out of the gem and the world came to. He squinted at the tip where a hair-thin swirl of smoke danced in a non-existent wind.

With his other hand, he removed a hand-drawn map from his breast pocket and unfolded it. On it was a depiction of the Fringe, the surrounding forest, the trade routes, Second City to the west, the barren wastes to the Far East, and the Ruins of

Third City to the south. And to the north, outlined in a massive blood-red X, was Stonehaven. Shaw laid the smoky thread along the map, which flung itself to a small dot on the Fringe, marking his location. The thread writhed like a worm before stretching east across the Valor, rising north and resting upon a small dot moving westward through the ocean, beyond the Maw to the entrance to the Valor...

As the dot moved, the line moved with it, marking the closest route between the two objects. The spell tracked the nearest magical essence and this one appeared to be on a Great Barge. Farther south along the Valor another dot moved near the Fringe.

He slapped the map together at the folds and shoved it back in his pocket. The Great Barge he'd been waiting for was approaching the Fringe and he wanted to interrogate its passengers for information from the Far East. He climbed down the spire, exited the church, and took the main trade route heading south into the town. He picked up his pace and the magpie clicked its beak with his footsteps. Of course, Shaw was the only one who could hear the magpie. The magpie took advantage of their internal connection.

"Stop that," Shaw thought to the bird in annoyance.

What do you suppose is on that Great Barge?

"Hopefully, information. My contact from the Far East said she'd be aboard this particular ship according to her message from a week ago. She sent an enchanted magpie, how fitting."

He recalled the magpie, which was fatter and only had two bulging eyes. When it arrived at the church through an open window, it jumped furiously on his head until he awoke, then vomited a small piece of parchment with four words on it into his hand. "Two weeks, Great Barge." Once he read the message, the bird attempted to swallow the parchment again and after struggling for several minutes, managed to get it down. The magpie hopped once before exploding with a small squeak and a pop in a cloud of feathers and blood.

Whoever she is, she is a very powerful mage. We need to be careful, replied the magpie, revolting slightly at the memory as if it was personally offended.

He ignored the bird.

What do you suppose is on the other Barge? it asked.

"Something not so terrible yet still fulfilling enough for you." The demon hadn't fed in weeks. Generally, the larger and more powerful the creature, the more energy the demon could replenish, reflected by the glow of the three rubies embedded within his arm. The more he drew from the demon's power, the weaker they both became. If he drew too much, the consequences were permanent.

It will never come to that, as long as you do not lose control, Arbiter, snapped the demon.

Shaw pushed on excitedly at the prospect of new information. He'd been on the Fringe for weeks. Since he'd awoken, he'd hoped for something, anything, to indicate the location of the Compendium. He pushed past merchants and others traveling the stone path heading south into the town. He turned abruptly eastbound and crested a small hill overlooking the shallow dock. Mid-afternoon winds blew hot across his face. He squinted against them, and rising above the swell of the river, he saw a thick wooden mast jutting toward the sky. The expected Great Barge was approaching quickly. Unlike some of the smaller travel vessels, Great Barges were loaded for bear and could be operated with magical assistance and a minimal crew of five. The Barges themselves were not magical; the captain directing the ship would use his powers to direct the wind. Shaw believed his contact from the Far East to be one of the five-hundred passengers tightly packed into the bowels of the ship. Unfortunately, he did not know which of the five-hundred she was...

He followed the crammed side-street and arrived on the main road within earshot of the shallow dock. Crowds had begun to shift from the central market to the dock. The life of the Fringe revolved around its trade along the river and the Great Barge was a sign of new wares. The Valor ran a deep, salt-water current from the mighty seascape to the north, splitting the barren wastes of the Far East and the Fringe. The river was strong, and vessels required extreme man-power to operate their manual oars and were often staffed by slaves, who were considered expendable. The slaves powered through the current until they passed out or died of exertion only to be replaced just as quickly. The Great Barges, on the other hand, were impressive, affordable, and relatively safe for common passengers.

The ship was within eyeshot and showed no signs of slowing. The ship glided swiftly across the surface of the swell, parting small waves to either side. Its triple sails flapped in the wind and then filled with a gust of air. The steady creak of heavy oaken boards shifting, the flapping of the ship's massive silver sails, and the slapping of waves against its broadside was settling. Above all the noise and the hustle on the crowded dock, a deep reverberating tone shook the air around him. The captain was calling the wind.

CHAPTER TWO

DEEP BELOW DECK, where the oceanic river waves did not take such a toll on his stomach, Cereal mopped the deck of an already wet boat. It felt silly to him, as the boat itself was constantly taking on water. When he asked the Master about it, he was slapped across the face and told to keep mopping. Begrudgingly, he mopped side to side between the shelves lining either side of the ship. The ship, called a Great Barge, was roomy, but that was for a reason. The Great Barge could transport two types of supplies: slaves or goods. Cereal was a slave, and he was tasked with mopping the deck with the supplies. He wiped sweat and grime from his forehead. It could be worse. Down below, slaves worse off than he manned giant oars designed to power through the waves and current of the Valor. Each side of the ship could seat thirty rowers and there was at least one replacement ready per rower.

It was quickly determined Cereal was too scrawny to row and so he was assigned to various tasks about the ship. He kept his head down, and his ears open. Long ago, he learned how much speaking out of turn could hurt. He was not always a slave. Once he was the son of a blacksmith, learning the trade and even learning to read and write Common. But when the King slaughtered his parents in the streets of Stonehaven, he was left to wander, alone. After traveling south through the Kingdom for some time, he was eventually caught by head-hunters looking for unclaimed orphans and sold on the Fringe to work the Great Barges, delivering goods to far off kingdoms and more.

Surprisingly, he'd gained weight since he'd boarded the ship. They had to keep the slaves fed in order to get them to work. He dumped a bucket of soiled water out a view port and ran a new bucket from a valve on a barrel as tall as the roof of the floor above. He dunked the mop in the bucket again and began working on the second half of the floor. He mopped alongside and around all the wares and the endless shelves filling the bowels of the ship. He dared not try to open them, else the Master would simply throw him overboard to drown or be eaten by something with scales. Cereal was simply biding his time. The ship was traveling north, powering through the Valor using men and spells to travel upriver. Soon enough, they'd port along the Maw, a basin with a rising whirlpool in the center and calm waters along its borders. Once they did, and the Master and the slaves went to sleep, Cereal would escape. He'd find a way back to the Kingdom, seek out the King and make him pay.

The Master came below deck again, holding a lash and a rod. His bald head almost touched the ceiling and Cereal had personally seen the man toss a crate loaded with spices across the room in anger. He hoped the man was only coming to bark more orders at him or to give him a few scraps of food. In the worst of times, the man would simply abuse and torment him out of boredom. If the King were not already on the top of his list, the Master would easily take his place.

He wandered over to the section of floor where Cereal was mopping, replacing the salt water on the floor with fresh water. The Master stopped in the area he had yet to mop, bent over at the waist and rubbed a fat grubby finger over the floor. He opened his mouth and shoved it in, lolling his tongue around it and smacking his lips.

"Missed a spot, boy," he said, grinning through his half toothless mouth.

"I have yet to mop there, Master," Cereal replied, keeping his eyes on the deck.

"That'll be ten lashes for your cheek," he said, slapping his lash against a wooden crate.

"Please, I just haven't mopped there. I'll mop there now," Cereal cried.

"Too late boy, you are too slow."

The Master pulled the mop from Cereal's hands and tossed it aside, then pulled his smock up and over his head, exposing his back. Cereal braced himself for the lash, waiting for the white-hot pain to scar his back, adding to what the King had left him not too long ago. He heard the lash whisk through the air behind him, and he flinched every time. In the silence, between the rocking of the boat, and the gentle slap of the waves against its broadsides, someone below deck screamed. It was muffled, but loud enough that the Master took an interest.

He looked at the boy. "We will continue this when I return."

He swung the lash through the air over Cereal's head and then lumbered towards the stairs to the lower deck on the far end of the ship. By the time he reached it, more screams and panicked voices could be heard as well as scampering feet. If people were running on the lower deck, that meant people had stopped rowing, and the Master was going to be even angrier.

Cereal retrieved the mop from the other side of the room, dunked it in the fresh water and continued mopping. For now, someone had the Master's attention. Or something...

CHAPTER THREE

THE MASSIVE SHIP was picking up speed. The gut-churning sound of the captain's spell shook the ground again, sending the crowd into a panic. Magic was well known to the land and there were many types of it. Those who used it were looked at no differently than those who practiced other dangerous trades. The spell the captain was using to call the wind was different. It felt dirty, like a fine grit on a pane of glass. Shaw kept his eyes on the Barge as it moved ever quicker through the water and pointed directly at the shallow dock. The murmur of the crowd turned to screams as onlookers realized the Barge was not slowing.

Shaw removed his tunic, revealing his identifying red hair and emerald eyes, unafraid; he'd be lost within the crowd. His stomach turned over as the captain's spell carried from the ship, across the water and to his ears. The ship-turned-battering-ram was powering through the Valor's current and barreling straight towards the shallow dock and the market square beneath. The ships sails were still and blocked out the mid-day sun. The unholy groan of powerful black magic flooded the air. Another guttural moan shook the cobblestone beneath his feet. He needed to act. Stopping the destruction that the boat was about to cause was impossible, but he still needed to get on board to find out what was releasing such foul magic. His energy was low, so whatever move he made, it needed to be minimal and precise. He thought about potential solutions in his head. He considered leaping onto the ship from below. Or attaching himself to the side and climbing aboard. Or just blasting a hole in the hull.

The third option is best, the magpie said, apparently sensing the commotion.

"Get out of my head."

We are beyond that; we have a special bond, you and I. I remember this one time, your wife appeared in your sleep, a beautiful woman by the way, dressed in a lovely purple slip. Her lady bits peeking through as she walked towards you, sprawled out in a pile of hay and horse dung...

"Demon, enough!" Shaw said aloud, blushing and reeling at the memory. It was true; the demon had access to his dreams and thoughts. It just did not need to make it so obvious it was watching.

The bystanders had almost completely evacuated the shallow dock. A few stragglers attempted to collect their things. Something caught his eye; a hooded figure, walking away from the scene, southbound out of the city.

In all this panic, that individual remains calm...That's more concerning than the ship, he thought.

The last of the crowd dispersed to various perceived points of safety. At this speed, the Barge would plant itself in the middle of the market common, destroying everything in its path as the wooden hull slammed through it all, breaking up as it came. He scanned his surroundings and allowed each option and many possible outcomes to flash through his mind once more. Finally, a most grim thought sparked an idea; he decided to consult the demon. This time, he'd need its help.

No, Pemazu said.

"It's the only way, he replied and lifted his gemmed arm to point at the ship. We need the Captain."

No. To do what you are thinking will leave you powerless to handle the Captain if he is something otherworldly.

"I've made the decision and we're out of damn options."

Walking the Thin Line this weak and in the middle of the Fringe? You have truly lost your mind, Arbiter.

"It'll take some time before we're sensed on the Line. By the time we have company, we'll have returned with the survivors and closed the Gateway."

You would risk an open Gateway for the mere possibility of information? The magpie's shrill voice pierced his ears. He'd had enough.

"Pemazu, open the damn Gateway!"

He slid his hand across the cool face of the familiar gems, and they pulsed in response to his touch. He had used the demon's true name, compelling it to action, bending it to his will. He saw the magpie appear to choke on something; its face was bulbous, and its neck feathers flared. The bird opened its mouth wide, as if to swallow the red of the gem from the inside. Black tar-like essence filled the three gems and Shaw's arm began to ache. He faced the Barge, its pointed bow now piercing the sun like a spear. The scent of sea-water, fish and sodden wood swamped the air. Shaw reared back, unlocking the dam within his mind which held back the building essence. He whipped his arm in an arc towards the incoming ship. Black demon-fire erupted from his hand in the form of a whip and snapped at the air, tearing a hole in the fabric of reality. The gaping maw of black he created steadily grew in size to match the ship. Swirling smoke formed along the brim of the Gateway as light itself was compressed and emptied into the void. He stood behind the Gateway, peering into its vast emptiness. The ship smacked the shallow dock and, in a shower of sea-water, various loading boxes and other deck-born supplies were tossed into the air. The Barge was not fazed by the structure and crested the stone ramp instead, exiting the water and gouging the ground.

As the ship made landfall, the Captain's song immediately began to wane, ending the slimy tones of black magic that filled the air. The Gateway appeared as a huge black pillar against the wooden backdrop of the ship. A mighty groan and the sound like a felled tree indicated the hull had failed against the stone ramp. Shaw stood motionless behind the Gateway as the bow entered the portal which hungrily accepted the remaining ship as it continued to move forward on momentum alone. As if it were entering a dark cave, the ship vanished in one smooth pass into the void beyond. Viewing the ship enter the Gateway from the opposite side was impossible, it did not function that way. He relaxed and let out a small sigh, not realizing he had been holding his breath. He looked at the Gateway, hoping he'd made the right decision.

Too late now, whispered the magpie. *Onward, walk the Line again, and remember, stay too long, and things far worse than me will eventually come looking.*

Shaw was very familiar with Gateways and the horrors that they led to. He thought back to what he could remember about the Thin Line from the Demonic Compendium. Retracing the pages in his head, he remembered how the thin vellum felt in his hands. Each page of the Book seemed to turn on its own as he finished reading the words on each page. Words and images of terrible, awful things jumped off the page and wrapped around his inner desires. The Book revealed the history of demons, of the human's plight to stop them, and the many First demons to walk the human plane. The Book took even as it gave. He remembered feeling drowsy and slow, wanting to drag out the time he had reading the book.

As he'd pull away from its unrelenting influence, it would

pull back twice as hard, forcing him to read and move through the stories between the pages. The Book was guiding him and showing him what it wanted him to see. He learned of many a demonic name and the appearance of their true forms. He learned what type of powers they could utilize to maim and destroy. He learned how their energy needed to be managed and how it couldn't be spent carefree. He remembered how to kill them and as he finished the chapter, the Book offered one final piece of knowledge, one final testament to its goals. The Book offered him unending power, revenge, solitude, and solidarity. The Book offered him his life back and showed him what the future would have been. The Book offered him everything. The Book offered him the opportunity to right so many wrongs.

Wake up. The Book is nothing but deceit, malice and hatred, never forget that, hissed the magpie in its ruby as it pulsed and shot pain down his arm.

"The Book is of your kind. It has been called the Great Equalizer in the past, has it not?"

The problem with the Book is its hatred for everything. Your kind and my kind alike. Do not underestimate it.

"I have read the Book and withstood its influence," Shaw replied with a slight hint of confidence.

Because it wanted you to, the magpie interrupted. *The Book has its own agenda. The Book chose you for a reason. The Book gave you your powers, Arbiter.*

Shaw shrugged in denial. He refused to believe the Book had manipulated him into making any decisions. It was not the Book that refused to die for so many a year. It was not the Book who fought for decades with only a notched sword and the image of his wife implanted in his mind.

He brought himself back to the present, tabled what he remembered from the Book and took a deep breath. He peered into the portal, its emptiness somewhat inviting, a peculiar effect of the Thin Line. It wanted you to be there. The longer you spent on that plane, the harder it became to leave.

Welcome back to my world, Shaw. Let us both pray to whatever gods answered you in the church. Let us not dawdle; my feathers are already tattered from your little stunt with the ship. Too much more and you and I will become more closely acquainted here, quipped the magpie.

"Pemazu, enough already. I am aware of your needs, which happen to mirror my own. Let us find the Captain and whatever information we can gather and get out of here, for surely the power it took to disperse the Barge will draw attention. Onward."

Remember Arbiter, do not look down and keep moving else the Line take you where it wishes.

Despite being a massive world of nothingness, the Thin Line had things *in it.* Unholy, fragmented gems littered what would normally be called the ground. While solid underfoot, neither human nor demon had seen the ground of the Thin Line directly and lived to describe it. It was a world between worlds. It was a desolate wasteland where the dead, undead, and everything in between restlessly waited. According to the Book, peripheral visions, reflections and even mirrors could be used to examine your surroundings. To gaze directly upon the ground and peer into the wild, swirling black nothingness would immediately throw the viewer beyond the Void and on to oblivion. The Compendium prefaced walking the Thin Line with warnings and tips to traverse its wonders.

It was a place filled with knowledge, for the dead keep their secrets. Small, sharp gems littered the area giving off a pulsing light, illuminating short distances around them. Luckily, what he was looking for was within the immediate area and returning to the Gateway from the Great Barge would be easy enough. To mark the area, he unclasped his boots and placed them next to the Gateway, careful not to let them be drawn into its mouth and spat back out on the Fringe. With care he kept his eyes faced outwards, scrounged around, and gathered up a handful of crystals. He shoved them into his boot, using them as a marker of sorts. He felt cool glass on his feet as he shifted from side to side and became familiar with the ground once again.

"More light, Pemazu," he thought as he rolled up the sleeve of his tunic and faced his palm outward.

More light means more attention, but if it gets you to move faster I will provide, the demon replied. The light amber glow from within the rubies grew and bathed the immediate area in an eerie glow.

"It was not a question. Help me find the Barge. Can you sense the Captain?"

I sense something; it is still far off but it knows we are here. The Captain is also nearby, and something else is with him. I cannot identify the energy, but it is not demonic.

"Where is it?"

Turn three half steps to your right, approximately one hundred feet in front of you.

The Thin Line warped your vision, encouraging you to look. Looking up would result in the person being taken to a far off peace; total serenity. For those who looked down, a much different fate was in store. Looking down would send you beyond the Void, where you simply cease to exist. All entities that hadn't moved and called the Line home would exist in almost solitude and reality itself bent around the individual. Their own personal bit of nothing; it was enough to drive one mad after even a short period of time. Even sound seemed to simply dissipate. Shaw was almost thankful for the demon's presence.

Following the demon's directions, Shaw took three careful steps in an arc and paced himself forward, counting each step meticulously.

Fourteen, fifteen, sixteen... Even his footfalls were silent. His ragged breathing escaped his mouth faster and his palms began to sweat.

Thirty-five, thirty-six, thirty-seven.

I hate this place, the demon rang out. Against the quiet of the Thin Line, the demon's voice reverberated and boomed within his head.

Even as the darkness pressed against his meager bubble of red light, Shaw still felt relatively comfortable here. He had read much of the Thin Line; what lurked further into the nothing, classifications, strengths, weaknesses, and names of the demons that called this place home. If the Compendium was as Pemazu suggested, sentient and goal seeking, it had shown him Pemazu's name for a reason.

Sixty-four, sixty-five, sixty-six.

There it was. The Great Barge; a behemoth of a ship, resting on its side. Here, on this plane, it looked lackluster without the mighty river challenging its integrity. It stood out against the black and through his peripherals, Shaw could see a ghostly path through the dark where the ship had made its way. It would rest here for eternity, one of the few man-made items unfortunate enough to call this place home.

Even here, the ship gave off a menacing air about it. On board, something terrible grew in strength. Black magic always found strength in the darkest and emptiest of places. The glow from Shaw's arm grew in response to the presence of magic and he brought it up to his face as he walked, looking for the magpie. The magpie was playing dead, its pink tongue lolled out of its beak along the bottom of the gem and its feet were contorted and twitching. A small plume of essence dribbled out from its mouth, adding to the performance.

"Really? Overdramatic much?"

I am not expecting us to make it out of here, consider this practice.

"Stop wasting your energy and help me pinpoint the Captain. Send out a Pulse."

Are you an idiot or is this your attempt to match my incredible humor? A Pulse will reveal their location, and ours. How do you like your magpie? Roasted, most likely... or raw like a savage?

"We will spend the next thirty years searching the damn ship if we can't pinpoint the Captain. Send the Pulse." Shaw was growing more nervous just standing around.

The magpie puffed up, drew in a heaping amount of air and slammed its face against the side of the crystal several times, plinking the glass surface.

He made a mental note and captured the image. The demon was a master of showmanship and sometimes, its taste wasn't bad.

The Pulse was simple but effective magic. The demon itself could cast the spell with minimal energy. He stopped a few strides away from the Great Barge. Though he was this close, he couldn't smell the ship.

The Thin Line is a peculiar place, he thought.

He turned his wrist outward and nodded at the magpie. The red light faded to a glimmer and for once, he felt alone and exposed. The demon was not what he'd consider a companion, but another presence in such an empty place provided some sort of comfort.

The light grew steadily, heating the crystals. He anticipated the oncoming magic and turned away to protect his eyes. Through his eyelids he could see the brightness of the magic building.

Now.

The spell's effect was instant. The magic passed through walls of the ship and clung to the outline of something inside before shimmering and fading away. The amber glow returned, and he opened his eyes. The magpie once again played dead.

"We've a problem Pemazu. I fear the Captain is gone but something else lives."

The bird did not answer him.

"Pemazu, can you sense it?"

The bird righted itself in the gem and hissed, a *Baulg*.

Shaw's heart skipped a beat. "Are you sure?"

The Pulse told me everything I need to know. Let us get on the ship. Maybe it is still hungry and will devour us quickly.

"Your optimism is my motivation, Pemazu. Onward, it's in the cargo hold."

The magpie clicked twice in response and resumed its feigned death position but provided the light anyway. Shaw rounded the bow of the ship and made his way to the port side entrance. The rough slide onto the shallow dock, across land, and through the Gateway had caused massive damage to the ship's hull and knocked several masts down. The center mast holding the main sail drooped close enough to the ground for him to reach it. With a heave and a grunt, he pulled himself up and walked along the beam leading to the main deck. He looked out towards what would be the deeper parts of the Thin Line. Off in the distance, through the mask of the void's constricting glow, a faint green light bobbed. He looked at the wrecked vessel's upper deck and attempted to find the safest point to access the center of the ship. A short distance from the broken center mast, the cargo hold netting had fallen away. Shaw ran the last few feet of the beam to gain momentum. At the broken end of the beam, he leapt purposefully towards the square cargo hold entrance cut in the deck and passed into the belly of the ship. On board, the world returned to a level of regularity. The haze caused by the Thin Line was lifted. With the return of his clear vision, his hearing was restored as well and the groans of the ship's interior struggling to hold integrity returned. Curiously enough, though the ship rested on its side, the world righted itself.

"Why are we not slipping towards the side of the ship right now?" he asked the demon.

This ship does not belong here. Its presence is abnormal. Precisely the same reason as to why your boots will help us locate the Gateway again, they stand out in this place.

Shaw glanced behind him at the place where he had left his boots, right next to the Gateway. Sure enough, they stood out as a tiny blip through the wall of the ship.

This place isn't how I remember it, Shaw thought.

Each entry to the Thin Line will be different. To make any progress here, you must remain. Did you learn anything in your thirty years here? the magpie said, laughing. It was an eerie sound, like rocks rattling in a pail.

"Thirty years on my plane, one hundred and eighty here."

He had always sheltered the memories of his lost time within the deepest vault of his mind. There, they couldn't resurface.

You should not harbor those memories, Shaw, they will give you wrinkles, the magpie clicked.

Shaw brushed off the slight and flicked the third ruby, causing the magpie to jump and bounce around inside the confines of the gem. The magpie swelled up and fluffed its feathers in retort, sticking out its long, barbed tongue. Grinning, Shaw pushed onwards. The innards of the ship were as one would expect for a vessel of its magnitude. Large wooden boxes stacked high and spools of rope filled almost every empty space. All was normal, minus the blood trail leading towards the end of the ship. He sighed and followed the line, sidestepping boxes of spices bearing shipping labels indicating that some of the goods were from beyond the Far East.

The torchlight flickered, giving the boxes the appearance that they were moving along the hull of the ship. Shaw assumed the torches were spelled to keep their light from dying out. Through the salted air, a pungent tang caused him to cover his nose and mouth. Death and decay had been committed to his memory since he was a child. Its scent was unmistakable.

"Where are their bodies?" Shaw breathed, surveying the area for whatever left the blood trail.

Consumed, most likely, Pemazu replied. *I have not seen a Baulg since one was summoned after the Battle of Third City to handle the abundance of corpses.*

"I know the name, but what is it? The Book never explained what they are, only of their demonic origin and the common advice to avoid at all costs."

The Book was wise in its advice then, Pemazu replied. *A Baulg is best avoided. They are the Great Consumers, the Bottomless Pits, the Insatiable. Baulgs are consumers of everything living, never satisfied, always hungry. They are resistant to most magic, including yours, Arbiter. In times of war, a Baulg may be summoned through a Gateway to consume the dead. The summoner would recall the Baulg, cut it open, and use the consumed body parts for necromancy.*

"It just feeds and collects."

No, Arbiter, I feed. It consumes, Pemazu said.

"You said it's of demonic origin. Can you feed off it? Replenish your essence?"

It would replenish me and give me indigestion for weeks...but you must kill it first.

"How?"

Do what humans do best. Hit it until it stops moving. Its essence will remain on this plane and then I can feed.

"I'll need the sword."

You mean my sword, the magpie mumbled as it preened the underside of a wing.

He moved through the center of the ship, following the rich, red blood trail. Bits of flesh and sinew lay about periodically. The Baulg had apparently ripped some of its prey apart before consuming it.

The Baulg will consume its victims in pieces. The summoner does not need whole bodies, just parts, the demon interjected.

The narrow path ended abruptly, marking the end of the ship and leaving him in the center of a large oval room. Golden tapestries, once proud markings of the ship's motherland, now lay tattered and frayed on the floor. In the center of the room, the creature rested amongst a pile of body parts in a pool of coagulated blood.

The creature disgusted him, which was saying a lot considering the things he had seen. Even the monstrosities on the Thin Line couldn't compare. He recalled the demon's words about Third City and understood the impact the creature must have had.

It dominated the middle of the room. It was a fleshy worm, several feet wide with arms grasping blindly at the ground around it. Every now and then it seized a piece of flesh or bone it had missed, shoving it aimlessly into a gaping hole in the center of its body. The creature gave off the suspected smell of decay and rot so pungent Shaw's nose itched. Luckily, the creature had yet to see him.

He ducked silently behind one of several pillars adorning the rotunda and raised his arm up to examine the crystals in it. Two lay cold, dark and dormant, but the third was filled with dancing red plumes of smoke. In the center of it all, a magpie with too many eyes was impatiently licking the glass with a forked tongue, obviously sensing the presence of the magical creature.

Ugh, must you? Shaw thought to the demon, disgusted.

It paused its furious licking for a moment to say, *hungry*.

"Just concentrate for a moment. We have the advantage; it hasn't seen us."

It does not see anything...it only hungers. It has known of our presence since we boarded the ship.

"Why has it not come after us?" Shaw wondered.

It is most likely confused. Not many creatures have encountered an Arbiter before. Your energy is both human and demon. Soon enough it will ignore its confusion and simply give in to the hunger.

A great slit in the creature's side resembling a mouth opened wide and it let out a tortured, inhuman moan.

Apparently, its attention is elsewhere. Perhaps there are survivors.

He peered over his shoulder to see what had caught the creature's attention. It flopped over and landed on the floor with a slap in the bloody pool. Its arms reached out, pulling and dragging the floor to worm its fleshy mound of a body towards a stack of crates at the other end of the room. Elongated hands and fingers swiped blindly about, searching for prey.

Look, the demon said.

A boy darted out from behind the crates as the hands nearly reached him. He ducked and dodged the remaining hands and beelined for the entry to the rotunda. Shaw took the opportunity to act while something had the creature's attention.

"Perr-da-ra-na!" Shaw bellowed, extending his jeweled arm. Blackened demon-fire erupted from his mouth, singing his tongue and throat. It crawled the length of his arm, fusing to his skin and bone, becoming one. The flames and coal turned a bright shade of green as the magnificent demonic blade took shape. In the place of his arm, a shiny hell-forged blade protruded from his elbow.

He leapt towards the creature, traversing the room in just a few strides, his footprints leaving smoldered imprints in the wood. In a coordinated half spin, Shaw drew back his arm and plunged it deep into the creature's side near its mouth.

Expecting the beast to recoil in pain, he extracted the blade and stepped back, swiping and severing several groping arms. Grey pus spewed from the limbs, and he had to sidestep out of the rain of filth. The creature seemed unbothered by the attack and the missing limbs and continued to search blindly for prey.

"Any ideas?" Shaw asked the demon aloud.

Did you ask it nicely to go away? Aim for its head next time.

"Which part of it is that?" he exclaimed, motioning towards the fleshy blob.

He stole a glance at the crystals in his arm. The third was fading. He couldn't maintain the demon-blade for much longer. Should he run out of energy, he and the demon would be trapped here together indefinitely.

Pale hands shot towards him and he drew down on them again. He was unable to dodge the rain of pus this time and it dampened his hair and tunic.

"Is there something you can do to help?"

The creature began to reach out again, dragging its slug-like body across the floor, leaving a blood trail.

You have the sword, use it. Imagine you had common steel; it would be useless versus the creature.

"Currently you're useless, demon...argh!" The Baulg had managed to grab hold of his leg. He plunged the blade through the creature's arm and into the wood of the boat. He twisted and jerked it loose.

In my unbound form I am eighteen feet tall. Do not take my humble appearance as weakness.

"Then do something!" Shaw yelled, diving and rolling behind the nearest pillar; now that he had drawn the creature's full attention.

A flurry of movement drew his focus to the entryway to the rotunda. The child from before had returned. *What is this child doing?* he thought. The boy was bent over with something in its hands. From the shadows, a fire grew atop a bottle in the child's hand. He tossed the bottle, arcing it through the air where it smashed against the fattest portion of the creature. A wave of fire enveloped the creature and bathed the room in intermittent light.

The creature arched its back in pain, gurgling and groaning. The child recoiled from the unexpected response and spun about, unsure of where to go or what to do next. He spotted Shaw and cut across the room, barely avoiding a set of hands.

Arbiter, burn it with Fyre! the magpie said.

"I can't control Fyre and we will expend all of our energy. The last thing I want to do is die here with you."

Agreed. I will not let you use the last of it, just do it now. Stop arguing and conflagrate the creature.

"Damn it, Pemazu!"

The child reached Shaw's pillar and slammed his back up against it.

"Move, child," Shaw growled, shoving the boy behind him. Shaw rounded the pillar to face the Baulg. It reared up and exposed its flattened stomach, high in the air. It used its arms to grasp the ceiling of the rotunda, pulling itself higher, preparing to drop its weight on them both.

He pointed his bladed hand at the creature's torso and tapped into the energy protected behind the wall in his mind. Like a river pressing against a dam, the energy appreciated any sort of release. He held the flood back, pressing his own will against it. The energy welled up quickly and he segregated a portion of it, only what he thought he'd need. It was alluring and addicting. He wanted more and he gave in to its draw.

More, Pemazu said.

"No."

More. You need more.

"No."

The power circled in his head, probing for weaknesses, testing for cracks. If he did not hold it back until the right moment, it would drain him of first the demon's essence and then his own. It wanted him to use it. It was a never-ending thirst. It was raw, unfathomable energy.

Shaw, you need more. It will not consume you. I will not let it.

The swirling mass of power lunged violently against the confines of his mind. He countered the attack and tried to contain it. The power was blinding and time stood still. He lost control and his vision turned to white.

Arbiter, you have so much to learn!

Out of the blankness of his failure to control the other-worldly energy, a towering black monstrosity leapt into his field of view. Clawed arms and blackened powdery wings wrapped around the river of energy, shaping it and forming it. The river lashed out with a tendril and the creature used its arms to press it into place once again. It was containing the energy, molding it.

"Pemazu," Shaw acknowledged. It was right; in his mind he could clearly see the demon's true form, three times his height, hooked and clawed arms, long enough to drag at its feet. Its four, tattered, veiny wings flapped periodically, spreading powder and smoke. A powerful, barbed tail stabilized the demon's torso.

A small bit of hope arose as he realized the demon would not let him fail in this moment.

"The last time I saw you as you were, we were on the Thin Line."

The last time you did, we made a deal.

"We came to an agreement. One which can't be completed until the Book has been placated."

I plan on honoring my end of the agreement, be sure to do so with yours. The demon flipped its head back and stared at him with a toothy upside-down grin. It opened its mouth wider, revealing a deep pit. The mouth gaped wider and wider, black replacing white. The energy became a distant, swirling dot. The demon, far off in the distance, still clung to it.

Shaw regained clarity, the rotunda returned, the boy cowering behind him and the pillars shot up through the floor. The tapestries lay as piles of colorful cloth around the circular room and in the center of it all, the faceless, shape-less, vile mass was rearing up, preparing to crush him. He stood against it; his arm extended outward, the hell-blade gone.

Against the grey facade, one ruby blazed into life, the magpie was nowhere to be seen. He reached into the well of energy again and found it instantly. It was no longer rushing and violent, but calm and contained. He reached out with his mind and the river greeted him and he smiled.

Now, Arbiter, Pemazu said calmly.

Shaw nodded.

The creature roared and released its grip on the decorative outcroppings of the rotunda.

He opened the floodgates in his mind, but this time he was no longer fearful of the cascade of power. It channeled through him and manifested as brilliant green and purple flames. The flames spewed out of the rubies and entangled his hand in demon-fire; the prickling warmth was comforting. He held it for a second, relishing the power's inviting and intoxicating embrace.

"Dorr-a-ra-doon!" Shaw infused the spell with demonic words of power and destruction. The demonic words mixing with his own voice sounded so strange to him. Deeper, warped and dirty, almost like the Captain's spell. The demon flames leapt from his outstretched arm and enveloped the Baulg.

The effect was immediate. The creature howled again in agony and began to fall with Shaw and the boy in its path. Stunned by the power behind the spell, Shaw was frozen; mesmerized by the power he called forth. The creature now bore down on him, crying out in agony. The boy…

He snapped out of it, dove to the right of the pillar and grabbed the boy in a two-armed death grip as he rolled. The crash from the creature shook the entire ship. It creaked and rocked, but maintained its integrity. A silver wisp began to rise from the creature's mid-section and hovered about like a milky cloud.

Shaw examined the toll the spell had taken on his energy. The third ruby, barely glowing, looked devoid of light. Inside, a lone magpie with too many eyes nestled with its beak in its feathers.

Pemazu, it's done, Shaw thought.

Obviously weakened, the magpie clicked once into its feathers.

Shaw examined the lump of rags that appeared to be breathing. Lifting an edge, he peeked underneath and saw it was the boy. A thin silver blade shot out from under the blanket, slashing wildly, only to return to the cover of the blanket.

"Enough of that," Shaw growled, dropping the corner of the blanket. "I am not to be feared."

With a shake in his voice, the boy replied, "I know what you are, Impius. Your foul tricks won't work on me. This blanket is spelled, you can't harm me."

His temper welled at the boy's slight. "Impius? I am no Impius."

"Lies. Fallacies. More trickery," the boy yelped, shivering. "I have seen the gems forged into your skin. You carry the mark of an Impius and have sold your soul for power."

Can I eat him? the demon eagerly asked.

Chuckling, Shaw allowed the child a moment of respite; he'd deal with him later. He rounded the pillar to examine the Baulg more closely. It dribbled pus and its skin was no longer flesh-colored, but blackened, burned, and smoldering. Shaw furrowed his nose at the smell of rotting and burning flesh and spoke to the demon.

"The creature is dead. Are you alive?"

Somewhat...this thing will taste disgusting. Death does not sound too unappealing at this moment.

Shaw rolled his eyes and smiled at the demon.

"Quickly. It was you who suggested haste, did you not?"

Rightly so...there are worse things than a Baulg on the Thin Line. One of which is approaching.

"Feed then, demon, we will gather the boy up on our way out. It appears only he remains. This is no place for a child."

Is that sentiment, Arbiter?

"The remains of sentiment," Shaw said. "I am trying to remember how to express pity."

Without a response, the magpie righted itself and shook about. Shaw angled his jeweled arm towards the floating substance hovering above the Baulg and whispered, *"Barronda."*

You become more fluent in my tongue daily, Pemazu said.

"Only with what you tell me."

The magpie opened its mouth wide, revealing a blackened pit in the back of its throat. The mouth grew wider and wider and encompassed the rim of the ruby. A low hiss came from the gem and the flowing essence leapt into his arm. In one swift inhale, the gem swallowed the essence from the creature and Shaw relaxed his arm. Three glowing gems embossed in fiery red light lit the rotunda. He looked through the gems like panes of glass and saw a black and grey magpie running furiously from gem to gem, disappearing where gem met flesh and returning to sight in the next. Its forked tongue lolled in a non-existent wind.

Shaw raised an eyebrow at the demon's antics.

He turned his back to the corpse and returned to the heap of rags hiding the frightened boy. He scooped the child up and wrapped the rags around him to prevent pricks from the child's blade. Cries came from the boy promising revenge, impending doom, and holy retribution. Shaw liked the child's enthusiasm, though foolish and ignorant. He retraced his path and then convinced the boy to climb out the ship on his own. He tied a piece of cloth over the boy's eyes and tossed him over his shoulder after he dropped them to the surface of the Thin Line. He need not let the boy look where he did not need to look. The haze of the Thin Line enveloped him, and he carefully set his eyes on the meager glow that marked his Gateway, and his favorite boots. The boy continued to voice his protest at being manhandled.

Silence the boy and pick up the pace. We are pursued, the magpie clicked, a level of anxiety in its voice causing Shaw to be a little concerned.

He jabbed the boy in the stomach and the protests stopped and became dry heaving. The message seemed to have been received as no sound came from the blanket for the remainder of the trip. They arrived at the Gateway and he looked through to the familiar dirt streets and huts of the Fringe. He squatted awkwardly without looking down and upturned his boots. He replaced them, then stepped through the Gateway into the mid-afternoon sun. Behind him, the Gateway closed in on itself and sealed off the otherworldly place once again.

Squinting out from beneath his eyebrows, Shaw looked up and surveyed the area. Time passed differently on the Thin Line. No more than a few hours seemed to have passed compared to what should have been an all-day expedition. The shallow dock was still empty, most commoners dispersed for some time before returning to peruse the area. Though the existence of magic was well-known throughout the land, it was still feared due to the risk and mystery in the details of spell work. A Great Barge disappearing during broad daylight would certainly clear the crowds for a day or more.

He dropped the boy to the ground with a thud. The boy untangled himself in a flurry before drawing his needle dagger. The boy snarled and assumed a fighting stance, obviously feigning courage. If the boy honestly believed Shaw was an Impius, he'd not be so courageous and ready to fight him.

"Relax, boy, you are safe and free from the grasp of the Baulg."

Frantically the boy said, "I am hardly safe from you, demon

whore," lunging in his direction, intending to stab him. Shaw sidestepped, causing the boy to trip over his own feet.

Persistent little thing, the demon said. *Perhaps we should ask him what he knows about the Great Barge and the news you were seeking.*

The demon had a point; the boy may have overheard something or seen something in relation to the Book. He looked the boy once over. He was filthy and probably a stowaway.

"Boy, before you attempt to stick me again, can you tell me of the journey? Who summoned the Baulg? Did anyone survive? What news of the Far East and their armies?"

The boy righted himself and lifted an eyebrow, confused. He placed the dagger in his waistband and, pulling it tight, looking down as he spoke. "That thing…everyone…they all…it ate them all…They barricaded themselves in the bowels of the ship…tried. All dead."

The boy is useless now. Let us take him with us, as there is someone approaching, I believe, chimed in the demon.

Shaw looked over his shoulder. Sure enough, a hooded figure was bounding from rooftop to rooftop, a silhouette against the afternoon sun. The figure was moving quickly, dead set on Shaw's location.

Turning to the boy, he asked, "What's your name?"

Sniffling and quickly wiping away tears, the boy replied, "Cereal…of Third City."

CHAPTER FOUR

PULLING his up hood against the sun, Shaw snatched the boy's arm up and picked up the pace northbound. He was pursued, and whoever or whatever it was, moved at an incredible speed. The boy issued no retaliation at his escort this time. If this boy, Cereal, was of Third City, he, or his family, may have the information he needed.

"Boy, we're pursued. Keep with my pace as we need to hide ourselves."

Panicked, Cereal looked around widely, his deep green eyes darting left and right. "Why must we hide? Who are you? What pursues us?"

Shaw growled, "Most likely an agent of the new King. The agent must know of the Gateway I opened. Perhaps, he even saw the events with the Great Barge. Most run away in fear at the sign of powers such as mine. This agent seems unafraid."

"You are obviously not an Impius, as they have no regard for life that I know of."

"You are correct in your assumptions, and I admire your courage with the Baulg. Turn here," Shaw said, steering the boy between two huts into the alley. He continued until the nearest outlet allowed him to turn northbound.

"A Baulg? I have never heard of that monster before."

"A Baulg is its true-name; common folk who tell tales of the Great Betrayal simply call it an Eater."

Shaw felt the boy nod, sniffling again. If the boy was of Third City as he said, The Great Betrayal and the Eater would be all too familiar. Shaw stopped mid-stride and listening intently, holding his breath in concentration. Hearing no quickened footsteps or pounding of feet on rooftops, Shaw and the boy continued onward.

"Where are we going?" asked the boy. Shaw felt the boy's gaze digging into the side of his skull.

"A church, where we won't be disturbed by whatever follows us. Then, once we have spoken, you will be on your way and you will forget what you saw today," Shaw said, issuing his plan in the form of a mild threat.

"But...I thought I'd come with you? You can teach me to fight, learn your skills. I saw what you did to that...bog."

"Baulg...and no, you won't be coming with me. I can't afford to spare the attention to keep you from your inevitable demise."

The demon chimed in in Shaw's head. *The offer to eat him still stands.*

The boy drew his dagger from his waistband, stabbing the air at an invisible enemy. "I can fight! I have my dagger, and you saw me make fire in a bottle!"

Slightly amused at the boy's ill-witted courage, Shaw replied sarcastically. "Indeed, your mastery of chemicals would astound even the greatest alchemists of our age!"

Feeling like he had finally shut the boy up, Shaw rounded the last corner, leaving the market to the west and seeing the large spire of the ruined church peeking over the rooftops.

"I'll tell the King what you are..." the boy said.

Stopping mid-stride, Shaw wheeled around and grasped the

boy by his neck, lifting him off the ground and pushing him against the wall of the alley. The boy struggled and clawed at Shaw's face. Shaw held him at arm's reach and said, "And tell him what exactly?"

The boy's eyes darted repeatedly to the exposed gems in Shaw's outstretched arm.

Do you intend to choke a child to death now, Shaw? That is evil, even for me. If not, I suggest you let him breathe, as his face is turning a lovely shade of purple, the demon said.

Shaw released the boy, who crumpled to the ground, gasping for air. Shaw bore down on him. "What would you tell our blessed King?"

"Noth...nothing...I swear..." the boy sputtered. "Empty threats. Nothing left...family...none."

"Follow me and keep your snide remarks to yourself. Threatening me? Pah! A child? The nerve...never in..." Shaw grumbled, walking off.

Shaw heard the boy get to his feet, dust himself off and continue on, keeping a short distance between them.

"Don't bother running either, Cereal. Whatever chases me most likely hungers for you, too," Shaw said, without looking over his shoulder.

With the church in view, Shaw examined the northern and southern paths that ordinarily poured foot traffic directly in front of the building. Seeing no signs of common-folk, he listened again for the sound of heavy footfalls on rooftops or the quickened patter of muffled footsteps on cobblestone. Feeling confident in their evasion of the unknown pursuer, and void of all prying eyes, Shaw ducked beneath the church's entryway barrier. Inside the church, the mid-day sun cast beams of light through the slatted roof. Holes from years of abandonment provided cascades of light randomly through the dimly-lit sanctuary. Shaw walked the familiar path behind the lectern and through the priest door, making his way to the top of the spire.

An unfamiliar scent grew stronger as he ascended the narrow, circular stairway.

Shaw breathed deep; he recognized the herb now, his memories returning. *That smell...rue...and ash...and the dead.* These were tools of a dark magic wielder. These were tools of the dead. Shaw put out an arm behind him to slow the boy from running into him. Carefully placing his steps, he ascended the stairs, treading lightly and purposefully.

Shaw stopped near the top, before his head crested the lip. He motioned for the boy to stay. Readying himself, he took a deep breath and pulled himself onto the landing. Wheeling around, preparing for an impending attack, he assumed a fighting position and scanned the room. Empty, except for a small wooden table, a set of chairs and a candle atop the table... a lit candle. The candle cast shadows about the room, flickering and moving at random, creating abysmal patches of dark. In the candlelight, one shadow refused to move.

Shaw rolled his sleeve, exposing the rubies.

Do not bother, your magic will not work on her, Arbiter, Pemazu said, unamused.

"Why do you think that? Wait...her?" Shaw thought, slightly confused.

"Hello, Shaw," the shadow said, slightly distorted but obviously a woman's voice.

"Reveal yourself, before I run you through!" Shaw said to the shadow.

"Come now. Is that any way to speak to your sister?"

The shadow dropped to the floor in small waves like falling tapestries. In its place stood a frail woman, a head shorter than Shaw. She was slouching slightly, her striking green eyes staring at him through her fire-red hair.

The initial shock of the shadow's introduction was overrun by disbelief. Confident in his knowledge of past events, Shaw questioned the frail woman. "If you're indeed my sister, why make yourself known to me now? Why did you use foul magic to pursue me? Why not approach me as any sister would?"

"You're still as dense as always. After the events with the Great Barge, I waited. It takes powerful magic to open a Gateway, and even stronger magic to return from that place." She quietly pushed out the final words. That place. The Thin Line. She knew of it. This must be his sister.

"If you're still claiming to be my sister, what is the truth of what happened during the events of the Great Betrayal?" Shaw said, gritting his teeth.

"Your brother, and my brother, our now glorious King, Jayecob, murdered our father, ran you through, and attempted to kill me."

"And how is it you managed to escape when so many couldn't?"

"The magic you saw me use today is called a Shroud. I learned it from the Compendium..." Her words rang out, hollow and grim. Mentioning the Book caused her to wince.

Shaw sighed. "Hello Princess Beggen Ostra. Time has obviously taken its toll on you as it has on me. Only my true sister knows of the Book."

Finally, he gets it, Pemazu said.

"Shut-up," Shaw said aloud.

"I'm sorry?" inquired Beggen Ostra.

He sighed. "We have much to discuss. Boy, gather yourself and come up here. We have questions for you."

Cereal meekly popped his head above the rim of the landing to survey the room. "We?"

Seated at the table, a single candle bouncing shadows off everyone's faces, the three sat in silence. Shaw, speaking only after he noticed the boy fidgeting uncomfortably on the wooden chair.

"Have you any food? This boy appears even frailer than you do, sister."

Beggen Ostra pulled a small hip pouch to her lap and retrieved a square of spiced mutton, unwrapping it and handing it to the boy. The boy snatched it quickly, shoving it into his mouth with fervor. Beggen Ostra raised an eyebrow curiously. Cheeks bulging, Cereal asked, "Wait, Beggen Ostra? Shaw? As in Princess Beggen Ostra and Prince Shaw?" His eyes widened with anticipation of the answer.

Both Beggen Ostra and Shaw chuckled at the delight in the child's voice.

"Who is your companion?" she asked Shaw.

Shaw scoffed. "Hardly my companion, more or less a liability. He has information from the Far East, and the Book."

The boy nodded several times.

"Does he have a name yet?"

"Indeed, Cereal…of Third City."

Beggen Ostra perked up, apparently more interested in the conversation now.

"But…you two are dead!" spat Cereal quickly, anxious to get the statement in.

"Hardly," replied Beggen Ostra. "Old, frail, but far from dead. Our grim Prince, however, is something else. Do you care to explain where you have been for the last thirty years?"

"Why is it you don't appear to be afraid of seeing me, dear sister?"

Beggen Ostra shrugged. "Magic has been awry since the Book came to light. I've learned that anything is possible."

Shaw nodded, instinctively rubbing the gems through the sleeves of his tunic. Pemazu was extraordinarily quiet.

"In time sister, I'll explain my absence. I'd like to hear from the boy."

With both Beggen Ostra and Shaw now turned towards him, Cereal began to speak. "Where would you like me to start off, Your Highnesses?"

"Please, formalities at this point are that, formalities, we need not reveal ourselves...yet."

Furiously nodding, the boy was obviously excited with keeping such a secret.

"Start with how you came to be Cereal of Third City. The Fall of Third City and the Great Betrayal were before your time. You can't be more than eleven years of age?"

"I am of twelve years, my lord"

Shaw rolled his hand for the boy to continue.

"My parents, my lord, they believed Third City was a legacy best remembered through its people and we best not associate ourselves with the events that took place. My father was of Third City and passed the name on to me before he was killed." Taking a bite of mutton, he said, "My mother made clothing. My father was a blacksmith."

Shaw leaned in, close enough to count the freckles on the boy's nose. "Tell me of the Great Barge."

Looking down, the boy said in a low tone. "Fleeing...after slavers took my family to Stonehaven to be sold. My father fought and we tried to escape...but my father was captured. The King tortured him himself while my mother and I watched. Then, the King's Guard took my mother. All of them..."

Shaw continued to listen. Beggen Ostra swore under her breath.

"She died then... and they sold me to work on the Great Barge as a deckhand. When the Baulg took the ship, I was able to make my escape."

Beggen Ostra turned to Shaw, who in turn nodded and made a face at the mention of the Baulg as if to say, "We'll talk about this later."

The boy paused, lost in his memories. He occupied himself by fiddling with his ragged tunic, picking at the fraying edges.

Beginning to get impatient, Shaw pressed him. "Did your father tell you of Third City? The Great Betrayal?"

"Indeed," the boy said, seemingly eager to help. "The Great Betrayal was between Prince Jayecob and you, my lord. There was a fight for the throne after King Armand died. Prince Jayecob won, and you fled to the Far East, my lord."

Scoffing and slightly disgusted, Shaw said, "Fled, the Far East...I'd never..."

"I know that, my lord, this is but the story I was told. I have seen you fight and the green Fyre you released."

Jumping up, Beggen Ostra pulled a silver-plated hip-sword from its scabbard. Blackened runes carved into its hilt and guard stood out over the glow of the silver. Cereal retreated to the corner of the room, afraid, as Beggen Ostra, though frail and elderly, moved quickly.

"Green Fyre, a Gateway. I know what you are and my brother you are not...Impius," she hissed, the edge of the blade just under Shaw's chin.

Without looking up at her, Shaw spoke. "I assure you sister, I am myself, though I am different. If you allow me to show you, I can explain everything."

Looking confused, she appeared to contemplate his request.

Beggen Ostra flicked her sword, motioning for Shaw to continue. Slowly and methodically, Shaw lifted his arm and turned out his wrist, unfastened the sleeve and pulled it up above his elbow. Three brilliant rubies lay embedded within his arm. In the center gem, a black magpie with too many eyes rested on one foot, listening. The other gems swirled with a red mist in the wind. Beyond the mist, a black emptiness flashed between the waves of red. Beggen Ostra leaned in for a closer look. The magpie, seeing Beggen Ostra staring at it, replied by sticking out a forked tongue until it spooled around the bird's hooked feet. The magpie made a rude gesture before hopping up and attempting to choke itself with its own tongue. She looked up at Shaw.

"Nasty little creature isn't it?" she said, not taking her eyes off Shaw. "Go on then…explain."

"Unfortunately, the boy's recount of events aren't as he and many others have been told. Our Great King is both a liar…and a murderer. Jayecob was sent to build and rule Third City on behalf of Stonehaven. In the course of his duties, he found the Book."

The room seemed to darken slightly with Shaw's words. The candle dimmed for a moment before returning to its usual brightness and dance.

"Jayecob read the Book and gave in to its power, becoming an Impius himself. He murdered the King, our father, before running his blade through me."

"How is it you sit before me then?"

"The Book….it brought me back. It wants me to do something. These things," he said, tracing a ruby with a finger, "they are both a gift…and a curse."

"And the fowl?"

Fowl! Did she dare say fowl? Pemazu squeaked in Shaw's head, plinking against the face of the gem, eyes bulging.

"A demon, Pemazu. I have taken him under my control."

We still have an agreement…tell her of the agreement, Pemazu said slyly.

"Do you still have a soul?" Cereal asked from the corner of the room.

Brushing the boy off, Beggen Ostra asked, "Are you not an Impius then, if you have a demon within you?"

"I am no Impius…I am what the Book calls an Arbiter, the first in over five hundred years."

"You always loved to be the center of attention. You are indeed my brother." With a slight smirk she sheathed her sword, plopping into her chair.

"More on this later, you're here now. We must discuss the Far East, their armies grow, and they aim to bear down on the

Kingdom all the while our King does nothing," Beggen Ostra continued.

"How are they crossing the Expanse? That desert is near impossible to navigate," questioned Shaw.

"They aren't...the Valor...using the Valor they commandeer our Great Barges, traverse the Maw, and bring them to the Far East."

"And my brother? He stands idly by as the Kingdom he was willing to commit patricide and fratricide to rule is so desperately threatened?"

"I have heard rumors of a final solution to the constant attack and commandeering of our Great Barges. What have you heard?" she asked Cereal. If he had been a stowaway, and had been to Stonehaven recently, he'd most likely have factual information. For silver, anyone on the Fringe would tell you what you wanted to hear. The Fringe was peculiar. If you were an undesirable, you'd be most welcomed. If you were royalty, well, Shaw remembered the words written in blood red paint on the archway. "The King, our redemption from filth." Ironic, of course, but fitting to describe the King's influence.

Cereal stood, wiping crumbs from his ragged clothing and brushed his uncut hair from his face. He stood as tall as he could, obviously delighted to be in the presence of royalty.

"My Lord and Lady, I haven't had such an honor in all my life. It gives me..."

"Speak plainly boy, and keep the formalities silent, we're no more royalty than you," snapped Shaw, who stood up, faced away from the boy and his sister, and walked to the shuttered window of the tower. The boy nodded again, rubbing his eyes. Shaw pushed back the shutters to let in the late-night air. By candlelight, time had escaped them and soon, darkness would creep over the Fringe. Lights would be put out, the market would die down, and the patrols would start.

"Perhaps we should continue this in the morning...The boy

obviously hasn't rested, and I myself am growing weary. Sister, will you stay here for the night?"

"Tonight, no, I must handle business of my own west of town."

"Dare I ask what business the disavowed princess might have late at night, especially when patrols of King's Guard rape and pillage freely?"

Beggen Ostra smiled a cool smile, her eyes glinting by the candlelight, full of youth ever-still. "In time, dear brother," she said.

She pushed back her chair, and, as she walked towards the circle stairs in the floor, she rubbed two fingers together above her head. A fine black powder seemed to fall lightly about her, clinging to her skin, clothing and armor. The deep black shroud that obscured her from vision early that day now obscured her even more in the dim light of the tower. Now an ominous black cloud appeared to be standing in the middle of the room, swirling slightly. Shaw admired her power. Magic such as hers was formidable and terrifying at the same time. She took great risk using spells that powerful.

Silently, the cloud rounded the banister protecting the stairway and made its way down the stairs, disappearing from view. The boy stood in awe, mouth slightly agape, his eyes unwavering.

"Boy...rest while you can. Tomorrow, I'll find you food and clothing at the market, and then you will continue with your story."

"My deepest gratitude, my Lord, I'll take this corner," he said, walking to the other side of the room near the table. He took off his ragged shirt to reveal many long pale scars across his belly. Shaw had seen these before, they were nicknamed "Marks of the King". Punishment for thieves and dissidents.

"What did you steal to warrant those?" Shaw asked, nodding to the marks on the boy's stomach.

"Nothing, my Lord. My father died before they finished his lashes for speaking out against the King. Since he was dead, I was given the remaining lashes."

Shaw stood stone-faced for a moment. Torturing children... Jayecob was cruel, but this was beyond him. As children, Jayecob had always been of temperament, preferring to fight first, ask questions later. His father, King Armand sent Jayecob to build Third City while Shaw was appointed Head of King's Guard, though Jayecob was the better fighter. Jayecob often voiced his complaints about the appointment, to which King Armand would reply, "We all have our duties and our place. In order to rule a kingdom, you must understand how one is built." Jayecob would in turn reply with a weakly placed, "Yes, father" before storming off, his angry retorts echoing the halls. King Armand would laugh it off, believing his youngest sons' behavior to be the result of his age. "Age and wisdom. One day they'll meet in that boy," he once said before plunking down on the throne, his armor and weapons resting upon the high-stone chair.

Shaw remembered that day in particular, because like most days, it began with Jayecob's outbursts and ended in King Armand's words of wisdom. But on that particular day, King Armand's words were silenced for good.

Shaw removed his outer tunic, throwing it to the boy. "Rest," he said.

Tearing up, the boy admired the craftsmanship of the tunic for a moment before laying his head atop it on the wood floor, his own ragged shirt balled up underneath an arm. Within moments, the boy was asleep. Shaw extinguished the candle and returned to the chair by the table.

From the darkness, a voice asked, "Where will you sleep, my Lord?"

"I have been sleeping for many years, boy. I'll sleep no longer."

CHAPTER FIVE

RAYS OF MORNING sun and a light chill woke the boy.

Shaw, lost in thought, stood watch by the entryway to the church. Moments before deciding to impatiently wake the boy himself, he emerged from the stairway rubbing sleep from his eyes, holding Shaw's outer tunic.

"Mornin', my Lord."

Shaw grunted.

I change my mind, seeing him in this light he is not very appetizing. Even the buzzards would pass up this scrawny meal, Pemazu chimed in.

The demon had a point. Eyeing the boy up, he did appear as if he hadn't eaten in quite some time, and he desperately needed a wash.

"Follow me, Cereal, you smell of fish. I'll also find you proper clothing, as payment for helping my sister and I."

The boy shrugged and held out Shaw's bundled-up tunic.

"Keep it, we will burn it later".

The boy hugged it tight, "Burn it?"

"Yes! Burn it! Did I not just say you smell of fish? It's a miracle you made it this far listening like you do."

"Apologies, my Lord," he said, head hung low.

Shaw grunted again. Pushing his back lazily off the wall of the church, Shaw walked towards the market square. He'd get the boy a proper bath, clothing and food before meeting with Beggen Ostra around mid-day. Under the cover of darkness she had returned, explaining she had found something and wanted to show him the following day. She did not stay and insisted it was a conversation best left in the daylight. She was as flighty and full of energy as usual, yet unusual for age as she must be nearing seventy years based on Shaw's calculations.

Shaw continued south, away from the church along the main road. When the sounds of the market arose above the sounds of travelers marching heavily on the cobblestone, Shaw side-stepped into an alley, dragging the boy with him. At the next cross alley, Shaw pulled the boy aside and set him against the wall of the building.

"Stay here, the market is busy and I don't want to lose track of you. Speak to no-one. If spoken to, bow your head and hold up your hands above your head. If given silver, thank them and sit down without another word."

The boy nodded quickly before plopping down. After speaking with him this morning the boy seemed even more eager to please. Confident the boy understood the beggar's customs, Shaw took the left-most path leading to the market. Glancing over his shoulder, he could see the boy swirling his finger in the dirt.

Shaw approached the cloth barrier marking the entrance to the market, flicked up his hood and double checked his sleeves. Pushing back a tattered cloth that served as a barrier, he stepped into the lowlight and followed the natural path rounding the outside of the square. He shouldered his way through the crowds gathered at the individual booths. Dealers held up their wares for auction, from demon-difference charms to infused weaponry. These items were, of course, useless, but to some, the hope of protection was enticing enough to spend all of one's silver. Magic is best defeated with stronger magic.

Shaw found the tradesman he was looking for dressed in a familiar but subtle two-toned travelers' cloak. He appeared non-threatening, which most likely aided his ability to move about while out *procuring*. Shaw knew otherwise. Underneath the traveler's cloak was a nasty pin-vest. A sort of body armor plated with short needles. The needles would act as a deterrent from assault. The poison they were coated with, however, would make sure the deterrent was permanent. Short, burly and lackluster, he was just the man Shaw preferred to do business with. He also seemed to have a knack for procuring odd items at Shaw's request, always without question.

"Hello, Garold," Shaw said lowly, approaching the man.

"Sir..." he said with a nod. The man examined Shaw for a second before retreating into his stall, returning a few moments later with a small, leather-bound pouch. It was knotted twice over and the dark leather was engraved with symbols Garold wouldn't recognize. Shaw knew them, however, for they matched those of the Compendium, and the language of demons. Garold held the bag gingerly between two fingers, almost as if it hurt to touch.

"Not easy to find this item, sir. Not cheap, either. Causes a tickle in the stomach it does."

Shaw looked at the bag more closely, noticing the runes crawling and changing periodically. Garold seemed oblivious to this. Shaw snatched the bag quickly from his hand and jammed it into an inner pocket. From his other pocket he withdrew a small pouch, dug out a small handful of silver coins, and handed them to Garold. He counted the coins suspiciously and raised an eyebrow questioningly.

"Your generosity is a blessing on these dark times," he said with hopefulness in his voice.

"Not quite. I need a day's worth of food, clothing for a boy of twelve, and shoes for the same."

Flashing disappointment, Garold grumbled and dug in the booth before throwing a deerskin jerkin, matching pants, and sandals out behind him on the dirt. In his hands he carried a small loaf of bread, wrapped in cloth, a deerskin water-bag, and another cloth containing cured meat.

"The meat?" Shaw asked.

"Goat, sir, these are hard times."

Shaw scoffed, then snatched up the items and left the stall. He retraced his steps, leaving the market behind him. As he walked, he felt the gems throb for a moment.

He has become suspicious. You may have to find another poor soul to gather your ingredients, Pemazu said.

"Indeed, he felt the runes on the bag. Though they don't affect me, the sickness to his insides he won't soon forget. Can you translate the runes to verify the contents before I open it?"

I can, but why should I? Have the boy do it.

"Your sarcasm isn't needed. The boy can't read your language," Shaw thought to the demon.

He can.

"No, he can't," Shaw said.

He can. The Book has identified him as the vessel.

"What? What are you going on about?"

He has read from the Book and it has chosen him. There was pure terror in his eyes when he saw your gems. They match the Book's. The gems throbbed again.

"Hmmm. This boy is unanswered question after unanswered question. We will get the truth soon enough. It's almost mid-day and my sister has something to show me. I'll question him in her presence."

Shaw stood impatiently, wares in hand, as a caravan of traders attempted to make way into the market square. Horse drawn carts piled high parted the sea of buyers as they made their way through. As the caravan cleared the path, Shaw peeked around earnestly to see if his charge was where he left him. Curiosity turned to slight panic and fury as he noticed the boy was no longer alone. From a distance, Shaw counted two children, roughly the same age staring at one another, inches from each other's faces. Shaw marched over, fully prepared to toss the boy's food into the fire for failing to obey him yet again.

As he approached, he started saying, "Cereal, damn it, see if I don't whip you my..." before stopping in mid-thought.

Cereal had his palms against the wall to either side and the other boy was inches from his face. Small, shaky breaths came from Cereal's mouth and he stared directly ahead in obvious terror. The other boy, about Cereal's age, wore ragged clothing and also had a head of jet-black overgrown hair.

The boy continued to stare at Cereal and turned to look up at Shaw as he approached. Stopping short, Shaw dropped his wares and drew his sword. The boy's eyes were black pits of nothingness, a toothy grin extended ear to ear and he hissed through his teeth, "Black spires black spires raise the night... TWO DEAD BOYS GOT UP TO FIGHT!" The boy finished speaking and Shaw lunged, swiping at the him and attempting to grab him by the hair. Instead, he grasped nothing as the boy's image fading into nothing, his words still lingering in his ears, a manic cackle bouncing off the walls of the ally.

Shaw righted himself and slammed his blade back into its scabbard in frustration.

Still, the Book taunts him! The boy must have read from the Book after all. It must be drawn to its readers.

He looked down at the frightened boy who still stared unwavering ahead, shaking. Showing empathy was difficult after all Shaw had been through; pity was easier to come by.

"C'mon now, boy, get up. You're fine. Pick yourself up now," Shaw said.

The boy remained steadfast and stone-faced.

Shaw grunted, put his hands underneath the boy's arms and lifted him to his feet. Continuing to stare through Shaw at the alley wall behind him, Cereal said lowly, quivering, "He told me things…awful…haunting things…I couldn't look away…I couldn't stop seeing….Who was he?"

"Not who…what," Shaw corrected. He paused for a moment before continuing. "You have read from the Book?"

The boy nodded. "Who was he?"

"That thing was the Book…the poor boy a vessel, his soul seared and shredded into tiny fractions of itself. What else did it say?"

"The same words rang about my head, my Lord. Spell won't work. Spell won't work. Spell won't work. What does that mean?"

"I'll explain in detail later. Here," he said, handing the boy the goods he had brought. "Just know this. If the Book…I mean, that *boy* returns, you run fast and far."

The boy examined the clothing and food for a moment and asked, "What does it want with me?"

"Nothing you need worry about. We will discuss it further away from prying ears."

Cereal nodded, content.

You and I both know what the Book really wants, Pemazu said.

Shaw thought back at the demon. "How do you explain that the boy has been chosen to be a vessel for the vile thing?"

Bluntly and quickly, so that he will have a choice.

"You and I both know that he does not have a choice once the Book has chosen him," Shaw replied.

He does…he can kill himself.

Shaw let the conversation die off and let the idea float for just a while longer. He did not know what choice the boy would make. Not much of a choice it was anyway. If he fought it, the Book would surely win, in time.

Addressing the boy by name, he said, "Cereal, follow me to the bath-house."

By the time Cereal returned, the mid-day sun was full overhead and sweat was running down Shaw's neck. He stayed outside the bathhouse in the shade of a propped-up cloth cover. Just another mysterious traveler seeking whatever goods the Fringe could provide. Cereal rounded the front of the bathhouse to where Shaw was sitting, eyes closed, but never truly asleep.

"I'm here, sir." he said.

"I know," Shaw said, opening his eyes. The boy was not such a gutter-rat now. He smelled of lavender and bees-wax. His hair was pulled back and tied loosely behind his head. He also wore the deerskin jerkin and sandals Shaw had purchased.

Shaw handed him his meager leather scabbard and belt, then gestured for him to put them on. Once he had himself situated, he looked rejuvenated and even younger than before. He held out his hands expectantly and Shaw smiled slightly before pulling the bread and goat meat from his hip pack.

With the sun once again at his back, Shaw moved eastward, heading deeper into the slums of the Fringe. Huts turned to shacks, and shacks turned to rows and rows of people simply sleeping in the dirt. Even the light seemed to reflect the poverty and seemed so scarce. A general level of dread floated over the place. Stalwart, Shaw ignored the prying eyes and Cereal hung close to his heels, eyes darting side to side, hand on his little dagger.

"Where are we going, sir?" he whispered to Shaw's backside.

"A meeting with my sister and someone who claims he can help us."

"Here? Why here, sir? Why not the church?"

"This person does not want to be seen in our company, nor near the marketplace. He values secrecy, as should you."

"Secrecy?" the boy asked, hoping to continue to pry for

information. He looked up to meet Shaw's gaze. He encountered a slight scowl. The boy asked too many questions. Upon seeing Shaw's reaction to his inquiry, he continued his scan of the area, tabling his questions... for now.

The path began to narrow and the cobblestone turned to dirt, marking the final turn in the directions Beggen Ostra provided. The two turned sharply to the right and into an even more narrow passage. The walls rubbed against their elbows and Cereal stepped on Shaw's heels several times, resulting in a short jab to the boy's ribs. After the third time, expecting the jab, he slowed his step to avoid it before speeding up again on Shaw's heels. He was obviously afraid. As much as he projected courage, his age showed.

Shaw and Cereal approached an opening along the pathway, where an all-encompassing darkness hid the doorway from the average eye in this gloomy place. Shaw moved through the opening in the walls of the passageway without losing his step and stood in front of the doorway. The doorway Beggen Ostra described would reveal a grotto warded to keep sound from escaping.

It was old wood and had metal-bound clasps on either side. Besides that, powerful wards of concealment hid it from the common eye. Shaw, however, saw it clear as day. Shaw spoke in the common tongue, infusing his words with a slight ebb of power.

"Ebandah."

The door responded by dropping its protective ward and unlatching with a muffled *thud*, breaking the ominous silence around them. Shaw pulled the door back and crossed over the threshold into a room with low ceilings and a small fire in the fireplace. The door slammed shut behind him with a loud sound before the ward replaced itself.

From a side door, Beggen Ostra entered the room silently, followed by a hard-looking man dressed in ornate battle armor.

His hand rested on the hilt of a large sword embossed with vibrant gems of every color. His other arm hung by his side, missing a hand. Over his armor the soldier wore a cloth vest with a large war-hammer stitched across the front. Shaw recognized this soldier as one of the elites from Second City. Shaw nodded in recognition; the man remained stalwart.

"Shaw, this is Daemond. He is second in command for the Stone Breakers in Second City. He has news of the King's plans and the response to the attacks from the Far East. He comes to us under risk of being charged with treason. He knows who we are."

"What would cause one of the Stone Breakers of Second City to turn against the King?" Shaw asked.

Daemond answered in a soft but deliberate voice. "The Stone Breakers of Stonehaven have their own interests; can I not have my own?"

"Whatever your interest, it must be of grave importance, considering the punishment for treason," Shaw replied.

He shifted his feet slightly and scanned the room side to side as if nervous he'd be overheard. "Second City is in the gutter of the land, and the Stone Breakers are young, foolish and ignorant of the King's dealings. I want out, and you two…" he said nodding to Shaw and Beggen Ostra in turn, "are my absolution."

Beggen Ostra spoke this time, a slight hint of annoyance in her voice. "Speak plainly, so they might understand what you want."

"I want command of the Stone Breakers of Stonehaven…"

"How do you propose we hand you the position? They are loyal only to the King," Shaw stepped in as he replied. He knew the Stone Breakers of Stonehaven were steadfast in their loyalty. He of all people would know, for he had taught them to be.

"When you two reveal the truth about the King, the Stone Breakers will fall in line and follow you, Prince Shaw."

Shaw scoffed. "Where did you find this one, sister?"

Beggen Ostra reached out and touched Shaw's arm. "It's true, they are loyal to the King, and the rightful King will unite them further. Daemond hasn't anything but contempt for the King."

"This isn't the first time a coup has been attempted..." he said, raising his arm, showing his missing hand. "I was demoted and banished from command at Stonehaven over twenty years ago. I rose up within Second City's Stone Breakers. I have the allegiance of the men there."

"What of the commander in Second City? Does he know of your plan?"

"No, and he won't. He won't turn against me, but the less who know, the better."

"You know this how?"

"He is my brother."

Shaw couldn't contain his laughter. They burst out, loud and deep-chested. So many years of suppressed contempt and anger for his brother manifested as laughter, causing him to keel over. He held up his hand to Daemond, as if telling him to stop, as he struggled to get the words out between breaths.

"My own brother ran me...through...killed my father...and seized the throne. My wife...my wife...is dead too. I lost everything because of my brother." His hysterics turning to spitting anger as the words left his mouth.

"My Lord, Princess Avana lives..."

Shaw's stomach flipped over and the words cut into his fury as easily a hot blade through churned butter.

"What did you say?" Shaw spat. His emotions welled up beyond his control. The gems in his arm shone bright enough to be seen through his tunic. The well of magic, sensing his lapse in control, threw itself violently against the barriers within Shaw's mind.

For one moment, Shaw gave up to the power within, the sudden blast of energy transforming his hand into a nasty, crooked claw. Shaw grabbed the soldier by the throat, lifting him high into the air, the sharp black nails digging into the man's skin. Desperately, he clawed at Shaw's now-green-and-black scaled arm. He kicked out and Shaw held him at a distance.

"No brother!" Beggen Ostra spoke. "He tells the truth!"

Determined to let Daemond suffer for his lies, Shaw released his grip just enough to allow him several shallow breaths. "She lives. She...lives. Captured...lives...Jayecob." the soldier gasped out, his face turning a shade of violet.

"She lives sir, I can attest," said a soft voice from the corner of the room. Shaw's overwhelming anger was temporarily lifted, and for a moment he had clarity. He looked at his own arm, scaled and grotesque, choking the life from a Stone Breaker...his brother-in-arms.

Shaw released Daemond, who crumpled to the floor, his armor clanking loudly. He fought for air, holding his neck, eyes bulging in terror at what had become of Shaw's hand and his demeanor in a matter of an instant.

"Speak boy," Shaw said, turning his back on his concerned sister and the clearly frightened Daemond.

"What are you?" the boy said, refusing to take his eyes off Shaw's mutated arm.

Shaw took a moment to truly look at the devastation his anger had caused. His sister, distrusting, a fellow Stone Breaker, wounded and scared, and the boy, not of thirteen years, terrified enough he couldn't move.

"A monster..." Shaw replied. His anger released with the realization that he was something to be feared. He was something mothers tell their children to be wary of. He was the thing that goes bump in the night...

Stop wasting energy on parlor tricks, Pemazu chirped. The demon's shrill bird voice cut through his concentration.

Ugh. For a moment, he had forgotten about the demon.

In silence, Shaw reached back into the well and instantly found where the power had leaked through. Without resistance, Shaw locked it behind the mental dam, causing his arm to shift back to normal.

"My powers...are different. I'm sorry," Shaw said with remorse.

Cereal walked forward cautiously. He reached out and touched Shaw's hand gingerly, using his forefinger like a stick poking at something dead.

"Relax, child. I am sorry. Now, please, tell me of my wife. Tell me of Princess Avana." Shaw dropped to one knee, catching the child's eye.

"When my parents and I were taken, the King's Guard first took us to the castle, to Stonehaven. Our cell was next to Princess Avana's."

"And you are sure it was her? What did she look like?"

"Beautiful, my lord. Crystal blue eyes, long brown hair...she wore a stone locket with an S on it."

With a surge of excitement, Shaw's heart began to beat frantically. How could she be alive? After so many years as a prisoner? It had to be her. The locket...he had given it to her when they married. It was the jeweled S of Stonehaven. Shaw had carved it from stone himself.

"She lives. I can't believe she lives," Shaw stammered, resting on the floor. He stared down at his hands in his lap.

Daemond, who had regained his composure, scoffed. "You believe this child but take not my word? Pathetic. Bring me to the brink of death...pah!" He got up and stomped through the doorway by which he had entered the room.

Beggen Ostra folded her arms across her chest. In the dim light, her skin looked even more aged and leathered than it had in the daylight. "This is what I wanted to tell you, brother, and you needed to hear it from all of us... privately."

"You could have told me in the tower..." he replied.

"You'd not have believed me had I not brought Daemond."

"I had the boy."

"How was I supposed to know of the knowledge this child has? It wasn't my place to tell you."

"How long have you known?"

"What?"

"How long have you known that she was alive?" Shaw questioned.

"Not long. Daemond made it known to me shortly before I saw you."

"How did you stumble upon a one-handed, treasonous Stone Breaker anyway?" Shaw asked, his voice reflecting his disbelief.

"He came to me in a vision...I found him."

"Ah, yes. Your powers have always been quite impressive." Shaw was aware of his sister's powers of foresight. For many years she was revered as the strongest battle mage of her time, both feared and respected.

"They are failing as my body does; this vision was a blessing and most likely my last. It was not clear, but Daemond's missing hand and chest tabard were. I met him as he travelled, and we discussed the situation in private. I told him I knew of his plan and wanted to help. He denied it, of course, but when I described how he was banished and dismembered in vivid detail, he came around."

"Greater than your otherworldly powers are your powers of persuasion, dear sister," Shaw said, a smile creeping out of the corner of his mouth.

"Well, I should at least properly explain my...reaction. Where did he run off to?" Shaw questioned, peaking into the darkness of the side doorway.

"That door leads to the other end of the grotto.... Let us find him. He most likely stepped out to smoke."

"Wait here," Shaw said to Cereal. "Don't move until I return. Eat." Cereal seemed to remember the meal he had packed away and dug it out of his pocket in a frenzy. Shaw and Beggen Ostra left the boy and closed the wooden door to the grotto behind him.

This doorway led to an intersection, and Shaw was soon cursing Daemond for not staying nearby, as the intersection was barren and there were no sounds of footfalls or heavy armor clinking. He took the center path, which was better lit and looked like it had seen foot traffic recently.

"It's unlike you to trust someone so blindly, sister," Shaw spoke softly, keeping his head and eyes forward, walking on.

"Hardly blind, I'd say. His needs are understandable, and his position with both Second City and the remaining Stone Breakers of Stonehaven may prove useful in gathering allies."

"Allies? What do you have planned?"

She chuckled. "For me? Resolution. For you? Revenge."

Revenge. Shaw was built for revenge. For many years, and many years beyond that, Shaw had relied on revenge, on the idea alone, to get him through. All those years in the dark, he plotted and schemed. He did not live for revenge. He simply refused to die on the Thin Line for the mere chance at revenge.

"Where did the stumpy man run off to?" Shaw asked, looking around. They had walked the length of the path, which met at the wall to another alley. Surely, he wouldn't have taken either of the turns, they were both clearly dead ends.

"I'll locate him," Beggen Ostra said. She closed her eyes in concentration. For a moment, Shaw thought she had fallen asleep and considered jostling her. Without warning, a large ripple came off her person, distorting the air like a desert heat wave and shaking the ground and the walls of the buildings.

The ripple disturbed the base layer of dust from the pathway, revealing the faint outline of boot-marks scaling the wall to their left. There were also outlines from handholds and footprints where someone had climbed up and onto the roof.

"That weasel!" Shaw exclaimed, preparing to climb the wall and chase after him.

"Shaw, wait! Look!" Beggen Ostra said, grabbing him by the arm and pointing above them.

Above the tops of the buildings, a brilliant red line shot straight into the air, pulsing every few seconds. "Shaw, what is that?"

Shaw was all too familiar with the signal. "His sword, the hilt. The gems are a warning beacon. It alerts the King's Guard that there is trouble and signals a pre-determined rallying point. There is no honor in treason. He means to gain favor from the King with our capture. We have to leave."

CHAPTER SIX

THE BRILLIANT RED line pulsed at regular intervals, ending in a mushroom shape against the overcast rolling clouds of a brewing afternoon storm. Shaw, Beggen Ostra, and Cereal ran single file through the mud-walled grotto, every few strides ducking quickly to avoid awnings and poorly made sunshades. The three ran in silence, breathing quietly and attempting to muffle their footsteps by landing softly and purposefully. Periodically, Shaw stopped to orient himself in the maze of alleys by looking up at the red beam. The beam gave a sense of direction, identifying the west side of the Fringe. Shaw regularly righted their path by orienting to the north-east, aiming to avoid the market, and they quickly made their way to the old church.

Shaw stopped, causing Beggen Ostra and Cereal to stop hard behind him, almost running into him. They both breathed rapidly. Beneath Beggen Ostra's armor, her chest heaved, making her age more apparent. Between rapid breaths of dusty air, she managed to whisper.

"The King's Guard is in Stonehaven. Why do we flee so quickly?"

"What is to worry of a one-armed Stone Breaker? He isn't

anything compared to you," Cereal asked as soon as she finished.

Shaw threw out his arm and pushed his companions into the shadows of a half-hung awning and spoke to them through his teeth.

"The Stone Breaker is of no concern to me, though he carries many years of experience, and the associated power. He will, however, target the weakest link to break the chain," he said, looking directly at Beggen Ostra. "He knows of your value to me, and our mission. Surely this will be immediately reported to my brother, who in turn commands an army of slaves, and along with those slaves he commands some of the best battle mages ever to have lived. He'll combine their strength, and with the help of their spells, the King's Guard will arrive within a half-day."

Beggen Ostra nodded along. "Ah yes, combining the strengths of multiple magic-wielders. There is great risk in pooling magic. A risk he will not have to undertake himself." She wiped the sweat from her brow and pulled the frizzing stragglers of her wispy hair behind her ears. She furrowed her brow in concentration, partially hoping Shaw would have an answer to bring their pursuit to an end. The King's Guard were not to be trifled with. If their strengths came anywhere near Shaw's, fleeing seemed to be the best option. Undoubtedly, they'd bring their war-dogs to pick up the scent; a greater distance from their pursuers will still not guarantee safety from the tracking skill of the war-dogs. Hearing that Shaw was alive after all this time would surely draw the utmost attention of the King, thus bringing the heavily armed and heavily trained King's Guard.

This time, it was the boy who spoke, and it seemed that his thoughts had followed the same pattern.

"Sir, I know somewhere we can go where the dogs can't follow."

Still looking down the alley, Shaw waited for the boy to continue.

"The Valor, south of the Fringe, there's an old Great Barge, long past its day. A dinghy remains attached to the side. After my parents…after they…I hid there many a night."

Shaw grunted.

Beggen Ostra replied, her voice reflecting some of the Shaw's doubts. "The Valor is dangerous, and Stonehaven commands a legion of vessels which frequent the river. A dinghy will make us an obvious curiosity. Why would such a small vessel risk traveling the river?"

Shaw grunted again. "It's a terrible idea. The Valor itself is one problem we can't continue to face. We can't stay on the river for long with the supplies the dinghy will carry. We must seek out refuge in Second City; they have no love for the King. Perhaps there we can find your traitorous Stone Breaker as well." A slight malice crept into his voice as he directed this jab at Beggen Ostra.

This time it was Beggen Ostra who grunted, a sound that was slightly odd to hear from an aging woman. It came out almost in the form of a question. Shaw took the general lull in conversation to consult Pemazu, who occasionally had note-worthy ideas.

And what are your thoughts? Shaw asked, his own voice rever-berating in his head for a moment. A light throb from the rubies embedded in his arm indicated that the demon was listening, but didn't guarantee a response. "You've been unusually quiet since the grotto. What do you believe we should do?"

The magpie took its time in its reply. *The dinghy is as you said: a terrible idea. But Second City has as much contempt for the royal family as for the King himself. My vote is for the river. Also, if you were attempting to move quietly, how about stifling your sword, as its incessant bouncing against your hip is even annoying me.*

It seemed that no one liked the idea of a crowded boat on the

Valor, and yet there were no other options. The river tended to weed out the weak, almost as if it were picking and choosing who was worthy enough to travel its massive swell. The river was the wealth of the land, but it held terrible secrets. Along its rocky bottom, creatures with many teeth and insatiable appetites patrolled endlessly. As the sun set, scaly lizards as large as horses basked in the warm shallows. If the wildlife granted you passage, the rocky outcrops, twenty-feet high, aimed to knock unsuspecting travelers off the decks of their ships or sink the ships themselves. As the stone itself grew, it created an ever-changing maze of deadly creatures, unbridled physical terrors, and those who make their living pillaging the unsuspecting.

Shaw led the way through the southwestern portion of the Fringe. Their surroundings mirrored the area they had just come from on the western side, but travel and trade were more prominent here, and the area itself seemed generally brighter. Cereal had taken the center position, leaving Beggen Ostra to guard their rear. Cereal kept a steady pace but the crew had to stop repeatedly to allow Beggen Ostra to rest.

Just before deciding their course, Cereal had asked another one of his questions, prompting a smack to the back of the head from Shaw and a light smile from Beggen Ostra at the question, as she seemed to value his curiosity but was disapproving of his timing.

"Why not spell yourself, as you did to pursue us?" he asked her, eyes wide and hopeful. Thus ensued the smart smack to the back of his head and Beggen Ostra's disapproving look.

"Magic is very taxing and will attract more attention than we already have. Besides, I'd not want to leave you all behind," she said with a wink and a flash of a smile. She liked how interested the boy was in magic and its potential. For many years, her name was spread about the Kingdom as an incredibly potent and cunning battle mage. Since the original Breaking, the beginning of the new Kingdom, she taught magic in all its glory to any who would listen. Magic flourished as the Kingdom flourished, until the Great Betrayal took history in another direction. Since then, like Beggen Ostra herself, magic had remained in the shadows, fading and forgotten.

Cereal seemed to catalog the information, satisfying his curiosity. His choice to take up the middle spot between the two seemed to reflect his current feelings towards them. On one hand, the boy appreciated and looked up to Shaw for saving him and felt like he owed a debt. On the other, Beggen Ostra seemed genuinely concerned and interested in him. Either way, he felt a connection to the rightful king and the forgotten princess.

Shaw's pace gradually increased as he led the way nearer the beam of light, attempting to circumvent the rallying point for the King's Guard and reach the south end of the Fringe where the ruined vessel rested. They planned to use the obscurity of the Fringe to hide their retreat, circle down south, sneak around the rallying point for the King's Guard, and push east towards the shipyard.

Along the way, a violent bubble shot up the red beam and marked the arrival of the King's Guard. The blast was much like Beggen Ostra's spell which originally located where the Stone Breaker had scurried off to, but this time, the ground shook and a wave of dust wove its way through the cramped alleys through which they traveled.

Beggen Ostra attempted to go into detail about the inner workings of the spell, but Shaw cut her off, griping about wasting time explaining powerful magic to a plain child with no magical talent. The result was Pemazu's mindful clicking of his beak, almost as if he were attempting to remind Shaw of the Book's contact with the boy. Indeed, the Book's connection and borderline obsession would grant the boy some amount of power…if he knew about it.

Shaw increased his stride again, causing the followers to

focus more on keeping with his pace and breathing rather than talking. He appreciated the silence, which gave him a moment to think about their next move. The dinghy was a temporary fix, one which Shaw firmly believed was an incredibly dumb idea, but it was the best option they had. Following the treacherous journey aboard a tiny lifeboat, on a river designed to sink all but the largest of ships and most competent of captains, Shaw rather looked forward to arriving in Second City, which was by nature only slightly more affluent than the slums of the Fringe. Since the Great Betrayal, Second City had been treated as a rodent in need of extermination; obviously the mad King's doing. The Kingdom was intended to unite in times of trial, and its enemies in the Far East had been taking advantage of the disjointed nation with quick and deadly strikes against supply lines on both land and water. Bandits raided the convoys, killing everyone and burning the supplies. On water, the crews were captured and flayed alive, their skinless bodies fed to scaly creatures. The Great Barges would be commandeered, taken north past the Maw and onward to the shores on the Far East, where the Kingdom's troops dared not travel. Learning to navigate The Maw had become a tool for mass incursion into the Kingdom, and the Far East was certainly taking advantage of it.

At times, Shaw remembered his time spent on the Thin Line and almost admired its simplicity. Anger drove him to the near brink of madness, and for many years only anger accompanied him in that place. For what seemed like an eternity, not caring if he lived or died, brutal, raw anger festered. Sensing his presence, many a creature attempted to consume his essence; over and over he struck them down. Until one, a monster of tentacles, teeth, and eyes approached him out of the darkness. Instead of attempting to consume him, it stopped its approach from the black and screeched and howled, testing Shaw's mettle. Shaw stood steadfast, a rusted, dented shield and a dull, unbalanced blade raised. The creature continued its tirade of screams, clicks, and inhuman moans before a vague memory broke through Shaw's concentration. This creature was familiar... The pomp and circumstance, the spectacle. Shaw had a fleeting memory - he had seen this creature somewhere...no...he had read about it somewhere. The Book. He had read about this creature in the Book. The creature, a demon, no doubt, had decided its prey was worthy of consuming and Shaw frantically ran through what he could remember of the Book. It had listed out demons by name, their appearance, their actions, their abilities...and their age.

Carefully remembering the pull of the Thin Line, Shaw kept his eyes trained on the creature, lest the ground drag him into the Void or the sky drag him into the unknown. He put the frantic searching of his memory aside for a moment as the creature lunged with its many tentacles. Shaw easily parried the suction-cup-laden tentacle and noticed that the creature seemed to be weak. Was it afraid? The demon lunged again and Shaw side-stepped, the creature lazily turning around to meet him, as though purposefully exposing its backside. Did this thing care to preserve whatever semblance of life it had? Was it trying to die? Shaw searched his memory again, not caring if the creature meant to be careless and slow, or if that was simply its nature. A flash of fleshy blackness ran through his memory for a moment. Shaw parried an advancing tentacle and gained some distance by hopping backward. The creature didn't pursue.

The creature resumed its routine of slapping and screaming. In an instant, a flood of information rushed through him. He knew this demon. He knew this demon's name...its full name. The Book told him its name, and with its name he could bind it!

The demon slid forward, tentacles reaching out like grasping vines from a deadly plant...

"Pemazu...." Shaw whispered to himself. The demon stopped and the screaming faded away.

He said it again. "Pemazu." This time, the creature brought its tentacles in on itself and appeared almost curious.

A third time he said the demon's name, this time confidently and from his chest, "Pemazu!" The demon began to slowly retreat in what Shaw judged as disbelief. He stepped forward, sword drawn with newfound confidence. This was the demon Pemazu. He was old, very old, possibly one of the First. The first of all demons and magical creatures, but something was different with this depiction of the terrifying monstrosity the Book had described. This version was much tamer...almost calm.

"Demon, I know your true name."

Responding with a screech, the demon continued its retreat.

"I have read from the Book and I know your true name!"

Shaw pointed his rusted weapon at the demon, a strange tenacity driving him forward. This demon was his pathway out of the Thin Line.

"You are Pemazu the Black, the Subjugator, the Defiler, the Empty. Et-al tre dua, tal-decal!" he cried, reciting the binding spell from the Book from memory. "From the Void I bring chains by which to bind you!"

The memory lingered for just a moment before Pemazu himself interrupted with a painful throb from the gems in his arm.

Let us be clear; I did not want to be captured. That was purely the Book forcing my inaction. I do not even like that particular form. The demon's shrill voice broke Shaw's focus on the memory. The timing appeared to be opportunistic, as the three of them were fast approaching the location where they'd be closest to the King's Guard. This was unavoidable, given the vast, dense forest they had come up against. This barrier prevented them from traveling any further south around the King's Guard without entering the woods. Of course, entering the woods near dusk would nearly be as treacherous as facing the King's Guard head on.

Shaw motioned to slow their pace. He looked around and spotted a small, crumbling hut, which appeared to be vacant. They hurried inside, ducking below the low-hanging timber ceiling. Inside, a thick layer of dust and the smell of decaying wood confirmed Shaw's assumptions about its occupancy. Cereal collapsed against the nearest wall; heaving and sputtering, he managed to get out, "How can you keep that pace?"

Beggen Ostra seemed slightly winded, but drank from her waterskin, unconcerned, and walked the hut, looking around. She kicked at an empty clay pot on the floor while Shaw peeked out the doorway. After a few moments, he pulled his head back inside.

"This is the closest we will be to them. As much as I'd like to thank Daemond for kicking off our mad dash through this wretched town to a tiny boat, we need to maintain our secrecy. The dogs can sense magic, so no spells of any kind."

That means you, too, Shaw thought to Pemazu. The warmth from the rubies faded and the face of the gems appeared dull and lifeless.

"I can see them from here. They're staged at the base of the watchtower at the north end of the intersection. We must move quickly so as not to attract attention; traveling at night would be suspicious. Cereal will go first. Walk quickly, as if delivering a message, and carry this," he said, handing Cereal a small, worn piece of parchment. "An errand boy won't attract too much attention, but you are too well dressed to pose as a servant or a beggar."

"Sister, walk slowly with your hood up, with a slight limp. They won't bother the elderly; nor will they suspect us to come so close to them."

Beggen Ostra nodded and pulled up her hood, hiding her wrinkled, expressionless face from view.

Shaw examined them for a moment longer, motioning for them to keep quiet, and peeked out the doorway again. Light was fading quickly, as was their opportunity to move about without arousing suspicion. A light wind began to blow in from the east, bringing a swirl of red dust dancing swiftly down the middle of the intersection. It briefly obscured his vision, and by the time he could see again, the King's Guard and war-dogs stood out starkly against the dark backdrop of the buildings and the blood-red of the fading light in the background. The King's Guard stood in a circle around a fire, while the war-dogs sat nearer the base of the watchtower. Above, Shaw saw two red specs glowing brightly against the black wall of the tower, appearing to float in midair. Shaw knew these to be the gems lodged in the tips of a powerful longbow. The bowman would use spelled arrows, with deadly results. He quickly counted the glowing hilts of the weapons worn at the hips of the King's Guard, and the spelled collars of the dogs. Six King's Guardsmen, two war-dogs, and a bowman. Obviously, the King did not whole-heartedly trust in Daemond's accusations, as only a small portion of the entire company of guardsmen was present. They laughed and joked loudly, a few of them drinking deeply from wine-pouches. Another uproar of laughter reached his ears as Shaw realized what had attracted their attention; the fire was not the only thing in the middle of the circle. On the ground, what appeared to be a small lump of cloth was issuing whimpers, high-pitched and easily heard between bouts of laughter.

One Guardsmen drank from his wine-pouch before dumping the contents on the quivering hump, inciting more cries. Shaw identified the voice as a young girl. One of the guardsmen broke from the group and untied the reins from the largest war-dog, bringing it to stand over the small girl, who continued to hide, tucking in the corners of the blanket covering her. The guardsman snapped his fingers at the dog, who looked up with both of its heads, and then down at the wine-soaked blanket. The dog seemed to notice the wine and proceeded to lick the blanket with increasing vigor. Another bout of laughter, and Shaw noticed the guardsmen holding on to one another. Obviously, they were not actively pursuing him.

Shaw pulled back inside, "They're distracted. Leave the girl and move quickly."

"What girl?" Cereal asked.

"Shut-up. Move."

Shaw flicked up his hood and ducked below the sagging roof. He turned right around the corner, followed by Cereal and Beggen Ostra. Shaw moved off, creating distance between them. Cereal and Beggen Ostra followed suit. The guardsmen laughed again; the other dog had taken interest in the girl. The dogs' green forked tongues licked at the blanket, lapping up the wine. The small spikes tore tiny holes in the blanket, wearing it away. The girl's whimpers and cries grew louder, more frequent, and deeper in tone.

Shaw checked on the others. Cereal was moving quickly, the parchment in one hand, the other in his pocket. Beggen Ostra lagged behind, shuffling slowly, The intersection was clearing and just a few wanderers and fewer trade-carts remained. Together they blended into the crowd. They made it to the middle of the intersection, where a gray fountain, dry and crumbling, sat, wearing away with time. A fading reminder of a once-prosperous nation.

The guardsmen's laughter turned to murmurs. Shaw sensed worry in their voices and strained to hear the girl's. Despite the lack of sound from the intersection, the girl's voice could no longer be heard. The murmurs of concern grew louder. The war-dogs were no longer licking their helpless victim and, instead, tugged against the handlers, attempting to get away.

"Do rah teh de rah...do rah teh de rah." A ghastly voice cut through the increasingly panicked guardsmen. Shaw heard several swords ring out of their sheaths. He stopped to peer against the black, the guardsmen outlined by the faint glow of the fire. The girl they were harassing was no longer in a heap on the ground but floated just above it, the blanket still covering her face.

"Do rah teh de rah....do rah teh de rah...." The deep, resounding voice was coming from the girl...

"Pemazu, what is she saying? It sounds like Demonic..."

'Into the Void,' over and over again, but we have a bigger problem. The demon's voice sounded as dire as his words.

"What is she?"

"Do rah te de rah....do rah teh de rah..." The voice grew louder, echoing off the walls of the buildings.

"Pemazu, what is she?!"

"Do rah teh de rah! Do rah te de rah! Do rah te deh rah!"

The guardsmen surrounded the girl, swords drawn. The dogs hung back, out of the circle with their handlers, poised and prepared.

A lone guardsman sheathed his sword and reached out to pull the blanket from the girl's face. He stepped forward gingerly and grasped the blanket. As his hand touched it, a blazing green light illuminated the intersection. The guardsman's screams cut through the air as he burst into violet and green flames, howling for another moment before falling to the ground in a smoldering pile of ash.

"It's an Impius! Run!" Shaw yelled to his companions, taking off without looking back. The guardsmen were attempting to stab and slash at the girl. As their blades met her flesh they melted down to the hilt, prompting the guardsmen to run in terror. The archer fired spelled arrows in succession, infusing each one with enough power to easily fell even the most armored individual. The spelled red arrows hit their intended target, lodging into the back of the girl, but appeared to have no effect. The girl turned slowly in the air and issued terrible laughter, rushing through the air towards the archer.

Keep moving! It is distracted! Pemazu chirped.

"What about the others?" Shaw asked, attempting to get as far away from the Impius as he could.

They are behind us, I can sense them. The Impius will consume the guardsmen and that will satiate it for now. Then it will seek out other prey, and it will sense me... The river will offer protection, or at least weaken it enough that we can destroy it. The Impius is impure, fresh waters should deter it.

Shaw carefully placed each step, maintaining speed but attempting to reduce the sounds his footsteps made so that he could listen.

Another scream and a yelp told him the Impius had finished with the archer and had moved on to the handlers and the dogs. A flash of green lit the area as Shaw made it through the intersection and onto the road, heading east to the shipyard. Hoping Pemazu was right, he continued on, passing the late-night stragglers who had begun to catch on to the commotion. He caught hurried footfalls and hushed voices whispering things like *magic, demon* and *King's Guard* as he made his way further east towards the edge of town. The late evening air was filled with the smell of fish and sea salt; when it hit him, Shaw almost felt relieved in knowing they were so close to enacting their foolish plan.

His relief was short-lived, however, when he heard the boy yell out from behind him, "Shaw! Help!" The boy's voice was shrill and cracking with terror.

Shaw turned around in the middle of the alley and started back towards where he had heard the boy's voice. He did not bother to worry about his sister; she had managed to stay hidden for over thirty years. Heading back the way he had come soon proved to be easier said than done. The Impius was wreaking havoc on the southern edge of the Fringe. Explosions rang out, shaking the ground, followed by flashes of green light. The Impius was relishing its new-found power and freedom; the demon must have easily broken the girl's will. At this point she was more demon than girl, and a demon with immeasurable power at that. He continued on, shoving people out of his way. Luckily, the panic was enough for them to want to avoid contact with someone running towards the commotion.

Shaw found the boy first, backed into a corner in a side alley just a short distance off the main road. The Impius blocked the path, separating Shaw and the boy. As he got close, Shaw tapped the gems in his arm, drawing Pemazu's attention to the here and now. Floating inches off the ground, the once-girl was quickly fading away beneath the grotesque outline of the demon's skin as it broke through the surface. Flesh and sinew fell off with every move the girl made and, according to the Book, the girl could feel the transformation take place. The kind of pain she was enduring must have been maddening. Even worse, the Impius appeared to have taken an interest in the boy.

The Impius hovered in a half-moon around the boy who had been reduced to a whimpering heap on the ground. Shaw reminded himself to confront the boy about his notorious behavior of giving up and rolling over. If or when the Book finally came for him, rolling over would not save him. Someday, he'd get the opportunity to fight, but if the Book came for him, nothing could save him but death itself. The Impius looked down at the boy, every so often reaching out a mangled hand then, pulling it back, murmuring to itself. The little girl's voice was gone and in its place was a voice sounding as Pemazu's did on the Thin Line. Only here, in this world, it was all the more eerie.

"Interesting little thing, aren't you? What are you, I suppose? I suppose it could be that which you suppose. Of course, it would, and you'd think that. Of course, I am not thinking, I am only supposing. Interesting…"

It has gone mad, Pemazu said.

Shaw glanced at the gems to see the magpie rubbing its eyes with a wing and yawning deeply.

"How do I kill it?"

Look for a gem, a single peridot. It will be somewhere on her body, normally on an arm or a leg. Destroy it. Then destroy the vessel and I will consume its essence, Pemazu said, a forked tongue flicking about in the bird's beak, tasting the air.

"Oh, is that all?"

Hardly, it uses the same form of magic that you do, therefore it cannot counter you and you cannot counter it. It is, however, ten times your strength, and is clearly insane.

"Do we eat it? It feels different, maybe kill it and then eat it? Yes, we should, a right choice you have made. Thank you. No, thank you. Always," it continued, babbling to itself.

We must hurry. Should the Impius make a meal of our scrawny friend there, I guarantee I would regret it later coming out the other end. Grown humans do not tend to carry much of a taste and the young ones have not had time to cure.

Shaw spoke to the girl, unsure of what to call her, or it. "Uhm, hello, little girl."

When the Impius responded, its voice seemed to resound all around him. It echoed in his head and against the walls of the alley.

"Little girl? Is that what I appear to be, Arbiter? Ahhhh!" it said, flipping around mid-air and beelining towards him.

He ducked and drew his sword, attempting to put himself between the boy and the creature. He swiped at it, but it moved quickly, only causing him to exert himself and eliciting a shallow, seething remark from Pemazu. Cursing under his breath, Shaw readied himself again for the creature. He stood half guarded, blade glinting silver in the moonlight.

"What shall we do? How shall we eat it? I'll eat it, oh yes, I will," the Impius trilled, its mouth moving differently from the words that it spoke. Small, bloodied chunks lopped off its face as it smiled. Piece by piece the girl was fading away; her body now resembling what remained of her soul.

He tried to recall what the Book told him. The Impius was a foul creature. It laid in wait near Gateways on the Thin Line, waiting to prey on those in the worst of pain. It took on the form of what it believed its victim would find appealing and trustworthy. In the victim's greatest pain, emotion or physical or some twisted combination of both, such as this young girl, the Impius would reach out, offering solace. It would lie. It would promise, and then it would take. Once granted permission, the Impius would rip the soul from its victim, scattering the pieces of it across the Thin Line, and in doing so, was granted enough power to force its way onto the mortal plane. The victim's soulless body would be the perfect host, empty, broken and faded, and the Impius would be in control.

Once occupying a body, it would wreak havoc, parading the victim's body around as a disguise. Overtime, the victim's body would deteriorate, leaving behind only the parasite, powerful and lawless. Once freed into the world, a black peridot marked their status as one of the damned, and according to Pemazu, was the chink in its armor.

When it dives again, swing for its left arm, I can sense the peridot, the demon chimed in matter-of-factly. *We need to make haste while it's still contained within the vessel. Once it has freed itself, it will swallow the peridot and it will become twice as difficult to subdue.*

"I value your insight as always."

My insight is only as valuable as your willingness to use it. Now act before it gets clever.

Shaw readied himself for the next attack. He shifted his weight to his front foot and kept his sword drawn high by his ear. The creature seemed interested by his willingness to fight and tilted its head to one side, the young girl's once rosy cheeks now a light shade of green, drooping lifelessly off the bone. The

Impius lifted its hand and with the other, began to peel back the skin, one finger at a time. The skin that still was somewhat intact stretched, warped, then finally ripped, revealing black, lizard-like scales underneath. At the end of each elongated finger a hooked black claw replaced human nail. Even in the moonlight, the light shining from the polished nails revealed their razor-sharp edge. The Impius dropped its hands, one normal, one mangled with a set of nefarious-looking nails to its side. Shaw watched as the last semblance of the girl faded in an instant and the demon's true self shone through. It was close to its full power, and soon, it would break through the constraints of its human host.

"Come Arbiter, test your mettle against my scales. I have withstood the pull of the Thin Line for eons; I am not one to so willingly give up this opportunity to destroy an Arbiter, the Book's little pet."

"I'll send you beyond the Void."

The demon didn't respond, and instead hurled itself at him, a half-human, half-demon smile stretched across its face. Shaw twisted and ducked, intending to bring his sword down on the demon from behind. His movement was swift and practiced, but the demon was incredibly fast. As he righted himself and attempted to plunge his sword into the demon's back, it met his sword with its scaled arm. A shower of purple sparks bounced through the air as they met.

A swift heel kick from the demon's inhuman foot caused Shaw to keel over for a moment. With an "umph," the demon brought its clawed hand through the air, catching him across his side. He cried out, seeing the gaping wounds caused by the demon's claws. Worm-like skin flaps hung from his side and warm blood trickled out of each of the five gashes, flowing into his trousers.

Intending to follow through with its attack, the demon slashed again. Shaw managed to parry the claw with his weak hand, his strong hand pressing down on the wound, haphazardly trying to slow the bleeding.

It has poisoned us, Pemazu said. *We cannot continue this fight alone, we need assistance.*

"You didn't mention poison. Ugh."

Should I need to? You were so confident in your monologue. 'I'll send you beyond the Void', Pemazu mocked.

"Shut up. We need to divert its attention and get the boy."

Now would be an optimal time to leave the boy to feed it.

"No. We need him....my vision...what's happening?"

Shaw keeled over, using his sword to prop himself up. He clutched the wound on his side and stared at the ground, wide-eyed. Everything was fading.

The Impius, apparently pleased with its handiwork, floated confidently towards Cereal again. Shaw fought to keep his eyes open as the demon, the boy, the cobblestone beneath his boots began to blur. He was fighting against the poison coursing through his veins.

I have to help the boy...I have to find my wife...my wife, he thought, his vision reduced to pinholes.

The boy may turn out to be useful after all, Pemazu said.

Shaw fell over; the weakness in his legs was overwhelming. As the light faded and the colors around him mixed and swirled, a curious image appeared before him. Two eyes, black as the night, looked over him. A shabby little boy with messy black hair stared at him; a toothy smile, too big for his face, showed tiny sharp teeth fighting for space in his mouth. As the world faded in on itself, the face got closer and closer until the black empty pits that were the boy's eyes were inches away.

"Hello, Shaw."

The Book had returned.

CHAPTER SEVEN

SHAW CRUMPLED IN A BLEEDING HEAP, still gripping his sword in defiance, with the final memory of his wife ingrained in his mind. Cereal was the Impius' focus initially, before the Book arrived in the dark alleyway. At first, Cereal thought it was coincidence, as the boy appeared on the high slatted roof of one of the buildings and looked down upon the chaotic scene. Only when the boy began to crawl the face of the building like a spider did he truly panic. Ignoring the Impius, he dove past the creature and attempted to wake Shaw by shaking him.

"Please, wake up, my Lord. It's here. It found us here." He needed Shaw to wake up. He couldn't fight them both, and he couldn't run. Without Shaw, he couldn't continue on to see the end of the King. He needed him.

"Found you? I think not, child. This creature," the boy nodded to the Impius, who cocked its head, "has been causing quite the ruckus, and I was all too curious as to who had released it. Now," the boy turned to face the Impius, who began to pick its teeth with a long black claw, "who summoned you?"

"I owe no explanation to you, but if you must know, her name is Tabitha and she is squuuuirming in here." The creature leaned in, tapping its temple. Another chunk of flesh fell from the girl's mangled face.

"Indeed, but I've lost interest in you, demon. I'd like to speak to Cereal. You may go."

The Impius scoffed and crossed its arms. "I think not, child," it said, mocking the boy. "I intend to eat this boy and then your Arbiter."

"You can't have these two. The boy is mine, and the Arbiter… this isn't his time. He is allowed to live, at my behest."

"Since when do you fight for the other side? This is the Arbiter, the Ender, the Balancer. He also has Pemazu the Black with him, I can sense him."

"I am surprised you managed to fell him as you did."

The creature shrugged, "He is blinded by hatred, and his power has made him arrogant. If my venom does not kill him, Pemazu will break his will in time."

"An Arbiter hasn't been broken since the writing of the Book. Shaw won't be the first. Will he die? Most likely. But cave, he will not."

The Impius watched warily as the boy walked over to Shaw, stooped, and slid up his left sleeve. He tapped the center ruby and it blazed into a brilliant red glow. The alley was bathed in a ruby red glow, revealing Cereal's location in the shadows. After the glow faded, the boy looked down at the magpie in the gem, who had begun to feign death. He put an effort into the performance, allowing a silver wisp of essence to leak out his beak.

The boy smiled. *Hello Pemazu. Your host is reckless.*

Indeed; unfortunately he does not yet listen to me as he should. He has potential. Pemazu righted himself, speaking to the boy without actually speaking.

The boy nodded, and Pemazu continued.

Are sure you need this scrawny rat as a host? Surely there is other, meatier fare?

This vessel is perfect but in time, it will fail as that one has. He pointed a thumb back towards the Impius, who responded with a rude gesture. *The boy carries such guilt and sorrow I can taste it... Hmmm, what is this?* The boy dug into Shaw's hip pocket and pulled a hand back in disgust.

"Ugh! Foul, tainted magic! Disgusting." The boy and the Impius both backed away to the far end of the alley, scraping their tongues as if they had bit into something rotten. For a moment, the two creatures seemed to react violently to the pouch.

Cereal saw the small pouch they had abandoned in the dirt. Runes in an unknown language crawled across its worn, leather surface.

Whatever was in that bag, neither the boy nor the monster seemed to be able to tolerate it, Cereal thought.

Weighing the unknown of the pouch against the two obviously inhuman children, he chose to risk exposing himself to grab the pouch, beginning to muster the courage to move his feet. The Impius and the boy continued their heated conversation alone, ignoring him for the moment. Sneaking cautiously from the perceived place of safety of the shadows and into the moonlight, he dashed the last few feet, reaching for the pouch. Behind him, the two children barely seemed to notice. He scooped the bag up and immediately felt the need to vomit. Clutching his stomach, which had begun to flip over on itself, he pulled the drawstring bag open without a thought. He peered into the bag, using the faint moonlight to see inside. In the bottom of the bag there was a small handful of red flower petals.

Roses! He had never seen roses before, but he knew of their power. His mother used to rock him to sleep with a rhyme about roses. A handful for the brave, a handful to save, off an evil might will stave. But would they work on these creatures?

He'd have to remove them from this terrible pouch, which he guessed was to protect them and ward off potential thieves. He grasped the bottom of the bag with the tips of his fingers, hard enough not to drop it, but soft enough that the sickening feeling was not overpowering. He hunched over the bag to protect the leaves from blowing away and flipped it over. The sickening feeling vanished as quickly as it had come, and was replaced with a creeping warmth, spreading from his innards all the way to his hands. The feeling was a relief from the gloom of the alley, and he felt emboldened to fight. He had hope in the petals. He had faith they'd work. Grasping them tightly, he closed the distance between himself and the monsters disguised as children.

"A handful for the brave, a handful to save, off an evil might will stave..." he said quietly to himself as he crept closer to them.

"A handful for the brave, a handful to save, off an evil might will stave."

"...Shaw may be a problem in the future..."

"If he is, he is your problem, Impius. I take no sides...."

"He is hunting the Book."

"He will never find it."

"He has before. You may no longer be able to leverage his soul at that point."

"I have him under control." The boy said authoritatively as he looked at the demon, unblinking.

"I can eat him."

"You won't."

"I will, and you won't be there to save him."

"A handful for the brave, a handful to save, off an evil might will stave."

"I already told you, I am here for the boy."

"You mean that boy?" said the girl, pointed a clawed thumb over her shoulder at Cereal as he continued to sneak forward.

"A handful for the brave, a handful to save, off an evil might will stave!" Cereal crunched the petals in his hand, reared back, and threw them at the children. They fluttered through the air before reaching the children's faces, inciting immediate howling and hissing. In a whirl of green, violet, and black, the boy disappeared, leaving behind scorched stones where it had stood. The Impius, however, appeared to smolder, the remaining skin on her face peeling back. She reached up, clawing at her face, scratching and reeling in pain.

"Argh! So hot! Where did you find such a wretched flower? I'll eat you first! I don't care if the Book wants you, I'll flay you alive and drink from your veins!" The girl began to erratically spin about, knocking into the walls and clutching her face. Cereal ducked behind Shaw's still-unconscious body, watching the creature writhe in pain. "I'll drink from your veins!" it said again before bursting into violet and black smoke, spiraling up into the late night's sky, then darting towards the west.

Cereal clutched Shaw's sword for reassurance, though its weight was beyond his use. The solid metal and runic markings offered some relief when he grasped the wire-bound hilt. Feeling something wet on his knee, he looked down only to immediately jump up. Shaw's blood, still warm, soaked through his pants. Cereal pulled the shredded piece of blood-soaked cloth away from the wound on his companion's side. Five long, finger-sized slices revealed pink and red flesh. Bits of bone peeked through the meat. Concern gave him the strength to overcome the queasiness gripping his stomach. He needed to find the princess; she could heal Shaw, she could help. He scanned the area wildly, beginning to panic. The alley was silent, save the slight whistle carried on the salty, humid air. The crowds had dispersed in the commotion, leaving Cereal feeling exposed and even more alone.

"Princess?" he hissed. "Princess?"

A rustle and a light tapping sound came from above. Expecting one of the monsters to be floating above him, he wheeled around, dragging the silver blade by the hilt across the stony ground. "I'll run you through!" he yelled, his bravery obviously fake. Only his scared echo responded. Even gripping the blade with all his might, he couldn't hide his tremors. He scanned the surrounding street and the rim of the rooftops, using the moonlight to see silhouettes of whatever might be there.

Nothing. The clicking continued. He strained against the silence to pinpoint the source of the sound.

Click click. Click click. Click click.

Whatever it was, it was on the ground, and getting closer.

Click click. Click click. Click click. He squinted against the dark.

"What do you plan to do with that?" a voice mocked. Scratchy and high-pitched, the voice came from below, close to the ground. Confused, Cereal looked down and was startled by a magpie with too many eyes standing on Shaw's unconscious form. It tilted its head toward him, looking as if it were waiting for a response. He counted three eyes on it. It clicked its beak open and closed before hopping up and down a few times, as though trying to catch his attention. Feeling stupid, he checked around him one last time for anyone or anything that could be responsible for the sound.

Timidly he looked down at the bird. "Are you talking to me?"

The bird opened its mouth and tapped its foot against Shaw's cheek. "No, you lemming, I'm speaking to the half-dead prince, who's not only bleeding to death, but has been poisoned. Put that nasty blade down and follow me."

"Are you Shaw?"

"I'll pretend you didn't ask that."

"You're the demon in Shaw's arm?" he asked, picking the bird up by a wing and examining it more closely. It jabbed him in the finger with a sharp beak and flopped to the ground, swearing.

"Follow me, leave Shaw, and the sword," the bird said, rearranging a few misplaced feathers.

"What? No. I can't leave him."

"You can, and you will. We can't help him, and I can't find Beggen Ostra."

"He's dying."

"Yes, but we can't help him here. I've slowed the bleeding, but I cannot conjure the complicated Impius anti-venom out of the air. Several of the King's Guard escaped the Impius. They'll take him to Stonehaven."

"What will they do to him?"

"Bring him back just enough to interrogate him, which is more than we can do. I am currently at the limits of my power."

"His sister-"

"Is nowhere to be found. She knows what she's doing. But unless you wish to join Shaw in the Howling Halls, we need to leave, now. I don't like the plan, but if it's any consolation, the King will not soon discard his brother. He'd sooner interrogate him until he has revealed all he knows, especially about me, then dispose of him."

"Are you what I saw in Shaw's arm?"

"No, I am a shadow, an apparition. I simply can't sit around waiting for something to happen. I find patience so uninteresting. Only in the rarest of times can I manifest on this plane. It just so happens that in his unconscious state I have a semblance of my power."

"What do I do?"

"Well, let's start with you following me…"

The boy sighed, "To where?"

"To the boat, obviously. Was that not that the terrible plan the three of you concocted?"

The bird was right. Perhaps Beggen Ostra was waiting at the dinghy. It was their agreed-upon plan, after all. He could make it to the dinghy and then bring her back to Shaw so he wouldn't have to be captured after all. The bird was knowledgeable enough of the situation, and at this point he was nearly out of options. The bird seemed to sense his agreement and took off towards the end of the alley, which met with the main road. He felt odd. He was alone, save for a talking bird with three eyes, leaving behind a dying prince in a pool of his own blood. Luckily, an option existed, and he was happy to have direction.

Cereal followed the eastern wall, dragging his hand across the stone. Something about the jagged bumps with intermittent breaks for doorways brought him in and out of his own thoughts. The bird made him slightly worried as it disappeared around a corner. Expecting to find a cohort of highly armed guardsmen he peeked multiple times around the corner and spotted the bird, still following the rightmost wall. For a moment, he wanted to laugh at how highly conspicuous a magpie walking the alley in the early morning was. He stifled his laughter in his hand and continued, keeping a few paces behind the bird. The air thickened with sea salt, and the path moved upward into a slight climb. The roofs of the Fringe ducked below the hilltop, and he breathed the salted air deeply, exhaling with a massive sigh. Though he was a slave *on* the sea, he was not a slave *to* the sea. He did not hold any ill will to the sea. Instead, he could pinpoint the day his parents were killed and the King set him on a course for revenge. A course leading him where he was now. He knew he couldn't let anything stop him from ending the King, even if it meant leaving Shaw behind.

"Calm yourself, child. I can taste your fear from here. Out here in the dark, the only things you need to be fearful of are the things that wish to be seen."

"That doesn't help at all," he replied to the bird, feeling worse than before.

"It was not meant to. It was meant to distract you from the happenings at the bottom of the hill. Shaw has been discovered and is being taken away. I can't lead you any longer. The extended distance from his body makes my essence itch. Soon enough, I'll fade and be forced back into the crystals. Continue onward to the Valor; you can find your way from there."

"What? You're leaving me?"

"I am without a choice, child. Follow the path, keep to the shadows, and don't tarry, regardless of what you may hear from below. Undoubtedly, they'll spell their travel, attracting the Impius once again. You should be out of its mind's-eye by then."

He stared blankly at the bird and ran through the list of options. None of them were appealing, and the thought of being entirely alone scared him. Waiting around for his companions to arrive would also be a horrible feeling, and something told him that the rose petals keep the demon and the boy at bay for so long. Soon, they would be able to shake the petals from their essence, recover and be ready to hunt him. He felt flushed and angry with the thought of losing yet another family to the King.

The bird stabbed him in the foot with its beak, punching a small hole through the thin leather. "Focus boy. Get moving. The King's Guard have him."

Cereal looked over his shoulder. At the bottom of the hill, the guardsmen were knocking on doors, and sometimes they did not wait for an answer before pushing their way in to search the buildings. One of the guardsmen called out to the others, beckoning them over. A short while later, they exited the alley, carrying Shaw's body on a stretcher.

He sighed. After what Shaw had done for him, he felt ashamed at not being able to do more in return.

"Go," the bird said, hopping earnestly.

He broke into a run, convinced not to let the bird see him wiping the tears from his eyes. He breathed in rhythm with his footfalls, relishing in the memory of the last time he was this close to the Valor before being enslaved. Years ago, his father had taken him to the main dock at Stonehaven and taught him about the many creatures of the water and the dangers of the waterway itself. He had once tried to return there, only to find a barricade high enough to block out the sun. His hatred for the King grew that day, feeling as though the King had not only taken his parents away, but was now attempting to take the few good memories he had left.

After finding the barricade, he traveled south, hoping to reach the Fringe. He stopped only to steal food and find shelter on the road. Upon reaching the Fringe, he was displeased in his ability to scavenge; it was not as easy as it had been on the road. There were more people, and the King's soldiers regularly took to the Fringe to abuse peasants, especially children. He was forced to continue south, using the Valor as his guide, and rationing his scavenged supplies. He eventually settled in the Ruins of Third City, unaware of where he truly was. He survived by trapping small game and by drinking from large ceramic jars that filled with rainwater.

That place. Never again would he return. He spent many a night in the Ruins, near frozen from an unnatural, lingering frost. It made the Ruins that much more foreboding, as there was not supposed to be such cold this time of year. The sounds of the day transformed as night fell. Twittering animals became howls and screams, and unknown things walked about the night, masked in darkness. He hid deep within the bowels of a monastery, in what he believed to be the crypt. He chose a sarcophagus for a bed; he was safer amongst the dead. Inside the monastery, the roof had collapsed, capping off the stairway with just enough room for him to squeeze through.

Eventually, he was forced to leave his hideout and flee to the river, as a monstrosity rampaged through the Ruins. It crumbled everything below its massive feet, further pummeling the remains of Third City into dust. The ground shook as it stepped through the Ruins, and he dared not take the seconds needed to look up at it. He just ran, faster than ever before. He ran blindly, in a panic, before tumbling down a smooth dirt path and into utter darkness. Once the momentum of the fall slowed, allowing him some control, he managed to dig his hands into the soft ground and slow his descent. He continued to slide downward for what felt like an eternity, and the darkness grew about him, suffocating him in endless darkness.

Only when he reached the bottom of the pit did he look up, expecting to see the face of whatever creature was chasing him. Instead, a lone beam of moonlight shined into the pit, illuminating his face. It was so far away, so hopelessly high, and the only thing awaiting him at the top was more of the same: terror and darkness. He remembered rolling onto his back, out of the light, leaving it to illuminate whatever it could. Without him in the way, the beam shined on something tucked into the earth. He could make out its outline, seeing just a corner peeking out. It looked like a book. *Why would there be a book here?* He looked around, squinting through the dark, looking for other books, or the shelves of a library, but found only darkness. Timidly, he inched along the floor, expecting another steep drop that he couldn't see. He slid easily; whatever type the dirt was, it was smooth and cold to the touch. He squeezed a small amount between his fingers, feeling it crumble to dust, leaving them smooth. The dirt felt like ash.

He was close enough that he could reach out and touch the corner of the book. Expecting the ground to drop out from underneath him again, he reached slowly and deliberately. His hand crossed the beam of light, illuminating it and showing that his fingers were indeed covered in a fine layer of ash. He ignored it for the moment and concentrated on the book. Curiosity drove him forward and in one movement he snatched the book out of the soft ash and hugged it tightly to his chest, wincing, expecting to fall again. The ground held firm, and he opened his eyes. He tried to relax the feeling of his heart pounding in his throat.

He was not in the pit anymore, but outside of it, sitting on the hard earth. To his right, the black hole leading to the long fall sat agape, waiting to swallow him up once more. Moonlight gave him back his vision, allowing him to see clearly once again. He looked down at the book. It was undoubtedly old, stained red in places, and was bound shut with layer after layer of thick wire. The surface of the book was carved with runes of some kind, and, to his surprise, they moved. The book was made of a hide-like material, thicker than a horse's and soft to the touch. His fingers left indents where he gripped it tight. *What type of animal was this?*

Remembering the creature that drove him into the pit in the first place, he tucked the book under his arm and surveyed the area. He'd finish examining the book later; now, he needed to find a place besides the Ruins where he could be safe. He thought of the Valor and considered following it north to the Fringe, perhaps trying his luck on the roads that led west to Second City. The outlying areas of the Kingdom were proving to be more dangerous than he had hoped. Perhaps he could find work in the stables. Either way, he knew he needed to go back to the city. Based on his trip south along the Valor, he estimated it would take him weeks to reach Second City by foot, and scavenging along the road would surely lead to his capture. There was only one road to Second City, and the roads were traveled by frequent patrols of the King's Guard who would be very interested in selling an orphan boy again.

Losing hope, he considered using the Valor as a final destination; he'd no longer have to scavenge, steal, and beg. What was there left for him anyways? The King took his parents from him and left him to the streets, knowing he'd most likely starve. He was tired, lonely, and losing hope. What the King failed to predict was his unwillingness to give up. His father, Martin of Third City, taught him the value of work, the value of morality and the value of fighting for what he believed in. He'd used these values to help him keep going, and it seemed he'd need them now.

Determined to continue fighting for his father, for his mother, for revenge, he set his mind to the task of finding another solution. He began walking east out of the Ruins, mindlessly dodging fading monoliths, destroyed and half-buried in the dirt. He focused on Second City and the road there. He knew it well; his father was a trader and would often tell Cereal of his adventures. He explained how he'd travel north out of Third City to the Fringe, where he'd stop in the market for a few days. From there, he'd take his horse and cart to the northwest, to Second City. He loved hearing about that journey; it was on these trips this that his father would hum softly to himself, puff on his pipe, and repeat, "We work to live and fight for our right to work." He'd beg for an explanation, and his father would chuckle deeply and simply say, "You will know in time, boy."

He still held the book tightly to his chest as a few tears escaped his eyes and landed on the cover. Once started, it seemed that they wouldn't stop. They ran down his cheeks and dribbled onto the top pages of the book, but he did not care. He continued east, toward the Valor. No ships ventured this far south anymore, and neither did the traders, not since before the Great Betrayal.

The gray ruins became more infrequent and the earth gave way to cobblestones the farther he walked. He was nearing the road that would take him to the Valor. He could follow it north and rest in the Fringe. He could keep to the road and scavenge wild berries and other food. He'd have to; he carried nothing but the book now. Perhaps it would be worth something to someone in the market.

His concentration and his tears disappeared in an instant at the sound of an ear-splitting howl from behind him. He froze in place, hugging the book so tight its wire bindings dug into his chest through his ragged shirt. His breath came in shallow bursts and his eyes locked unblinking in his skull. The howl came again, this time closer. He mustered as much fortitude as he could to make himself look at whatever was behind him.

Slowly, he twisted his body around, unable to move his neck. What he saw turned his shallow breaths into heaving, chest-deep gasps for air.

A great black bull charged towards him.

Its horns were covered in spike-wire and tan flesh lines stood out against its black hide where it had been whipped. Its hooves dug great grooves into the dirt as it rampaged toward him. It was close enough now that he could feel the ground shake. It was much larger than any bull he'd seen, easily double the size of a normal bull. Its muscular legs pushed off the ground with enough force on the stone walkway to crack the cobblestones beneath its hooves. Cereal met its eyes as it charged. His eyes full of crippling fear. The bull, hunger. And anger. This was not an ordinary bull. This was a Gollox; an ageless rage-fueled animal used by temple guards from long ago, and it obviously had an interest in him.

Its charge did not slow and Cereal remained frozen. Every muscle felt as though it were locked in place and shivers made their way from his hands down to his feet. In his fear, he neglected his grip on the book and it fell to the ground with a thud. He looked down to see that the book had opened and the wire lay strewn about, as if cut by invisible hands.

The bull's pace slowed, but it continued to charge. It was just a few hundred feet away, and its massive size was no longer distorted by distance. The terrible beast snorted and howled, ending with a high-pitched whoop.

Cereal thought at first the pages were blank, but words in an unknown language began to bleed out of the pages. The words worked to captivate his attention and he felt he must read the words written there. The beast charged at him, yet he couldn't look away from the page. At that moment, he did not care about the bull, or the beast in the Ruins, or his stomach warning of hunger. In that moment, he only cared to read. He fell to his knees and stared hopelessly at the foreign words. He couldn't read Common, but he could recognize the figures, and these were not of common writing. He knelt with the book at his feet and attempted to decipher the words written there, to discover something. The book wanted him to read it, and he wanted to obey, but he couldn't. Even still, he couldn't take his eyes off of it, and now the words were no longer flowing and instead, inching their way off the page and onto the ground below. Like tiny bugs, they crawled toward him in a single file and up onto his legs. Now, it felt as if he was again locked in place but this time not from his fear, but the book itself. Like ropes, the words tied his wrists and ankles.

He tried to scream as he sat helpless in his own body, watching from behind his own eyes, but not a sound would come out. The words crawled the surface of his skin and made their way up his arms and onto his chest. Expecting pain of some kind he prepared his mind, but instead, the words provided warmth and took the chill from the air. The words were comforting and warmed his body wherever they crawled, which seemed to be everywhere. Like being submerged in a warm basin, he felt his body begin to heat from his toes, to his legs, and up the rest of his body. Still, he sat paralyzed and help-less; somewhere in front of him a charging bull would run him through. He lost hope in fighting against whatever force locked him in place. He lost hope in understanding what the words said or what they were doing to him. Instead, he gave in and closed his eyes. He was tired anyway, and this seemed like a better way out then starving to death. The Gollox was on top of him one moment, and the next, he was at the shallow docks of the Fringe with a slave-master, the book nowhere to be found.

CHAPTER EIGHT

THE VALOR RAGED and frothed with rain from the northern mountains. Its strength was well known throughout the Kingdom for sinking even the strongest of ships, and forcing creatures from its depths to the shore, seeking reprieve from its undertow. One such creature blocked Cereal's path as he made his way to where a beached Great Barge laid, forever run aground. On board the beached vessel was the dinghy, he hoped. He saw the creature from afar as he crested the final hill before reaching the Valor. Stone marked his path, one of the less-beaten ones leading out of the Fringe, which gradually thinned to dirt. Closer to the Valor, patches of green under-growth threatened to consume even that, and Cereal had to rely on the growing smell of the sea to guide him through the night.

Somewhere up ahead, something moved in the dark. The creature made clicking sounds like hundreds of tiny beetles scampering at once. He knew creatures like this. They hunted with sound both on land and underwater. He'd encountered one with his father while traveling the Valor, hauling supplies from Third City to sell in the Fringe. The one he'd seen was nearly dead, riddled with arrows, and even then, it was not to be taken lightly. His father had called it a shambler. Only a few sailors traveling the Valor had reported encountering one, and most had only seen black and brown algae-covered carcasses with six appendages. In the other cases, the sailors had reported that whatever it was had clicked loudly enough to be heard under still waters, and had leapt out of the water, pulling crew members off the deck and into the depths with hooked appendages. Most of these reports had been dismissed as sailor stories until recently, when the cool waters of winter drove them out of the deep to the shallow, populated shores of the Fringe. From there, the reports of man-sized creatures with armored hides and the ability to hunt with sound spread quickly. Far Eastern folklore spread by refugees described a monster raging in the Maw, which caused the waterway to rise. Locals knew better, and understood that the high mountains bordering the north-eastern section of the Valor gathered water from the mountain range to the north and summer rains, dumping it into the river. The creatures were rumored to be the remains of an ancient species that occupied the outer rim of The Maw, but frequent trade ships providing easy food sources had coaxed them out of the deep and into shallow waters.

He hid behind a large stone off the eastern side of the path. His father had taught him that to hide from the creature's vocal hunting technique, one needed to find solid fixtures to hide behind. This stone would work perfectly until the creature went off to search another area, or until he found a way around it. He crouched instinctively in the lowlight, even though he knew the shambler couldn't see him. A series of clicks came from the creature, and he ducked his head behind the rock again. He looked around in the low light for something to throw, hoping to cause the shambler to run off in search of the sound. He scooped up a handful of rocks, adjusted his pack, and leaned back, to throw them off into the thick brush on the western side of the road. A thickly-calloused hand grabbed his wrist and another covered his mouth, stifling his yell. The hands turned him around to face a hooded figure, and even in the night, he could make out the smile and bright green eyes of the Princess. She released his arm and shook her head, holding up a finger to be quiet.

She eyed the shambler, ducked below the rock, and pulled her cloak aside to reveal a menacing crossbow strapped across her shoulder. Alongside it was a quiver, several pouches, and a silver dagger engraved with words in an unknown language. Its hilt was inlaid with multiple decorative gems. She noticed the crossbow was nocked with a thick black bolt, red metal gleaming at its tip. She grabbed Cereal firmly by the shoulders and turned him to face the stone, then steered him off to the side. She shook him, indicating that he should stay put.

He began to tremble nervously with half his body exposed. Beggen Ostra rubbed her hand across his cheek. Her comforting touch helped him, but he still didn't know why she was making him stand outside the safety of the rock. The shambler wandered directly up the road and was close enough he could make out its six appendages, each one razor-sharp and reflecting the moon. He imagined them tearing into his flesh, then multiple rows of teeth grinding away on his bones from the feet up.

He felt something heavy on his shoulder. The crossbow came into view as Beggen Ostra put it on his shoulder and adjusted its weight so the head of the bow was to the left-front of his face. She readied her shoulder against the butt stock and aimed the front sight at the shambler's torso. Based on the angle, Cereal thought the shot would go directly into the stone in front of her. He attempted to shift to the left, assuming she didn't know she'd miss. As he started to move, Beggen Ostra pushed down on the crossbow, digging it into his shoulder. He took this as an instruction to stay still.

He tried to look back at the old woman, hoping for a clue as to her intentions but another soft hand on his other shoulder gave him the reassurance he needed. The shambler was just feet from the rock now. It smelled strongly of saltwater and ammonia. The shambler clicked; it was loud enough to make him wince. He readied himself for Beggen Ostra to pull the trigger on the crossbow and did his best not to shake fearfully and throw off her aim. He gripped his fists and stood tall. The shambler rose to its full height in front of the rock, towering over them. He could make out several sets of pincers set into its rounded head. Something caught his eye before he could voice his concern. There were runes crawling along the body of the weapon.

Beggen Ostra made her move before Cereal could tilt his head out of the way. She whistled loudly and the shambler zeroed in on the pair, hidden behind the rock. It scrambled over the stone in search of its prey. In that moment, Beggen Ostra dropped to a knee, angling the crossbow upward towards the shambler's head, and pulled the trigger. The force of the bolt leaving the bow was so strong that she momentarily lost control and it leapt from his shoulder.

The drawstring caught Cereal across the cheek, splitting it open, and he dropped to the ground, clutching his bleeding face. The bolt found its mark and skewered the shambler directly under its pincers and through the top of its head, sending a spray of neon blood and bits of tissue into the sky. Cereal writhed from the pain, desperately pressing his hand to his cheek as the taste of iron filled his mouth. The shambler's carcass fell next to him, but he didn't care. All he could think about was the pain radiating from his face to the area behind his eyes. Beggen Ostra dropped the crossbow and knelt next to the scared and bloodied child. He felt her warm hand pressed against his cheek as she applied pressure.

"Cereal, I need you to calm yourself. I can heal this, but not if you move and not if you break my concentration."

Between sobs and sniffles he managed to nod. He fought through the pain enough to stop writhing and to pull his hand away from his cheek. He pressed his tongue against the wound inside of his mouth to try to stop the blood from seeping into his throat. It stung for a moment, but he remembered what Beggen Ostra said and held it there, hoping she'd hurry.

"This will hurt before it gets better. I need you to keep still and remember that I am helping you. Do you understand?"

He nodded and tensed up. He was glad she told him it would hurt otherwise he'd have jumped in surprise and broken her concentration.

When she touched him again, the feeling of hundreds of pinpricks overwhelmed the throb of the wound. The two sides of the wound met in the middle and his eyes welled up with salty tears, which dripped into the cut, making it worse. Even still, he held on for what felt like several minutes, though in truth the entire spell took only seconds. He was able to open his eyes toward the end of the spell to see Beggen Ostra crouched over him, her eyes black as night. His cheek felt better, and the pain was reduced to an annoying throb. He touched the wound and felt the raised skin of a scar.

She stood up first before helping him to his feet and greeting him with a hug. She looked at him for a moment and said, "I am glad you made it, child, and I am sorry about your cheek. I love this device, but as I age, my grip weakens. I had to spell the bolt's flight to pierce the shambler's hide. The Impius sure made a mess of things, and coming across this creature was just bad luck."

"It was horrible. It wanted to eat me, but a boy stopped it."

"A boy? What boy?"

"A nasty boy. So nasty the Impius was afraid of it."

"Hmmm. Did the boy have a name?"

"No, but it did say that I belonged to it."

"Don't worry about that for now, child. Tell me of Shaw. Did he make it past the Impius?"

"No ma'am, I was told to leave him. I was told the King's Guard would heal him up at the castle."

"Told by whom, child?"

"A talking bird, ma'am. The one who told me to meet you here."

"What kind of bird? What else did it say?"

"It was black and white and had three eyes."

"Hmm, more mysteries." She paused for a moment, thinking. "Either way, the talking bird gave you directions here which led you to me. A blessing in itself, honestly, even with the bad luck of encountering this creature." She pointed at the creature twitching on the ground in a pool of green blood.

He turned away from it, pressing his tongue to his cheek, a memento of their encounter with the monster from the depths of the Valor.

"We must travel north from here, through the forest and beyond the Fringe. There is an outpost, high upon the face of the stone walls containing the Valor, hidden by dense forest. Though lost to the eye, it isn't lost to my memory. With the King's Guard occupied and Shaw captured, my plan will need to be put in motion sooner rather than later, and that outpost is the first step."

"What plan, ma'am?"

"One I have been carefully developing for thirty years."

"What are we going to do?"

"*You* aren't going to do anything."

"What are *you* going to do?"

"I am going to kill the King."

Traveling the brush that lined the river proved slow and frustrating. Cereal and Beggen Ostra slowly pushed their way through, as it was incredibly thick and had many thorny and unforgiving plants. Trees and brush worked together to block out the moonlight, forcing them to rely on their sense of touch. Beggen Ostra kept him to her left to prevent him from misstepping and tumbling into the Valor below. They were several strides from the edge, but Beggen Ostra still aimed to ease his fear of falling.

* * *

They traveled in silence, stopping only to drink from the apparently never-ending supply of water from Beggen Ostra's waterskin and nibble on her apparently waning supply of dried meats and fresh legumes. Cereal began to think her waterskin was spelled. He never got around to asking her, his attention drawn by hunger pangs, and he began eyeing the pack Beggen Ostra had pulled the meat out of. After several hours, he began to lag behind as the night's events piled up and pulled on his remaining energy. Beggen Ostra would have continued on forever if Cereal hadn't said something. He hissed her name through his teeth, unsure if he still needed to be silent for fear of additional shamblers stalking the upper reaches of the Valor.

"Princess…can we rest?" he hissed after tripping over a sapling and sprawling out across the forest bed.

"Apparently, we already are. You may speak up, child. There are no other creatures in the area," she said, yanking Cereal to his feet. She brushed him off before finding the clearest area to set herself down. She kicked a few leaves and twigs out of the way and unclasped her belt. Her sword, crossbow, food packs, waterskin and several other pouches clattered to the ground; she carried a lot more on her belt than he realized. He admired the old woman for not only her magical abilities but for her cunning attitude and ability to move nimbly at her age.

"How do you know there aren't any more of those things?" he asked, mimicking her by sweeping sticks and leaves from the forest floor, clearing a space for himself.

"Because we'd have been eaten a long time ago." She smiled at him, apparently amused by her own sharp wit. She took off her traveling cloak and laid it in the clearing before spreading out on top of it with her hands behind her head. He did the same, lying on Shaw's cloak. He looked up, half expecting stars, but instead gazed up at a thick canopy of trees where every branch had fought for sunlight.

"I'll wake you when we need to move again. We should be at the outpost by mid-afternoon. It will be easier to move through this brush in the daylight."

"What about Prince Shaw?"

"After I send my message from the outpost, we will ride north through the Fringe and rendezvous at the Northern Barrier with... friends. From there, we will retrieve the Prince from the castle, if he hasn't taken his leave already."

The way she said *friends* had him worried - as if she did not believe her own words. He was not sure who the old woman's friends were, or what plan she wanted to set in motion, but he trusted her. How could he not? She and Shaw were the only ones to show him any kindness, and genuinely made him feel welcome. The Fringe was second only to the Ruins as the most terrible place in the Kingdom for a parentless child. He was sure that the King knew this, and orphaning him in the Kingdom was part of his cruelty. Cereal began to drift off to sleep, warmed by Shaw's cloak in the crisp, damp air. Beggen Ostra kept her ears open from the other side of the clearing, easily picking up a few words Cereal mustn't have thought she'd hear.

"King Jayecob, I am coming."

Beggen Ostra admired the boy's courage, of course, but his absoluteness worried her. She knew of the King's power and had obviously heard the story of Cereal of Third City and the torture-killing of his parents, but she also knew how revenge can blind one from thinking clearly. Even her brother, the Prince, who she remembered having a level head and clear heart, now appeared cold and driven only by revenge. He may say he relished the news of Princess Avana being alive, but it did not mean that was what drove him now. She'd seen the result of his anger, when his arm had transformed in the grotto. Whatever he was, he called himself a monster. What could be worse than a monster driven by revenge? Similar thoughts helped bring her to mind to rest, and sleep came easily. With her final thoughts of the outpost, standing poised on the face of the rock adorning the side of the Valor, she relaxed into a dreamless sleep.

* * *

Cereal awoke, startled by a branch snapping near his head. His eyes flashed open and his hands scrambled at his belt for his dagger. He found the pommel, still damp with the cool morning chill. He struggled with it for a moment before ripping it out and rolling around on the ground, looking for the source of the sound and holding the dagger weakly above his head. He could make out something dark moving through the brush, heading away from the river. He twirled around, holding his dagger out in front of him defensively and inching towards where Beggen Ostra was sleeping.

After a few steps he stopped and stole a look to his feet, where she should be lying. He found only the clearing where she'd obviously slept the night prior. Whatever had snapped the branch continued onward through the thicket, following the natural path. Cereal ran to his cloak and scooped it off the ground. He looked around for other directions in which Beggen Ostra may have gone, but the thicket was dense and offered only the single path other than the one that brought them to the clearing. The same one the sound had come from. He relied on her ability to both navigate the bramble and push aside the thorn-laden vines, which allowed him to follow her, albeit much slower. Beggen Ostra seemed to have pressed additional vines down into the brush, which allowed him to step over them before the thorns reached up and threatened his nether regions. She'd followed something out of the clearing.

Whatever had traversed the path was obviously unaffected by the large thorns, and had in fact aided in clearing the path by stomping the vines down and pushing stray tree limbs aside. He stalked the path, dagger in hand, walking on his toes and masking his footfalls. He scanned side to side, worried that something from the dark might push through the thicket at any moment. He imagined things with long arms and unseen mouths reaching from the darkness and pulling him in, consuming him before he could scream for help. Another branch snapped ahead of him, and the smell of horses drifted faintly above the wet leaves and damp earth.

Cereal wondered what a horse would be doing this deep into the brush. Perhaps it was lost? Or perhaps something had scared it? Whatever it was, it was large enough that it wasn't bothered by the thicket.

The branches above let in more light and the path grew wider and more forgiving to drifting elbows. He still kept his dagger raised, but his arm was getting tired, and he'd broken a sweat. Encouraged by the widening of the path, he moved more quickly and with less fear of making noise. Normally, he wouldn't follow an unknown creature down a dark wooded path alone. In this case, the clearly defined path and the smell of horses made him feel a little more at ease; he didn't think that whatever was ahead of him was dangerous. The path opened up and spat him out onto a dirt road heading north. Cereal's fears of a monstrosity stalking the woods quickly faded as he saw what he'd followed out of the clearing.

On the west side of the road, sniffing lazily at a few measly blades of grass, was a colt with a rich black coat, braided tail, and matching mane. He noticed that the horse lacked scars or signs of battle. It wore a riding saddle with two saddle bags with a clear finish and hand-stamped designs. Each strap securing the bag to the horse was inlaid with gleaming gems in red, blue and green. He admired the beautiful creature; as of late, he'd only seen death and destruction and creatures from the deep. To see something pure and innocent was a wonderful change. He felt his spirits lift, and approached the horse. It eyed him with a tuft of grass hanging from its mouth and froze. The horse knew what the dagger was. He tucked his dagger into his belt and tried to make an approach again, hoping not to scare it, and to be able to touch its coat.

"Easy. Easy now."

The horse snorted and resumed scavenging for grass in the tall weeds. He approached it by its front legs, precisely where his mother had taught him years ago while working in the stables of some nobleman in Stonehaven. Working in the stables was not the most memorable of times in Stonehaven, but he hadn't been abused, and the stables were warm during the winters. The winters were harsh and unforgiving, especially for those considered undesirable. With the Great Betrayal and the destruction of Third City, the King sent hordes of troops to the Ruins to scavenge supplies and come to the apparent rescue of the residents there. It was not discovered until their arrival at Stonehaven that the rescued people were to be commissioned as slaves, with the debt of their lives to be repaid. He spent many a day this way, and over time found comfort in the horses, because their lives were not all too different from his own.

The colt let him touch it, meeting him at eye level, assessing him before looking for more grass. He rubbed its silky coat for a minute, then dug around in the saddlebags, hoping to find something that might reveal the horse's owner. To his dismay, both saddlebags were empty. He heard the sound of heavy boots falling on dirt and peered up the road from between the horse's legs. To his joy, he easily recognized Beggen Ostra's travel coat, and as it shifted side to side, he could make out the corners of the vicious crossbow and her silver-plated sword. Cereal scrambled around the horse to meet her on the road. She had the skin and meat of something furry in one hand, and a full waterskin in the other. She tossed him the waterskin, which he graciously accepted.

"I see you've met Madrigol, my oldest friend," she said, nuzzling the horse's neck and playing with its mane. The horse explored her waistline with its nose, attempting to reach something along the back of her belt in the smallest pouches. It snorted and scooted closer, nudging her and stomping its front foot.

"Alright, alright, you great beast, hold on."

The horse snorted in reply and backed up. Cereal thought it looked like a dog, waiting for scraps. She dug under her cloak to the pouches behind her and tossed the horse a small white cube. "Don't get used to them. This is my last one. I swear I have found all the sugar in the Kingdom and fed it to you."

The horse snorted again, flicked its tail, and continued its search for more grass.

Cereal was amazed at the horse's apparent personality and smiled. "He is an amazing horse, ma'am. He has such a personality. How long have you had him? He looks young."

She shrugged, pulling twigs and leaves from its mane and smoothing rogue hairs.

"I don't know how old he is. He is my oldest friend, but he is Prince Shaw's horse."

Cereal's mouth dropped open. "By the gods, he must be fifty years old." He stared at it, wide-eyed.

"Watch your swearing, boy. A bit more than that; I don't know Shaw's age exactly. He may not even know himself. From what I've deduced, time moves differently where he's been."

"Madrigol, how old are you? Fifty?" The horse flicked its tail, whipping Cereal in the side of the head.

"Fifty-one?"

The horse whipped Cereal in the head again.

"Fifty-two?"

It snorted and dropped dung before drifting off down the road and rummaging for more grass.

"He is fifty-two," she said, a massive smile hidden behind her hand as she stifled a laugh.

"Where did he come from?"

"I sent for him days ago. He likes the forest west of the Fringe. Sometimes he roams as far as the mountain ranges to the north and follows the coast until he makes his way back to the forest. He takes care of himself. Except when it comes to sugar cubes; he can't seem to find those."

The horse snorted from further down the road.

"How did he know to meet us here?"

"He's intuitive. He's a lot nicer to Shaw, but he is swift and loyal to the Royal family. I haven't called for him in years, so I am surprised he came."

"I admire you, Princess. Your skills, even with age, are unmatched."

She laughed "Indeed, in my prime I was capable of many feats. I fear with age, my skills wane as my body does...but my mind is still fresh."

"Will you teach me some of what you know?"

"If we find a time, I'll teach you as I taught all children in the halls of Stonehaven...when the Kingdom was still new and the world brighter."

"I'd enjoy that."

"So would I, child. But for now, we have to make it to the outpost before dark. Madrigol will move swifter than any horse, but afterwards he'll need to rest for many days. We will be on our own to make it to Stonehaven in time."

"In time for what?"

"Through the night, I thought of Shaw's capture and I realized that there's more to this situation. If he is recognized and already weakened at the time he may not be able to escape, even with his power. We must help him, and he must set my plan in motion. If we aren't swift, The King may kill his brother again."

Once Beggen Ostra finally coerced Madrigol into cooperating and allowing her to ride him - in exchange for two sugar cubes in the future - he threw the horse equivalent of a temper tantrum upon finding out that he also had to carry Cereal. The horse snorted, stomped and rolled in the middle of the dirt road as Beggen Ostra tried to bargain with the beast. In the end, she promised two additional sugar cubes and two apples before the horse stood up and allowed her to rub his nose, signaling some sort of agreement.

"Two sugar cubes. Two! Where am I going to find two? It was hard enough to hunt the first one down, let alone finding two more! I'll never argue with a horse again. Next time we'll risk the damn river before I let an undead glorified pack donkey bargain with me."

The horse apparently understood what she said and took offense to her comments. It responded by shaking off its saddle and packs before laying on top of them and staring Beggen Ostra in the eye; whether challenging her or waiting for an apology, Cereal couldn't tell. He sat near the side of the road, nibbling on dried meat, entertained by the exchange.

"Oh, you know I didn't mean that," she exclaimed.

Madrigol snorted.

"Alright, fine. I'm sorry! I didn't mean it. We both know how much we appreciate all that you do for the family."

Another snort.

"For me. Fine. All that you do for me," Beggen Ostra corrected herself. Either she could understand him, or he could understand her, or both. Another one of her mysterious magical feats. Cereal hoped one day she could teach him to talk to Madrigol.

"Get on, child. Once he moves, he won't stop until we reach the outpost."

Beggen Ostra sat atop the horse and left room in front of her for him to sit. She left a stirrup empty and held a hand out for him to grab onto. He stepped up and she pulled him swiftly into the saddle. It was surprisingly comfortable, and Madrigol did not seem to mind the extra weight. He wondered what other capabilities the horse had.

Madrigol shifted side to side, testing the weight on his back before turning off the road aiming directly for the forest wall. Beggen Ostra sat unconcerned and hummed softly to herself. Cereal expected the horse to dump them both off into the wall of thorny trees out of spite, but he did not give any indication that he planned to do so. Instead, he picked his pace up to a trot and Cereal bounced with the rhythm of the horse's movement. The forest grew closer, and the horse only picked up speed, now at a gallop. Trees blocked out the morning sun breaking over the crest of the land as the horse whinnied and snorted before leaping into the tree line. Cereal turned away and closed his eyes, expecting his entire upper body to be cut up by the thorns adorning every branch and tree.

Instead, a gentle wind blew across his face and what felt like strands of hair tickled his cheeks and ears. He opened his eyes timidly and the forest came into view. He still sat atop Madrigol, but it looked like the forest bent and twisted away, inches before the horse and its riders crashed through. Each branch and leaf ducked and weaved out of the way. He no longer needed to match the hard impacts of the horse's gallop and instead only leaned forward on the saddle, sitting on a pillow of air.

He guessed it was enchanted to ease the pain of riding rough. Beggen Ostra was unsurprised by the forest's avoidance of the horse and riders and sat tall on the saddle behind him. The forest ducked, twisted and weaved out of the way of the travelers, and Madrigol picked up speed. He breathed harder, pushing off the forest floor, each step flinging them through the thicket with increasing speed. They seemed to move so quickly, the branches and leaves wove together into a never-ending stream of green. He felt himself slipping backward off the saddle and Beggen Ostra pushed up against him, grabbing a hold of the saddle horn. She whispered into his ear, "Almost there."

Maldrigol snorted and whinnied, the forest rushed by, and the sound of strong wind filled Cereal's ears. He felt dizzy; he was moving too fast. His stomach began to knot up and he felt like someone was pressing in on his neck. His eyes began to droop as the horse pushed harder, and his body felt heavier with each lunge forward. He closed his eyes, praying for it to end. He felt as if someone was sitting on his chest. He couldn't breathe. He closed his eyes, begging for the horse to slow just a little. Then it was over. The weight lifted from his chest and he could breathe again.

Brilliant sunlight bathed his face from a treeless sky and the sun shone brightly through his eyelids. He opened his eyes to great plains of grass and rolling hills. He looked to the east and saw the high-top ridges adorning the banks of the Valor. High on the peak, plateaus covered in lush forest created massive mushroom-like steppes up the face of the stone wall. He recognized this place; he'd traveled through here before. Just up ahead, no more than a half-day's ride should be the clear road headed east to Second City, but there was no way he could be here. Not this quickly. He knew, unlike many, that if he were to climb the steppes and cross the Valor, he'd be able to look to the southeast upon the great barren wasteland of the Far East Desert. He also knew he'd be able to see the remnants of the Stone Breaker Expanse between gusts of thick sand walls and whirling dune devils. It was a series of great stone shields, raised by the Stone Breakers from the earth to protect them from the stinging winds of the desert as they fled slavery and came to start anew. Every child was told of the incredible feats of the Stone Breakers, their escape from slavery, the building of the three cities, and then of the Great Betrayal that followed.

He stared wide-eyed in wonder. The journey from the eastern edge of the Fringe to the road to Second City normally took at least four days of hard riding, but they had made it in what felt like minutes. Looking at the location of the sun in the sky, however, it seemed as though hours had passed.

"How?"

The old woman chuckled and rubbed the horse's neck. "Madrigol is an incredible creature. But he isn't without limits. He'll need to rest for many days and nights now."

She dismounted the horse and dropped to the ground with a slight groan. Madrigol looked back at him with his big brown eye before plopping down and tilting to the side, allowing him to hop off with ease. Beggen Ostra rolled her eyes and dug into her hip pack, retrieving a red apple and tossing it to the horse. He caught the apple in midair before standing up and wandering towards the nearest patch of green grass.

"I'll have your sugar and apples the next time I call for you."

The horse turned around and took its time walking back to her. It leaned in as it approached and nuzzled the old woman.

Cereal thought it was interesting for the animal to show such affection when, only minutes before, it had thrown a tantrum like a small child. He raised an eyebrow at it as she let go of the embrace. He thought he saw a tear in her eye but, if it was there, she wiped it away quickly. The horse walked to him, and bowed its head, allowing him to rub it. It nudged his hand with its wet nose and he opened his hand to pet it. Instead of allowing him to do so, the horse dropped the slimy apple core into his hand, whinnied, and trotted off, looking pleased.

Beggen Ostra giggled to herself, dug into her pack and pulled out a crinkled piece of parchment. She examined it for a minute, checked the position of the sun and started off towards the north-east. She pointed to a particularly high steppe.

"The outpost is there. The Stone Breakers set it up as a guard tower to send out messenger birds if anyone else should try to use the Expanse to cross the desert. Time has swallowed the outpost from view. Along the steppe is a hidden path through the mountain and into the outpost."

"How do you know about it?"

"Because I made it. From the outpost we will send for help. After that, we've a five days' ride to the Northern Barricade, east of Stonehaven, where help should be waiting. With that help, we will rescue Prince Shaw."

"I thought you said he may have already escaped."

"If he has, that'll be even better. I have business at the castle, he'll be able to help."

"Will you kill the King then?"

"No. I have heard terrible rumors of the King's doings; I need to see them for myself. If they are true, we've bigger problems than the King. There will be a time for him soon enough."

Cereal did not know what could be worse than the King himself, but he trusted the woman. He shifted his belt, checked the lashings that secured the pouches, and nodded at her. She nodded back, turned towards the great steppe, and marched on. He looked back just in time to see the great black colt, rolling around in the pasture at the bottom of the hill.

CHAPTER NINE

WAKE UP. Shaw, wake up. I know you're dreaming of something sweet, but you need to wake up. We are here.

Pemazu warmed the gems in Shaw's arm hot enough that he jumped up and shook his arm violently, looking for burns.

Why, demon? he thought, looking around and trying to piece together the pieces that his memory had held on to.

Because while you were dreaming of flesh and sweat, I was busy attempting to burn off the Impius venom in your blood. I have managed to take the edge off, the King's Guard has done the rest. You are welcome, by the way, for not allowing us to die.

"All I remember was being scratched. Everything else is a fog. Where are we?" Shaw sat up from the floor, rubbing his eyes as if he'd been asleep all night. He was in a white, stone-walled room with bars on one side. Outside the bars was more of the same white wall.

The Howling Halls.

"Stonehaven? How? Where is my sister? Cereal?"

After the Impius got its claws on you, the King's Guard found you in the alley. They transported you here using the lifeblood of a few slave mages. Along the way, I was able to burn off the Impius venom.

Shaw pulled up his tunic and examined his side. Five raised purple scars ran from his ribs to his stomach. He touched them gingerly. They were tender and slightly warm, but felt generally okay.

"What of Cereal and my sister?"

I gave the boy directions to the boat; I am assuming your sister will meet him there.

"Did the Impius get to them?" Shaw asked.

No, it was distracted.

"By whom?"

More like by what. The Book has a real interest in the boy, Pemazu said.

"The Book? It appeared again?"

Indeed. This time, it stopped the Impius from eating the boy. It is determined to have him as a vessel.

I'll address that problem later, Shaw thought. *It won't truly come for him until its other vessel has fully decomposed.*

That leaves us with another problem.

"What's that?"

We cannot use our abilities in this cell. Or in the Howling Halls at all, for that matter. There have been many powerful wards placed in the stone itself, Pemazu said.

Shaw sat up. He was familiar with the layout of Stonehaven, and had heard many of the tales of what happened to prisoners in its halls. He had helped build Stonehaven many moons ago, but he was not involved in the creation of such an elaborate and ornate prison. This was his brother's doing.

Down the hall, screams rose from a dull moan to an elaborate echo. Each scream was amplified by the smooth stone walls and high arched ceiling. Whoever was screaming, they did not let up, and soon it sounded like a terrible choir of pain.

Shaw got up from the stone slab bed and walked to the barred entrance of the cell. Down the hall, a large circular window provided light to the eastern side of the hall.

Hundreds of cells, identical to his own, lined it. He shook the bars, testing their give. They rattled only a bit in their stone housings. No keys were used to enter and exit these cells, only a portal created from outside the hall would allow for any movement.

Shaw sighed and plopped down on the bed again. Soon, an agent of the King would come through a portal with a cohort of armed guards, and, without his weapons or his powers, he was no more than an outnumbered and under-equipped prisoner.

Whatever the guards were doing to interrogate or simply torture their prisoners, it was working. The screaming resumed.

Well, at least we have entertainment, Pemazu said.

"Do you have any ideas, or is sarcasm the only thing I can expect from you at this point?"

I believe my humor to be somewhat refreshing, considering our predicament. There are more options than you realize.

"Oh? What might those be? Because as I see it, we're at the mercy of whatever comes next." Shaw tapped his foot, irritated.

There is a weakness in this fortress, and there is help on the way, Pemazu said.

"Unless you have an army on standby, we aren't leaving this cell except in pieces."

I may not have an army, but rest assured, help is coming. I told the boy where to find you.

"Excellent news, a child knows where to find Stonehaven. Well done, demon," Shaw said.

The child lives and was well on his way to the river when I left him. And I did not see your sister's body, did you?

The demon was right; he hadn't seen his sister, or her body. She was not one to die so easily.

"Let's assume she found the boy. She is but an old woman and she grows weaker every day."

She may be old, but she is cunning. Do not underestimate that woman. It seems to me she has many cogs moving at once.

"What do you mean by that? What do you know?" Shaw asked.

I can only assume.

"Then assume," Shaw said.

Fine, if I must console your curiosity. Your sister knew of you from the moment she sent that first messenger bird. Your sister, the last remaining descendant of the Royal Family, besides your dearest brother, of course, has remained out of mind's eye for over thirty years. Why has she not fled? Taken a Great Barge beyond the Maw to the open waters? How did she come to consort with the Stone Breaker from Second City? Where does she go every night? Your dearest sister is divisive, and a mystery deeper than the Maw itself. Your sister has a plan, Pemazu said.

"Fair enough, but does her plan involve my capture and inevitable death at the hands of my brother again?"

It is possible she may have forseen this; she does have many gifts.

Shaw pondered the demon's ideas for a bit longer. Beggen Ostra had run off many times since their reunion on the Fringe, and she did seem at ease with Shaw's unexpected return from death. Perhaps something was already in motion.

The air thickened and Shaw felt a ghostly pull on the back of his tunic. He turned around to face the center of the cell, where the air was shimmering and cracking, like a broken window in mid-air. Shaw recognized this as the tell-tale sign of a portal opening. He backed himself to a wall instinctively, but knew it was pointless. Whoever was coming through the portal could see him now, readying to fight. Shaw crouched into a defensive position, preparing to strike. The cracked window in the middle of the room began to fall to the ground in pieces before shimmering for a moment and fading away. Behind each piece, a black void floated. He recognized that familiar blackness, how empty and lonely it was. Whoever was on the other end of the portal, they were using the Thin Line as the bridge.

Another portal cracked into life behind him and he dove to

the other side of the cell. He was trapped; two more portals cracked in the remaining corners. Shaw readied himself to fight any and all who came into the room. If they wanted him, they'd need all that they could bring. As if reading his mind, a red-scaled, gloved arm shot through each portal, followed by a golden boot, white pants, and matching tabard. Each arm was followed by a shoulder, then a steel-plated head, each sporting a scowling metal mask. Finally, four Stonehaven soldiers with matching hammers crowded the room, surrounding him.

One soldier stepped forward. Above his mask, stamped into the metal of his helmet, was the letter "I". Shaw knew what this man's job was. He was specifically trained to extract information using a warped, tainted form of magic, and the I on his helmet meant that he was very skilled at it. All four soldiers lunged, each grabbing one of Shaw's limbs. He thrashed and kicked, trying to free a hand. He frantically checked their belts and backs for weapons. It was useless; none of these soldiers needed weapons in this prison, their armor and their numbers would be enough to control even the most unruly prisoner.

Shaw kicked and rolled as the guards dragged him to the metal bars at the end of the room. He managed to free a hand for a moment and swung at the guard holding his other arm. He connected with the soldier's helmet, only causing him to bruise his hand and the guard to tighten his grip further. They threw him violently against the bars and held him down. The soldier with the "I" on his helmet, the mage, stared at Shaw for a moment before turning to his left arm and whispering a spell behind the metal of the helmet. There was something off about the spell, like a sharp note held for too long. Each word seemed to twist and entangle with the last, forming a sour knot of power. Shaw couldn't make out the words, but knew them to be some form of black magic, something that had to be manipulated and tainted in order to work in the warded walls of the prison. Shaw wondered how much of this man's soul remained intact after learning to use such magic with such control. The mage finished the spell, and its effects were instantaneous. The metal bars of the cell warped and twisted themselves around Shaw's hands and feet. Like snakes, they writhed, then tightened, then shifted and tightened again, until Shaw could do little more than wiggle his fingers and toes. He sighed and quit fighting, conserving his remaining strength instead. At some point, he'd be released to rest. This man aimed to torture him for information. A prison this elaborate was not an execution chamber, though he supposed one most likely existed nearby.

"Leave," the interrogator said, inches from Shaw's face. He could smell rot and decay from behind the man's helmet. The tainted magic was taking a toll on him.

The other guards bowed slightly and backed away, sliding into the dark windows in the center of the room. Each one seemed to get sucked through the portal, their uniforms and armor twisting and coiling as their bodies shifted from view and the windows caved in on themselves. In seconds, Shaw was alone with the interrogator and the portals were gone.

The interrogator removed his helmet, and Shaw understood why he wore it in the first place. His skin, once tight and drawn up, now sagged on the bones. His lips appeared purple and withdrawn against his remaining teeth and, through the gaps, Shaw could see his blackened tongue. The man's hair was no longer gray and full, but now laid in stringy patches. The black magic hadn't seemed to affect his eyes, though, which remained a striking shade of blue. Shaw stared back at the man, wondering if he knew that he did not have much life remaining in him if he kept using magic this way.

Pemazu gagged and retched.

I can taste the foulness of the magic emanating from his skin, Pemazu said.

"He has been using spells like this for some time. It must be how he can use them within the walls here."

How do you plan to get out of here?

"This man has an obvious weakness," Shaw said.

How do you figure?

"He gives up pieces of his soul in search of information. He'll do anything for information. I say we give it to him, because we have information he'd lust for."

It is a terrible idea. He will torture it out of you momentarily, or kill you for sport, Pemazu snapped.

"The magic is killing him. He'll willingly take anything we give him without needing to torture anyone."

We will see. Just make sure he does not touch the gems. Touching them makes my essence crawl.

"Well, we wouldn't want that, now would we?" Shaw said.

The interrogator removed his gloves and set them aside neatly on the stone bench. He rolled up the sleeves of his tunic all the way to the shoulder plates of his armor. His arms resembled his face - his skin was sagging and appeared faded and aged.

"Who are you?" the man hissed, his mouth barely opening to allow the words to slip between the cracks of his teeth. Shaw guessed that speaking was incredibly painful for him.

"That depends on what you believe."

"My beliefs have no place here. I have a task to complete. I can't leave until that task is complete. Who are you?" He inched closer to Shaw's face.

"Well, I am a farmer by trade, but obviously that isn't what you found me doing. I have three daughters and two sons, all of whom love the King and all his glory-"

The man balled his fist and swung at him. Shaw predicted the outburst and slid his head slightly, causing the guard to ram his fist into the iron bars.

"Argh!" He reeled back, rubbing his knuckles. "Aoa shloat chnar reht," he hissed. The words flowed together, melding with one another as they left his mouth. He winced in pain as hair-thin black needles burst from his fingertips, dripping vibrant red blood on the light stone floor. The interrogator extended his fingers and the needles danced in a nonexistent wind before righting themselves again, stiff and straight.

"Let me show you how I extract information from those who end up in my prison. The King has questions, and I am sworn to provide answers."

"You are no more bound to the King as the King is bound to his stolen throne."

"Still you are defiant and disrespect our King. No matter. Information will leak out of you like a bucket with holes." He moved closer and, for once, Shaw was afraid. The iron bars were tight around his wrists and ankles, Pemazu was powerless, and his own powers were stifled. It seemed he was without options.

"What do you wish to know?"

The man chuckled dryly, "We will get there, in time."

He reached up and angled the little black needles at Shaw's arm. Shaw closed his eyes, unaware of what pain was soon to come. He felt a feather-like feeling on his arm and winced as the interrogator cut away his sleeve. Completely still and starting to shake, Shaw clamped his eyes tighter. Still no burst of pain. Shaw opened his eyes a sliver, then the rest of the way. The interrogator was hairs away from his arms, staring into the rubies embedded in his arm, the shadowy needles inches from his skin's surface.

"These gems. How are they in your arm?"

"What is your name?" Shaw jumped on the opportunity.

"What?"

"I'll tell you about the gems if you tell me about you. What is your name?"

"What do you care of me?"

"That's another question. I can answer that next. Do you want to know of the gems?"

"Yes. Yes of course. They are gorgeous, and there is a tiny bird inside one of them. It's making rude gestures at me."

"Would you like to know of the bird, too?"

"Yes. Tell me of it." The interrogator smiled wickedly, cracking his dry, peeling lips. Blood formed in the cracks and ran into his mouth.

"What is your name?" Shaw tried again.

"Viktor..." he hissed. "Now tell me of the gems."

"I was born with them. They are a part of me."

"What of the bird?"

"That was not our deal, Viktor"

"Oh, yes, of course. What is your request?"

"What city are you from?"

"I am... I was... from Third City." He bowed his head for a moment. Then looked up, eager to ask Shaw more questions. Still, the black needles were just hairs from his wrist. "What is the bird? A raven of sorts?"

"A magpie actually. It's a demon."

"Interesting. How is it contained within the gems?"

"My turn, Viktor. Did you have family in Third City?"

"Yes of course...How do you control it?"

"It's bound to me. You know of the Great Betrayal?"

"Yes, I am familiar with the story. Does it talk?"

"Only to me," Shaw said. "You said you are bound to the King, how are you bound?"

"He has my son," he said solemnly. "I must continue this downward path if my son is to live. Where are you from?"

"Here... Stonehaven, but I have been away for quite some time. Where is your son now?"

"Enslaved in Stonehaven. He is a cleric's runner boy. Why do you care?"

"I can help him, and you."

"You can't even help yourself. How can you help him?"

"Do you want to know the greatest bit of information I can offer?" Shaw asked.

"Yes," he said eagerly.

"War is brewing, and I am bringing it to the King's doorstep," Shaw said coldly. He hoped this would be enough to spark the man's interest.

"Oh, is it now? An insurrection? You are a no-name, a drifter with interesting gems in his arms." He flicked the needles on the ends of his fingers.

"I am more than a drifter. I can help you and your son."

"If you can, I'll soon find out how. I have much enjoyed our conversation and our light-hearted, however futile, exchange. If you have anything hidden away, I will extract it now."

Viktor plunged the needles into Shaw's forearm and they spread out, writhing beneath his skin. Shaw cried out as blazing pain shot up his arm, and he clenched down on his teeth, feeling them crack. The needles wiggled and churned, digging into his soft muscle. Shaw was blinded by the pain and he bucked against the metal bars, trying anything to get away. He felt dizzy, and then sick to his stomach from the pain. It was constant and unending, as if the needles themselves were pressing on the nerves in his arms. He clenched his fists tight, praying for it to stop. Eventually, he couldn't stand the pain any longer, and he passed out. The room folded over on itself until nothing but darkness remained.

CHAPTER TEN

THE FIRST STEP was by far the easiest to climb, but more remained, and Cereal wondered if Beggen Ostra was kidding about climbing to the second. He looked up at the rocky underside of the massive stone outcrop, jutting awkwardly from the side of the mountain. Cereal knew that on the other side of that mountain range the mighty Valor raged and frothed, contained against a matching mountain range. The steppe that Beggen Ostra had suggested they reach hid a watchtower lost and forgotten with time. It was here that Beggen Ostra aimed to reach and set a plan in place, a plan she'd been working on for many years.

She put her hand on his shoulder and steered him toward the face of the mountain. When they had climbed the first step, it took them both some time to recover. It was difficult, but manageable with the two of them working together. They approached each additional steppe with a plan. Beggen Ostra would hop up the step, then pull Cereal up. This worked until the steppes grew too large; from then on, each one required Beggen Ostra to tie off one end of a rope from a nearby tree. She'd then toss the hooked end to a tree on the steppe above and climb it. Cereal would untie the rope from a tree, make a noose, tie it loosely to his belt and climb it to the next level.

Now, they stared up at the underside of a stony outcrop hundreds of feet above them. Still, Beggen Ostra seemed unconcerned, though unless she had a lot more rope hidden somewhere, Cereal did not know what her plan was. They weaved between the few trees on the plateau and over the rocky outcrops that were like tiny barriers standing in their way. They walked in silence, except for when Beggen Ostra occasionally mirrored the trills of tiny birds. Overall, she seemed happy to be on the steppes. He suspected that it had something to do with her earlier comment about making the outpost itself, and the hidden path to it.

The mountaintop was even more intimidating than the steppe, knowing it continued for a hundred feet below and hundreds more above. The stone face was light brown and slightly cool to the touch, despite the morning sun bearing down on the back of their necks. Beggen Ostra ran her fingers along it as they followed it to the north, humming louder now. Cereal followed in step, taking in every bit of the sight before him. To his right, a mountain, rising without end. Below him, vast plains. To the west, Second City, poking its towers above the sprawling forest a great distance away. The old woman dragged him onward with a firm but comforting grip on his hand. He couldn't help himself from stopping and admiring the Kingdom from a distance. Underneath, even he felt that something grew and festered, and it started and ended with the King.

"Here." Beggen Ostra stopped at a point in the mountainside where the walls met at an unusual indent. From a distance, the indent would appear as part of the rock face, but up close, it was obviously carved out. Beggen Ostra disappeared into the indent, and for a moment Cereal panicked.

"My lady? My lady?"

"Here, child."

Beggen Ostra's head appeared to be floating in midair on the side of the indent, until he realized upon walking inside that a perfectly cut path led up and into the mountain. Beggen Ostra stood on the bottom of an impossibly steep staircase aimed into the heart of the mountain. The stairs were slightly lit, shedding light on the steps until the darkness from the mountain swallowed them from view.

Cereal hurried forward and grabbed onto her coat tail as they headed deeper into the darkness. She confidently took each step as if she'd done it hundreds of times in the past. He closed his eyes and relied on her forward movement upward through the dark and his grip on her clothes to guide him. She continued to hum, which comforted him in the dark. She kept a regular pace that he had trouble keeping up with. By the time they had reached the top of the stairs, Cereal was winded and Beggen Ostra was almost dancing with excitement. The top stair opened to a stony platform that the old woman confidently stepped onto before guiding Cereal up behind her. Once she was sure he was safely behind her, she leaned her weight onto the stone wall. A line of light shot up from the floor as sunlight poured into the path. He shielded his eyes, but not before the sunlight caught him off-guard. Cereal squeezed his eyes shut tight, but Beggen Ostra seemed not to care, and pushed the hidden door further open, exiting the path.

They stood at the base of a graying tower as tall as the mountain itself. Trees and leafy vines covered the majority of its surface, and the same trees and vines covered the stony mountain face. These steppes were significantly larger than the last. When Cereal looked out past the rim, he couldn't see any towers of Second City, and instead saw endless blue sky. He looked closer at the trees; individually they were unimpressive, but collectively they made an outstanding canopy and barrier to the stony outcrop. Now he understood, standing at its base, how such a massive structure could easily be missed. The tower was carved into the mountain itself with various holes, which he assumed were windows, now being overtaken by vines and saplings. He stood staring up at it, mouth agape.

"Close your mouth, boy, lest a bird decide to roost there."

She brushed past him and made her way to the west side of the tower, where a large tree had overtaken the entryway and sprouted up the middle of the tower. She skirted the tree to the left and climbed an enclosed stone stair running clockwise up the wall of the tower before ending at a wooden hatch. Cereal followed her closely, astounded by how such a massive structure could have fallen out of memory. He found it quite beautiful, even though it had been invaded by the large tree in the entryway. They stopped a few steps shy of the wooden hatch, and he was surprised to see a thick metal lock securing two solid metal poles to the stone itself. It almost appeared as if the tower had been built to lock something inside.

Beggen Ostra turned to him. "On the other side of this door is a creature, taken from the Far East, across the Stone Breaker Expanse, and eventually placed here, in this tower. It's an observatory, but how it observes is what is most important, and is a closely guarded secret. The creature here, while not exactly friendly, shared a common enemy in the Far East, and in exchange for the opportunity to strike back at the heart of the Far East, it provided us a gift of far-sight. We'd bring it trinkets, gifts, and news of our continued effort to build our new Kingdom and strike at the Far East, and it was content. However, after the Great Betrayal, I am afraid that no one remained to bring it good news, or news strong enough to maintain the bond. I am hoping it remembers me; it always seemed most fond of me, possibly because I brought it items infused with magic, kids' things."

She paused for a moment as if remembering before looking back at Cereal, a serious glint in her eye.

"A few things to remember. If it addresses you, don't

address it directly; always ask a question. I found its most attentive when it feels it's of use. Besides its ability to see and a few other gifts, the creature has a certain affinity for birds, and has an odd connection to them. That's how we will send my message. The problem we will most likely encounter is how thirty years of solitude may have changed it. It will test us."

Cereal swallowed nervously, and the lump that had begun welling in his throat at the beginning of her speech was now thick and distracting. He was scared, even by the old woman's side, and whatever was on the other side of this door had been there, in solitude, for over thirty years. He truly hoped the old woman knew what she was doing, and that this risk was worth whatever message she had to send. He clenched his fists in an attempt to hide his building fear.

"And if it has changed? If it doesn't like us?"

"It will probably eat us out of spite. From my understanding, it does not even need to eat."

"Can I stay here?"

"No. It has never been known to eat children, and if it eats me, I need you to send the message."

"What is the message?"

"Remember these words exactly. Two dead boys got up to fight."

"What does that mean?"

"It means Prince Shaw is going after his throne, and we're to help him."

"How are we going to help him get his throne back? The King has an army of Stone Breakers and all things terrible, " Cereal said.

"We have many friends throughout the Kingdom who believe in the true King, and the true King can rally such friends."

"We'd need an army, or more!"

She chuckled. "Indeed, child. Now, stay behind me, and remember what I told you."

She faced the hatch again, raised her hand to the lock, and took in a deep breath. A small pulse shook the top step as she whispered something under her breath, and little bits of stone and dust landed on his head. Cereal felt the spell like a thick spot in the air before it expanded outward as a pulse. The lock clicked open and fell off the loop, and Beggen Ostra grabbed it in midair. She grasped the large metal bar holding the door shut and pulled it to the side, freeing the door and causing it to drop open.

The room up above was dark, other than a small fire burning in the window off to the right. Cereal recognized the flickering of shadows caused by a hearth fire, and was slightly confused as to what kind of creature this was that ate people, but had also lit a hearth fire. Beggen Ostra pocketed the lock and pulled herself up and into the room. Cereal followed suit, but she reached down and pulled him up the rest of the way by his tunic. They stood in the center of a large circular room, and every inch of wall, from the floor to the expansive ceiling, was covered in a single ornate painting. Every few feet, the painting would change styles, from vibrant and full of life to dreary and depressing. Then, the scenes shifted to depict incredible battles, followed by bloodied fields of dead soldiers. Cereal recognized the uniform of the soldiers, red and gold, with the famous Stone Breaker hammer. These graveyards were scattered every so often between pictures of the green steppe, the plains of the Kingdom, and even a to-scale picture of Stonehaven. He couldn't help but admire the intricacy of the painting, but was sad that every moment of peace was interrupted by yet another battle.

"Where is it?" he whispered to Beggen Ostra, not seeing anything in the room but the small fire lit off to her right and the painted walls.

"Look up and remember what I told you," she whispered from somewhere behind him.

Cereal looked up, and immediately the desire to run and hide washed over him, replacing his slowly-building fear with outright terror. Just above him, a tree-like creature grew out of the walls and converged in the middle of the room, strung up by thick vines. Its skin reminded him of that of an aging, barkless tree, smooth and grey. It had several of what he'd call appendages, but each one funneled into one of the vines stringing it up in the room. He looked up at what would be its feet but instead, a thick knot of vines writhed about, like a ball of mating snakes. It seemed impossibly heavy to be strung up by so few vines, and it seemed to be almost as tall as the ceiling, though Cereal couldn't see how far up it went. It was like a tree, but it moved.

Beggen Ostra ignored his initial shock and chose to speak to the creature. She stood directly under the knot of vines, looked up and spoke softly and clearly. "Where have I been for many a year?"

It responded with a voice like two pieces of wood scraping together, ominously from above. "Have you left me here? Am I uninteresting?"

"Are you not glad to see I have returned?"

"Where have you been? Why did you leave me here?"

"Didn't you know the Kingdom is in disarray? What happened to the Royal Family dead? Do the Far Eastern armies threaten our borders yet again?"

"Am I to believe that you did not think to release me? Did we not have an agreement?"

"Don't you remember the terms of our agreement?"

"What gifts?" The vine ball stopped writhing.

Beggen Ostra reached into her pocket and withdrew the lock to the hatch that led to the room they were in. She lifted it to the writhing ball, like an offering. Several vines shot out and wrapped around her wrist and the lock before lifting her off the floor.

Cereal jumped in surprise and pulled his dagger out of his belt and moved to slash at the vines.

"Did I say to move?" she snapped at him.

He stopped, but did not put his dagger away.

"What did you bring me?" The gritty voice emanated from the tree creature again.

"Don't you recognize a puzzle?"

"What puzzle? Is this a simple lock?"

"Is it a simple lock, or is it the lock to this tower?"

"Do you aim to deceive me? Have I not been imprisoned for thirty years? Have I not been tricked into cooperating? Have I not continued to aid you, despite the fact that we barely share a connection?" The vines tightened around her wrists, and she winced. Still, she shot a glance at Cereal, showing that she knew what she was doing.

"Do I aim to trick you? Or do I aim to release you?"

"Would you release me? Why?"

"Is it possible I wish to release you onto this new world so you may seek out all the puzzles you can desire?"

Cereal was glad to see the vines release their grip a bit, as her hands had started turning a light shade of purple.

"You'd dare ask my help, after trapping me here for so long?"

"Could I have left you here? With no puzzles, and no news of the world?"

"Could you have?"

"Will you release me, so we may discuss?" she asked meagerly.

This was it. Cereal could tell she was priming the creature for this question. He only hoped it had remembered her and appreciated her gesture to release it, though he was not sure that was a good idea either.

All at once, the vines unraveled from her wrists, but the lock was pulled up into the mass. One by one, the vines plucked themselves from the walls and tucked into the mass. When only two vines remained, suspending it from the ceiling, the creature lowered itself to the floor. Once grounded, it creeped and twisted, wrapping vine on top of vine until two leg-like appendages formed, then a torso, then two, arms, and finally a head with tiny impressions for eyes. After a moment, the vines stopped swirling and hardened, creating the semblance of a man, though its arms were slightly elongated, and its head was flat across the top, and too wide.

"Now you're just showing off for the boy." Beggen Ostra chuckled, massaging her wrists.

Cereal quickly turned his head toward her, afraid; she hadn't spoken in the form of a question. Half expecting the vine creature to attack them, he raised his dagger, shaking.

"Put that away, Cereal."

"But…you said…"

"Don't worry with what I said before. This is Agatha; she may not be a friend of ours, but she doesn't appreciate the slavers in the Far East, or she finds them uninteresting with nothing to share. We've survived her test." She brushed herself off and dug into her pocket, pulling out two entangled pieces of metal and handing them to the creature. It reached out, and tiny vines in the place of its hands began eagerly working on the metal puzzle.

"As I said, the Kingdom is besieged, inside and out. The King, his eldest son, and his son's wife were killed by Jayecob, Shaw's brother, thirty years ago. The reigning King is brewing something, something terrible, deep within the castle. I have heard rumors of it being a final solution to the war with the Far East."

"That sounds like a good thing." This time when it spoke, its voice was higher-pitched and less scratchy. Cereal saw several vines scraping together near its neck where its voice seemed to be coming from.

"You'd think so, but that's the story the King twists. I believe his war machine is but a con, a fallacy. I believe he aims to destroy everything."

It pulled the two pieces of metal apart and dropped them to the floor. She dug in her pocket again and pulled out another puzzle; this one consisted of square blocks of several colors set in a wooden frame with a single empty space. Agatha snatched it out of her hands and used its vines to quickly slide the pieces over and over.

"We need to act. I need you to call your friends, and I need to *see*."

"You ask a lot, but bring so little." It tossed the finished puzzle aside and loomed over her, one viny hand held out, like an expectant child. Beggen Ostra was ready with another puzzle; this one Cereal recognized as a simple wooden box with no visible markings.

"A trick?" It looked up from the box.

"Not a trick."

It resumed sliding its vine appendages over the box's smooth surface. Cereal looked at the woman who winked at him quickly and smiled.

"Agatha, call to your friends, and help me *see*, and you will be released to seek all the puzzles of this world. If you don't help us, I fear there won't be a world to puzzle over."

"No tricks. You will release me?"

"Have I not always kept my word? I promised to return when I was able."

"You did." It pondered the idea for a moment, still gripping the box and turning it over and over again with its vines.

"Will you help us one last time? This time as friends?" she asked, and closed her eyes.

Cereal felt the familiar pressure in his chest as Beggen Ostra readied another spell. This one she aimed at the outward-facing wall of the tower. She began to whisper something to herself, her brow furrowed in concentration. He felt the pressure continue to build in his chest and the hairs on his arms stood up. All at once, she released the welling power, resulting in a cascade of blinding white knife-shaped objects manifesting from her hand and embedding themselves in the wall. For a moment they lit the room before exploding outward, leaving a gaping hole in the tower, revealing the night's sky. She dropped to her knees with her hands on the floor, heaving. Between her deep breaths she spoke to the creature, "You are free... go... but please... we need your help... this last time."

Cereal looked at Agatha, who had apparently ignored Beggen Ostra's incredible show of power and was furiously searching for a way to open the box. It looked up from the box and at the old woman, who looked frailer than ever.

Cereal rushed over to help lift her off the floor. He pulled her by the arm so she was standing again.

"You say there are many puzzles out there?" It turned to the hole in the tower.

"Many. Much more intriguing than anything I can bring you."

After a moment it said, "I'll help. What do you wish to see?"

"Show me Prince Shaw."

"The Royal Family is dead?"

"Shaw has returned."

"How has the Prince returned?" It faced her again.

"One of the many puzzles out there." She nodded to the hole in the wall.

"Very well." It turned away from her. The vines that had once hardened to resemble skin transformed into their usual gray color and wiggled again. It put its arms out to its side and leaned its head forward. The creature's arms flattened and expanded, as did its legs and torso. Beggen Ostra approached it, matching her arms and legs with the creatures, and leaned forward. Vines snatched her up and pulled her into the creature's body. Additional vines wrapped around her until only bits of her tunic and armor poked through the gaps. It lifted its head and engulfed the old woman in more vines. For a moment, everything was silent, but Beggen Ostra showed no signs of distress from within the creature. Unexpectedly, a thin black beam shot out from the creature's face as an empty black line against the night's sky. First it aimed directly east before the creature turned its head, pivoting the beam toward the north... to Stonehaven.

"He is in the Howling Halls. He is being tortured by Viktor, the interrogator. My magic can't penetrate those walls and neither can his. But yours is different. Yours is older, and stronger. You must help him," she said from within the confines of the creature. Her voice was only slightly muffled, but Cereal caught the hint of the grinding sound as she spoke.

"Is this what you wish? Or will you have me call to my friends? I'll grant you one."

She hung her head, pondering, "Everything fails without Prince Shaw. Help him. I'll find another way to send the message."

The creature titled its head at her for a moment. "Very well." The beam widened and sparks shimmered from its head and traveled along the beam out into the night sky. In rapid succession, three balls shot out from the creature's face and rode along the beam off and into the night.

"It is done."

The beam cut off and disappeared. Just as she'd entered the creature's mass of vines, she exited, and it resumed its human-like form, picking and prodding at the wooden box again.

"Thank you, Agatha. You will always be a member of our Kingdom." She nodded at Cereal to climb down the hatch.

"The boy..." it said softly as Beggen Ostra put her feet through the hole.

She looked down at Cereal near the bottom of the steps then back at the creature.

"What of him?"

"Something festers within him. Like a rot, hidden beneath the dirt."

"Thank you, Agatha. A lot weighs on him."

"What was your message for my friends?"

"You have done enough Agatha, go, and be free."

"I'd like to know."

"Two dead boys got up to fight."

She slipped through the hatch and met Cereal at the bottom of the tower. She found him climbing over the fallen tree which blocked the entry into the tower, and he leaned back to stretch in the cool night's air.

"We did not get to send your message, ma'am."

"No, but we did find the Prince and, hopefully, Agatha gave him a way out."

CHAPTER ELEVEN

SHAW SCREAMED AGAIN as the needle-thin tendrils dug into the muscle in his forearm and wrist, writhing and wriggling, stabbing at each nerve. Shaw's hand involuntarily clenched and his nails dug into his skin, drawing blood. He bit down on his teeth so hard he felt like they'd crumble.

Viktor slowly retracted each tendril from his skin, and they wiggled and straightened and pulled, like a dog on a leash. The shadowy tendrils relaxed and flexed on the tip of Viktor's finger as he eyed Shaw closely with his retracted eyelids and bloodshot eyes. If Viktor still had normal gums, Shaw would have expected him to be smiling right about now. Instead, only the smell of rot escaped from behind his teeth as he clicked them together. Obviously pleased with his work, Viktor whispered another spell, and the tendrils drifted off like wisps of smoke.

"What is your name?" Viktor asked, inches from Shaw's face.

"It's of no concern," he said between pained breaths, trying to sound as defiant and absolute as possible.

"If you don't want to give your name, I'll extract it from you." He began the incantation to summon the tendrils again, but was interrupted by a thud from the outside wall of the hall. Viktor looked behind him for a moment before turning back and, this time, pulling Shaw's tunic aside.

Our opportunity is coming. Be ready, Pemazu chittered in his head.

"What do you mean?"

Something has weakened the wards within the stone walls, and I think more are coming.

"What has enough power to do that?" Shaw asked.

Who cares? Get ready.

Viktor stared into Shaw's eyes. He could see through the gaps of his teeth the man's blackened tongue flopped, dry and bleeding a little in his mouth.

A second thud impacted the wall; this time, it sounded stronger and closer. Viktor looked at him again and raised a thinning eyebrow.

"You wouldn't happen to know anything about that would you?"

Shaw smiled.

Now.

A third impact shook the side of the building and tiny cracks appeared in the wall of the cell in front of him. Shaw dug into the well of power trapped behind the dam in his mind. Since he'd been trapped here, the well was inaccessible, and he felt cut off from its welcoming, addictive power. Like a cascade of water over the edge of a cliff, the well graciously answered Shaw's request and flooded his body with warmth and energy. Shaw pressed his will on either side of the river, constraining and molding it to his will. It pushed back, attempting to spill over, testing his mettle. Shaw held on, filling the well fully before he concentrated the power with a spell.

Viktor's eyes drifted from Shaw's to the gems in his arms as the foremost emptied its usual red glow and the magpie drifted to the middle gem. The magpie made a rude gesture before opening its mouth wide enough to encompass the rim of the gem and disappear from view.

Shaw infused his words with the power from the well, and the effect from his spell was instantaneous.

"Orhen dro rah."

In an instant, his skin crawled with a burning, tingling feeling and began to crack and twist under the bars that held his hands. Dagger-like claws burst through his fingertips, black scales replaced skin up to his elbows, and his toes cut through his boots with hook-like claws. His brilliant emerald eyes rolled back in his head and were replaced with deep empty pits.

His voice rang out hollow and empty. "My name is Shaw."

If Viktor still had eyelids, Shaw believed he'd be a mix of surprised and scared. Shaw pulled free of the metal bars, gripping and disfiguring the metal as he pulled away from it. First he pulled one crooked claw free, then tore the metal on his other arm and his feet.

Viktor stumbled backward over himself, scampering to the other side of the room.

Shaw stepped onto the stony floor with his hooked feet, each nail clicking individually, gouging the stone. Viktor spat out the incantation to open the glass-like portal in the middle of the room and crawled through it. It quickly began to close in on itself, but Shaw managed to dash forward and jam a clawed hand through it. The portal failed to close over the scaled skin, whereas the average person would have simply lost their hand. He held the portal open, then jammed his other hand through. He turned his hands out and pulled, forcing the glass window open and making space for the rest of his body. He pulled it wider and slipped a clawed foot through, followed by his other foot and, finally, he dropped the rest of his torso and head to the other side.

He was in an armory of sorts. The lower sections of suits of armor rested on racks with their upper halves mounted next to them. Various weaponry, spelled and not spelled, decorated the wall in a way that was both functionally accessible and aesthetically pleasing. Viktor, the interrogator, was retrieving a halberd from one of the walls while two additional guards pushed back from their chairs and drew their swords. Across their chests was the standard Stone Breaker hammer on a background of gold and red, but instead of the beautiful gray of stone from Stonehaven, the hammers were dyed black, the mark of the new Royal Guard. These were Stone Breakers who had earned a black hammer from their exploits in battle. Exploits which included the killing of innocent women and children fleeing Third City.

Viktor had retrieved the polearm and was rushing at him, holding it high and preparing to bring it down on him. The Royal Guards moved to either side and Viktor swept the weapon in a wide arc in front of him. Shaw hopped backward, the blade inches from cutting his chest open.

On the left, Pemazu warned, sounding slightly amused.

The guard jabbed and Shaw sidestepped, hooked a claw under the hilt of the blade, and ripped it out of his hands, where it soared through the air and landed somewhere behind him. He drew a short sword and stepped back, waiting for Viktor to strike again.

Watch your right. Must I do this for you?

The second guard had mustered enough courage to chop at him with an overhead strike. Shaw crossed his arms and met the blade above his head where it sparked against his scales and slid off. He reared back and kicked the guard in the chest with a clawed foot, causing him to sprawl backward. Viktor dropped his halberd and caught him.

All three will strike at once. You must finish this quickly if we are to escape. Soon they will raise the alarm, and my power is draining.

Shaw glanced at the gems in his arm, two of which shone bright and brilliant red, but the third lay gray and dormant.

One of the guards yelled to the others, "What is it?"

"I did not even scratch it." The guards began to discuss hurriedly between themselves, trying to decide what to do.

"As one!" Viktor commanded, lifting the halberd and seeing that the other guards were in agreeance. Together they nodded and raised their weapons, this time intending to close in on their opponent from three sides. With the wall to his back and his attackers to the front Shaw needed to end this quickly.

Blind them.

He agreed with the demon and prepared a Pulse. Those who were caught in the wake of the spell at this range would be blinded by it. The gems in his arm glowed deep red and heat radiated outward from them, warming his skin.

Viktor lunged the moment the spell was prepared. He swung the bladed weapon down while the two guards slashed from the side. Shaw managed to dodge the halberd again and parry one of the swords with a scaled arm. The third guardsmen sunk his blade in the table behind him.

Shaw raised his arm and released the pulse, shielding his eyes in the crook of his arm. The guards yelled out, but no additional strikes from their bladed weapons came, and only the sound of their wailing could be heard. Shaw looked up and saw all three soldiers wandering around the room, crying out with their hands pressed against their faces, blood dripping out from between their fingers. He looked at the men, blind and scared, scrambling to feel their way through the room, bumping into tables and each other. One wailed like a child, the other mumbled to himself, and the last sat prodding at his eye sockets in shock and disbelief.

You should kill them. The King will kill them for being useless to him now anyways.

No, he thought, *no soldier should die like this. I know my brother. He won't care if the body is blind or not; he only cares about their usefulness as a whole. He may put them to work in the mines or the stables.*

He stooped down to talk to the guard sitting and prodding his missing eyes. Sensing something in front of him he asked, "Who…what are you?"

"Tell anyone what happened here today, and I'll come for more than your eyesight. All of you."

Terrified and confused, they each nodded in turn.

"Now you must answer me, Viktor, or I'll take your skin off in strips."

The blind, whimpering man nodded.

"Where is the Book?"

Why would he know of the Book? Pemazu questioned.

"The spells you use. They are from the Book, are they not?"

Viktor spoke softly from behind his hands. "I don't know of any book."

"Who taught you those spells?"

"The King. He taught me personally."

"Did you ever see him with a book? Bound with wire, with gems like those in my arm?"

"No. He was looking for something like it for many years, but he gave up."

"What is within the walls of the castle? What is his *final solution*? Tell me of the war machine. What is he preparing for?"

"I can't reveal that."

"The next thing I'll take is your tongue and your ears. You will be a sightless, speechless, deaf blight, left to wander…"

"He aims to quell an insurrection!" Viktor blurted out.

"Don't say more brother," the other guard cried out.

"Speak," Shaw demanded, scratching Viktor behind the ear with a claw.

"Second City. Second City aims to take the castle. A rogue Stone Breaker named Daemond. The King knows about it and plans to obliterate all of Second City. He grows something within the castle. Something terrible."

"Who else knows of this insurrection?"

"Just the King and the King's Guard. He prepares his army in secret for a mission unknown."

"How many is his army?"

"Legions. They are amassed everywhere; insurgents, traders, barmaids. They wait for his signal."

"How does he communicate with them?"

"He has a system, three floors above us. It's fueled by desecrating the bodies of the dead…"

Dark, foul magic. The room may prove useful in getting us out of here, Pemazu said.

"How long? How long until he strikes?"

"Weeks…"

Shaw stood up. "Tell no one of what you encountered here today. Tell them you were simply bested and blinded by a thief."

I should have eaten them.

"Let us head for the communication room to find out what we can," Shaw said.

"I have one final question and I'll leave you alive to be found later. Where are my possessions?"

"The center door."

One of the guards nodded his head towards the middle of three doors.

After locating his sword, armor, traveling pouch, boots, and a few other useful items. Shaw left the three blinded guards bound and gagged in a storage closet and exited down the hallway to the right.

He made his way down the main corridor, taking note of the changes since he had last roamed the halls. Once lit with hundreds of candles and torches, now a minimal number provided light in the darkest of corners. The tapestries and paintings that once decorated the spaces between torches were faded and torn from neglect, and a lowly musk hung about the warm air.

Overall, the castle seemed strangely vacant. No guards roaming the halls, no hustle and bustle of those conducting business within the castle, no passersby aiming to speak with the leader of the Kingdom. He was thankful the halls were empty as in his present form, he'd surely raise cause for concern.

He moved quickly but purposefully, checking each store-room and side room as he passed. Most were unlit, as if the emphasis on lighting was minimal in this main hallway. Shaw also noticed that the castle had changed structurally since he'd been gone. Thirty years shouldn't have left cracks in the stone. Especially if this hallway was a reflection of the activity the castle had seen as a whole.

Shaw found the stairway he was looking for. The Stone Breaker had said that the communication device was above them, and the stairway spiraled up and back over the room had he just left. He took the steps two at a time, tapping the gems in his arm to provide just enough light to see the next. He also checked the glow, noting Pemazu tapping a foot in the last gem, with the second only half-filled with light, indicating that his time in this form was limited. The claws on his feet dug into the stone, keeping him from slipping on the smooth surface as he picked up speed in the narrow stairway. The stairway opened up onto a landing, and something caught his eye. The landing led to another hallway, even darker than the last. At the end was a great archway, with thick stone pillars blocking off the majority of the passage. This hallway was an entirely new addi-tion, and the pillars seemed to have been built in a way to let someone see inside, but not let something out. He decided that finding out more about the King's doings was worth the precious time, and the risk of running into more guards. He felt the gems in his arms throb painfully.

We do not have time for this. We are running out of energy.

"We need to know of the King's war machine. If he manages to destroy everything, the Book will be useless anyway."

That Book is the key to everything. Do not disrespect its power, Pemazu chirped.

"That Book is responsible for all of this!"

You are wrong, Arbiter. Your brother's pride, ego, and desire are responsible. The Book does not take sides.

Shaw rattled his arm, causing the bird to bounce around the confines of the gem, leading to more swearing and more painful throbbing. He continued on the west side of the hall, keeping the pillar-blocked chamber in view at all times. As he neared it, he noticed a small room off to the right, sealed tight with a studded metal door. He made it to the archway, and it was as he'd expected; the entrance to a large room, and the pillars were not wide enough to get a hand through. He looked through, but it was too dark to see anything.

I could give you light to see, but I am not so sure I would want to see, if I was human, the bird cautioned.

"What do you mean?"

What is happening on that side of these walls is something foul, horrid, and unforgivable, Pemazu said in a morbid tone.

"Well, those things may differ between us."

No, even for me. The fact that I do not believe in good does not necessarily mean that I am evil.

"Twist and turn your words how you please, demon, I know what you are."

And yet you choose to share an existence with me. What does that say about you?

"Even the best of us have moments of weakness."

The bird made multiple gagging and vomiting sounds before hopping backwards as a glow rose from within the gem.

It grew brighter and brighter, warming his arm until it felt like it was burning his skin. He held his arm up to the space between the pillars and allowed Pemazu to finish the spell. A tiny bauble of light drifted out from the gem, between the pillars and into the dark beyond. It moved through the air like a small bug caught in the wind, but eventually found the center of the room. From there, it grew in brightness until all but the most stubborn shadow was snuffed out.

Shaw first saw what he thought were people, standing feet from each other with their heads bowed. Then he noticed thin black tubes, leading from their eyes, noses, and mouths to a larger, thicker tube on the floor. He traced that tube to a central pot with a glass porthole in the side. At first, he thought that whatever was in the pot came from the people standing about the room, but he soon discovered the pot wasn't filling with the thick, green sludge. The tubes protruded from the bottom of the pot. It was emptying its contents into the people in the room through their eyes, noses and mouths.

Can you see, Arbiter?

"What am I looking at? What is being done to them?"

Argomancy, Pemazu said.

"What is Argomancy?"

A crude and ancient magic. While necromancy is a classification of magic dealing with the dead, Argomancy is performed on the living.

"What is happening to them?"

It looks as if your brother has perfected the process. Argomancy takes years...and this process seems to have reduced it to months. I can sense the presence inside them, Pemazu said.

"Stop speaking in riddles."

Argomancy twists, tortures and molds the soul of the living...using a combination of chemicals and black magic...he is making demons.

"Demons? How? You can't exist without making a trade. A soul for power. Your kind can't exist on this plane without us."

Argomancy removes that requirement and breaks a soul beyond recognition. This is why the Book brought you back, Arbiter. This is what is upsetting the balance. The King has a demonic army under his command. While they may not be truly demon, they will have our power...and our unrestrained anger, Pemazu said.

The bauble of light faded, leaving the room dark once again, and he pushed back from the pillars. Shaw walked over to the room with the solid metal door and peered through. A hole was cut through the wall to accommodate a thick black tube, which led back to the Argomancy room. Unlike the other room, this smaller one was well-lit, and in the center sat a metal coffin. Metal chains wrapped around it, and the thick tube was attached to the top.

The conduit. The centerpiece. Whoever is in there is one of us...and incredibly powerful...

"We need to get in there. Take it all down. Kill the conduit," Shaw said.

How do you propose we get through this door, get into the coffin, and, finally, destroy whatever demon is fueling this?

Shaw thought to himself, *Pemazu had a point.* He was close to drained and needed to return to his sister and the boy. He could use their help to find the Book.

What makes you think the Book will help? The Book takes no sides, Pemazu said.

"The Book won't help directly, but it will have ideas."

Let us hope so. I am growing bored.

Shaw reluctantly turned away from the chamber and the conduit room and headed back to the stairway at the other end of the hall. As he was about to continue his way to the top, torchlight lit the stairway from below, and the sound of thick boots and chainmail echoed up the chamber. Knowing that he'd be unable to move upward quickly enough, he chose to stand on the other side of the doorway, lying in wait.

The soldiers, like the ones from the storeroom below, were wearing Stone Breaker tunics with a blackened hammer and wore large battle axes across their backs. They rounded the corner and pulled the axes from their backs. Shaw moved on them from behind, quickly crushing their metal helmets in his clawed hands before slamming them both into the wall. They both crumpled without a sound and, without a place to hide them, he knew that he'd need to move quickly if he was to see the communication device. Taking the steps two at a time again, he hurried his way up three more circular stair rounds and poured out onto another stairway landing with a closed wooden door.

Expecting another guarded hallway, he readied himself to strike as he opened the door and, once still, found himself alone in the tower. He remembered many years ago that every tower and every stair was filled with people who had business in the castle. Seeing it so empty, so barren, made him wonder what else had faded away under the new King's rule.

He slid inside and shut the door behind him. Thankfully, this room was left unguarded and unlocked. He supposed the two guards he encountered on his way up were most likely assigned to this entire region of the castle. Either the King did not expect much opposition, or the guards themselves were scarce. Based on the overall decaying quality of what he'd seen, he guessed the latter. Determined to interrupt the King's plans as best he could, he took inventory of the room and how the apparatus before him appeared to work.

A large circular platform took up most of the space, with markings in what he believed were demonic etched into the stone around the platform. Four windowed, stone sarcophagi, also marked in demonic, made a square around the circular platform, closing it in. Inside each sarcophagus was a corpse, or what was left of one. Its eyes and ears were removed, and every inch of skin was carved with deep demonic runes. Along its stomach was a large incision with hasty stitches. Shaw noticed that its insides were hastily shoved to the bottom of the stone coffin and whatever clothing they might have worn at one point was piled high in the corner. This room had been used many a time.

Necromancy begins when the person is alive. Their skin is marked, then they are killed and their souls used to cast spells of immense power. This type of magic has been dead for many a lifetime, Pemazu explained.

"Where did he learn it?"

Most likely from one of us, or the Book itself.

"The Book did not have anything of necromancy in it," Shaw said.

The Book is different to each of its readers, you know this.

The demon was right. The Book had appeared differently to him. It had taught him nothing of necromancy, and instead taught him spells of binding and keeping. The other powers seemed to have come from the demon.

"What can this do? Can this help us talk to my sister?"

Yes, and I believe it can transport you as well, Pemazu explained.

"Transporting me won't do me any good. I must gather more information. Surely someone here knows of the Book."

And do you not think the King would have interrogated everyone to find that information? We must regroup. We've seen the King's war machine. We know he has insurgents planted throughout the Kingdom. It will not be long until we are found, Pemazu said, trailing off.

He hated to agree with the demon but trying to make his way through the castle unseen, especially with his power drained as it was, would certainly end with his recapture.

"How do we use this device?"

Say the spell written around the platform, then envision your sister. According to the inscriptions. It will transport us to whomever you envision, Pemazu explained.

"Is there something else?"

This magic...it has a cost...Viktor knew the cost of using such magic and chose to use it only under duress. It's more addicting, and more dangerous, than anything you have ever felt. Once you start, you must stop, or I fear our relationship will end rather quickly. Though at this point I dare not say that would be a bad thing.

"What cost?" Shaw asked.

I do not know, Arbiter, but there is a reason this magic has been dead for thousands of years.

He let the demon's words sink in for a few moments. He was limited on options. Fighting his way out of the castle was the least attractive of them and would inevitably end with his recapture. There were roving guards and soon, one of them would locate their fellow soldiers and sound the alarm. If this device was able to communicate with Beggen Ostra and Cereal, he needed to call for help.

Arbiter, I have read over this spell. It appears to be linked to another location. A similar device rests in the Pit.

"This can transport us there?"

Yes, but remember, Arbiter...the cost...and are you ready to go back to the Pit?

Again, the demon brought up a valid point. It had been thirty years since the events of the Great Betrayal. Since the events that had plunged him into an anger-fueled, wandering existence on the Thin Line. Since the events leading to the death of his father, his mother, and, as he'd believed at the time, his wife and sister. The Pit was not only a haven for these memories, but also the tainted ground upon which his brother, Jayecob, had opened a portal, releasing a demon from the depths of the Thin Line leading to the destruction of Third City.

"I fear that we're again without a choice. I don't think I'll get such a chance to leave this castle behind again. I'll return soon. Hopefully whatever my sister has been planning will help once she learns of what is happening within these walls."

I do not fear anything living, but I may make an exception for her, Pemazu said in a hushed tone.

"What? You, scared of a little old woman? She has but a fraction of her power. You should have seen her thirty years ago."

I do not fear what she can do. I fear what she is willing to do.

"Again with your riddles, demon. Enough for now. Let us leave here."

Are you going like that? Pemazu said sarcastically. He of course meant Shaw's current transfigured state.

"I suppose not."

Shaw concentrated on the flow of power surging through him and quickly found the well. Confined and channeled, the power made a river, slowly fueled by the overflowing well. Carefully, he concentrated on capping the well, cutting off the flow of power. As the river reduced to a trickle, and then to the faint splashing, his arms and legs returned to normal. Claws became feet and hands, and scales became skin. Shaw opened his eyes and flexed his hands and feet. He pulled his extra boots and gloves from his pack and slipped them on. After securing his belt and sword, he stepped onto the platform and prepared to cast the dark magic.

He glanced at the gems in his arm. Only one continued to glow brilliant red. The magpie with too many eyes puffed up its feathers and blew a massive raspberry.

Shaw rolled his eyes, then circled in place, reading the incantation.

"It's written in demonic, but a few of the words I don't know."

Simply read it off as it appears and do not tarry. The power is infused in the words and the corpses around us. No need to use our own. We have also been discovered, and something of great power has arrived at the castle.

"You can sense it?"

Yes, it is incredibly powerful, and old.

"You're old," Shaw snapped.

Not compared to this thing. Hurry!

Shaw took a deep breath and let it out, preparing to read off the incantation. In a loud and commanding voice, he recited the words. *"Angra torant ranoa torant angra."*

Each word stung his tongue like tiny bugs pricking him. Each word also had an effect on the corpses in the boxes. As he spoke, the corpses began to violently thrash about, further distorting what little humanlike features they maintained. Each word flowed from his mouth more quickly than he expected, as if he couldn't wait to spit the next one out. The platform shook slightly at first, but by the end of the incantation his legs wobbled and his eyes jarred in his head. The room began to twist and bend, crisscrossing and turning in on itself. He closed his eyes as his stomach followed suit, tumbling and cramping. He felt like he was going to vomit. Pressure built in his head and he squinted through the pain, trying to see what was happening.

The room was almost entirely a blur now, but through the distortion he could make out the shape of the door to the chamber opening and the vague outline of someone in shiny gold armor pointing at him. At this point, he was drifting backward, pulling away from the room like a bird flying off from a mountainside, but below him there was only black, and above him, only black. Whatever was happening, it reminded him of the Thin Line, and, for a moment, he panicked. He'd been betrayed. The device was dragging him back to that place, to the endless wandering, to the great void where he'd be stuck forever. Desperately he tried to fight the pull of the spell, but his hands were heavy and his legs stiff and immovable. He was trapped again, and the world was spinning in on itself around him. He closed his eyes, the image of his wife, breaking up the darkness.

Shaw sat up excitedly, breathing heavily and covered in sweat. For a moment he'd forgotten where he was, but the events of the last few days drifted back to him. The Howling Halls, Viktor, the Argomancy room, the thing in the coffin, the room with the bodies. How long had he been asleep?

He blinked his eyes a few times, adjusting to the low light. Wherever he was, it was dimly lit and the air was sticky. Something sour filled the air and there was a slight dripping sound in the distance. Wherever he was, it was big; even his breathing echoed.

"Pemazu, where are we? Pemazu?"

The demon didn't answer. He slid his sleeve over his forearm and tapped the gems. A faint light grew from the gem lowest on his arm. It grew and gently lit the silhouette of the magpie. It was resting on its legs, its head drooping slightly.

I told you that device had a cost, it chirped weakly. *The Pit...it was buried long ago...*

"Why? All know the story of the Great Betrayal. Why bury it?"

Your sister buried it. I would presume to bury whatever is here...I can sense the remnants of her magic here...and something else.

"How do we get out?"

We cannot. We are beneath many buildings that used to stand in these Ruins. Courtesy of your sister.

"You can get us out. Open a portal to the Thin Line. Or we can blast our way out."

I told you that device had a cost.

"What do you mean? You can't do anything?"

The device took what it needed from me. Even with the foulest of magic the basic principles still apply. You must give in order to receive, Pemazu said.

"So, what? We're trapped here?"

Perhaps not. We can try to make our way through the rubble, but avoid the center of the room, at least until I have regained enough strength to figure out what it is. It is a strange bit of magic.

"Is it dangerous?"

Probably, but that is just the way things are, are they not?

CHAPTER TWELVE

THE MAGES LAID on their backs in a circle, with their heads towards the center of the platform. Each wore cloth robes, ceremoniously tailored to be form-fitting, showing off the skill and physical prowess of the mages. Magical prowess, accompanied with physical strength and conditioning, led to more controlled and targeted spells. Targeted and controlled was what the King needed right now.

The King himself stood in the middle of the mages, in the center of a room designed to amplify their power. He was a burly man, towering above most. He kept his jet-black hair shaved down to the skin on the sides of his head, leaving just enough on top to pad his helmet. Between his height, his armor, and his striking blue eyes, he was impressive. He believed in the importance of appearances and believed they should match one's status. Unlike the lowly mages on the floor, the King was clad in gold-plated armor with studded jewels. Offsetting the gold, a blackened broadsword was slung tight across his back, and a two-tailed alley cat sat upon his shoulders, flicking its tails with impatience. The King stood proud, content to let the mages wait for his command, because as King, he waited for no one.

He had taken up his armor and gathered the mages upon hearing of a prisoner's escape from the Howling Halls. A prisoner who had enough power to escape a magic-proof room, blind several guards, and knock out two more. A prisoner who managed to use his device to transport himself outside the castle walls to the far end of the Kingdom. Whoever this prisoner was, he'd invoked enough fear in his guards they'd not dare speak a word of his name or appearance. By chance, he explored the north-most tower and located two guards at the base of the tower who had clearly been attacked. His companion had notified him that the device had been activated, piquing his interest to where he felt he should investigate the disturbance himself. Normally, he was above such petty tasks, but his guards had proven to be incompetent.

The cat spoke to him, injecting its thoughts directly into his mind. Its voice would be described as soft, should he have actually heard it on the physical plane.

There is a taste in the air. One of us.

"What do you mean, Amekath?" he thought back.

I mean that whoever came through here has a demon with them.

"Impius?"

Doubtful, the taste is too clean. Impius are destructive and rancid. An Impius would have eaten the guards as well, out of boredom. The cat rubbed its twin-headed tail against the back of his neck.

"Whoever they are, I intend to meet them, then find out everything they wouldn't tell Viktor. You will have to assist me if Viktor was unable to extract anything."

As you wish. The cat shifted on his shoulder. *Do you wish to take the guard with you?*

"No, it has been some time since I have left the castle. I can appreciate the solitude from the incessant nagging of peasants."

I would hardly call what we have solitude. The cat yawned.

"Indeed, but at least you shut up, even when you're hungry."

Jayecob, I hope after all I have given you, you would still yearn to hear my voice, Amekath said.

"You have paved the way to a new, prosperous reign, our army is growing, the device is producing; but this incursion is fueling my curiosity. Let us see who has bested the guards."

Jayecob shifted his armor higher up on his shoulders, checked the placement of his broadsword across his back, and picked up his helmet from the floor, tucking it under his arm. He did not trust any of the people who laid at his feet. He looked at the mage closest to him, his eyes showing a hint of fear. These mages were aware of the spell they were about to use and the power it required. Should they not be able to muster enough, the spell would continue to take whatever they had to give. Sometimes, it took too much. Consequently, lives were often lost in the use of this spell.

He nodded at the young man on the floor, who spoke the first string of words in a complicated spell. Each mage was responsible for his own portion of the spell. Because of the nature of the spell, each piece pulled from the mage's life-force. Once the spell was in full effect, he'd be granted vision of a few precious seconds in time. The King intended to see into the past, but a specific past, one which involved Viktor, his interrogator. He intended to see what Viktor saw, if only for a moment, but he needed the combined power of these mages to do so.

All six mages chanted their portion of the spell in unison. The language was that of demons. Like chittering rats, their haunted melodies wove into a grotesque song of power. The mages need not know what they truly said, only to recite the words and give in to the internal tug of energy drawn from them. The King lifted his helmet and placed it over his head, securing the faceguard. The armor was impressive and intimidating, designed to accentuate the muscles along his arms, chest, and legs. Overall, the King was an impressive figure; with the addition of gold-plated armor, he was the embodiment of power. Only slightly off-putting was the presence of the two-tailed feline, riding upon his shoulders. After thirty years, however, no one had come to question its presence; magical creatures were more and more common since the destruction of Third City. A thin, net-like web crisscrossed across the eyelets of his helmet and obscured the room. He felt exposed, though he was clad in the highest quality of armor, so the cat kept watch, eyeing each mage in turn, studying them, as if each one hid a blade beneath their robes. Throughout their many years together, the alley cat had always watched over the King, as it had a greater purpose for him.

The spell's melody became muffled as each mage shut their mouth in unison. The spell continued from within their throats as they hummed each syllable between closed lips. The King was fully enthralled in the spell now, sifting through moments of time, looking for the right one. After a few seconds, Jayecob opened his eyes and the ethereal net over his eyes fell from his view like leaves, before evaporating. He sucked in air through his nose and removed his helmet, tucking it under his arm once again and stepping off the platform.

He thought to the cat, *I believe something from your plane is wearing my brother's skin as armor. Perhaps to taunt me.*

Your brother? Did you hear anything to indicate that it was him?

"No, I only had the sight. It was him, or his body, or a phantasm of some sort. But I couldn't mistake the scar above his eye, or the fiery scowl across his face. The details were all too clear", Jayecob thought.

Where is he now?

"The Pit."

Then leave him. That crotchety old woman buried the place long ago, Amekath said.

"I can't. I must know what creature taunts me, disrespects

my brother's honor. He was a fool, and weak, but he doesn't deserve to have his body pranced around, especially in my castle. I'll go to the Pit and see that my brother's corpse rests there or find whatever mocks me in his name."

There is no way out of the Pit, the demon said dryly.

"That's what you're for."

The King left the room behind, noting that only three of the mages got up from the floor, and even they were drained of color and glassy-eyed. He circled around the nearest bend, making his way down a long hallway towards the eastern tower. His boots clanked and echoed in the drab emptiness of the central corridor of the castle. A guard hurried toward him from the opposite end of the hall, knelt upon nearing, and spoke in a hushed voice, "My Lord, we've interrogated the guards who fell to the intruder. They dare not speak his name, but did reveal he had three large rubies in his arm. That's all they'd say. They are currently... indisposed."

"Thank you, Rogir. Carry on. Notify the Captain that I'll be taking leave and returning shortly."

"As you wish, my Lord." The guard bowed and backed away, continuing down the rest of the hallway, headed for the courtyard.

"Amekath, what are the rubies he spoke of?"

Hopefully a figment or product of hysteria. If not, it may not be so wise seeking out this intruder without the Guard.

"I can more than handle myself. I razed Third City to the ground. I seized the throne from my weakling father and my pacifist brother. I have brought this Kingdom beyond a cataclysm and into new light. I have set the wheels in motion to end the war with the slave traders in the Far East. I need not worry about an intruder with pretty jewels on his arms."

He finished his internal rant sounding slightly wicked and overly confident. The things he'd said to the cat were a common thought, one which drove him to continue with his plans.

The cat curled its tails to either side of the man's thick neck. *Indeed, but you were not without my help... and I answer to a higher power. As do you. Never forget how you got here.*

He ignored the cat, though it was right. He hadn't accomplished all that he'd done through good will and good fortune, and a debt was still owned.

Arriving at the bottom of the easternmost tower, he took to the stairs and closed off his mind to further incursion by the cat. He was aware of his debt, but there was work to be done, and he'd see it through before his debt was paid.

He shoved the solid wooden door open to a room with a platform and several sarcophagi in the corners of the room. Thick black cables met at a center platform and markings were etched around it in a circle. He stood with his knees slightly bent, preparing for the incoming pull and twist as magic sent him to a place he hadn't been in over thirty years. He was only slightly nervous to be transported by the device. He'd only used it for sending messages across the Kingdom. Now, he'd use it to once again to send him to deep beneath the earth. A place, even for him, that was dark and haunted with the memories of things he'd done in the name of the Kingdom. He read off the incantation, the bodies jumped and flailed in the sarcophagi, and the room faded to black, sending him off to a place long left buried.

CHAPTER THIRTEEN

ONLY AFTER HE was sure the old woman was asleep did he sneak off on his own, following a peculiar scraping sound coming from somewhere outside the tower. Despite knowing the creature Agatha might still be in the area, Cereal and Princess Beggen Ostra chose to bed down for the night at the base of the tower behind the large tree which blocked the entrance. That way, they were safe from the elements and had a makeshift barrier for protection, though he doubted anything, or anyone, would come up that far on the mountainside.

He awoke from a nightmare, the same one he'd had for several years, since his parents' deaths. In it, he stood by helplessly as his mother was tortured and then killed in front of him, followed by his father, and finally, when it was his turn, the mad King would smile a big, toothy grin, throw him to the ground, and pounce on him, plunging his massive sword through his chest. Spiders would pour out of the wound and crawl up his stomach, piling into his throat, choking him, tickling his tongue with their many legs.

He awoke, violently thrashing, clawing at his own throat,

only to find that his blanket had made its way into his mouth in the night. He looked around stupidly, expecting the old woman to be staring at him, disappointed or disconcerted. Instead, he found her sleeping deeply with her back to him, her sword close at hand.

He sat up, rubbing the sleep from his eyes. It was just before dawn, and light was beginning to drag its way over the horizon, reflecting off the clouds growing in the distance, creating a purple and blue facade. Still high on the steppe, he could admire the morning glow without a care as to what the day would bring. As long as he remained on the plateau, it was just him and the horizon.

Something scraped against the outside of the tower. He could hear it coming through the walls. At first, he put it off as mountain rats, birds, or some other secluded creature, but the sound was ceaseless, and he was already up. He drank from his waterskin, listening to the scraping continue.

Wide awake and curious, Cereal reattached his sword belt and left the pack with his food and water behind. He stepped quietly over the sleeping woman and rounded the knobby base of the tree, heading off to the left, where the tower met the stone face. The scratching grew louder as he drew nearer. In the early morning, when not even a bird chirped, he was surprised at how loud the scratching sound was. The rounded exterior of the tower blocked his view from the blind corner on the other side and he found himself touching the smooth tower in reassurance. Though he was slightly afraid, his curiosity took control and he felt the distant support from Beggen Ostra, should he call for help. He knew he could trust her. He had seen her move. When the time came, he felt that she could be there in an instant, despite her age.

The source of the sound was enough to cause Cereal to draw his sword, take a stance, and charge around the blind corner. Near the base of the tower, where stone met rock-face, a young boy with black hair squatted, barefoot and clothed only in an oversized shirt and trousers. Cereal noticed the glint of a blade reflecting the low light of the horizon, and the boy was using the blade to carve at an old metal-bound box with strange writing on the side.

"Do not run, and please, put that thing away. You will lose us an eye," the boy said without looking up from the box. "I do not suppose you can provide aid in opening this box? It seems when I chose a vessel this time, I did not take into account the physical limitations."

Cereal did not listen and kept his sword up, though his wrist was limp with fear and the tip drooped slightly. Trying to appear fearless, he spat out, "What do you want?"

Instead of being strong, it came out as a cry.

"Dear boy, have we not discussed this already?" The boy twisted his head to catch Cereal's eye.

The indefinite emptiness of the boy's eyes was astounding. How something could be so dark, so empty, but so full of life was confusing and intriguing?

"I need a new vessel; soon enough, this one will fail, and I need another lined up. It is not such a terrible existence. We share a body, of course. Your life would be significantly longer, considering I care about self-preservation, and, judging by how you hold that sword, you do not."

"I'll never be your vessel," Cereal said, with added gusto.

"What kind of existence will you have otherwise? Do you really believe your companions care about you? The old woman needed you as a means to an end, to enact her plan in the shadows should she fail. She is a usurper; how well can you trust her? What of the fallen Prince Shaw? He seeks nothing but revenge and cares not for anyone but himself. He rescued you out of necessity, out of some sort of subconscious reflection of his own failure. Do you not understand? I move the pieces in the background, and in the end, my goal is balance."

"You are evil, embodied as a boy."

"I can be, and I have been, depending on what is needed. There are greater forces at play, boy. Things you cannot begin to comprehend. But I can offer you something more. To be a part of something, for once in your life."

"What do you mean, offer me something more? You only want my body."

"When I inhabit your body, you will be empowered and omnipotent."

"What happens to me?" Cereal tapped his chest with his sword hand as he asked.

"You are still you, but I am also you."

"What else can you offer?" he asked coyly.

"In what way do you mean?" The boy perked up from the box, kicking it aside.

"You obviously need my permission...which explains why you keep coming around. Without my permission you have no way to enter my body, do you?"

"Don't tempt what you know nothing of. Persuasion is just a word for trial and error. I'll discover what means most to you, and with it under a knife, you will give me permission."

He walked to Cereal, standing toe to toe. They were of similar heights, which put them eye to eye.

"I want to kill the king."

"Hmm?"

"You wanted to know what means most to me. I'll tell you. I want the King's head, just as he took my parents' heads, making me watch."

"I cannot do that for you"

"But it can be done?"

"Of course. But not by you directly."

"Then who?"

"The Prince, of course."

"Get away from him!" Beggen Ostra appeared from around

the blind bend of the tower, sword drawn, a black tar-like substance dripping from the blade and sizzling as it hit the earth at her feet.

"Ah, yes. The old woman. Time hasn't been good to you."

"Enough from you. Cereal, come to me...Step away from it." She motioned for him to come to her side, pointing the blade at the boy. Cereal retreated from the boy, not turning his back to him.

"Do you really think you can trust her, after what she let happen?"

"What are you talking about?"

"Cereal, ignore it. Come to me," Beggen Ostra pleaded.

"Please, no blade can harm me."

"No, but I can sever your head, sink it in the Bone Bottom Crags, and toss your body into the Maw. That should slow you down," she spat.

"What is he talking about, m'lady?"

"I have no idea. It speaks in riddles meant to confuse even the brightest of scholars; ignore it."

"She knows, she has always known. Why do you think she cares so fondly for you? Your father was a blacksmith, was he not?" the boy asked.

"Yes," Cereal said, his courage dissipated by the memory of the marketplace.

"You stole a golden chalice for your family, melted it down, did you not?"

"Yes," he said, even quieter.

"Noble, bold. I know not someone so willing to risk it all for their family. I'd have done the same."

"What do you know of family? Don't listen to it, Cereal!" Beggen Ostra pleaded again, her hand extended, Cereal caught in the middle.

"There was someone else in the market that day...someone who could have helped. Someone strong enough to save you and your family. Someone who watched from the shadows as your mother was tortured and killed, followed by your father, for a crime they did not commit. And yet, with all of her power, this person sat by, watching, afraid. Did you not...Princess Beggen Ostra?"

The boy looked over Cereal's shoulder at the old woman.

"I did not have a choice. Please Cereal...you must understand. The King...his power...the guards...I was without a choice."

"Do you see? She takes you under her wing out of guilt...not because she cares about you...She hides behind her guilt."

"Cereal...I was without a choice...you must understand. When Shaw found you...I wanted to help you because I saw you needed me...I did not learn of your identity until later..."

"That was not my parent's debt to pay..." he said to the ground, tears running rivers down his cheeks. He put his sword away and hid his face with his hands.

The boy reached out and put a hand softly on his shoulder. "You are right, of course, you're right. Because you know what you did was wrong, and you feel that their death is on your hands. But you have a chance to make it right. With my help..." The boy reached out to Cereal.

"Cereal...please child...don't listen to this wicked-tongued fiend. It speaks only to swirl the thoughts in your head."

Cereal met the boy's gaze with his own. "What can you do for me, if I say yes?"

"If it's to take the King's head yourself, I cannot do that...but I can provide help to someone who can. Say yes, and I'll help Shaw any way I can. I have to maintain the balance, and he is my Arbiter...the equalizer...the balance."

"What are you blabbering about?" Beggen Ostra asked the boy, her eyes locked and her brow furrowed in anger.

"Did you really think you were the only one with plans at

hand? Shaw is my creation. I brought him back from the Thin Line."

Cereal and Beggen Ostra gasped in unison. They had always wondered how he'd been brought back. They had assumed it was a magical concoction or spell. Shaw had mentioned that the Book had had a hand in bringing him back, but not this level of involvement.

"So, you see, in the end, Shaw will enact my will, and my will is to maintain balance. Now, I am but a manifestation of what you'd describe as the lighter side of the Book. However, I am not without a temperament, and I am not on a side. We are not friends. You are all a means to an end, and that end is balance. Say yes, child; allow me to inhabit your body, and I will assure you, I will see to the end of the King."

Cereal thought through what the boy was offering. Opportunity, revenge, to be somebody, to help someone else. What could he do now as a boy? He was simply a tagalong for the prince and the princess. They had had to pull him out of more situations than he could count. His family was gone, and what he believed was a new family seemed to be born out of pity rather than genuine care. With what the boy was offering, he could see the King fall, and his family avenged.

"I want to see the King bleed. I want his blood to wash over the stone courtyards of Stonehaven and his devil-dogs to lap at it. Then I'll say yes."

The boy cocked his head, "A deal? Interesting...you are more than I thought of you, Cereal of Third City. After the King falls, you agree to say yes?"

"After he falls."

"Then prick your finger and let us mark our deal in blood. Only in blood can it not be broken." The boy pulled the tip of Cereal's sword from its place on his belt, sliced his palm, and held out a hand, though no blood ran from the wound.

After hesitating for a moment, he did the same, though his

hand bled fresh, crimson blood. The boy grabbed Cereal's hand, allowing the wounds to touch.

"What have you done, boy…" Beggen Ostra said, now obviously sad, choking up as she spoke.

"It's done." The boy turned to leave.

"Wait! You were supposed to help Shaw." Cereal cried out, tears in his eyes.

"I am, or, rather, the creature Agatha will."

This time, Beggen Ostra spoke, "What has Agatha got to do with this? She won't help us any further."

"Do not worry about that. I cannot take action, but I am excellent at influencing others in the direction I need them to walk. I'll speak with the creature Agatha; she has a message you need delivered, doesn't she?" The boy turned on the last word, stalking off into the tree line, heading for the drop off to the earth below. How he planned on getting down, the two did not know.

"That was a foolish choice, boy," Beggen Ostra said.

"What do you care? Without me, your plan would have failed. Now the message will be sent, and we can have our chance at the King."

"I'd have found another way."

"If time isn't on our side, then no, you'd not have. I did something when you couldn't, or wouldn't. Remember that when that thing is prancing around in my skin. I'll find a way to undo this."

"No, you won't." Cereal lifted his arm, showing what looked like black lines, tracing his veins from the cut in his hand. "Whatever it did, it gave us a time limit."

"Indeed. I'll find a way to get you out of this!"

"Will you? Or will you stand by and watch?" he said with a snarl.

"That isn't what happened-" She tried to go on, but he interrupted her.

"-I don't care. I care about what happens next. Where do we go?"

"If the Book has set the wheels in motion with Agatha, we need to make our way to the Fringe."

"What is there?"

"Hopefully...an army."

CHAPTER FOURTEEN

SHAW HELD his arm high against the dark, using the red gems to provide enough light to see just a few feet in front of him. The Pit was a vast cavern, deep underground but strangely warm. He couldn't tell how wide it was, though he'd been following the outer rim for some time, and heeding Pemazu's advice to avoid the center of the room where something of great power lay. He took note of the ash covering the floor, there was inches of it. Whatever happened here after he'd gone...it had burned.

Someone is coming, Pemazu said to him.

"Coming? How? There isn't a way in or out. We're trapped."

Not entirely; there is a draft, up ahead.

"You're just mentioning this now?" Shaw questioned.

I just felt it.

"Wait, a draft? You can't feel anything."

A draft. The remnants of something powerful. It is up ahead, and leads upwards. We may be able to follow it. What did you think I meant?

"Nothing, never mind. Can we make it over to the draft before whoever is coming arrives? I doubt they mean us well if they intend to follow us here."

Of course they do not mean us well. And to answer your question, no. The draft is only the remnants of something powerful, most likely a spell, but it will do us no good in getting out of here if I cannot examine it for longer than a few moments. Make your way to the center of the room, let us see whatever is there.

Shaw turned away from the wall, holding his arm ahead of him to illuminate the ground as he walked. Each step kicked up more ash, leaving a ghostly cloud swirling around his feet. The Pit began to angle upward towards a mound as he continued toward the center. He also noticed how incredibly suffocating the room would be without the light provided by the crystals. Though vast and open, the Pit had a way of closing in, feeling tighter the longer one stayed. The dark itself seemed endless should one not know to walk in one direction until one found the outer wall. The light from the gems protected him from such darkness and claustrophobia, but it did not stop his mind from wandering. Soon, he'd be trapped with whoever was coming, and very little of his power remained. Anything with enough power to make it here surely had enough power that Shaw would want to avoid them.

He discovered near the top of the mound that the ground was no longer covered with ash, but was thick and dragging, like wading through a marsh. The substance stuck to his boots, slowing him down. He dug his toes in deeper, trying to maintain a grip as he slid backward a little more with each step. His hike turned into a crawl on all fours, as he had to use his hands to try to keep from sliding. His breath came quicker the closer he got to the top, though due to the lack of adequate lighting, he had no idea where that was.

Hurry. Pemazu sounded agitated.

"You are welcome to help. Possibly give me an idea of what's coming? Or how about what I'm climbing for?"

If it is what I think it is, you will thank me shortly. As far as what is coming below, you will not thank me, for obvious reasons.

A resounding crack echoed through the cavern, shaking the hard surface beneath the ash so hard that dust jumped as if it were frightened of itself. The sound came from the bottom of the pit, near where he'd started his trek up the mound of sludge. A forceful wave disrupted the air and followed the sound, hitting Shaw from behind, toppling him forward as he made it to the top of the mound. He brushed himself off and pulled clumps of muck from his boots. He stood atop a hard spot on the mound. Beneath his toes he could make out what appeared to be a stone slab. He shined his arm over the raised square, highlighting the familiar gold and red crest surrounding the Stone Breaker maul.

Slide it aside.

Eyes wide in anticipation, Shaw found a lip near the top of the slab where he could get his fingers between the slab and the surrounding stone. He dug in and heaved it upwards. Immediately, the taint of death and decay drifted upwards through the opening he'd made. He covered his nose with his sleeve, breathing through it. He used his other arm to hook under the slab again and tried to heave it backward. After realizing that he couldn't move it without the use of both hands, he decided to suffer through the smell, held his breath, and pulled hard once, leaving an opening just large enough for him to fit his arm in. He dropped to his knees and slid his gemmed arm through the crack. Inside the compartment, in the faint red light, a book-shaped object wrapped in a blackened cloth was visible.

In disbelief, Shaw tugged at the cloth and, holding his breath in anticipation, pulled the object from the hole and set it on the stone floor in front of him. He carefully unwrapped the corner of the package, uncovering the pale-gray skin of The Demonic Compendium. Its familiar runes crawled across the surface. Thick metal straps held it shut, and in the center of the cover, three large rubies, matching those in his arm, swirled with a mystical red dust. For so long he'd dreamt of the Book, yearned for it, hoping to stumble upon even so much as a clue of its location. While he searched he had done things, sometimes terrible things, things that stalked his memories like a patient predator. He hoped the end of his quest could justify the means. This book held the answers to what he was, how he had come to be...and how to defeat the King...

"Brother!" a voice, throaty and gruff, echoed through the chamber. "It must be you here. Amekath tells me either you have returned from the dead or you're an imposter, wearing his skin. Either way, come down, we've much to discuss."

Shaw gasped, breathing in the sour decay-laden air, and immediately broke into a coughing fit.

Rewrap the Book. The cloth is spelled to hide the Book's presence. Put it in your pack. I'll find us a way out of here, Pemazu said to him.

"Is it really my brother?"

Yes, and he has Amekath the Tainted with him...she is older...much older than I, far more powerful though she does not have my relaxed demeanor.

"Is he an Arbiter?"

No...he feels like an Impius, though without the decay and building insanity.

"What do we do?"

Face him. Stall him, Pemazu stated.

"For how long?"

Until I can locate the draft. Perhaps I can draw from it and get you enough power to fight.

"I thought you said Amekath is stronger than you?"

She is. Spell for spell. But she is a dimwit, and Jayecob does not have control over her like you have over me. Something is off about their connection, but I cannot place it. Wits will win us this battle.

Shaw threw the cloth covering back over the Book and twisted his pack around to the front to store it. Hastily, he shoved the Book inside, wrapped the pack around his back and covered it with his cloak. He checked the positioning of his sword, rested his arm comfortably on the hilt, finding some solace in the coolness of the metal.

He realized he was unusually hot, sweating actually, but unsure if it was nerves or the effort he'd exerted moving the stone slab. Either way, he wasn't ready to let his nervousness show in front of his brother, and he wouldn't lose again. Too long did he fight his way through the endless monotony of the Thin Line, only to be sent right back in the exact same circumstances. He'd face his brother, but this time, he was prepared.

He examined the gems again; only the third shone with any light. Inside, the magpie sat on its legs, content and resting. He began his hike down the mound, trusting in his footing and refraining from using the light from the gems. In the dark, his ears became accustomed to the sound of his boots falling and sliding on the mound, as well as his own shallow breathing.

The ground leveled out and caught him by surprise. The trip down seemed infinitely shorter and was less of a burden on his legs. He scanned the area, searching for any source of movement or sound.

"Amekath, give us some light."

A ghastly glow grew and moved upward, shining a dull white light on the hilt of a sword, a hand, and the reflection of full coverage armor, appearing dull and faded in the light, but Shaw knew better. His brother was invested in appearances; hence the fact that he wore armor plated in enough gold to feed half of Stonehaven for several days. The ball of light sat above them, highlighting both brothers. One tall, decorated in ornate armor, meticulously crafted to accent his thick arms and powerful legs. The other highlighting the grim expression of contempt and a resounding deep-seated hatred.

"Hello, brother."

"Hello, Jayecob. Again, we meet in this forsaken place."

Keep him talking, I am attempting to connect to the draft. It's stronger down here.

"Again indeed. If I had known you were alive I'd have arranged for a more formal setting. I see you found your way into my castle."

"Not by my own accord; I have no interest in that place. I have interest only in you."

"In me? What is done is done; you got in my way. And now, again you stand in my way."

"In your way of what?"

"Amekath tells me there is something of power at the top of this mound."

"You have mentioned this Amekath several times. Is this your new bride?"

He chuckled and drummed his fingers on the hilt of his sword. "Amekath is much like your Pemazu, but older...and far more powerful."

But not nearly as handsome.

"What else do you know of Amekath?" Shaw replied.

She is old, very old. Possibly one of the First. I have heard of her on the Thin Line. She has only come to the mortal plane once before. Ahead of you, towards the right. I think I found it.

Shaw sidestepped away from the mound, attempting to circle around inconspicuously.

"Do you intend to run me through again, brother? It isn't very often that someone can claim they have committed fratricide twice on the same brother."

"On that topic, how have you returned? Amekath tells me you are no Impius, and you did not make a deal. Please, enlighten me?"

"Let us discuss it over an evening meal. Perhaps on the Fringe? There is a nice marketplace that hasn't quite fallen into ruin like the rest of the Kingdom under your rule."

"Brother, you know as well as I do we are beyond civil

discourse. I am aware of what you saw in the halls of Stonehaven. My solution to the pests…and the usurpers who still aim to dislodge my place as King."

We will not have a lot of time once I tap into the draft…Amekath will feel me within moments. You will not have long to act.

"What do you mean by act? What exactly do you want me to do?"

I sometimes forget that this is new to you. Once I tap into the draft, your power will temporarily be replenished. Hit him with everything you have. If you need to leave, follow the wall behind you until even you can feel the draft. There will be an opening.

"These pests and usurpers you speak of are simple peasants. Hungry, tired people, who lack the support of their King. They see your lavish parties celebrating your life of mediocre accomplishments and your ornate armor while they starve."

"I have united people who came from chaos!" He slammed his fist against his chest as he spoke, leaning in, his eyes bulging beneath his dark eyebrows.

"At what cost? What have you accomplished that father had not?"

"Father was foolish and slow to act. The enemy steals our boats and he still aims to make peace? Pathetic." He spat on Shaw's feet.

"And Beggen Ostra?"

"A bleeding-heart humanitarian! She'd have given away all of our food and medicine to refugees if we had let her."

"We were once refugees, brother…"

"And now I am a King. Why can you not see what I see, brother? I see a crumbling nation, attacked from within, on the brink of war, lacking unification. I'll bring them together under the power of Stonehaven." He beat his armored chest with his fist and spit flew from his mouth. "I'll show them why our family was chosen to lead our people out of slavery. I'll unify our nation once again."

"At what cost?" Shaw couldn't bottle in his anger. "At what cost, mighty King? Was my wife part of your unification? Murdering her and your entire family? That's what you call unification?" He spat the last few words out, gripping the pommel of his sword so tight he was losing feeling in his hand.

"Your wife...was an unfortunate necessity."

"Say her name!"

"Avana...I am deeply sorry about Avana." He bowed his head. "Of the mistakes I have made...your wife was one of them...but you must trust me, brother, every death has a purpose."

Arbiter...there is not enough power in this draft. We cannot defeat Amekath with recklessness anyways...

He shook in anger. Raking his knuckles across the pommel of his sword over and over each time, the short blast of pain was like a wet blanket on a raging fire. It smoldered and smoked underneath, but the flames atop were stifled.

Calm your fire, Shaw. Live today...fight tomorrow.

"Will it end as it started, Shaw? With my blade running through your heart? Even with your mediocre demon by your side, you are a bug beneath my boot, just as you were before..."

As they exchanged emotion-fueled words, he'd managed to circle around, one step at a time so his back was to the opposite wall. Jayecob now stood at the bottom of the mound and he was now no longer barring their path. The demon's words echoed in his head and he knew it was right. Live today...fight tomorrow.

This is as close as we can get. Now. Go now.

Shaw transformed his right arm into a crooked, twisted, scaly claw and lunged in an instant, reaching out to gouge at his brother. Jayecob was slightly startled by the attack and turned his body away as Shaw slashed at him. The claw met golden armor and easily tore a gash through the decorative layer, exposing the steel underneath. Shaw pulled his sword from his belt with his other hand and swung it in a backwards arc. Jayecob managed to pull his own sword from his back and deflected the Shaw's blade, but not before the face of the blade struck the top of his hand, bruising it. Jayecob dropped his sword and Shaw flipped around and took off towards the wall of the cavern in a full sprint.

We have limited time in the draft. It is infusing us for now. Transform and climb the wall to the opening. Quickly. Amekath has healed your brother's hand.

As if to confirm Pemazu's statement, a blackened spear flew past him, narrowly missing his arm. Black smoke-like tendrils surrounded the lance and dissipated as the weapon stuck into the wall in front of him. A second lance flew by, this time clipping his shoulder. The wound began to throb but not painful enough to slow him down. He felt warm liquid drip into his tunic.

Shaw ignored the nagging throb and, instead, focused on drawing from the well of power within and channeling it to his will. The draft maintained the color in two of the three rubies as he used the energy to transform his other hand and his feet into the blackened, hooked claws that would allow him to grip the wall. Instinctively, Shaw dropped to all fours, increasing his speed and allowing him to maneuver out of the way of the spelled lances. The wall was fast approaching.

Pemazu maximized the red light from the gems, highlighting where the ground met the wall. Shaw leapt to the wall from several strides away and dug into the stony surface with his claws. The hole Pemazu had mentioned was not far off. He could see its black pitted outline on the surface of the rock wall. He was at the entrance to the tunnel within seconds, and Pemazu dimmed the light, just enough that Shaw could see a few feet in front of him. He was reduced to reaching forward, digging into the stone with his claws and pulling himself along. The tunnel was tight, and if he lifted himself up his head would hit the ceiling.

Crawl to the end. It is a long way, but it probably goes towards the surface.

Shaw stopped every few minutes to listen, hoping that he wouldn't hear his brother somehow squeezing his way into the tunnel, or worse, the sound of a lance flying through the tunnel to skewer him. After some time in the tunnel, a resounding crack and reverberations from a powerful spell told him that Jayecob had found a way out of the Pit...most likely relying on Amekath. After a while he stopped checking and, instead, focused on pulling himself forward while the draft lasted. Attempting to move through the corridor without the use of his claws would be terrible. Though he did not speak, he could hear his brother's words in his head...Avana...his wife...was killed... for what reason? What did he mean by "every death has a purpose?" And how did this add up to what Daemond had said in the grotto...that his wife lives?

A little while later, after crawling through the suffocating tunnel, Shaw emerged into the dark of the night from beneath the leg of a broken statue of a Stone Breaker. He pulled himself up and looked at the hole; unless it was properly examined, it could easily be written off as a hole dug by an animal under the statue itself. This did not surprise him, but standing in the Ruins of Third City after thirty years, the flood of memories of the battle did. He remembered the countless bodies thrown about as the monster, summoned and released from the Thin Line, tore through the city. He remembered how it had swung its mighty fists, tearing through the city walls, raining stone down upon its victims. He remembered Jayecob, standing atop a church, reading from the Book, laughing maniacally as the entire city burned and crashed around him. He remembered his sister amongst her fledgling wizards, trying to gather their combined strength to banish the creature back to the Thin Line. He remembered confronting his brother in the Pit and the cold steel of his blade, making its way through him. He remembered

Avana being dragged away, somewhere off in the darkness…and then he remembered nothing. The sound of his brother's voice, echoing his wife's name, ate at him from the inside. He hadn't spoken her name since he'd returned.

We have the Book. You should read it.

"Shut-up. We need to regroup and warn Second City. Whatever Jayecob is planning, the attack will come from within."

Who would you tell? Pemazu asked.

"Daemond."

The treasonous bastard? I still plan to eat him…

"We share a common enemy," Shaw said.

Then I will eat him after, Pemazu chirped.

"If you don't mind the aftermath…fine…but I don't wish to hear you complain."

It will be worth it.

A chittering brown bird darted past his head, and then came around for a second pass, this time running into the back of his head. It tumbled and fell before Shaw caught it and lifted it up to eye level to examine it.

"A friend of yours?" he asked the demon with a smile.

The magpie puffed up and bulged out its feathers in response.

The little brown bird came to and flapped about, trying to regain its bearings. It stood in Shaw's hand for a moment before opening its mouth. From deep within its stomach, Beggen Ostra's voice came out. "If alive. Church. If dead. Never mind." Once it had finished expelling its message, the bird shook its head violently before taking off into the night sky.

Your sister is quite potent with her means of sending a message, is she not?

"Indeed," Shaw replied. "To the Fringe, it's four days walk following the eastern path."

He took in a deep breath of brisk night air, thankful to be out of the age-old air of the Pit and the heavily laden air of the tunnel. He held the well back in the confines of his mind and, slowly, his scaled hands and feet transformed back to their human equivalents. He began the long journey up the northern road, beyond the barrier and onward to the Fringe, but not before eyeing the gems in his arm. Two dark, one brightly lit with a sulking magpie sitting in the middle of it.

CHAPTER FIFTEEN

IF THE FRINGE had ever been considered a safe haven for smugglers, burglars, thieves, and rats, now it appeared to be even more so. Shaw arrived several days after climbing out of the Pit, having followed the eastern road beyond the barrier segregating the Ruins of Third City. When he arrived on the Fringe, the tension in the market was palpable. Traders now whispered between peddling their wares. More swords were sold than spices, more phony protective charms than saddles. The Fringe itself reeked of *war*. Before he even entered the city, travelers heading to the south seeking safe haven in the wooded areas or grasslands whispered of Second City's army marching on Stonehaven. When he arrived in the market, they didn't whisper. They spoke with concern and hushed talks of magical interference. One child, a refugee from the Far East, bore pink scars across his back and legs. When Shaw questioned him about it, he said, "It isn't those in plain sight you need to worry about." Shaw brushed the boy off as just another casualty of war. He'd need to dig deeper, or travel to Stonehaven himself, and that was not happening with Pemazu as drained as he was.

He passed through the market specifically to catch the gossip and check in on his favorite procurer. The chubby, greasy man was nowhere to be found, and his cart lay empty. Obviously, with war comes panic, and panic on the Fringe was like standing in a bug's nest, waiting to get bitten.

Beyond the market, near the shallow dock, Shaw arrived at a familiar church, the ruined monolith of an unknown religion that worshiped an unknown god. Inside the church, up the spire and in the tower, he was pleased to find Beggen Ostra and Cereal, sitting around a small fire, boiling something scrawny.

Upon opening the hatch to the tower he was first greeted by the overzealous child, who hugged his leg. Shaw noted his traveling coat lying on the floor, exactly as it had been when he had first handed it to the boy. His sister, on the other hand, simply nodded and continued to stir the stew, every so often tasting the broth. Shaw dragged one of the two chairs to the makeshift circle and sat in it, exhausted from traveling.

He stared into the fire a while, admiring how simple and forever-different fire could be. He appreciated the different ways the flame would lick the air, then swirl in on itself and lick the air again. On the Thin Line, there was not a fire to break up the endless drab facade that had followed him throughout his journey.

Beggen Ostra doled out the boiled meat in tiny bowls to herself and Cereal. Shaw refused his and instead stood and peered out the porthole to the north-east. Rolling hills blocked his view of Stonehaven, but he knew, beyond those hills, an army would soon collide with the walls of the castle. Mages with no sense of self-preservation expended every bit of life-force they had on the most devastating of spells. Stone Breakers battled Stone Breakers, raising pillars from the ground to topple over and crush each other. And somewhere, far beyond the wall, high in the tower, was his brother, adorned in golden armor, enjoying the spectacle. War was messy, but from afar, it might seem entertaining for those with no stake in the outcome.

"Second City has rallied their army and marched east and then north to the walls of Stonehaven. Rumor from travelers stated they did not make it to the wall before they were attacked. Attacked from within is all they said."

"What do you mean from within?" Shaw replied, still staring out across the flat tops of the buildings in the Fringe until his vision was blocked by rolling hills.

"I was hoping you'd tell me. Maybe discuss with me the events at Stonehaven and everything."

He knew what she meant by *everything*. Obviously she wanted to know how he had escaped from Stonehaven, and why it took him three days to arrive on the Fringe after he'd received her message. She was a cunning woman; he knew she was also calculating travel time. It was three days on foot from the Ruins of Third City to arrive on the Fringe, while it would take four to travel from Stonehaven. Shaw had arrived in three.

"And I was hoping you'd know something of the help I received in the Howling Halls." He glanced back, smirking.

"Perhaps we both have secrets worth sharing."

"You first, dear sister."

"I spoke with Agatha."

"The treant? The barbarous miscreant we dragged across the desert so you could talk with birds? Why on earth did you go to her? I'm surprised she didn't consume you. She has been in that tower for quite some time now, has she not?"

"Indeed, for the last thirty years, but you know how she likes current events, and she has always had a sort of affection towards me."

"And what did the beast do for you?"

"Well, it's more about what I did for her...I released her."

"Is this a joke, sister? You let that thing loose? We locked it in a tower surrounded by overgrowth for a reason. A creature of that power need not roam our lands unchecked."

"How do you think you were able to escape, brother? Agatha

weakened the walls of the Howling Halls so you could bypass their wards."

"At what cost?"

"What?"

"At what cost?" he said, clenching his jaw. "The creature doesn't work without making a deal. That's how things are around here, apparently. In order to receive anything, you must make a deal."

"She only agreed to help me because I freed her. Don't be so thick."

"I'm still quite surprised she didn't eat you."

"As am I. My original intent was not to visit her so she could free you. I had other plans, but you had to get yourself caught, thus turning my focus."

"What plans?"

"You will see, at dusk…" She trailed off. "There was a cost… not for your release, but for my plan."

Shaw raised an eyebrow, and she continued. "You must understand. I had but one choice. Save you, or enact my plan. *Thirty years* I have been plotting and scheming, all ruined when you got caught."

"Don't blame me, sister, for whatever maniacal thing you had cooked up. I had to fight the Impius alone while you hid in the shadows."

"I did as I was told. Stay hidden. I can't fight an Impius, and I doubt you can. We aren't as strong as we once were."

"You have no idea, sister, what I am capable of."

"Capable of getting caught, apparently. But don't think there was a cost paid on my part." She turned and looked at the boy, cross-legged on the floor, picking scraps off the animal bone.

"Show him your hand, Cereal."

He looked up, slipped a piece of meat into his mouth, and held out his palm, revealing black spidering veins running upward as far as his elbow.

"He made a deal..."

"He *what*? With what demon? What were the terms?" Shaw turned around to face his sister. "How could you let this happen?" Deep lines cut into his face as his anger built. He knew what this meant. The black spider veins were a sign of an other-worldly poison, a timer, counting down the time one had left to control one's own body. Once the lines traveled the arm, up the neck and to the eyes, the demon was free to inhabit the victim's body, and their soul would be condemned to walk the Thin Line for eternity. The timer moved slowly, depending on the deal; this one seemed to be of a slower pace.

"I did not have a choice, brother. He did not listen to me, and the boy...the boy has such a wicked tongue."

"What boy?"

"The boy, Shaw..." She looked down at the floor, saddened, tears welling in the corners of her eyes.

"The Book? You made a deal with it? Look at me." He addressed the boy, who had tucked his knees up to his chest.

"The King must die, and I must make amends for what I did. The Book said it would see to it."

"You idiot child! The Book will help no one! It only thinks of itself. It doesn't feel. It doesn't care for your plight and your reckless sense of honor. What were the terms?"

Beggen Ostra spoke up for the boy. "It agreed to our terms. When the King falls, the boy will be its vessel. We can undo this; this gives us time. This also means the Book is in line with our goals."

"Have you not been listening? The Book has its own agenda. If you made a deal, it will only benefit the Book."

"Even so, we know it won't get in our way, and it may even help us. It forced Agatha, somehow, to send my message."

"Your bird-message only managed to smack me in the back of the head and give me a useless line of poetry I had heard once before. Nothing followed."

"The message wasn't meant for you. You will see, tonight at dusk."

"Well, we may not be at a total loss. We can use the boy as leverage. It only seeks him as a vessel...and I have something which may help us later." Shaw swung his traveling pack around, unclasped it, and dropped a square-shaped object bound in blackened cloth on the ground. As it hit, the hollow thud reverberated in the air, and the fire itself seemed to cower for a moment, threatening to go out before rising up once more.

Beggen Ostra gasped and fell backwards, landing hard on her rear and shimmying backward until her back touched the wall.

"You know what this is, don't you?"

She nodded, wide-eyed. Terror gripping her by the throat.

"Why not tell me how this came to be...in the Ruins of Third City...warded by powerful magic...warded against detection... buried in a Stone Breaker tomb...bound in a cloth...with your seal on it..." he asked, emphasizing each phrase by unwrapping a portion of the flesh-colored book, revealing it a section at a time until the entire thing lay uncovered near the fire. Three red gems on the cover shimmered and swayed in the firelight, and runes in an unknown language danced across the surface.

He revealed a scorched seal, gold and red, with a Stone Breaker hammer on one side and a scale on the other, encased by a string of fig leaves. He showed her the seal before wrapping the Book up in the spelled cloth once again and shoving it into his pack.

She continued to stare at the spot where the Book had been, her lower lip trembling. Cereal still hugged his legs, terrified as he watched the confident, resourceful woman reduced to a whimpering mess. Anything that scared her this badly should make him run in fear, but for some reason, a sense of familiarity washed over him as the cover was revealed.

"Tell me, sister. I have been hunting the Book since my

return, and even before that. It has obviously been buried in the Ruins for a very long time, and I know of only one living mage with the kind of power it would take to bring half a city down on it and still leave a way out."

A small whimper escaped her lips.

"You knew where to find it. You used my name and my return for whatever plan you have concocted, knowing full well the power this Book has...and yet you failed to reveal that you knew of its location. You scheme and plot and scurry in the shadows, but the greatest tool of all lay hidden away. I'll give you one chance to explain yourself before I chalk my own sister up as yet another casualty of war. Betrayal seems to run in the family, and I'd hate to be different."

Shaw was standing over her now, the limited light from the dying fire outlining the hard lines on his face, making his eyes appear black and his mouth a curved snarl.

She gripped her bony knees to her chest and spoke down at the floor. "That Book...is the embodiment of evil...Jayecob read from it...brought an entire city to the ground...killed everyone with some creature from the darkest corner of the Thin Line. You read from it and now look at you! You don't eat! You don't sleep! You are hell-bent on revenge and even the thought of your own wife still being alive barely phases you! I read from the Book too, Shaw. I tried to look for answers, and instead...it twisted my mind. It showed me things...things I can't even describe. Things that still keep me up at night...so much so...I tried to end my own life...but I couldn't...the Book would not let me. That boy showed up and looked at me with its great, voided-out eyes and forced me to untie the rope from my neck. So I buried it as deep as I could and protected it...even from the boy himself. So forgive me if I did not reveal its location to the Kingdom once again, because the last time it was free our family was slaughtered, hundreds of thousands of people died, and Jayecob emerged as he is...deranged at best!"

She finished with conviction in her voice, tears pooling on the wooden floor beneath her feet. She obviously believed that what she did was right, despite Shaw's attempts to find the Book.

"While it was noble of you to try, *I* can read from the Book to find answers to all of this. It has the answers on how to defeat Jayecob...and how to help the boy...and how to free me from its control..."

She sniffled, "What do you mean...and you? I thought you knew what you needed from the Book. Isn't that how you returned to the land of the living?"

Quietly, he said, "There is more to it. You will want to sit. And Cereal...not a word, else I end you before the Book does."

The boy nodded rapidly, intrigued.

Shaw breathed deeply before continuing. He first spoke of the events of the Great Betrayal...his brother's blackened broadsword running through his heart, the last images of his wife being dragged away, his father's upper body face-down in the mud, his lower half somewhere unseen. He recalled the Thin Line...the endless days of wandering, counting every second of every minute of every hour, tirelessly. He could count forever, as he did not sleep, he did not tire, and he did not hunger. All of which weighed down on him because his mind was never truly at rest. He spoke of his festering, bloated anger and his undying thirst for revenge. And for the first time, he spoke of the demon Pemazu and the moment in which he bound it to his will, tore open a Gateway and forced himself back onto the living plane. He took with him nothing but his sword, stained in otherworldly blood and bent from countless years of fighting everything that crawled from the dark of the Thin Line, clawing at what semblance of life he still held. Upon arriving on this plane, he recalled the notches in his sword...one for every year he counted...one hundred and eighty years he fought in that place...one hundred and eighty years he clung only to his deep-seated hatred for his brother.

By the end of his story, the fire had burned out and Shaw had rolled up his sleeve, showing them the gems in his arm before willing them to light the room in a low amber glow. "The Book has its own task for me. I am bound to this demon, and him to me. If I am to die, I'll be cast into nothingness forever. There is something worse than death, and that's for the soul to be lost, unable to move on. That's what I face if I fail. The Book offered me a chance. It showed me what I needed to see in order to bind Pemazu to my will, to return to life and dislodge my brother for good."

Shaw held out his arm for his sister and the boy to examine it. As the two leaned in, a magpie with too many eyes winked at Cereal, who smiled back at it, as though he was a friend who had just told him a secret.

"So you see, sister, the Book contains the answers I need to rid myself of its grasp. I don't want to be its puppet any longer, inadvertently or not."

Beggen Ostra prodded the gem with the magpie in it like a dead thing she had found. The magpie stuck out its forked tongue in response and eyed the woman as menacingly as a magpie could. "I have seen these gems before on an Impius, yet I am not convinced you are one. You are much too...sane."

"Indeed, sister, but you are misinformed on a minor detail. An Impius swaps souls with someone in a time of great pain and despair, such as the young girl we saw. As she crossed over, she was intercepted by a demon waiting near the border of life, and it offered her a deal in exchange for her body. They are marked by a peridot...a small black gem."

She shrugged. "The Book should be buried, but you obviously can't be reasoned with. If you must, bring it with you and come with me; the light will be fading soon, and I have waited thirty years for this." She stood and packed her things. The boy stood by the fire until they were ready to leave together and pointed at it when it looked like they were going to leave it burning. Beggen Ostra simply clapped her hands and breezed past the boy to the tower stairs.

Shaw snatched his traveling coat from Cereal as he walked by, despite the boy's protests and muttered comments about gift-giving. He only responded by slapping the boy upside his head, reminding him that it was him who it would fit, and he'd get the boy one of his own someday. This seemed to calm the boy, and he settled for a thin cloak Beggen Ostra retrieved from her pack, thankful that it did not smell. Beggen Ostra also covered her head and led the two northbound, away from the center of the town.

They passed over the north-eastern roadway leaving the Fringe and headed north-west along the tree line until the wall of trees gave way to a less-traveled path. Beggen Ostra continued to lead the way north until they were guided only by her footsteps and the moonlight as the sun faded beyond the horizon. She seemed to know her way, despite the thicket and bramble reaching up from the forest floor. The path was well-traveled, it seemed. Unfortunately, the wood was thick and the path narrow, leaving only room for a few travelers to stand abreast.

After what seemed like several more hours, Beggen Ostra curved off the path to the right, between two trees which appeared to be leaning against one another. To an average traveler, the trees would be easily missed, but to someone such as this old woman, they were a welcome sign. As if light weren't hard enough to come by already, inside the thicket, all light was blocked out by branches overhead, fighting for sky-space. By this point, Shaw was pulling up the rear, mostly keeping Cereal from falling as he traversed gnarly roots as thick as his skull. A few minutes later, the thicket thinned, and they emerged in a clearing. And they were not the only ones occupying it.

Beggen Ostra approached the center of the clearing where a funeral pyre was built. Atop it, some poor soul's body burned, forever safe from demonic influence or any other magical malady. Around the pyre, four hardened men stood in silence. One drank deeply from a hip flask. Another stood stout, the tip of his broadsword down in the dirt, his hands rested on the hilt. Each man was dressed differently. One wore the tabard of the Stone Breaker, another a black and red tabard with a woven stallion on the front, and the one with the broadsword wore a simple suit of armor, one arm exposed for maneuvering in combat. Shaw noticed beyond the pyre, on the opposite end of the tree line, another man crouched in the shadows, a massive longbow strung across his back, silver arrows mounted on leather straps on his chest.

Beggen Ostra approached the rag-tag group like time-lost friends. First she removed her hood, then nodded to each man in turn, save the man in the shadows. Shaw kept his eye on each one, also returned the customary nod, as one would do during a funeral. Beggen Ostra broke character for a moment to hug the largest of the group, the man with the broadsword. She was tiny in comparison, having to stand on her toes to meet his cheek with her own, even considering the fact that he'd stooped low to the old woman. She smiled at him and he gave a corner smile back. Overall, Shaw felt the exchange to be entirely uncomfortable. Friendliness in this day and age was hard to come by, and this crew was obviously hardened by combat and other tribulations. He gave them each the appropriate once-over and relied on his sister to explain what they were doing in the middle of the woodland, at a funeral, with men from obviously different groups. Beggen Ostra spoke first, "Gentlemen, it has been a long time coming, but I am glad you are here when I called."

The man from the edge of the clearing stood and approached the group. He was skinny, but walked with confidence and poise. Shaw could tell, of everyone in the group, this man had the potential to cause the most problems.

His arrows and bow. Both spelled.

"I know."

His jacket, too.

"I can see that," Shaw said.

Actually, everything he is wearing is spelled from detection by those like me.

Shaw stared at the man from across the pyre. In that kind of darkness, even though his eyes were barely reflections of the fire, he could feel the man staring back, eyeing him and reading him. Pemazu was right; Shaw could see the runes crawling across his leather tunic, pants, and traveling boots. His bow ached with power and his arrows shone with some type of poison on the tip, offsetting the silver with a hint of black. Shaw took a moment to scan the runes; a few he recognized, a few he did not. Runes of destruction, tearing, ripping, severing, and confusion crawled the length of the bow, while runes of speed, agility, and dispersion ran along his boots. What he found most interesting was the fact that the runes were written in demonic. He realized what this man was. He was a demon-hunter.

One of the men, with a Stone Breaker Tabard and a mess of curly hair stepped forward. Beggen Ostra nodded at him to speak without waiting for the demon-hunter to join them. "Go ahead, Trepin."

"Princess, myself and my crew received your message, but I am afraid with Second City attacking Stonehaven…well…you can see we've already suffered losses," he finished, looking up at the pyre. "The King has something amiss at his command. Griss had to put ol' Rogir here down."

"What are you saying?"

"I am saying, ma'am, that this is a war we need not fight, just not yet. We stand behind you, we always will, but I strongly disagree with moving forward at this moment."

"Does everyone feel this way? Shall we cast our lot and see where the dice land? Step forward with your opinion, Griss."

The demon-hunter stepped forward first and spoke in a surprisingly deep voice. "Princess...the King has a magic I haven't seen before. Rogir was in a demonic state. Only a spelled arrow took him down, and even then, he tried to rise. It took four additional arrows."

"Speak plainly, Griss"

"The King amasses a demon-army. I'll follow you into the depths of the Maw myself, ma'am, but I agree with Trepin."

"And you, Tomas?"

The black-and-red-robed man stepped forward. In the fire-light, the stallion across his chest reflected so the horse shimmered. His robes were obviously made with great skill. Skill reminiscent of those with plenty of gold to spare. "I stand behind you ma'am. Civil war will weaken and distract the main part of King Jayecob's army. This may present an opportunity to strike."

"Michael? Do you feel the same?"

"You must know that Trepin and I answer together, and I have to agree with Trepin, my Lady. Stone Breaking isn't necessarily a strong magic against an army, let alone a demon-infused army."

Beggen Ostra scoffed and focused on the man in the suit of armor. "Adius, my friend. Tell me what say you? Will you trust me?"

"My Lady, I pledged my sword to you long ago. I knew this day would come, and yet, I still stand here, by your side."

She smiled at him. "It appears we have a tie that Rogir would have broken...rest his soul. We lack a final vote. Luckily I have brought in another to our cause." She turned to Shaw and held out her hand, motioning for him to step forward into the impromptu circle around the pyre. Not knowing entirely what was going on, he stepped forward anyways, taken aback by the pomp and circumstance in these trying times. "I motion to vote…Prince Shaw into our little coup."

Several of the men shifted where they stood, indicating a level of unease.

Adius whispered. "Ma'am, the Prince is dead and has been for many a year."

Beggen Ostra smiled wide. "You must know by now that dead is just a word. Brother, your hood."

Normally, he'd have disagreed with her use of his name, let alone revealing him to total strangers, but for the sake of trust in his sister, and a massive amount of curiosity, he removed his hood, revealing his mess of short bronze hair, emerald eyes matching his sister's, and a scar running from his eye to the length of his cheek and down his neck. The scar was a rumor, a hushed topic of discussion behind closed doors that said King Jayecob had marked his body upon death. His emerald eyes, however, could never be mistaken for anything but royalty, for they were unique to the Royal Family.

The reactions were varied. Adius scoffed at the old woman, flashed a smile, and nodded again at Shaw. The two Stone Breakers, Michael and Trepin, dropped to their knees, bowing, and Griss, the demon-hunter, shrugged and took a seat in the grass, fiddling with an arrow. He spoke from the ground, "While I admire your effort Princess…what does a fallen prince bring besides more questions? What vote can he cast at our table? I should wonder if he was in league with his brother and thus somehow escaped death."

"I'd just as soon wear my brother's head as a hat. Since his isn't readily available, I'll settle for yours," Shaw snapped back. "I can, however, agree with you on one front. I cast no vote at this table because I know nothing of this table. You speak so openly of subterfuge and a coup, yet I see no army standing behind you, because that's what you will need to defeat the army before you. I see marauders, haggling over a derelict dream at best.

Care not who I am, because I care not who you are. I aim to return to that castle and take my brother's head myself."

"Which parts of the castle have you been in? Surely there must be a benefit to royal blood," said Griss.

"There is no bond between my brother and I. That died in Third City. I have been through the Howling Halls and the north-eastern tower, as well as the central corridor with some sort of chamber with some sort of foul magic inside. The halls themselves were almost empty."

"Of course they were empty, they were preparing for battle. Second City walked into an ambush...they were tipped off," Trepin interjected.

"What sort of chamber?" Griss asked.

"What do you care? I have no vote here, and I may as well be in bed with my brother, according to you."

"What chamber?"

"A room with tubes and people. Thousands of them."

Argomancy.

"Argomancy," Shaw repeated to the group.

"I know everything there is to know about demons..."

I doubt that

"...and I have never heard of this Argomancy," Griss said confidently into the fire.

Beggen Ostra stepped in, "Gentlemen, allow me to discuss the specifics. I motion for my brother to cast his vote as well, as he has seen the inner chambers of Stonehaven, and obviously shares our contempt for The King."

She looked to each man individually, who took a moment to think before nodding. All but Griss, who simply grunted, shrugged, and tossed a stick into the fire.

"Dear brother, since the Great Betrayal, the King has retreated inward, leaving Second City to govern itself. Inevitably, they eyed the seat of power. The Fringe and the remaining Kingdom, however, fell on the shoulders of the men you see here. Their...crews...maintained their own bylaws, and they have many men at their command, all trained and ready to fight for a noble cause."

Shaw crossed his arms, unimpressed.

"Trepin and Michael speak for The Stone Breakers in Second City that remain loyal to the rightful King...you. They are worn, but loyal, and just as sprightly as myself."

"Still loyal after thirty years. The veteran fighters must be near eighty!"

"Yes...as I said...worn, but they also don't forget."

"Tomas leads the horse traders from the plains to the south of the Fringe."

The man with the black and red robes took a drink from his flask and raised it in recognition.

"Adius commands stalwart protectors of the Valor. They accompany traders beyond the Far East to protect from pirates and others. He commands a loyal group of well-equipped fighters."

The armor-clad man tapped his sword on the ground.

"Griss...is our resident demon-hunter. He is but one of many demon-hunters settled outside of the Ruins, and he commands their loyalty."

The demon-hunter threw another stick in the fire.

"So you see, dear brother, over the last three decades I have been gathering together those still loyal to the crown, or at least those who would see to the downfall of Jayecob."

Shaw scoffed again and replied shortly through his teeth. "Mercenaries. Thieves. Hunters. And old men. You gather not an army, sister, but a joke. Who did Rogir command? A group of salty fishermen? Jayecob commands an army with ten-fold the people of the Fringe on the average day! How do you expect to conquer that?"

"I don't expect to. I expect you to."

"And where do you and your friends fall into this?"

"We were hoping you'd tell us."

"Pah. You haven't a clue, sister! What if I hadn't come? What if I had simply remained in the shadows? How would your plan unfold then?"

"I'd have taken the King's head myself, as I do every night in my dreams. But I am a realist, and I have you, and you have friends. This isn't just a dream, but a mission." She finished by stepping back, leaving him standing amongst the ragtag group of men, each looking at him eagerly, as if he were to reveal some hidden solution to their problems.

"Look, I stand before you as a man, eager to lop off the King's head and storm the castle, but he has an army, and from what I have seen, it's an army infused with demonic energy. This isn't a war anyone need fight."

Griss stood up. "Who said anything about a war?"

"Is that not what you intend, sister? Civil war?"

"Oh, no, dear brother. I aim to have these men do what they do best. Lie, cheat, steal, kill, and so much more. I am aware that this isn't a battle we can win from outside the walls of Stonehaven, so we will bring the battle inside the walls."

"And these men? And those loyal to them? What will they do?"

"Distract the King's Army. Make one man feel like a thousand. Meanwhile, a select few of us will see to our beloved King."

After Beggen Ostra finished her speech, she gave them a moment to discuss things amongst themselves. Neither Shaw nor Cereal cared much for their meeting, or whatever it was that they were concocting. Adding to the confusion was the overall expectations from the group if their already-difficult mission were to be accomplished. Did they expect to occupy Stonehaven together? The man with the horse on his chest would live near the stables and Griss would stalk the towers with his bow? Meanwhile the Stone Breakers would do what?

204 | THE RISEN PRINCE

There was also the issue of those Stone Breakers, King's Guard, and other valuable fighters who would uphold their allegiance to the King, despite the revelation of Shaw's return. Overall, there were too many moving pieces, and five makeshift warriors did not seem like enough men to break through the castle's defenses to take on the King alone. Shaw did not like it. Cereal, on the other hand, soaked up everything the men had to say. The only reason he was near Shaw instead of with Beggen Ostra and the men was because when he tried to join the circle, he was promptly shooed away.

The meeting did not finish until the pyre itself had burned out and only coals remained. At once, the men dispersed to different sections of the clearing and exited through natural openings in the tree line. Beggen Ostra left the circle and beckoned Shaw and Cereal to follow. While he was waiting, a final question drummed up inside his head and he couldn't wait to ask his sister about it. They hadn't made it through the bramble line before he asked, "Sister. Those men. I counted five total. What would you have done should Rogir have been able to vote, and he chose against your plan?"

"Dear brother, I had Rogir poisoned weeks ago. His demise was only mildly coincidental. He was never going to vote in this meeting."

Shaw was shocked at her cruelty, and the ease by which she admitted to what she'd done. He had obviously underestimated the old woman, and she managed to surprise him at every turn.

"And who did Rogir speak for?"

"Rogir was the Captain of the King's Guard. Daemond's brother, who has disappeared in the last few weeks. This leaves the King's Guard in temporary disarray as there isn't a third appointed, and the trials for a new leader will take some time. So you see, brother, the cogs are moving our war-machine forward as well."

Again, he admired his sister's confidence. She leaned heavily on loyalty, promises, and morals, all of which seemed scarce in these times. With civil war to the north, Shaw did not have great confidence in the loyalty of men.

No more was said about Beggen Ostra's master plan, other than that more would be revealed, and soon; civil war is an excellent distraction, and she aimed to capitalize on the King's divided attention. As they approached the northern road into the Fringe, off in the distance, protected by darkness, leaders of sects around the Kingdom plotted the demise of the King.

CHAPTER SIXTEEN

WAR DRUMS AWOKE the majority of the Fringe, including Shaw, Cereal and Beggen Ostra. The group was holed up in the tower of the church again, as it was a spot proven to be secluded and somewhat safe. Churches seemed to be less often frequented, temples abandoned, and more men and women turned to pleasures of the flesh and sin to stifle the desire for faith. If one were seeking pleasures of the flesh, one could find what one needed on the Fringe. Prostitution, gambling, thievery, cut-throats, traders...you could find anything on the Fringe. And when war-drums sounded, those who catered to the pleasures of the flesh and sin perked up like a dog hearing a dinner bell. The group huddled in the tower, however, their ears perked up for a different reason...dismay. Shaw peered out of the porthole; while it had originally been designed to allow the sound of a bell to travel from the tower, it now made an excellent viewing port from the northern end of the Fringe down the market to the buildings on the southern end. The drums came from the west and, a little while later, from the north. The drums continued through the morning and the ground shook, marking the arrival of the first of thousands of soldiers.

Shaw admired Second City's Army out of display alone. Their gold-and-red-blazoned tabards reflected slightly with the mid-day sun as rows upon rows of shiny helmets flashed as they crested the hill. In unison they marched to the beat of the drums. Each drumbeat shook the church, so much so that Shaw began to wonder if the church could take much more abuse. It was an impressive display, and the army was not lacking showmanship. Obviously, the leadership had great confidence in the war they intended to start. Shaw knew better though; a number of things yet stood in their way, from what the King had brewing in the chambers of the castle to the powers he had acquired to the wealth in manpower, supplies, and weaponry at his disposal. When they had escaped oppression from the Far East and established the new Kingdom, it was his father's wish to consolidate power within Stonehaven, establishing Second City and Third City as extensions of the main city. Aid, supplies, protection, they all trickled down from Stonehaven to prevent exactly what was happening now...civil war. Since the fall of Third City and the death of the royal family, Second City seemed to have taken it upon themselves to flourish. When these two armies collided, he did not want to be anywhere near them.

This war, there will be many dead. Many dead means much sorrow, and with that sorrow, my kind will be tempted, Pemazu said to him softly, probing Shaw's concentration with his shrill voice.

"There is a chance at stopping this before it begins, if we can get to the King."

Second City is here for supplies, Pemazu stated.

"I can tell; that isn't a war beat. They aim to bed down here. An army of that size would not be able to move through the forest. It's a smart plan; whoever commands Second City knows the impact taking the Fringe will have."

The impact of this war goes beyond the Fringe...you know that.

Cereal came up from behind, rubbing the sleep from his eyes and yawning. He had his traveling bag in his hand, rummaging inside for something to eat. Shaw pulled a piece of dried meat from his belt pouch and tossed it to the boy, who eyed it, contemplating turning his nose up at it before putting it into his mouth whole. He had already proven he could take care of himself. He had already shown he could make things happen.

Beggen Ostra was also digging in her pack, but instead of retrieving meat, she pulled out a medium-sized leather pouch and carefully laid it on the floor at her feet. Shaw pulled himself away from the window, hypnotic as the view was, and went to speak with his sister about their next steps. He stood over her as she pulled miscellaneous items from her pack and laid them on the wood floor in front of her. She pulled out a bird's foot first, dried and gray, which immediately sent Pemazu into a gagging fit. Next was a spoon mounted in a brick of wax, followed by a tuft of horse's hair.

"Madrigol's," she said, showing it to him.

"That spritely horse is still alive?"

"Very much so, and he still has an attitude. He obviously misses you."

"I don't doubt it. That horse and I went through quite a bit together," Shaw chuckled.

"He helped us reach the steppes quickly; even let Cereal ride him."

"How many sugar cubes do you owe him?"

"Pah! The beast wanted two, and then a promise of two more later! Haggling with a horse...never had I thought I'd stoop to haggling with a wild animal. I have no idea where I am going to get two more cubes. Do you know what I had to do to get the first two?"

"Madrigol will call you on your debt. I'd be ready when he returns."

"He'll forget about the cubes the next time he sees you. I

have a gift for you, brother." She motioned to the spoon, tuft of hair, and dried bird's foot.

"Your incantations always do impress me, but I really think we need to focus."

"Incantations. Something about that word reminds me of some simple conjurer. I bring you a gift. A while back, in the grotto, I brought you Daemond, who had news of your wife. There were many years you wondered what had happened to her. This spell's key ingredient is you. It may show us more of that night."

Shaw's heart dropped. He had been focusing on his revenge and their plans simply to ease his mind of the pain of losing his wife, and the further pain of rediscovering that she was being held captive in Stonehaven. Up until now, he had redirected his focus to Beggen Ostra's plan. He remembered the Book in his pack. After Beggen Ostra was finished with whatever she was doing, he'd consult it for answers, though he was not entirely looking forward to reading it again. With it safely in his possession, he decided to let it wait just a few moments longer.

"What spell is this, sister?" He knelt next to her, looking at the side of her face. She seemed to have aged even further after the events with the Impius, as if time itself was waiting to catch her off-guard in her sleep. Deep bags rested below her emerald eyes, Shaw's eyes, and crow's feet had settled permanently in their corners.

"This will give us a brief look into the night on which your wife was taken. This is one of many preserved utensils I managed to gather as I fled the castle." She gestured vaguely toward the spoon on the floor. "I already cast a spell on the spoon you had eaten with in order to find you," she said, looking at him for a moment, then back at the items on the floor.

"I was curious as to how you had located me in the first place. I always assumed you didn't know it was me, and you were simply taking a gamble communicating with me while you were in the Far East."

"The only gamble was what kind of condition you were in upon your return. Things don't seem to stay dead, and you wrote to me of your search for the Book. I could only hope it was you."

"How did you know based on those facts alone?"

"Once I saw you I knew it was either you or Jayecob. And let's be honest, you are much skinnier than he is."

She had a point, though he did not appreciate the slight. Jayecob was burlier; he always had been. Perhaps it was this fact that had fueled Jayecob's rage, causing it to grow even stronger when his smaller brother was placed as Captain of the King's Guard while Jayecob was sent to raise Third City from the ground.

Shaw inhaled deeply at the memory and waved his hand, begging her to continue without further slight or without eliciting further memories.

"Tell me of this spell."

"It will give me precious seconds of a selected point which you are a part of, even things you yourself may not know. I can take you with me. That's why I have waited for your return. When I used this spell the last time, I used Jayecob's spoon. I saw him killing you. But I needed to know where he got his power, not how you died. The spell also showed me someone pulling themselves from a great pit of black tar. I assumed it was him." She took a deep breath and looked at him sternly. "This spell will allow me to see things as they pertain to you, not necessarily things attached to your memory."

He looked away from her as that particular memory rushed into his head. He remembered the tar pond, its sticky web trying to drag him back down while every inch of his skin burned and peeled away, only to regrow and start the process over again...until he was finally free...gasping for air.

"I'm sorry; I'll need you to focus on the moment you saw her last. Only then can I drive your focus. If you lose focus of the memory, this will fail and the spoon will no longer have a connection to you. Do you understand?"

He nodded.

"Cereal, I need you to protect us. We will only be gone minutes, but we will be vulnerable. We're trusting in you to protect our bodies. Can you do that?"

He beamed at her request, drew his tiny sword, and pushed a chair over to the stairway leading downward.

"Good boy." She turned back toward Shaw.

"Are you ready, brother? Can you picture the moment we need? Be specific, pull all that you can into the memory. I need to see what you see."

She sat cross-legged, the assortment of items at her feet. Shaw trusted that she knew what she was doing. Judging from the items she had, she'd be stepping into the realm of darker magic. Magic that relied not just on a well of internal energy, but also on unnatural means. This type of magic would befoul one's soul if used improperly or without boundary. Perhaps this is why she said they only had a few select moments in which they could see.

He reached down and touched his sister's bony shoulder, creating a connection between them. For the first time, he forced himself to recollect what happened that night in Third City. He first remembered the cool dampness in the air, peculiar for that time of year, almost as if the weather itself knew what was coming and was dreary in response. He was standing in the entrance of the citadel, a dome-topped stone monstrosity built as the central keep to Third City. He looked behind him, noting that the surrounding buildings were half-raised from the ground, and only pockmarks in the dirt marked where towers and other fortifications were to be built. He remembered this scene so very clearly.

His memory faded and returned moments later with a flash of golden armor and wispy white hair entering the staircase. His memory flashed again; this time, it was his wife walking down the stairs. He could recognize her pale, beautifully unblemished skin and tightly-wound braid from across the sea. She smiled at him as she descended the staircase, holding her gown in one hand and using the other to beckon to him. He wanted to reach out, to scream and tell her to stop; remembering it was only a memory made it all the more painful. This was the moment they needed. The moment when Jayecob found something beneath Third City. The moment marked as the Great Betrayal.

Outside of his memory, he squeezed his sister's shoulder, marking the memory and signaling her to begin the spell. Almost immediately, the feeling of falling washed over him, and he closed his eyes to keep from getting sick. Into the memory they fell, and he squeezed his eyes tighter. He was sure his nails were digging into the old woman's shoulder, and he softened his grip on her slightly. He felt her cold hand reach up and cover his, comforting him. Moments later, the falling feeling disappeared and the ground struck his feet from below, causing him to wobble, or at least feel like he was wobbling. She tapped his hand with her finger and he opened his eyes to a horrific scene.

His father's head lay next to Shaw's own body. Both of them were obviously dead. A massive still-bleeding wound soaked the ground around him. He looked to his left. Avana was no longer smiling at him. Instead, a look of sheer terror crossed her face as Jayecob, now adorned in his father's armor, dragged her, bound and gagged, by her hair off into the distance. Further and further they went until there was nothing but his body and his father's head. He couldn't move. He couldn't speak. He could only watch in horror.

He felt Beggen Ostra's hand comfort him once more, and her finger tapped his shoulder lightly. The world flashed again, blinding him for a moment. When he could see, he was standing at the end of a long hallway, a hallway he recognized...the hallway in Stonehaven. A door slammed in front of him and Jayecob entered the hallway, again, dragging Avana by her hair. She fought and kicked at him, trying in vain to get away. He wanted to reach out. To help her, to save her. His angst turned to anger as Jayecob reared back and slapped her across the face so hard she went limp. His rage boiled over in an instant. He wanted to scream. His heartbeat matched his anger and pounded in his chest. And still, he looked on as Jayecob tossed Avana over his shoulder, limp and unconscious.

The world flashed again, but this time, he stood in front of a solid steel door with a small window to peer through. He strained to move his head to see more clearly, but it was locked in place. His brother was facing away, his golden armor blocking most of the view. For a moment, Shaw was unsure of where he was, until he remembered the room with the metal coffin...the room next to the Argomancy chamber...the room with the many pipes leading to a central point...the metal coffin.

Jayecob moved out of view for a moment, revealing Avana, bound and gagged, lying in the coffin. Tears streamed down her face. She bucked and fought to get free, but to no avail. He tried to catch her eye and she looked right through him. The coffin slammed shut, and no more could he see his beautiful wife. Instead, he looked upon a solid wall of metal, thick chains wrapped around it, sealing it off for good.

The world flashed one more time, and as his eyes adjusted, he could tell that he was no longer in the memory but inside the tower of the church. He was drenched in sweat, all the way through his tunic to his traveling coat. Beggen Ostra sat calmly on the floor by a series of scorch marks where the tuft of hair and bird's foot had once been. The spoon was gone; the wax casing appeared to have melted, forming a small pool on the floor that was starting to dry. Cereal still sat near the stairway leading to the rest of the church, his attention fixated on the hole in the floor.

He felt like the afternoon had gone by, but by the look of the sun in the sky, and by Cereal, who did not seem to have moved, only seconds had passed. He was breathing hard, as if he'd been sprinting. Coupled with the sweat soaking through his clothes, he felt the tax the spell had taken on his body. Emotionally, he was both drained and mortified. Avana…she was in that chamber, in the coffin. He had been so close to her! Panic overcame his emotional distress like a misjudged wave. He leaned on the wall, staring at the floorboards. Was it not enough that his life, his family, an entire city be taken? But now, he had to subject his innocent wife to whatever would befoul her in that chamber? Sweat dripped from his brow and pooled on the floor.

Beggen Ostra sat back and stared up at the ceiling. She was not nearly as sweaty, but she still furrowed her brow in concern, and her lips were pressed tightly together. She knew Avana had been taken; everyone who told the story of the Great Betrayal knew what had happened to the Royal Family. But nobody knew the extent of what had happened. No one knew the finer details, the details best left buried. She wondered if the truth was worth the heartache they were both feeling. She cared for Shaw, deeply, as should any sister, but there was something brewing within him, and she was afraid of what may come from this knowledge.

"I have to go. I have to find her. I have to help her, rescue her…from whatever it is," he said between breaths.

"Shaw, brother, we must be careful; we have plans in place that can help her. Now isn't the time to be hasty."

His rage began to swell and bubble, starting in the pit of his stomach and ending in his throat. How could she even suggest they wait? Knowing that Avana was being held captive, tortured and alone, in that coffin…

"There isn't anything that drives me forward other than

finding Avana, and now that we know where she is, you suggest we wait?"

"How do you suppose this will work? Barge into the castle? Storm it yourself? You barely escaped the last time. I may not know the intricate details of that demon inside you, but your gems are not so bright, and the bird looks like it had been caught in a storm. You're in no condition to fight, let alone take on an army by yourself. Look outside. Second City will provide the distraction from the outside. Our friends will provide the diversion within. We must be tactful." She tried to console him, putting her hand on his back, only to pull back, surprised by how clammy his skin was.

"Tell me sister, would you wait if it was someone you loved in that coffin?"

"I'd do whatever it takes. If that included waiting for the right opportunity, so be it."

"When is the right opportunity? When will we strike? I am strong enough now.

No, we are not, Pemazu chimed in.

"Shut-up."

Listen to the old woman.

"Pemazu. Shut-up."

"We will strike when Second City does. Our friends aim to gather within a night. Until then, is there a way to restore your demon? I know little of demons and less still of what you are."

"There is; we need to find something with magical properties. Something that can be killed and drained."

"Like a Baulg."

"Yes, Cereal, like a Baulg."

The boy was listening intently to their discussion. As disrespectful as he was, Shaw admired the boy for remembering what had happened with the creature.

"What is a Baulg?" Beggen Ostra asked, with slight intrigue in her voice.

"Something we should hope we don't encounter on the battlefield. For now, we need to find something to consume." He paused for a second, thinking. "Perhaps it's time Madrigol left this world."

"Leave the horse be. We will find something else."

She did indeed find something else. After leaving the church around mid-day, she headed to the east side of the Fringe to the docks and from there, she took a narrow sandy beach path south along the Valor until they came across a wider basin, tucked beneath the cliff. From the road, it would be nearly invisible, but from the beach, several nests with large bugs scurrying across their tops made the ground look as if it were moving. The nests were shaped like miniature hilltops topped with a half-buried rotting animal carcass that dribbled thick greenish liquid.

"Shaker nests. They have some magical properties. Perhaps you can use them?"

Shaw looked at the bugs nibbling on the animal carcasses with large retractable pinchers.

These things...will taste so bad...

"Is she right?" Shaw asked.

Yes, she is, but do you know how many I will have to consume? Do you know what this will do to my feathers?

"Do you want to feed or not?"

No...yes...but let it be known I am not happy.

"Are you ever?"

Only when I am killing men.

Cereal and Beggen Ostra sat on the beach and watched Shaw stab and skewer the bugs until they were all dead; by the time he was finished, the tide had started to come in. They had several laughs as the bugs realized what was happening, displayed their pinchers, and chased Shaw out of the nest. He had to return several times over in order to avoid being bitten. Once all the bugs were dead, Shaw pulled back his sleeve and allowed

Pemazu to absorb the silver wisps of essence that trickled faintly from each bug. The ghostly trails twisted in the air before being sucked into the gems in his arm. Pemazu made a variety of noises, ranging from a howling cur to a dying horse. After he had absorbed the last bug, he disappeared in a whiff of red smoke, and the gems resumed their usual amber glow. Cereal appeared entirely confused throughout the process, but Beggen Ostra was obviously intrigued. The look on her face told him that she had many questions to ask, and that she was struggling to keep them to herself.

"Ask later, sister. For now, let us prepare, as you promised you would. Your friends, where will they be meeting us?"

She pushed herself to her feet, stiff from sitting. "Their people are already here, scattered on the Fringe, blending in. We will meet with them at dusk. Until then, what do you suggest we do to prepare? Are you ready?"

"I'm not. I need to consult the Book."

The color drained from Beggen Ostra's face. She was terrified of it, but Shaw knew he had to know all there was about Argomancy, and possibly figure out what the King planned to do with it. The Book could also tell him about whatever demon Jayecob had with him.

"If you open that book, I won't be anywhere near you."

"Sister, I need you by my side whilst I read from it. It has a way of drawing you in. Please."

"No, Shaw. That Book is evil. It's tainted and black. I won't be near it."

"The Book twists its readers if they are vulnerable. It did not affect me thirty years ago. It won't do so now."

That is what you think.

"Quiet, else I make you eat bugs again," Shaw said.

"Fine...I'll be near you for moral support, but this isn't the place."

The three hiked back toward the Fringe again, arriving in

time to see troves of soldiers walking south from the main road. They traveled in groups of twenty, marching in unison, their metal-plated boots clicking on the cobblestone. The entire company of soldiers had arrived by early-evening, swarming the countryside. News of the soldiers' arrival had traveled fast, and the market was overrun with traders and those looking to make a sale from the influx of potential customers. Now, it seemed as if every corner of the Fringe had a stand, displaying their wares. They each put on their hooded tunics and covered their faces. The soldiers were uninterested and instead focused on goods to purchase, brothels to visit, and wine to drink. It made going unnoticed manageable, for which Shaw was thankful; he was confident that Second City would have no love for him either. He knew that, were he in their position, the entire Royal Family would be held responsible for leaving all but Stonehaven in poverty, letting the Far East ransack their trade-ships and allowing an entire city to be destroyed.

The ruined church was again unoccupied, whether from superstition or from the appearance that it may cave in at any moment. The three sat on the landing this time, leaving more room than they would have in the tower. Since they were inside, they were less likely to be spotted through the porthole in the tower. Beggen Ostra lit a small fire in the stone fireplace on the landing. Shaw moved to the corner of the landing with a table and chair and sat down. He wiped the dust off the table before reaching carefully into his traveling pack and removing the cloth-covered Book. He sat it in front of him and prepared to read from it for the first time in one hundred and eighty years. This time, he was not seeking solutions, he was only seeking information; He'd handle the solutions himself. The last time he sought solutions, he was brought back from the dead with three gems in his arm and a debt to pay.

CHAPTER SEVENTEEN

BEGGEN OSTRA SENT Cereal off to the marketplace to restock their supplies for the next few days. She handed him a handful of coins and shoved him out the door, telling him to find dried meat, refill their waterskins, and find several days' worth of dried fruits and vegetables. Normally, they'd try to carry non-spoiling fruits, but she had reason to believe they'd not be returning to the Fringe for quite some time. Either that, or the army bedded down just north of the town would bleed it dry.

Shaw reminded Cereal to keep to himself, keep his head low, get what they needed, and then return. He said that by the time he returned, he'd be done with the Book. He dumped the silver in his pocket and scurried out the front of the church, happy to have a job, happy to be useful. As of late, he had felt that he was mostly a burden on the two adults. Besides feeling somewhat useless, he had other things on his mind, which he refused to tell them, lest they stop giving him jobs altogether. His dreams were steadily becoming odder, with visions of dead and evil things tormenting him throughout the night. The dreams would not initially begin this way. They'd change as the night grew older, and he couldn't stop them from coming. So when Beggen Ostra had a job for him, he took to it earnestly.

Cereal was not even out the front door of the church before Shaw had the Book out, unwrapped, and was working on the flat metal bindings that kept it locked shut. He had reassured her prior to removing the spelled cloth that there was enough magic on the Fringe that no one would be able to discern the Book from anything else that might be there. She stood a few feet behind him, lightly rubbing her arms as she hugged herself, a look of concern set in deep in her wrinkled face. Shaw had also noticed that she hadn't managed her hair from the day prior. It sat unkempt, and strands were falling out of her usual tightly-kept updo. He wondered if she'd slept at all during the nights since he'd retrieved the Book from its hiding place in the Pit.

The Book was unusually inactive. Previously, unknown runes, identifiable as Demonic by only a few, had been scattered and crawling across the Book's surface. They were inset into the pale, fleshy-colored cover itself and as the runes would move, they could be felt, sliding under your finger. But now, the letters lumbered as if they were weighed down by something unseen. Shaw continued to wrench and pull on the binding, but the metal was rigid and very sharp. He wondered if it was Jayecob who had bound the Book shut, or possibly his sister. Whoever it was, he did not care; he simply needed it open.

The Book is behaving oddly. I have never seen it so...lackluster, Pemazu said.

"What do you know of lackluster?"

Fine, undermine me. But have you even thought to read the runes?

He hadn't. In fact, he'd only concentrated on opening the Book and had forgotten that it was sentient. It was alive, and whatever may be on the cover may help him open the bindings, which he was sure were magically enforced at this point. It made sense that the Book might offer information on how to open it on its cover. It wanted to be read. It wanted to spread, like a disease in a crowded stable, it wanted to move from person to person. But Shaw also knew that the Book was never direct about anything. It was sly and cunning. Every move was pre-planned. It played the game; you were simply pieces of the board. The Book was the step on a ladder that decided when it wanted to break or if it wanted to hold your weight just one last time, and break when the next person got to it.

If I was not so sure of who you were, I would almost say you admire it, Arbiter.

"You don't know anything about me," Shaw stated flatly.

I know everything. Do you forget, we share body and mind?

"No, I haven't forgotten, but it doesn't mean I need or want a reminder. Don't you have a nest to build or something to occupy yourself?"

One day, Arbiter, you will need my help, and you will ask for it, rather than demanding it, and only then, you will see things from my perspective.

"Let us hope not."

He ceased fiddling with the metal bindings and focused on the runes instead. Some of the words were useful in discerning what the Book was telling him, some of it was jumbled up and useless. He could read a few words and of these, several formed repeatedly, making him think it was conveying a message of some sort. He picked out a few runes that made sense for the situation: doorway, Gateway, territory. For good measure, he picked out a few more random words: gauge, sanction, balance.

You missed a few. Brazen, bull, testicles...

"Shut-up Pemazu!"

Why not try 'two dead boys got up to fight'?

"Why would I try that?"

Because that is what it says along the spine. How about we switch? I will be the Arbiter and you be the demon.

Flustered, he flipped the Book over and, sure enough, "two

dead boys got up to fight" had formed along the spine. This was not nearly as interesting as *how* it was written. Instead of demonic runes, the words were spelled out in Common. The Book wanted him to read it and that made him even more nervous. He spoke to Beggen Ostra over his shoulder, "Two dead boys got up to fight."

Three resounding pops with residual twangs told him that the bindings around the Book had been released. Again he looked up at his sister. "Was that not your coded message? You hid the Book; it only makes sense that you bound it too. How long were you going to watch me struggle with these bindings?"

"I was hoping you'd give it up and leave it at the bottom of the Maw."

"It does us no good there."

"It certainly does us no good here, either."

"Sister, I have never seen you so afraid of knowledge."

"Don't suggest that that's *all* the Book is."

"I suggest nothing, I'm simply stating that I'm not afraid of its influence."

"Brother, it already has its grip on you."

"I belong to myself. Nothing controls me. I control the demon. I read from the Book. I choose."

"I hope you are correct, dear brother. Let's get this done; Cereal will be back soon."

He dragged himself and the Book across the floor until his back hit the south-most wall on the landing. With his feet crossed, he sat the Book on his lap, gripped both sides firmly, and opened the cover. He heard Beggen Ostra gasp as he did so, and he ignored her. As he had expected, the pages were blank. He ruffled through them, rubbing each one between his fingers for a moment before turning to the next blank page. He knew to keep going through the pages and wait for the Book to show him what it wanted to. When he had first come across the Book and realized that it appeared differently to whoever possessed it, he attempted to influence it into showing him what he wanted to know. After countless attempts and much wasted time, he gave up and pushed it away, only to see the words "Hello, Shaw" write itself on one of the pages from an invisible ink well. It was then that the Book began to show him things. Things that started him on the path he was on now.

He flipped another page. *Come on*, he thought.

He waited another moment before turning the page. Nothing new appeared. Instead, the runes from the cover of the Book began to move under his fingertips. Faster than before, they twisted, turned and crawled their way from the front of the Book, under the turned pages and then began to push their way through the center spine and onto the page.

The words stopped crawling in the middle of the page and spelled in Common, "Hello Shaw." His stomach turned over and he gripped the cover tighter and his knuckles turned white.

Hello...it has been quite some time. He thought, trying to sound as in control of his emotions as he could.

It has. What do you want?

"I need to know how to defeat Jayecob, and Amekath. How do I stop the Argomancy? How do I free Avana?"

I cannot help you with these things, the Book said.

"What can you help me with?"

I cannot help you with anything, I do not take sides.

"You say you don't take sides, yet you created me."

You are an Arbiter, the Balancer. That is what you were made to do. Bring balance.

"Then help me maintain the balance. Jayecob disrupts the balance with his war, his genocide, and his Argomancy."

Again you mention Argomancy. It has not been done successfully in centuries. Your brother is foolish to attempt Argomancy.

"I have seen it with my own eyes," Shaw said.

The word "Lies" quickly rearranged itself on the page.

"I don't lie. He has a chamber, there are people there, and

they are under spell and alchemy. There is a central conduit, in a metal coffin."

Destroy the chamber, the Book said.

"Not until you help me."

You don't have a choice, Arbiter. Do as you are tasked.

"I have a choice, and I am not taking commands from a book."

If you defy me, I'll ensure you never escape the Thin Line, and you will never truly die. You will wander for eternity.

Shaw's heart jumped in his chest as he remembered in an instant the feeling of directionless eternity that was the Thin Line. He glanced at the gems in his arm.

"Why did you show me the name of this demon? "

You were chosen.

"Why? Why was I chosen?"

Because you care for nothing in this mortal world other than revenge, and revenge is required to reestablish the balance, the Book said.

"I care about my wife, and my sister, and my Kingdom."

Just as you have read from my pages, I have read from your heart. You care for nothing but to quench your own thirst. Your wife, your family, your Kingdom aren't anything but afterthoughts. You are so blinded by your anger you cannot see the truth about yourself. I chose you to be the Arbiter because you must not be swayed by emotion.

"You know not of who I am," Shaw thought.

I chose you, and I made you. You are who I want you to be, just as you will do as you are commanded. Destroy the chamber, destroy Jayecob, and you will free your wife. What happens to this wretched land after that, is in your hands.

"Fine. But know this. I will always choose her. The chamber will come second."

Foolish man. You are not the only one who answers to someone else. There is a war, between your kind and demons. There are things in this world that neither side should have access to.

"Like Argomancy?"

Yes, the Book said.

"What happens if I fail?"

There are things worse than death.

"And the boy?"

What of him?

"I care for him. Choose another vessel."

I have chosen him; he has already been marked.

"Choose another," Shaw said.

I won't. It's done. It's final.

With those last words, he had nothing more to ask the Book. It had told him what it needed him to hear, nothing more and nothing less. He did not have to agree with it, however. The idea that revenge was his only compass now; it was simply not true. His wife was the reason he came back, the reason he had refused to die for all those years, the reason he continued to fight.

Perhaps you thought you came back for your wife...but according to the Book, you came back to gather revenge for your wife, and those are two completely different things, the magpie mused.

"You know not of my desires, Pemazu."

And you know only of my desire. Remember my desire when the time comes, because it will.

"I'll honor your wishes. It isn't very often a demon asks to die."

I am old, very old, and I am sure I am not the only one who feels the way I do. Unlike you, when we die, we just end up back on the Thin Line. At least you have somewhere after, somewhere final. The only beauty in my death is that, if it is at your hands, Arbiter, it will be permanent.

"Normally, I'd feel bad for you. If you were human."

You feel nothing, which is why you were chosen, Pemazu said.

"Now you sound like the Book."

You should try it.

Shaw slammed the Book shut and the metal straps wrapped themselves around the cover, between the gems, until they connected themselves once more. The ends glowed red, as though from an unknown source of heat, welding themselves shut. Shaw knew there was more than just metal and a solid weld keeping this book shut. There was powerful magic at play. His sister's magic. He looked over his shoulder, ready to report what the Book had told him. To his surprise, she was leaning over him, wide-eyed and staring down at the face of the closed book.

"What did you see, sister?"

"I saw what you saw. What it wanted us both to see."

"The Book lies. I care for more than revenge," Shaw said.

"Then when the time comes, do what's right to bring balance."

She turned on her heels and walked down the stairs to the bottom floor, each step sounding heavier than the last. She made no effort to hide her concern with what the Book showed them both. Until Cereal returned, she remained downstairs while Shaw contemplated what the Book had shown him. It hadn't directly said that saving his wife was impossible, or that enacting revenge on his brother was out of the question. It had simply said to destroy the chamber. He knew the Book was right, to some extent; despite his lack of interest in anything beyond saving his wife, he knew the Argomancy chamber had to be destroyed. From what Pemazu had told him of its history, and from the Book's foreboding message, he knew that some magic is best left buried.

Cereal returned by mid-afternoon, obviously pleased with himself, beaming as he entered the church with his arms full of supplies. He brought them to the landing on the second floor and dumped them out on the table for himself and Beggen Ostra to organize and pack. He was intuitive enough to discern, based on what Beggen Ostra had asked him to gather, that they'd be traveling for some time. Shaw took a look at the supplies for a moment before meeting his sister downstairs.

"When do your friends expect to hear from you?"

"They are already in place. Within the ranks of Second City, within the inner city of Stonehaven, hidden amongst the commoners of the Fringe, staged at strategic points along the protective walls of the castle. They wait for my signal, and we wait for Second City to begin their attack on Stonehaven."

"And what will they accomplish?"

"In case my agents and their professions aren't obvious, one thing is. These aren't front-line, hardened soldiers. These men won't win a war, nor are they expected to. This war ends with the death of the King. These men have a single purpose: to cause enough chaos and mayhem so that you might get a chance at entering the castle and be able to handle your brother, uninterrupted."

"It seems you have planned for every contingency, sister."

"I wish I could say I agreed with you, but war is unpredictable, and only being unpredictable will accomplish this mission. I wish the battle raging on would be enough to cover your incursion, but I'm afraid it wouldn't."

He did not like the idea of relying on distraction, subtlety, and mass chaos in order to get to his brother. But if there was one thing he could expect, it was a level of showmanship from Jayecob. He fully expected the King to be sitting upon his throne, devouring platefuls of exotic meats and fresh fruit as the battle raged below. He'd expect nothing less than perfection out of his commanders; they knew the lash, or worse, waited for them if they should fail and still manage to survive. At some point during the battle, he'd grace the backlines with his presence, walking amongst the dead, pretending to care. After his little display, he'd return to the safety of the keep with his King's Guard standing as a final line of defense. If all went according to plan, Shaw would only have to fight his way through the

King's Guard in order to reach the King, and he should have help.

Beggen Ostra interjected his thoughts with a question, "I see you did not find answers on how to help Cereal." She looked up the stairs to the landing and smiled at his back. He was occupied with the supplies on the table.

"I need to conduct the mission it has given me; once I'm standing in front of the chamber, I'll have room to bargain. It did mention something I found particularly curious."

"Which part?"

"The part about answering to a higher power, to something else."

"Perhaps the Book isn't the only one pulling the strings. There is quite a bit of magic, old magic, in these lands."

"I agree. Let's handle our brother, and from there, we can help the boy."

Shaw shoved the Book into his traveling pack. He had considered hiding it in the church, but allowing it out of his sight once again would not give him the type of assurance he'd need that the Book would be safe. The Book was not dangerous in and of itself; that was the misconception about it. The Book was only dangerous if the wrong person had it.

Cereal appeared from the back room, wearing a thin leather tunic and greaves, his sword jammed through his belt and his pack shouldered, his head held high. The two adults looked at the boy, looked at each other, and then smiled and laughed, for the first time in a very long while. They laughed from deep within their chests, so much so that tears grew in the corners of their eyes. The boy looked absolutely adorable. He had shed his tunic and had taken it upon himself to purchase the leather armor, but he failed to take note of the size of the armor before purchasing it. The tunic that came with the armor draped below his knees and he had obviously attempted to make the greaves a manageable length by cutting the legs down. He appeared to have sewn the pants together at the top in an attempt to make them a more manageable size, but only succeeded in creating a temporary stitch; as he had strutted into the room, the stitch had given way and the pants had dropped to the floor. He pulled them up high on his waist and dashed back into the side-room, mortified. Overall, the two adults needed the moment of mirth, because soon after, the floor began to shake with the sound of war drums. Second City had begun their march on Stonehaven.

CHAPTER EIGHTEEN

It took Second City's army three and a half days to get within eyesight of Stonehaven. The army moved as a single unit, like a giant caterpillar making its way across the landscape. Riders rode alongside foot soldiers, who bore standards with the colors of Stonehaven, defiled with black smears. Near the back of the formation, war-machines trudged along. Great black wooden contraptions trundled forward on spiked wheels, pulled by ten horses each. While the majority of them were catapults, in the center of the formation, a metal-tipped battering ram, was suspended between two trusses and dragged by yet more horses. The formation was an impressive display of force by Second City, as their troops stood several thousand strong. Coupling the manpower with the machinery made the journey from the Fringe slow, however. The machinery was forced to travel alongside the cobblestone road, as the spiked wheels couldn't grip the smooth stone. The horses didn't seem to appreciate the stone roadway either, slowing the pace of the entire army. The natural terrain of the roadway leading north to Stonehaven was an ever-changing challenge for the military leaders to overcome.

Shaw, Beggen Ostra, and Cereal took to the rear of the formation, traveling with tradesmen and others who aimed to capitalize on the war. Looters, beggars, mystics, men of religion, prostitutes, and many others straggled behind the main body, spreading rumors of the war and even placing bets. The three hid themselves among these undesirables. Shaw often wondered if the man to his left or the woman to his right was one of Beggen Ostra's allies, donning a disguise, prepared to strike at any moment.

Stragglers from the Fringe, Second City, and elsewhere in the Kingdom arrived at the encampments each night. Some brought more goods to peddle, while some were eager to take up arms and fight Stonehaven. Each night also brought more free-flowing spirits as men and women alike drank to their heart's content from a seemingly bottomless supply of alcohol. Shaw, Beggen Ostra, and Cereal did not partake. They needed their strength, their wit, and their preparedness, all of which would be tested when they arrived within eyesight of Stonehaven's towers, where the army set up camp.

The war drums died off sometime after dusk, signaling the end of the march. Soldiers immediately began raising shelter, starting fires, and downing their equipment. Shaw and his companions had traveled lightly, carrying only woolen mats to lie on and their bags to lift their heads from the dirt. They made camp easily, starting a fire to stave off the bite of the cool evening air and lying down to rest from a final day's march. The entire encampment had a low buzz of activity at all times. Simple conversations, background noise, people walking and laughing made up the majority of it. It was when this low chatter turned to screaming, yelling, and the sound of unsheathing swords that Shaw's head popped off his bag. He pulled it around and grabbed a torch then went to shake the others to wake them.

"Sister, something is happening. Wake up. Sister." He shook

her shoulder and eventually her eyes opened a crack to look at Shaw's face as he held a torch above him.

"What's happening?"

"I don't know, but there's a disturbance, possibly an attack of some sort. Is this your doing?"

She sat up on her elbows and whispered, "No, this isn't my doing. This is something else." She looked around and turned her focus towards the north end of the sprawl. "Can you feel it? Something is amiss. There is always some amount of magic in the air when many users gather, but up there, beyond my vision, there is a surge of energy."

I can feel it. The power in the air. It tastes...thick...dirty.

"Pemazu says there is something in the air, something about the magic. He says it tastes dirty."

"He is right to say so. I am sure of what I feel now. Somewhere up ahead something is causing the disturbance." As she said this, a soldier bearing a golden standard with white ribbons burst through the tent line.

"We're under attack! Move towards the city, now! The assault begins!" He ran through the encampment, stopping every few paces to repeat the message. Others awoke upon hearing his cry, quickly taking up arms, donning armor, and bringing only the necessities for battle. Somewhere up ahead, the drummers began their beat, signaling the march and, according to the messenger, the attack on Stonehaven. Cereal was awoken when someone running past connected a boot with his shin, causing him to howl and draw his sword, looking around suspiciously for the culprit.

"What is happening? Are we moving out?"

Shaw gathered up their blankets and strapped them to their packs, "Yes, but there is a disturbance up ahead. The attack seems to be in response to it, premature and haphazard. We're moving now; be prepared for anything."

Cereal shouldered his pack and helped Beggen Ostra with

hers before taking position between them. Together, they followed the natural flow of the encampment northbound, weaving between tents and dodging cooling coals in the dirt. They were some of the last to leave the encampment, as evidenced by the last of the army cresting a hill far off in front of them. On the other side of that hill lay Stonehaven: fortified white-stone walls thirty feet high, thousands of archers, massive ballistae mounted atop connecting towers, and, somewhere on the other side, their army lying in wait.

The encampment was eerie and quiet now that it was left unoccupied. No chatter or laughter or the sound of filling glasses broke the ambience of the bugs chittering in the night or the birds calling weakly to each other. But up ahead, the war-drums continued on. Shaw aimed to follow the trail left by the army, but stopped mid-stride as movement from one of the tents caught his attention. Looters would have no interest in this encampment; the wealth to be gained was from the bodies of the dead. He cut off the path and headed toward the tent on the outermost edge of the encampment. It was a multi-person tent, with a peaked roof and a fur carpet blocking the doorway. Something inside was pushing outward on the canvas walls.

Something...off...is in that tent, Pemazu warned.

Shaw drew his sword and snuck around a weapon rack and a camp fire until he was just to the side of the carpet-covered doorway. He motioned for Beggen Ostra and Cereal to stay behind him, and each of them drew their swords. Something snapped and creaked inside, like a log splitting followed by an ungreased door opening. His heartbeat was in his ears as he tried to concentrate on what was in front of him and run through the possible scenarios in his head. He settled on simply being calm and quick about his movements. He used his free hand to slide a corner of the carpet aside so that he could see inside.

The canvas tent was dark, the remains of coals, orange and

lackluster, smoldering in the dirt. A shaft of moonlight lit the coals from a vent-hole in the room. The entire tent was filled with smoke, blocking his vision, but a groan told him that someone was still inside. He pulled the carpet off the doorway. He stepped aside and waited for the person to come out, assuming they had simply gotten lost in the smoke of the tent. What came out of the tent, however, both startled and confused him. A man, obviously not a soldier, stumbled out of the tent. He shambled as he walked, and Shaw noticed that one of his legs was broken at the kneecap, leaving it jutting out to one side. The man's skin was blackened by the smoke and soot of the fire and his clothes were stained in black and blue blood. The man turned towards Shaw, and he saw a fresh cut running the length of his neck. Discolored blood was caked along the line where the skin had been severed, and the man's head leaned backward, stopped by the remaining sinew, as he looked, mouth agape, at the night's sky. A moan escaped the slash in the man's throat.

This is what I sensed. This is no longer a man. It is something... something else. It feels almost like my kind, but only faintly.

"What is it?" Shaw asked.

Well, from the looks of it, it used to be man, but I cannot sense his energy, his life-force...

"Shaw, get away from it." Beggen Ostra called to him, worry cracked her voice.

"Why?"

"Because it isn't human. It's very clearly dead and yet it moves. Get away from it."

Shaw backpedaled, holding out his arm and pushing the others back with him. "How is it moving? Pemazu says he can't sense its life-force."

"Because it doesn't have one. I felt something earlier, something off, and I realize what it is now. It's the same feeling I get when I am around you. There is a demon in that body."

Well, a part of one.

"Pemazu says it's only part of a demon; would somebody please explain?"

"Ask the demon, it probably knows more."

I do, and she is right to ask me. I feared this was what the King was doing in that chamber in the castle. Argomancy corrupts the soul, twists it, bends it, until it folds in on itself and turns into this creature. One of them...becomes one of us.

"He said it used to be human, but Argomancy has turned it into a demon."

Beggen Ostra nodded and looked down. She spoke to the ground and Shaw could see her trying to understand the creature. "That makes sense. When someone dies, the soul leaves the body, but with Argomancy, the soul never leaves. It becomes trapped, warped beyond recognition."

"But why did this one just show up? Why did the others not notice anything?"

"They must have put this man in the tent when he died earlier. He must have just turned. This may have been a trap. Kill him, then leave him to turn before Second City can begin the assault."

"What can Jayecob gain from having such a creature?"

Beggen Ostra drew her sword and lunged at it, driving her blade through what would be its heart. It responded by reaching and flailing its arms, desperate to grab hold of any part of the old woman. She leaned back and kicked it square in the chest, and it stumbled and fell over. She held her sword up in the moonlight. It was bathed in a blue and black blood, thick, and coagulating quickly. Her sword began to smoke and smelled of burnt hair. She dropped it out of surprise, where it smoldered in the dirt and began to melt the dirt itself. Shaw leaned in close to examine the sword as well. The metal bubbled and groaned. It was melting before their eyes. Shaw and Beggen Ostra looked at each other, and Shaw spoke first.

"These soldiers, they must be the ones I saw in the chamber."

He looked at the man again, then at the sword. "Soldier dies… soldier comes back…soldier dies again…weapons become useless…"

"Second City won't be focusing on the dead. They won't have a chance to prepare for an internal attack."

"We have to warn them."

"No…this is just what we need."

"What?"

"We need chaos…this is chaos."

"Second City will lose the battle! They can't fight magic like this."

"Then let not their sacrifice be in vain. Find the King and win the war. Perhaps killing him will stop the transformation."

The source. The Book said to destroy the chamber and the source. Perhaps the King is the source.

"I have to destroy the source, just as the Book mentioned. This is what it was talking about."

"No doubt you will have to get through the King to get to the source…no matter."

Shaw's eyes opened wide with realization. "The King IS the source. He needed a demon powerful enough to power the Argomancy. He must have used the demon Amekath." With confidence he said, "The plan remains. We will still need your people. Can you have them assist me in reaching the King?"

"I can try once the battle begins. It will cover my magic, and I can't risk it until then."

"Okay. Good. Once the battle begins, cast your spell. Have them meet me near the southeastern tower. There is a doorway leading into the tower and from there into the wall itself."

Beggen Ostra nodded and Cereal's hand shot up.

"What do I do?" he looked at them, wide-eyed and hopeful.

"Your place is here, boy. Hide in the thicket on the other side of the encampment. There is plenty of food and water to gather, but keep to the woods and await our return.

"But I want to help you."

"You are doing your part here. By staying alive. The King will use every opportunity to gain the advantage, which includes hurting children. We can't risk you getting in the way."

For the first time, true tears dripped from his eyes and wet the dirt by his feet. He sniffled and smeared his nose, trying to hide his sadness. Beggen Ostra dropped to her knees to console him. She pulled him in close and he nuzzled her neck.

"I want to be with you and Shaw. I only have you. Please don't leave me here."

"The front line is no place for a child. We know you want to help, we know you desire to avenge your parents, but we also know what the battlefield looks like, and it isn't safe for you. We need you here, ready for us when we return."

He sniffled and wiped snot on his sleeve, unconvinced. "I want to fight."

"We know, and soon enough, the fight will come to you. But for now, render aid, and whenever they ask who you stand with, you tell them you stand with Prince Shaw."

He seemed newly invigorated with the task he had been given, especially since he'd be able to identify himself as standing with Prince Shaw. Though he wondered if anyone would know what that meant, given that most had thought of him as dead for over thirty years.

"One last thing: show me your arm."

Cereal slid up his sleeve to reveal the place where he had pricked his finger. The blackened veins spidered further up his arm now, past his elbow and into his armpit. Beggen Ostra turned it over to examine both sides, then pulled his sleeve down for him.

"The Book has given us a time limit. The blackening of your veins is ticking down how much time. There isn't much time, but then again, we all might be walking the Thin Line if we fail." She grabbed Cereal by the shoulders and steered him to look at the hole left by the creature's acidic corpse. "These people, these creatures of Argomancy, they can't be allowed to fester and grow like an untethered blight."

Shaw looked at the small hole where the creature had melted the earth to a smooth glasslike finish, then up at his sister.

"There is enough chaos for a lifetime in these fields. Come sister, we're lagging behind. Cereal, we will return, and when we do, I'll bring you the King's head myself." He pushed out a weak smile, bending the scar on his face as he did so.

The boy smiled back, his big eyes reflecting the remains of the moon slowly being dragged downward beyond the horizon. He stalked the narrow walkways of the camp between tents until he found one with a comfortable looking pile of furs and a decent spread of meat, fruits, and drink on a table inside. He untied the canvas flap, allowing it to fall before tying it off at the bottom. He laid on the pile of furs with his sword lying on his chest and stared at the ceiling above until he drifted off. Sometime later, when the sun was high and the birds chirped, the sounds of battle filled the air, and not long after, the screams began.

CHAPTER NINETEEN

SECOND CITY'S army lined the backside of the final hill, protecting it from the view of Stonehaven's guard towers. Commanders shouted orders to arrange the shield bearers to protect the front line, followed by a row of swordsmen and, finally, the magic-wielding Stone Breakers. Each group was distinctly marked with standards at either end of the massive warfront. Siege engines of all types, dragged by horseback riders and guarded by more Stone Breakers, made up the middle of the formation. Commanders, bowmen, advisors, and mystics made up the rear of the army. Three massive ballistae were spread evenly across the back lines. Each one was twenty feet wide, with six wound ropes forming a draw string and two pegged cogwheels on either side. Based on the size, the ballistae seemed to be able to launch entire trees.

Hours of battle formations and assault preparations came to an abrupt end. Then, after a moment of complete silence, the ground began to shake as the army pressed the attack as one. Shaw and Beggen Ostra stood beyond the mainlines, intermingling with the scavengers who intended to benefit from the bloodshed. Ready to risk getting hit by a stray arrow as they rush out to the dead, grabbing up everything they could hold and running back. They sat calmly in a circle of trade carts, sipping on their waterskins and swatting bugs off their sweat-laden necks. While the morning air had been crisp, the temperature had steadily risen until the sun was in full force, bathing the bystanders in waves of heat.

Somewhere among the commanders, a second trumpet call signaled for movement of the siege engines. The hills echoed with the sounds of battle cries, whoops, and war drums. The army marched to the beat, climbing the hill while the siege engines began to move toward the east, around the hill. Second City aimed to take the high ground with support from the ballistae while attacking the main walls of Stonehaven with the other siege engines. Shaw was familiar with this battle plan, as it was a weakness he'd discussed with his father many years ago. Shaw and Beggen Ostra purposefully straggled behind, maintaining their guise and biding their time. Soon enough, when the battle raged, Beggen Ostra would give some sort of signal, telling the insurgents to begin skirmishes all along the wall. She hadn't discussed what the signal was specifically, other than saying it would be obvious. It was only at this point that he began to feel nervous, similar to the way he felt when he had escaped the Far East. Why this day and this battle drew those memories, he did not know. Instead, he tried to direct his nervousness into productivity by keeping an eye on his sister, who only now seemed to be having trouble moving as they followed the slow-moving force to the top of the enormous hill.

"Is there something wrong, sister? Surely you aren't weakening when the battle is finally before you?"

"I am now thirty years your superior; don't give this old woman grief."

"I always imagined you to be bitter and dragging in your old age."

"I have plenty of energy left in me, especially for this day. Will these ballistae pierce the wall?" She asked.

"I don't think that's what they aim to do with them. There are supportive ropes just on the other side of the drawbridge, and these bolts are metal-tipped. They don't mean to go through the wall, they mean to drop the bridge by attacking the wheels supporting it."

"A frontal assault? That's a suicide mission. The Stone Breakers will draft massive slabs of stone out of the ground to protect the hole."

"Indeed - and Second City has brought a battering ram as well. But...I don't think that's the goal. Second City's Stone Breakers are near the front, the ballistae and battering ram are in plain view. Stonehaven's towers will clearly be able to see the majority of their plan, if not all of it. I believe this all to be an elaborate ruse."

"For what?"

"The Stone Breakers are near the front line. I don't think they mean to breach the wall...I believe they intend to go over it."

"How do you know this?" Beggen Ostra questioned.

"It's what I'd do. Stonehaven was created to be impenetrable from a direct assault, and Stone Breakers lining the wall would see to this. So, if you can't go through it...why not go over it?"

Beggen Ostra examined the rows of soldiers ascending the hill. The ballistae were manned, but unguarded, the battering ram had only a small company to give the guise of protection, and the horsemen were limited. All of which would be unusual for a front assault. Those leading the advance managed to crest the hill, and the spiked wheels of the siege engines and war machines stopped them from rolling back down. Another trumpet sounded, signaling for the bowmen to nock their arrows, the ballistae to draw back, and others to prepare for the initial onslaught. From the other side of the wall, a drumbeat began, followed by the whistle of thousands of arrows flying over the battlements. Above the drums, and above the screaming of arrows, came the cries of men and women from both sides.

Far behind the lines, Shaw steered down the eastern side of the hill, following the siege engines as they made their way around the hilltop and nearer the dead zone directly beneath the wall. A large company of soldiers hid under the canopy of what should be the largest siege engine, and it was with this group that Shaw and Beggen Ostra managed to blend in seamlessly. Second City's army, upon closer inspection, seemed to be made up not only of soldiers, but of anyone willing to pick up a sword and fight. Stonehaven's tyranny and oppression had driven even women to take up bows and garb themselves in leather armor, ready to do anything for their cause.

Up close, under the canopy of the siege engine, hundreds of people hid, protected from arrow and sun. Shaw and Beggen Ostra easily slid underneath the protective wooden slats, as they were not the last ones to arrive. Shaw looked up at the device and admired its ingenuity. A metal-dipped tree, cut to a razor point and filed down, was suspended among hundreds of ropes, each one on a simple pulley. When pulled in unison, the spear would be pulled back and then driven forward, obliterating anything in its path. It was dragged by thirty horses, each with two of Second City's Stone Breakers at their side. There was quite a lot of effort put into the act.

Shaw and Beggen Ostra gathered among a few other outlanders, those who wore no clear uniform, their side was derived by the directions of their swords. Next to him, a soldier garbed in actual armor and Second City colors of red and gold walked calmly yet ready, and deep in thought. Shaw looked up at the man, who was nearly four inches taller than him. He appeared to be a normal soldier of Second City, with a bridged helmet protecting his head, a short sword sheathed on one side, and a full sword on the other. Unlike soldiers he'd seen in the past, this one had several holes punched through his armor, some on his left, a few along his spine, and a few on each of his legs.

That is where the hoses attached. He is one of them.

"I can see that. He looks…lifeless," Shaw said.

Technically, he is. I cannot sense any life-force, not even the faintest. This is a very elaborate ruse. The King only needs to inflict minimal casualties for this to work in his favor.

"Well, we must make haste then. I hope you are prepared."

As I hope you are, Arbiter. Today you face great challenges. Remember the objective and we may both survive this day so that I may die tomorrow.

"Again with the optimism. How I appreciate your sarcasm."

I am optimistic. If you succeed, we both win.

Beggen Ostra tapped his shoulder and motioned with her head at the soldier with the holes in his armor. She had noticed him, too. He nodded back at her. Under the canopy, people chatted freely, unconcerned with the battle ahead of them, almost free-spirited about it. They talked about what they would do after the battle, their plans and those who awaited their return. Shaw thought about how much blood would be spilt this day, and how unaware these people were. He did not blame them; they were peasants among soldiers. Shaw scanned the underside of the ram for more soldiers and quickly picked out fifteen, all motionless, waiting for the ram to be pulled forward by the horses ahead. Somewhere on the hilltop, a trumpet sounded three short blasts. From the western side of the hill, another trumpeter mimicked the call and finally, a horseman pulling the ram pressed a trumpet to his lips and returned the call. The battle for Stonehaven began.

Once clear and full of sunshine, the air was filled in an instant with thousands of arrows from archers hidden behind battlements all along Stonehaven's protective outer wall. The whistling of the arrows sounded like a thousand birds screaming at once. The Stone Breakers and other magic users on the front line of Second City's army cast spells to deflect the arrows, sending them clattering uselessly to the ground. Second City responded with their own volley of arrows, the sounds of which overlapped with three loud twangs as the ballistae atop the hill loosed tree-sized bolts at the front gate of the castle walls. The magic-users atop the wall also cast spells to protect themselves from the rain of arrows, but they were not prepared for the might of the ballistae. The bolts impacted the side of the gate, aiming for the weak stone that covered the wheels holding the gate up. The trumpeter for the battering ram blasted two short notes and one long note, and the ram began to move forward towards the castle wall. They were relying on the canopy to protect the ram from overhead attack while it made its way towards the front gate. The archers would have to expose themselves from the battlements in order to target the ram. It was a valiant plan, despite the fact that it was only a distraction.

As though to confirm Shaw's theory, the front line of Second City marched forward, shields drawn up to protect themselves and to protect the Stone Breakers. The war drums pounded atop the hill, providing audible momentum for the assault. He watched from the underside of the ram as the frontline sustained volley after volley of arrows. Every now and then, a misplaced arrow connected with flesh through gaps in the protective line. The line would immediately huddle together to replace the fallen soldier. A quick, triple note from Second City signaled their next move.

A great surge of magic energy, centered on Second City's army, shook the very essence of the air itself as hundreds of Second City's Stone Breakers dug into their individual magic wells. Together, they channeled the energy of the ground, and focused on the image they wished to create. In unison, they released the energy into the earth itself, and the effect was incredible. In one coordinated attack, hundreds of Stone Breakers channeled the same image of squared stone monoliths and directed them at the castle walls. Hundreds of white pillars burst from the ground, at an angle, and speared the top third of the protective stone wall. Shaw was incredibly impressed by the strength of the coordinated efforts and power of that many Stone Breakers. In one strike, they had hid the ram from view, whilst guarding the ballistae from volleys of arrows. He was amazed to see that this was not the intended goal of the maneuver, but one of the side effects. The soldiers protecting the Stone Breakers continued to march forward, then up onto the smooth stone surface. As their boots touched stone, instead of muffled marching, Shaw heard what sounded like hundreds of metal swords tapping against shields.

They seem to have metal spurs attached to their boots, to help them climb the surface of the stone into the city. I doubt the King predicted this, Pemazu squawked.

"You sound impressed by the feats of men."

Hardly; even I know of your precious Stone Breaking and how you covet its abilities and tout its energy efficiency. But look before you Arbiter, magic that powerful has a cost.

Shaw looked back towards the point where hillside met stone monolith. The Stone Breakers that had raised the monoliths all laid about the ground, clearly dead. He'd been momentarily deceived by their skills into thinking they could survive such a powerful spell, and he'd been deceived by his now-heavy heart into minimizing just how many casualties this war would have. The ram continued to move. They were coming up on the tower with the door hidden along its backside.

Beggen Ostra fiddled with something under her robe as they continued to move forward. He looked around, but no one seemed to notice nor care; the effects of battle had started to take hold on them. Some cried, some talked themselves up, and others maintained their composure, focused on what lay ahead. Beggen Ostra pulled a small red and yellow cylinder, about the size of her palm, from under her robe and nudged Shaw with her elbow, motioning for him to follow her. She moved against the herd, pushing her way to the rear of the ram. Once she was close to the edge, while still being hidden from the archers, she whispered something, igniting one end of the cylinder.

"This is the signal. Our men are hidden on the lower levels. They will do their part on the other side of the wall where undoubtedly an entire army awaits us. I need you to get us through that door," she whispered and pointed at a studded bronze door just larger than a man, tucked into the backside of the tower. He nodded, still looking at the smoldering cylinder.

"Something I took with me from the Far East. Watch this," she said, tossing the cylinder out into the open between wall and the ram. The cylinder smoldered for a moment and then went out, but what followed both shocked and intrigued him. Miniature stars, bathed in flame, shot from the tube into the air, higher than the wall itself. Hundreds of tiny balls, surrounded by dazzling reds and golds, burst as they reached above the wall. All eyes turned to the display, and he could see some confusion, fear, and amazement in the eyes of those who stood beneath the ram.

Beggen Ostra tugged on his sleeve before rounding the corner of the ram, into the open air and stepping quickly to the tower door. Remembering his part, he tapped the gems on his arm, signaling Pemazu to pay attention. The gems throbbed and he concentrated on the steady stream of power emanating from them. As he ran, he channeled that power back down into his hand and held it there in a balled fist. His hand shook with the power, and he struggled to keep it from breaking away from his control. It wanted to escape. It wanted to disperse.

They made it to the bronze-plated door, and he pressed his palm to the bolt securing the door to the wall itself. The energy willfully leapt from his hand, guided by his thoughts and will, and connected with the lock. The lock creaked and groaned before it lurched and moved to the side. He pulled the door open and held it for his sister before shutting it and turning around, prepared to meet Stonehaven soldiers.

To their surprise and relief, the tower was unguarded. He suspected that most of the soldiers were either inside the wall preparing for a breach or along the wall with bows. The battle raged louder as waves of soldiers scurried up the stone monoliths to breach the wall. Along the battlements, bowmen struggled to aim into the sun to target Second City's soldiers. The attack was so violent and aggressive, Stonehaven's own Stone Breakers were unable to rally in such a way to counter the massive conjunction of magic. Soon, the ground battle would be taken to the interior of the castle as the ram breached the front gates. He looked eastward down the tunnel and saw a few pathetic torches, desperate to stay lit. In the shadow of the torches lay the guards charged with protecting the narrow corridor. Shaw looked at the dead soldiers then back at Beggen Ostra. The old woman simply nodded down the hall. If they followed this path, it would take them directly into the keep. He drew his sword and took off at a jog.

Along the walls of the tunnel were doorways leading to unknown parts of the castle, and Shaw knew he needed to be prepared in case any soldiers came through them. The narrow tunnel would make fighting difficult and at times, they needed to move in a single file. Surprisingly, his sister kept up with him with minimal complaint. After a few more minutes of running, the torches became scarcer and the noise from the battle raging outside the walls was reduced to a low rumble, with sporadic shakes as the ballistae launched their massive bolts at the front gate. After rounding another blind corner, they came upon an archway with a large wooden door and Beggen Ostra said, "Stop here for a moment."

She pulled another cylinder from her robes, cast the same minor spell to light it, and then nodded at Shaw to pull the door open. He cracked the door and as he did so, he realized that the door led to the central courtyard. There, at the ready, were rows and rows of Stonehaven soldiers. Some with bows, axes, spears, but all of them clad head to toe in armor. Every so often a stray arrow would drift into the courtyard and a soldier would step aside for a moment before falling back into formation. These soldiers were different. He examined them more closely and saw an identifier that told him who they were. On each of their left shoulders was a maul and sword, in gold and red, a sigil marking them as the King's Guard, the elite of Stonehaven. They stood at the ready, prepared to counter the opposing forces who were slowly battling their way further into the castle. Soon, the intruders would be in the courtyard, where the finest soldiers of Stonehaven would be waiting.

He pulled Beggen Ostra over to look at the men in the courtyard. She stared at them for a moment before pulling back. To his surprise, she did not share his look of concern.

"King's Guard," Shaw prompted her.

"I know."

"Second City can't fight them, even if they take the castle walls, they are too spread out. Even organized, it would be a difficult battle."

"They won't need to fight alone." She brushed past him and tossed the smoldering cylinder into the courtyard. As one, the company drew their shields in front of them and jammed them into the dirt, creating a solid protective wall. Luckily, she had pulled the door shut and they remained unnoticed.

"That's the second and last one. If our allies are out there, they serve to draw the King's Guard away from the courtyard. Now...we wait. They'll cause enough of a disturbance and force the King's Guard to move in. That'll give us the time we need to make it into the castle."

"That's relying heavily on the idea that they'll do as you expect. What happens if it doesn't work? Or if our allies are unsuccessful?"

"Then let's hope you have enough left in you to fight them all, because we will need everything you have."

Out of habit he looked at the gems in his arm. All three were shining bright red, and in the center, Pemazu was preening his feathers, looking unamused.

"Let's hope it doesn't come to that."

He looked around for a moment before sheathing his sword and sitting on a wooden box, near the door, but not near enough to be caught unaware should it open unexpectedly. The tunnels seemed as though they had been unoccupied for a while now. They waited in silence for what seemed like hours, before a cascade of screaming, running, and the clattering of weapons drew their attention. Shaw went to the door to peek through again, and was immediately taken aback by what he saw. The screams and other sounds came from soldiers, but which soldiers specifically couldn't be distinguished. Soldiers from Second City and Stonehaven were piling into the courtyard in a steady stream, and the scene was a mass of chaos, exactly as his sister wanted. Soldiers from both sides, disorganized and scared, sought protection in the courtyard. He did not know what they were trying to escape from until he looked closer at the soldiers themselves. Some were missing limbs, some held melted weapons covered in a thick dark liquid, and others suffered burns to their faces, armor, and just about every part of their bodies. They helped each other, carrying those who couldn't walk and supporting those who were hurt. Somewhere on the other side of the courtyard, the ballistae continued to pound on the retaining gate, unaware of what was happening inside the castle walls.

Shaw saw the soldiers working together and decided it was time to ask what was going on, since both sides had been on the battlefield to kill one another. A soldier from Second City came barreling towards him, a clear look of distress imprinted on his face. He bore many small scars across his face, but his eyes reflected humbly. He wore the markings of leadership on his helmet, but it appeared to be too big for his head.

"Please, we can't stop the burning. Have you a healer or other mystic familiar with dark magic?" Shaw noticed the soldier bore the blackened maul marking him as a soldier of Second City. Soot and blood covered the majority of his uniform.

"What's happening? Why has the battle stopped?" Shaw asked.

"The dead, our dead and theirs, something is happening with them. They rise, and after they rise...the blood. It's something to do with the blood. It melts our weapons and our armor. Stonehaven suspects treachery, foul magic. They refuse to fight us and we the same if this is what happens to our dead. The dead don't deserve this, nor do the living. Please, have you a mystic or know of one in your caravan? You are obviously not soldiers, and we don't care which city you belong to," the soldier pleaded.

"What of your leaders? Do they not command you to fight?"

"I am all that remains. The rest are all dead, or one of those...things. They were the first to die. We suspect treason. They died by their own personal guards, just as we breached the wall. I have no one to command if they won't take orders. They are too scared to fight."

"And what of the King?" Shaw asked.

"He gives commands from the landing. Stonehaven reports they haven't received any instruction other than to continue the battle."

"How many are there?"

"Thousands...thousands of them remain. We can't kill them, but they kill us. We have fallen back to the courtyard to make a final stand. If they breach the courtyard, they can make their way into the castle and through the remainder of the keep. Meanwhile, the King sits idly by, watching from above. We may fight each other, but women, children and the elderly, be they from Stonehaven or Second City, it doesn't matter...they need not witness this." He spat on the ground.

"Why are you telling me all of this?" Shaw questioned.

The man looked confused for a moment, but continued, "Near the rear of the formation was a boy, no more than twelve or thirteen years. He ferried arrows to the archers. When asked, he said he stood with Prince Shaw of Stonehaven. He also told us to find an old woman on the battlefield, Princess Beggen Ostra, and that you'd be together. Now, I know the kind of magic that flows through this Kingdom, and I know of the powers of the Princess, so I'd not doubt nor be afraid in seeing you here. I ask again, do you have a means to end this madness?"

Beggen Ostra stepped forward, "No; we encountered it earlier, at the rear camp. Was there a response to my signal? The device in the courtyard?"

"No. We saw it get thrown and it made stars in the sky, but nothing happened after that. We assumed it was something from a mage somewhere."

"None of our allies saw our signal." She turned to Shaw. "Or they were dead, or worse."

"What do we do?"

Both his sister and the soldier looked to him for answers, and a handful of scenarios flashed through his head, each one seemingly worse than the last.

"What if we barricade the front gate and the courtyard? How many Stone Breakers remain?"

"Almost none: a handful at most, and a small contingent of battle mages. But we'll never make it to the gate. It was overrun immediately after the ballistae felled the gate."

I have an idea, but you are not going to like it, Pemazu interjected.

"My options are limited, and it seems there are no sides anymore, only dead or alive," Shaw replied.

Well, if this does not work, it was clearly your idea.

"Just tell me."

Remember the Great Barge? Do it again, Pemazu said.

"You mean I should have you do it again? I thought you said opening a Gateway was a bad idea."

It is, but it seems that the lesser of two evils is still a better option.

He thought it through again. He could open the Gateway near the entrance of the courtyard and funnel the creatures onto the Thin Line, then seal the Gateway once it was clear. He looked at his sister, then back at the soldier, "I have a plan, but you must keep everyone back, and you must trust me."

"What is it? Just say the word and my sword is yours. I may fight for Second City, and I know not how you stand before us, but I know the King is at the heart of this, and I know that good people stay in this castle."

"Magic caused this, and magic can end it. Keep everyone back. Trust me." He looked at his sister. "Stay with them, see who you can help."

She can help.

"What?"

She can help; teach her the spell.

"Not a chance," Shaw said.

Teach her the spell, cast it together; it will conserve my power. We will need it later.

He hated relying on others, but this was no time to argue, so he'd have to trust the demon...for now.

"Actually sister, come with me." The old woman nodded, and Shaw turned to the soldier.

"You, soldier, what's your name?"

"Goren, commander of the Stone Breakers of Second City."

The traitor Daemond's brother.

"Goren, I met your brother Daemond once."

He scoffed, "My younger brother has always shot high and landed short. Rumor has it he caused a useless excursion of the King's Guard to the Fringe, managing only to get a few of them killed. From what I heard, he boarded a Great Barge headed north. Haven't heard from him since."

"Well, I hope you are more reliable than him. Gather your mages and the Stone Breakers from either side, any who are willing to fight, and have them ready."

"I will, my Lord. Who do I tell them is giving the new orders?"

"Tell them Prince Shaw has returned for the throne."

With that, Goren turned on his heels and ran towards the large group of people huddled by a crumbling fountain near the back of the courtyard.

"What do you have in mind, dear brother?"

"We're going to open a Gateway to the Thin Line as those creatures breach the courtyard doors. Once the majority of them have been dealt with, we will use the Stone Breakers to seal the courtyard and take our fight to the King. With his death, hopefully the remaining creatures will die."

"The Thin Line? The place where you were…"

"Trapped, for over one hundred and eighty years. Yes. Time moves differently there. But don't worry, we won't be going there ; we will simply give the creatures a place to go where they can't continue to spread their blight."

"Okay, teach me the spell."

"Let's head towards the courtyard door, I'll tell you the spell along the way."

By the time they reached it, the heavy wooden door was already beginning to bow with the weight of the creatures from the other side. Shaw ran through the instructions with Beggen Ostra again, who relayed it back, confirming that she knew the spell. He pointed for her to stand quite a bit away from the door, giving him time to run to her once he pulled the metal beam from its brackets, which would unlock the door and let the creatures through. Once she was in place, he took his place by the east end of the door with his hands on the beam.

"I wouldn't do that if I were you," a voice growled from behind him. He did not recognize the voice and drew his sword as he spun around. He ended up staring down the shaft of a silver-tipped arrow, nocked on a large black bow, held by a man covered in leather armor, each piece crawling with demonic runes.

"Hello, Griss."

"Hello, Shaw."

"Come all this way just to lose an arrow in me?"

"Not you." He loosened the tension on the drawstring and lowered the bow. "My arrows are intended for those things on the other side of the door, but unfortunately, I don't have enough for all of them. Do you plan on opening those doors and killing us all? Because if so, allow me to leave first and watch from above. It isn't very often I get to witness a prince die."

"We have a plan, a place to send all of those things. But you must trust in me, and my sister."

The door creaked and one of the beams of wood snapped, sending wood splinters through the air.

He shrugged, "Well, at least we die in battle. What would you have me do?"

"Pull this beam on my command and stand behind the door as it swings open. Once we let them flow into the courtyard, my sister and I will handle the rest."

Griss pulled the silver arrow from the drawstring of the bow, slid it into a pouch on his chest, and strung the bow across his back. He took his position at the right side of the door with his hands on the beam, and Shaw took his place next to his sister. Griss nodded, and Shaw nodded back. He looked at

Beggen Ostra, who smiled a wrinkly smile at him before readying herself to cast the spell. Shaw searched the back of his mind for the well of energy, circling and swirling, begging to be released. He felt a wave of energy emanate from his sister as she did the same. Together, they focused the power into a useable form, pushing it through their hands, pressing in from all sides with nothing but their will, molding it, shaping it. Together, they stepped back and opened their hands, releasing the pent-up energy. Black demon-fire shot from Shaw's right hand in the form of a massive whip, and from Beggen Ostra's right hand, a whip of crackling red took shape. At once, they reared back and snapped their hands into the air, and the whips followed. As they did, Griss tugged on the bar until it fell to the ground with a hollow thud, and the wooden doors burst inward. The spell accomplished what it was supposed to, and a large window opened in the very fabric of reality, twenty feet high, with jagged edges that seemed to suck at the air itself.

Hundreds of soldiers from Second City and Stonehaven ran through the open door, howling. Some of them were missing limbs and flesh. Others had arrows sticking out of vital organs or bore stab wounds in the crooks of their armor. Together they charged, howling and screaming from torn lungs in one endless voice. They charged mindlessly towards the rip in reality and began to pile through. The narrow corridor funneled them en masse. This went on for minutes, long enough for Griss to find his way around the Gateway and back to Shaw and Beggen Ostra. Together they watched as soldiers from both armies hurled onto the Thin Line. Shaw couldn't stand to watch as they entered that place. He knew what awaited them there. The endless wandering. Demons and worse, all seeking what semblance of life they might have. The sheer viciousness of trying to survive...

You can help them still, Pemazu said.

"What are you going on about?" Shaw replied.

I can feel your sorrow. I can taste it.

"What of it?"

You are an Arbiter. You can send their souls onward, just as you can send me onward.

"Why do you care?"

I do not, but your emotions are giving me indigestion. You cannot help them now. But once you destroy the source, you should be able to restore their souls.

"Good to know."

Shaw walked to the back end of the courtyard to see how the remaining people were faring, leaving Griss and Beggen Ostra to stay near the Gateway and continue to watch the funnel. It had slowed, but it was still a steady stream of soldiers, and he felt it was necessary to leave someone posted.

Among the wounded were more soldiers, healers, mystics, mages, and even a few Stone Breakers. All of them wore a fear about their faces that was more than the war alone would account for. His estimate was a few hundred soldiers remaining, and only a handful of magic users. Near the back, he spotted a graying soldier with the markings of the King's Guard on his shoulder. He motioned at the man to come closer. The man shifted the armor with his shoulders and moved through the crowd so that he was within speaking distance of Shaw. As he got closer, his age was more apparent. Deep wrinkles cut into what tanned skin was visible under his helmet.

"What is your name?"

"Pasket, of Stonehaven. King's Guard."

"Where are the other King's Guard? Why are you not with them?"

"Those cowards have retreated to the inner chambers of Stonehaven, leaving men, women and children behind. We fight battles, where one army conquers another, and the world moves on. That's honorable. But today, black magic destroyed all chances of an honorable death. An honorable death is all a warrior can ask for. An honorable death and a worthy opponent. When warriors don't die and the dead are not dead, what reason have we to fight? On this day, our King has shown us his true colors as he hides, watching as his own people are slaughtered. There is no honor with our King, but there is honor among men. So I stand and fight with the men, and I hope to die when the time comes." He paused for a moment, looking toward the swirling rift at the far end of the courtyard. "You are a mystic, or a mage, are you not? That doorway is of your creation? You seem to have spared us all a terrible fate."

"It was I, yes. And your cause is noble. I hoped you could tell me where I can find the King and how many of the King's Guard he has with him."

"You can't breach the castle. Not from the courtyard."

"Breaching the castle is the least of my worries. How many has he with him?"

"Twenty, minus myself. So nineteen remain. He can be found in a chamber, deep within the castle, at the end of a long hallway."

The Argomancy chamber. How fitting, Pemazu thought to him.

"We just need to breach the castle."

Shaw's attention was immediately diverted to the Gateway as his sister's voice, shrill with panic cried out "Shaw! Something comes!" He turned around and took off in full sprint. He knew what she meant by *something comes.* The Gateway was exactly that; a Gateway, and if something was coming through from the other side, that meant it was powerful. He needed to get there and close the Gateway. Beggen Ostra stood to the side of the odd rip in space that covered the doorway to the courtyard, and Griss had an arrow nocked and was slowly backing away towards the rest of the group, his eyes latched onto the Gateway.

Hurry, begin to close the Gateway now. If she can see it, that means it is too close.

"What is it?"

Demon. Big.

"Bigger than you?"

Do you really want the answer to that question? Hurry.

As he ran, he did what he could to tap into the river of energy gushing forth from his life-force; this time, he was attempting to constrain it, and direct its power away from the Gateway in order to close it. The closer he got, the harder it was for him to reach out and locate the river. It was as if it was behind a dam. It was visible, but he couldn't *feel it*. It was a drifting thought, inaccessible, but still there. He made it to Beggen Ostra's side; her eyes were wide as she looked into the Gateway at the thing slugging its way into view. Shaw gripped her arm and began to walk backwards, back towards the handful of warriors, huddled together in a makeshift defensive formation.

It is too late.

"Why can't I close the Gateway? What's it doing to our power?" Shaw questioned.

Something is holding the Gateway open...What do you call the blood drinking worms?

"Leeches?"

Yes. It is a Leech. You must not access your power; you are only feeding it, and it grows by the instant.

"No magic, it'll only absorb it." he said to his sister. He looked back at the warriors protecting the group and yelled. "No magic!" Then he turned back. "What do we do?

Ask the Book. Read it and learn how to banish the demon. Just as you would me.

"I thought you said no magic?"

This is not your magic, nor mine. This will be the Book's, Pemazu said.

Shaw removed his pack and dug through it until he felt the cloth wrapping that enveloped the hard cover. He set it out in front of him just as a massive hook-clawed foot stepped through the Gateway, appearing to come out of the air itself and step out onto the dirt. Each clawed toe was as tall as he was, and the shiny black foot was twice as long. This demon, this Leech, was gargantuan.

CHAPTER TWENTY

WHATEVER SENSE OF LOYALTY, honor to country, or dedication to a cause that used to motivate the remaining soldiers in the courtyard was lost upon seeing the demon step through the Gateway. The three initial clawed toes were followed by thick legs, black and moss-green, reversed like a bird's, but thick and muscular. The demon's legs connected at a torso as thick as a horse is long, and a barbed tail dragged on the ground behind it. It stepped out from under the constraining edges of the Gateway and pulled the rest of its body through, using the walls of the courtyard as handles. It had four hands, each one equipped with clawed fingertips, filed to needle points. Its head was that of a boar's, yet devoid of skin or muscle, as if it wore the bones of a boar's head for a helmet. As it finished pulling its tail through the Gateway, it opened its mouth, reared back, and let out a half-scream, half-yowl that shook the very foundations of Stonehaven itself. As it did so, Beggen Ostra looked at Shaw to speak but was drowned out by the creature's cry.

"What have we done?" she mouthed.

The demon surveyed its new surroundings, surprised by the feeling of the physical plane. It shook its head from side to side, peering over the walls of the courtyard, down the steps, and into the vale below where a few of the newly risen soldiers of Argomancy straggled behind. When Shaw and the others had realized what was coming through the Gateway, they had taken up defensive positions at the back wall of the courtyard; the closest doorway bared by rubble and the other by the demon. Here, they were at least somewhat hidden by a half-retaining wall and various decorative shrubs. A bow twanged by his ear as Griss loosed a silver arrow. It connected with the demon's leg with a weak thud.

"I am almost certain I prefer the half-dead soldiers," he whispered.

The creature continued to stomp about the courtyard, curious and uninterested in the people hidden within arm's reach of its razor-sharp claws. As it stepped nearer to examine the corner of the courtyard where everyone was hiding, Beggen Ostra reached out a hand until she was just inches from its armored leg. She pulled it, her terror seeming to age her by the second. She looked to Shaw, as though she were using her eyes to ask him what to do. He stared back and did everything he could to not appear terrified. He needed to stay strong, to solve this problem, though he wasn't sure that it was worse than the original problem. As if to answer his thoughts, the demon seemed to realize that it was constrained by the walls of the courtyard and balled its clawed hands, bringing them down on one corner of the wall nearest them. Heavy stone and wood collapsed around the people hiding in that corner of the courtyard, and, like tiny bugs in the torchlight, they scattered.

Griss took up a defensive position behind the door to the exterior wall, which was now lying off to the side. He nocked another arrow, aimed higher on the demon's body, and let it go. It struck the demon in the eye socket. The arrow had found its mark.

The demon staggered back, bringing a hand to guard its

wounded eye before swinging its great head side to side, looking for the culprit, but Griss had already hidden behind the door again. Beggen Ostra took note of the demon's reaction to Griss' arrow and readied an easy and, hopefully, effective spell. She held out her arm and, using her other hand, traced a line from her pointer finger down to her elbow. A silver line appeared there, shimmering slightly. She stood up from her measly hiding place behind a large shrub and aimed herself at the demon like she was holding an invisible bow. She drew her other hand back, aimed down her arm to her finger, and loosed her unseen arrow. The silver line on her hand leapt out, taking the shape of an arrow as it did, and connected with the demon's other eye.

She looked at Shaw, "Griss and I will keep it distracted. It must not leave the courtyard. Find a solution." She hid behind the shrub again; the demon, angrier than before, opened up its great bony mouth and let out another scream, causing the few people in the courtyard to scatter along both sides, hoping to put distance between them and the increasingly violent monstrosity. The demon, noticing the flurry of movement, reached a claw toward the retreating crowd, ready to slice open a young woman who was straggling behind the others, but not before another silver arrow connected with its head, causing it to roar and shake its head in pain. This time, Griss did not return to cover fast enough; he just managed to roll out of the way as a mighty fist brought a section of stone down on his hiding spot.

"Pemazu, how do I banish it?" he thought.

Why bother? This is the worst possible scenario, Pemazu said.

"Enough with the negativity! Can you not be a demon for once and just give me a straight answer?"

He felt the bird plink its head against the glass of the gems for emphasis.

The last time a demon was released on your plane. It. Destroyed. Third. City.

"And that demon was sent back to the Thin Line. It can be done again. But I need to know how."

You think it was sent back to the Thin Line, but nobody knows what happened other than the fact that it was there, then it was not there.

"We can argue about history later. For now, I just need to know how to kill it," Shaw stated.

You cannot. This is not some minor demon, or even an Impius. This is a Leech. It felt the massive surge of power and death and sorrow from this battlefield. It is incredibly powerful. Something no ordinary magic can handle.

"Then perhaps we need extraordinary magic. The Book has that kind of power. A different kind of power, such as the kind my sister seems to use."

Consulting the Book again? Is this another calculated risk, Arbiter? Because, from what I can see, your last calculated risk allowed a Leech to walk the physical plane. Watch out.

The Leech was being repeatedly pelted with arrow and spell to the point that it was now lashing out, slamming its fists on every section of the courtyard until nothing remained. Shaw managed to sidestep as a clawed fist passed right by his face before tearing through a section of roof, landing next to him. He lashed out and kicked one of its knuckles, but it did not seem to notice. The fist went back through the hole it had just created, and the Leech looked about the area, expecting another arrow to the eye. It was slow, but they were running out of places to hide. As much as he detested asking for help, especially from the Book, he was out of options. Soon, this monstrosity would leave the courtyard and make its way through the rest of Stonehaven, destroying everything in its path until the only thing that remained were ruins. Just like Third City.

He found a spot behind some fallen stone and a wooden

piece of roofing, dropped his pack, and tore through it until he reached the Book. He looked over the piece of roof, checking on his sister and the demon-hunter. They continued to distract it, firing at regular intervals, Beggen Ostra with her mystical arrows, and Griss with a seemingly unlimited supply of silver arrows. Shaw did not waste another moment; he pulled off the protective cover around the Book, and noticed that its spine was still imprinted with the same words as it had the last time he'd read from it: "Two dead boys got up to fight."

The metal clasps glowed orange on their welds and popped open. The three red rubies embedded in the cover swirled as he looked into the large one in the center, surprised to see his reflection. He flipped open the cover, expecting to have to practically beg the Book to communicate with him. Instead, the words "Hello Shaw" were already written on the first page, though the characters quickly shifted.

Blundered again, I see, the letters spelled out.

"I am not without fault. Those creatures, the Argomancy things, they'd have destroyed everyone, everything. I had no choice," he thought to the Book.

We always have a choice. It's the content of our choices that decides the outcome.

"I need not a riddle. I need a solution. You brought me back to bring balance. That thing isn't balance."

I cannot intervene, the Book repeated.

"You said you needed to maintain the balance; this thing threatens to destroy an entire city and everyone in it."

And the Argomancy chamber. And the source.

"That's what this is? This thing is a backup plan?"

In case you fail.

"I won't fail," Shaw stated.

You may. This demon will not. It will destroy, and continue to destroy. It cannot be stopped.

"A demon of this might has been stopped before."

And to this day the world is out of balance because of it.

"What does that mean?"

The world is still out of balance, even without the Argomancy, even without this demon. You have failed, the Book said.

"I haven't and I won't fail! I'll take this monstrosity to the Thin Line myself, even if I must walk there for eternity! Then you have no demon, and no Arbiter to carry out your deeds." He had raised his voice for a moment, forgetting his need for secrecy. Fortunately, the demon did not notice and was still occupied with taking the courtyard apart, piece by piece, raining wood and stone down on the area.

"I'm running low on arrows here! If you are going to do something, do it now, Shaw!" Griss yelled as he slid on his knees between the demon's feet, shooting an arrow up at its face as it looked down at him. The arrow caught it in the demon's open mouth and it coughed purple flames and a few plumes of smoke, smelling strongly of sulfur, before roaring and attempting to squash him. He dodged the demon's balled fist and it shook the ground as it came down on the stone, inches from his backside. He ran through its legs towards the adjacent wall where a few thick pillars remained to hide behind.

"Help me, and I won't fail. Help me save these people. Save everyone. I can save everyone," Shaw begged.

True, but the risk is too great should you fail, the Book said.

"Then I'll drag the creature back through the Gateway myself."

You won't return.

"Neither will the demon. Without me, the Argomancy continues."

The words faded from the page.

"Do you understand? I'll take this beast with me," Shaw thought.

You won't. Your kind seeks self-preservation.

"Not when something threatens to take all that we care for."

The words, *I have a proposition. A deal, as it were,* appeared.

"Name it."

Don't stand in my way when I come for the boy, I know you plan to.

"Leave him out of this."

The offer stands, and time is running out.

Shaw looked over his shoulder in time to see the Leech crunch through a soldier's armor and consuming his upper half and tossing the man's lower-half aside. Shaw turned back and thought of Cereal. Then, he envisioned the scores of people who would die if he didn't banish the demon.

"Fine! Tell me how to banish this demon."

Signed in blood, Shaw...

He looked around, spotted a nail jutting out from a board, and jabbed his palm at it, then smeared it hastily across the page.

Silver. Silver can destroy its tether. Note the shadow leading into the Gateway, but you must do it on the other side, the Book said.

Shaw glanced at his silver sword and knew what it meant by *the other side.* He had to lure the demon through the Gateway and banish it there.

"Tether?" He wondered.

This demon cannot exist on this plane without its tether. It needs a host. It is rooted to the Thin Line. You are your demon's host. Return it there, then sever the tether.

"How do I get it to go back there?" Shaw asked.

The name you bestowed it, Leech; give the Leech what it wants. With enough magic, you should be able to draw its attention.

With those final words sprawling out of a hole in the center of the page, Shaw slowly began to close the Book, but more words formed on the center of the page.

Bo-reng ah de rath...to destroy.

"What spell is this?"

You will need it, the Book said.

"When?"

The page remained blank. Frustrated, he slammed it shut, covered it with the cloth, and repacked it beneath the rest of his possessions.

I have never been afraid, Arbiter; it is not a feeling I know. But if I could, I would be afraid of that spell, Pemazu said.

"Why?" he questioned.

The power in those words. They are in my tongue. Remember... magic of this strength has a cost...

"A cost I am willing to pay. The Book gave it to us for a reason."

You would think that, but you know that the Book only cares for itself, despite what it may tell you. What if this spell is meant to consume you? The demon will still be loose.

"It's a risk we must take. I don't have another option," Shaw said.

You gave the boy up to the Book...you really do not care for anyone.

"I am doing all of this for everyone! Don't patronize me, demon."

Very well. But if your sister finds out that you allowed the Book to take the boy, I fear it may be the end of us both.

"She won't. Now, how do we get it through the Gateway once more?"

The Book said give it what it wants. Give it power.

"Where can we get enough to draw its attention? My sister's power seems to affect it, but I doubt she is strong enough to keep its attention."

It looks to me like your prayers have been answered.

Shaw turned his head, seeing a flurry of dark robes and flashes of light as a small cohort of mages joined the fight. They came from the courtyard entrance, skirting the Gateway and casting a variety of spells. A few more joined the fray from their hiding places, mustering courage at the sight of the other spell casters.

Shaw stuffed the Book back into his bag and shouldered it, leaving his cover and running towards the others, "Turn it towards the Gateway! Move it around!" he yelled, waving at them. Some of the mages heard him and began circling around the demon as they cast spells, each one connecting with its scales and then fading away as the demon absorbed it. The mages didn't seem to notice how ineffective their spells were, but did notice that they had gained the creatures attention.

"Come to me! Come to me!" he yelled, running up to the Gateway, putting himself between the rift and demon. "Come to me! Gather together. Save your spells. We need to strike as one!"

Scared and tired, the other mages gathered around him, panting and looking drained and pale. They had used up a lot of their energy already. They obviously did not have much fight left in them. They needed to draw its attention as one.

"Beggen Ostra, get behind it. You too, Griss. Get ready to hit it with everything you have! We need to push it into the Gateway. We will draw its attention."

Beggen Ostra nodded and began whispering something. Black clouds crackled in her hands and waves of power shot out from her, kicking up dust. As she did, the air became warm and thick, and the taste of copper coated his tongue. Griss opened a long vertical pouch along his back and pulled out black-tipped arrow. He nocked it and nodded he was ready.

"Mages, on my count, give it everything! We need to bring it forward just a little more." The demon was about three strides from the Gateway. It looked down at the Gateway and prepared to move safely off to the side.

"Give me a hand here, Pemazu."

If I must.

"Three! Two! One! Give it everything!" He turned back,

snarling at the mages behind him. Each one conjured spells from the pits of their minds, drawing on their own essence to channel and cast the spells. Flashes of light in vibrant reds, greens, and whites lit the sky, unaffected by the daylight. Each spell collided with the demon, only to be immediately absorbed. Instantly, two mages died, and another lost consciousness, but the spells had an effect. The demon's attention moved from the Gateway to the men on the ground. It opened its bony mouth and howled. Shaw didn't wait for it to rear back and hit him. Instead, he ran through the demon's legs and stopped at its heels.

"Now!" he signaled his sister and the bowman.

"Give me the sword and let's hope."

You know what to do, Pemazu said.

"Perr-da-ra-na!" Shaw bellowed, extending his jeweled arm. Blackened demon-fire erupted from his mouth, singeing his tongue and throat. It crawled the length of his arm, fusing to his skin and bone, becoming one. The flames and coal turned a bright shade of green as the magnificent demonic blade took shape. In the place of his arm, a shiny black hell-forged sword protruded from his elbow. He was relieved that magic granted by the Book actually worked.

He smiled and gave a manic, voice-cracking battle-cry and plunged the sword into the demon's leg, piercing its armored hide with the enchanted weapon. Griss loosed the arrow, and it caught the demon under its bony head, near its neck. The arrow pierced the skin and kept going, flying off into the distance. Whatever it was tipped with, it went through the demon's armor. Beggen Ostra released whatever spell she had concocted by slamming her hands together. A black cloud of soot launched from her hands and hit the demon in its back. The combined effort toppled it forward and it lost its footing, tripping and tumbling directly on the Gateway. Thunderous noise echoed in the courtyard as it stomped backward trying to regain its balance before it fell into the Gateway. It cried out, almost as though it were in pain, howling and screeching until the last bits of it faded away and the courtyard was silent.

Shaw relaxed his arm and pushed the demonic energy back behind the dam in his mind, returning his hand to normal. Beggen Ostra ran past him to check on the mages. Griss ran over to him to talk and take a count of his arrows, expecting another fight. "Is that it? Is it gone?"

"Unfortunately, no. It's still near, somewhere on the Thin Line. I need to go there and destroy its tether. I have to go now before it recovers and comes back through."

"Where is the Thin Line? It can come back?"

"The Thin Line is the plane demons walk upon. If I don't banish it, it will only be a matter of time before it seeks to come back through. Especially with how much magic we just fed it. I can walk the Thin Line and destroy its tether. Then it will cease to exist."

"I am glad that's your mission. I'd rather kill them on my own terms."

"You did well. What was that black arrow?"

"Demon claw. I found it in the Ruins of Third City, after the battle," he said.

"I need to remember that."

"When will you go?"

"Now; I can't risk it coming back again. Will you ferry the people in the wall towards safety? There are still creatures out there that were not sent to the Thin Line. We don't know how many of those things the King created."

"If they'll come with me. Many of them will feel safer in the castle," the demon hunter said.

"There are still undead soldiers within the castle."

"I'll try my best."

"Thank you, Griss."

"Thank you, Prince Shaw. Best of luck. I expect you to be seated upon the throne by nightfall."

"I appreciate your optimism."

He put his hand on Shaw's shoulder for a moment, nodded, then ran towards the hole leading to the exterior wall of the castle, picking one of the injured mages up by the arm and helping him limp towards the hole.

Beggen Ostra slid her hands over the dead mages' eyes and crossed their hands on their chests. She stood up and stretched her back.

"Are you hurt, sister?"

"In body, no, but my soul aches. The echo of these mages' spells still circles here. They gave everything."

"Let it not be in vain. I need to finish banishing the demon."

"How?" she asked.

"The Book told me to walk the Thin Line, find its tether, and destroy it. From there, it will no longer be able to return to our plane. We fed it enough magic, it will come back through where the veil between the planes is thinnest. After I banish it, I'll return through the Gateway and close it for good."

"You are really going back there? At the Book's behest?"

"The Book isn't making this decision. I am. I need to finish what I started. I have walked the Line before. I am not afraid," he said.

"I am. We still need you. The King isn't out of reach."

"I won't be gone long."

"As you wish, brother."

CHAPTER TWENTY-ONE

"THE WORST PART of being here isn't the fact that I am here again, but that it hasn't changed since the last time," Shaw thought to Pemazu.

Perhaps you will feel sorry for us, now that you know what we must endure for eternity.

"Still no."

He had left Reggen Ostra to help Griss round up as many of the living as he could and shuttle them out of the castle towards the rear lines of the battle. The great war machines had long since been abandoned when soldiers began to rise from the dead and their blood began to melt weapons, armor, and flesh alike. Now, he was once again facing the endless black void, lit by tiny glowing shards, while sound was muffled around him and ambient light was just as scarce. The Thin Line took advantage of wandering eyes and punished those who strayed beyond using their peripheral vision. Should he look up, he'd be immediately taken, body and soul, to somewhere unknown. Should he look down, the Line would bring him to its furthest depths and hurl him into the Void, where even the Book couldn't reach him. He kept his eyes locked forward and removed his boots, setting them by the Gateway, a beacon to mark his way home. The boots did not belong and would be a guide should he find himself out of eyesight of the Gateway. Despite not knowing what a tether should look like, he found what he thought it was, and immediately felt stupid that he hadn't asked the Book for a description. Knowing the Book, though, he doubted it would have told him what the tether looked like anyway.

The glowing shards, which lit the glass-like surface of the Line, were scattered over the ground, faded and weak-looking, leaving some areas in shadow. Shaw looked off into the distance, following the faded rocks. He noticed that they created a string, easily followed. He started walking, humming to himself; the absence of ambient noise was maddening. He followed the glowing stones, noticing that they faded the further he walked. He identified the tether as the shadow upon the glassy floor. The longer he walked, the thicker the shadow became, and the thicker it became, the more it looked like he could touch it. He walked, following the tether, using his expanded vision to keep it by his left foot.

"How far must I walk?"

Until the tether is taut. You must cut it clean, the bird chittered.

"Wait, how do you know this?"

I am only assuming. It makes sense to completely remove the demon's connection to your plane.

The tether thickened as he walked, becoming an unmoving snake, but it still appeared to have slack to it. Onward he went, step after step, until the snake was as thick as a tree trunk, and taut.

"Pemazu, light."

The demon complied and the gems in his arms radiated a small amount of heat before the red glow grew from a speck of light to a glorious curtain of red, illuminating the area. The gems' light caught something in front of him, a dark mount of scales as tall as a man. He squinted against the dark, the gems casting shadows on whatever was out there, until he realized it was the Leech, laying on its side.

Quickly! Before you wake it. Cut the tether. Do not look down.

Shaw drew his sword without a sound and turned his body to face the black, tree-like tether. He kept his eyes on the Leech, expecting it to rise at any moment. He brought the sword down on the tether. He was taken aback when he did not meet resistance and the sword vibrated in his hand as it slammed into the surface of the Thin Line. The tether shimmered for a moment before disappearing, fading away into nothing. Still, the Leech did not move.

He sheathed his sword, took a calculated half step to his left and set out towards the Gateway, a blip of light against the drab facade of the Thin Line. Off to the side of the Gateway, his boots gave off an unusual glow, just as the rocks did. For once, he allowed himself to relax. He'd leave this place behind, never to return again. He neared the Gateway and was close enough that he was able to see some color from the other side. He picked up his step; he was so close. A glint of gold darted across the entrance of the Gateway.

"What was that?"

The bird did not respond.

"Pemazu, can you sense anything?"

Amekath...

* * *

Jayecob's golden-armored leg stepped through the Gateway, followed by another leg, and then the rest of his body. A hideous smile dug into his face behind the protective face-plate of his helmet. His black broadsword in hand, he stood, barring the way through.

He mouthed the words, "Hello brother." Shaw did not respond, knowing full well he couldn't be heard. Instead, he drew his sword and prepared for the fight for which he'd been waiting for over one hundred and eighty years.

There was something wondrous and culminating about meeting Jayecob here. He should have almost expected it. With the spectacle in the courtyard, surely Jayecob would have seen the commotion from the landing above, watching as a demon of great power came onto the mortal plane. Watching, and waiting, as his combination of necromancy and alchemy took hold, turning his own soldiers into walking shells of themselves. Surely he'd have sensed the powerful magic from his sister and the demonic magic from Shaw. Shaw should have expected this; he should have prepared his mind for this. Now, he'd take his revenge on his brother, and the stakes were so much higher.

Jayecob struck first, drawing his two-handed sword up and over his head, hacking at Shaw crossways as he closed the distance between them. He still barred the path to the Gateway but managed to push Shaw further back towards the emptiness of the Thin Line. Shaw watched his eyes, to see if he might hint at wavering, if he might look any direction but forward, but they were steadfast and as piercing as always. As if he was staring through his brother and into the demon within.

Your brother is strong, and your normal blade will not be able to take a strike from his broadsword. His is of demon-weld.

"What about your sword?"

It will hold, but it will drain us. Amekath is much stronger than I am. You need to end this fight quickly.

"With pleasure."

"Perr-da-ra-na!" Shaw bellowed, extending his jeweled arm. His mouth said the words, but in the confines of the Thin Line, he was the only one who could hear them.

The spell worked, fusing demon-fire with his arm until it created a sword of demon-weld as well, black and shining, just like Jayecob's, but smaller.

His armor and sword make him slow. Use it to your advantage, Pemazu advised.

"Since when are you a combat expert?"

We share body and mind, Arbiter. I am simply relaying what you would do.

"Then why say anything at all?"

Shaw sidestepped another overhead slash as the blade struck the glass-like surface inches from his feet. He kicked at the blade, hard, causing Jayecob to lose his footing. He hurried into a guard, but Shaw was quicker. He jabbed at the space under his shoulder-cap, where the armor connected but the leather was still visible. Blade met flesh, but only for a moment. A trickle of blood ran down the front of Jayecob's chest plate. Shaw backpedaled and crouched, preparing to strike again. Jayecob wiped the blood with his hand, looked at it, and smeared it across his face. He looked manic now, and impossibly angry. He opened his mouth and issued a battle-cry, veins stuck out in his neck and throat, but the silence continued to surround them. Shaw kept his footing, always looking forward, waiting for Jayecob to strike again so he could counter.

Jayecob took two steps forward and brought the blade around in an arc. Shaw managed to jump back, feeling the blade tug at the front of his tunic. Jayecob swung the blade around again for an immediate follow-up strike. Shaw dashed wide to the right, jumped, and slammed his demonic blade forward, aiming for his brother's unprotected neck. Jayecob reared back, causing Shaw's blade to glance off the rounded armor. He landed on his knees, shooting pain up his thighs to his hips. He barely managed to bring his sword arm up in time as Jayecob brought his broadsword down upon him. Demon blade met demon blade. Though no sound came from the blades, he imagined for a moment that they'd be screeching as the perfect edges scraped together.

Two dead boys got up to fight.

"What?"

The poem, from the Book in the market. Two dead boys got up to fight, Pemazu said.

"What about it?"

That was the message your sister sent out to her bandit friends?

"So?"

It means the Book knew this fight was going to happen...and so did your sister.

* * *

Shaw tucked and rolled, ending the sword-lock and effectively resetting the fight, breathing hard.

"This doesn't help us! How much longer can we keep this up? He seems tireless."

I told you, Amekath is much more powerful than I.

"What do you propose we do?" Shaw asked.

You could release me.

"Not a chance."

Then I have no options. But I do know that the demon from earlier, the Leech, is on its way here, to the Gateway.

"I destroyed its tether."

You did, but it does not mean it ceases to exist, only that it cannot exist on your plane.

"Great."

Jayecob obviously sensed it too; he looked down the Line, feeling the demon moving in their direction. It was moving quickly, sensing the two sources of power. Jayecob checked his position near the Gateway, keeping just a few feet in front of it. He looked at Shaw again, his ocean-blue eyes meeting his brother's emerald green. Together, they'd have been perfect reflections, equal halves of their father. But here, in this place, they weren't so different at all. Dark heart versus dark heart. Black against blacker.

You could at least try to act confident, for my sake.

"Again, you find an opportune time to get in my head," Shaw said.

And you find an opportune time to feel sorry for yourself; are you not one hundred and eighty years old? Act like it.

"Thank you, demon, for your kind words."

Whatever it takes, Arbiter, as I am tired of this place. My essence aches. The Leech will be here in moments. You cannot hear it, but I can feel it growing closer. We need not be the first thing it sees.

Shaw stole a glance over his shoulder. A great shadow was moving towards them, like the shadow of an ancient tree in the dark. It blotted out the abysmal gray of the Thin Line. Jayecob used the distraction to jab and Shaw barely stepped out of the way, the blade whooshing under his elbow. Jayecob pulled it back, but swept it upwards as he did so, opening a deep gash under Shaw's right arm.

"Argh!" Shaw cried out, tucking his arm tightly against his side. He felt his own warm blood quickly soaking his skin beneath his undershirt. It stung; distracting, but not impossible to fight through. The cut was not very deep, but it weakened his concentration. He took a defensive position, brought his blade up in front of him to check the gems. Only one kept its glow; inside the magpie sat, stoic.

The demon is here. Take up a position out of range of your brother but next to him. He won't risk a three way fight, and neither should you. You will need to work together to destroy it. Amekath should likely advise him of the same.

"Why would he not just leave? Continue this fight in the land of the living?" Shaw asked.

Here, you are alone. That is how he wants you and here, if you die, even the Book cannot bring you back. Amekath must know this.

The bone-faced demon lumbered into view, dragging its clawed hands on the ground, its mouth agape. Shaw remembered what its roar sounded like. Seeing it go through the motions soundlessly was unnerving. Jayecob swung at him weakly as he ran around to stand off to his side. The Gateway was still behind him, but Shaw was now off to the right. He looked forward, using his peripheral vision to see the demon, but he could only keep sight of its torso and hands. It swept its claws in a wide arc in front of it. Jayecob closed the gap, ducked under the demon's wrist and pierced it between its ribs. Shaw ran forward as well and plunged his blade into the demon's heel, drew it out, and slashed at the thick tendons, severing them.

The demon buckled, flailing in pain, its clawed hands reaching out, sweeping, grasping, and slashing blindly. The combination of his strikes, Jayecob's and Griss's arrow seem to have taken its toll on it. Alone, Shaw would have had trouble destroying it. Only his demonic blade seemed to have any effect. Jayecob's as well. Separate, they were strong. Together, they were to be feared.

This is why you are the Arbiter. You are equipped to restore the balance.

Jayecob closed the gap further and ended up directly underneath the demon, shoving his blade upward into the demon's stomach. He backed out and Shaw slashed at the demon's other leg, aiming for the thick tendon on its heel. The demon fell forward and Jayecob placed the hilt of the blade on the ground. As it fell, Jayecob repositioned the blade so it landed with its chin centered on the point. The demon's head sunk down the length of the blade and it lay motionless on the ground. Jayecob climbed on top of its head, wrenched it around, and pulled his sword out sideways. He jumped off, landing heavily next to the demon's carcass. He scraped the edge of his blade on the carcass and circled around it, taking up his place guarding the Gateway.

Well done. We may win this after all.

"Do you have some bit of information I don't?" Shaw asked.

Do I not always? I just absorbed the remaining essence from this demon.

Shaw's heart leapt. He brought his forearm to his eyes. Sure enough, all three gems were filled with dancing, swirling red smoke, and the magpie was dashing from gem to gem, again excited and nervous. He dropped his bladed hand down to his side and smiled. He could continue this fight. He had already wounded Jayecob; he was still but a man. This wasn't over.

Jayecob looked at him and cocked his head slightly, possibly confused as to why Shaw might be smiling. He found out moments later. Shaw let the rampaging river of energy flow just a bit. It was tucked safely away in the confines of his mind, protected by sheer will power. He relaxed the dam in his mind, and demonic energy flowed through him. It took the form of overlapping scales; perfect hexagons replaced skin under his clothing, turning it into tough, demonic armor. His unchanged hand ached. It cracked and became misshapen. Knuckles moved and set in impossible places. Fingers elongated, nails grew out, becoming thick and pointed. As a final part of the transformation, his nails and the skin on his hands blackened to match his scaled armor. Jayecob looked at him unamused.

Rejuvenated and less worried about how much energy he was using, he went on the offensive. He dashed at Jayecob, slashing with demonic hand and blade. Jayecob struggled to deflect and parry the onslaught of quick strikes. Shaw jabbed high with the blade and followed up low with a clawed hand. The demonic hand easily tore through Jayecob's gold-plating and through the steel underneath. Jayecob twisted his sword to deflect the clawed hand and kept a defensive stance with his blade. Shaw's strikes came quicker, more violent, and almost reckless. He dodged a sweeping strike from Jayecob's blade and carved out a corner of his brother's shoulder. Claws sank into armor, like piercing cloth, and met flesh. Shaw squeezed and pulled away, tearing flesh from bone. Jayecob's face contorted in agony, and he became enraged. His eyes reflected manic ferocity; he gnashed his teeth and spittle flew from his mouth as he gave another silent battle cry.

Shaw backed off and shook the blood and tissue from his claw. He took a defensive stance, preparing to dodge the broadsword again and continue the flurry of quick strikes. Jayecob clutched his wounded shoulder, blood dripping between his fingers, his sword held loosely in his wounded hand. Jayecob stared back at Shaw, and a calmness washed over his face, replacing the blind anger and fear, masking the pain. He dropped his sword to the ground, reached behind his back and tore at the straps to his armor. The golden chest plate fell away, revealing a plain, blood-soaked leather tunic. He unclasped his vambraces and greaves and ripped off his helmet. Together, the golden pile of armor was especially jarring, given the amount of blood Jayecob's shoulder had dripped onto it. Jayecob pressed his hand to his shoulder, and his chest rose and fell heavily. He looked like he was deep in concentration, or planning his next strike. Shaw was confused as to why he'd remove his armor. Jayecob was an excellent fighter, even when laden with heavy armor. Shaw guessed that Jayecob was slowed from it so much he couldn't keep up with his own barrage of slashes.

Moments later, Shaw realized why Jayecob had removed his armor. Jayecob dropped his hands to his side and transformed himself. Blue scales burst from his skin and crawled up his arms, over his shoulders, and halfway up his neck. Thick, gnarled horns grew from his head; feet became hooves, hands became claws, and his arms became elongated. The only thing that remained to identify him as a man was his face. Shaw saw a face that was that of his brother, but something else had driven his brother out. On the surface, he was Jayecob. But underneath, he was something more, and his body had begun to reflect it. The demon that was once his brother stood, a seven foot tall monstrosity guarding the Gateway. Its arms were so long that its knuckles touched the ground, and its legs were jointed backwards like a bird.

Now, he looked more demonic than human.

Amekath has taken over.

"That thing is Amekath? Is Jayecob in there?"

He is an observer in his own body. Fight Amekath or flee, unfortunately I cannot make the choice for you, Pemazu stated.

The demon charged, dragging its clawed hands on the ground and bringing them up at the last minute, gripping Shaw by the throat and forcing his head upwards, trying to get him to look up into the Thin Line. Claws dug into his neck, and its grip was impossibly strong. He mustn't look up. He shut his eyes, pulled back his bladed hand and thrust it forward, sinking it deep into the demon's chest. It let him go and he collapsed on the ground, managing to keep his eyes shut, lest he look down and be taken away. He pulled himself to his knees, then to his feet, and opened his eyes again just in time to bring his arms up and parry two clawed strikes. He locked his sword hand between two fingers of one of Amekath's hands and interlocked his claw with the demon's other claw. It became a battle of strength; Shaw and Jayecob were head to head, shoving each other back. Jayecob increased his grip, attempting to crush Shaw's hand. Jayecob broke the deadlock and slashed with a free hand, catching Shaw's stomach and ripping three fresh slashes into it. Shaw keeled over, pain washing over him in waves, and still he kept his eyes forward.

That was a stupid mistake; you are getting complacent.

"That isn't helping," Shaw said.

You are losing too much blood. You will faint soon. Amekath will consume us both.

"I can't defeat him. He is too strong."

Indeed, Arbiter, but you were given tools. Use them.

"What tools?"

Perhaps the spell the Book gave you? What else do you have to lose? We will both die here shortly, Pemazu said.

"I can't risk using that spell. We don't know what it does and there is too much waiting for us on the other side."

For you, maybe...

"We still have an agreement. I'll uphold my end."

I expect so, Arbiter, but first you must get us out of here. If you choose to use that spell, now would be the time to pray to whatever god you wish.

His brother, or Amekath, whoever it was, paced before the Gateway, waiting to continue the fight. He was taunting him. He wanted to best him yet again. He wanted Shaw to fight back for as long as he could. Shaw cradled his wounded stomach, applying as much pressure as he could. Hot, stinging waves of pain flooded his body with every heartbeat and his vision began to blur. He raised his claw in Jayecob's direction. Jayecob, or Amekath, paced and smiled, waiting for Shaw to attack again. It was obviously pleased with the wound it had caused in Shaw's stomach. He was not sure if the demon was aware of how much damage it had caused, because it still paced, expecting a retaliatory strike, giving Shaw the little time he needed to prepare for the spell. Amekath must have sensed that he was starting to cast something, because it charged, raising a hook-clawed hand high above it with elongated arms; but the attack was too slow.

"Bo-reng ah de rath!" Shaw yelled silently into the abyss, his arm shaking as he released a flood of power; everything he had left was channeled into the spell. The gems in his arm drained of energy and light; Pemazu was forced to scurry to the gem bottommost on his arm and huddle there, with only a glint of light remaining. Though the expenditure of energy was unexpectedly rough, like a raging torrent, he still managed to hold on and continue to channel the spell.

The demon that was his brother was not expecting a spell, nor one of that magnitude, and it collided with his stomach in a torrent of red and black flames, writhing like a ball of snakes. His brother tried to shake it off of him, brush it away, pat out the flames, but all to no avail.

His arm burned from holding up its own weight. Everything was darkening while the thing that was his brother silently writhed and howled in agony. The spell continued to take from him, to draw on Pemazu's energy and his own. In seconds it would consume him entirely, and he'd be forever lost on the Thin Line.

A glint of silver flashed in the corner of his eye. A shadow among shadows darted from the edge of his vision. A cloud of moving shadows stood next to him. Perhaps he was imagining it. Perhaps, in his final moments, this was the thing to take him beyond. Perhaps this was the Book, ready to collect on what it had laid claim on. He was ready. Jayecob was defeated; the flames melted his flesh away, eating at the scales, exposing the essence underneath, and still the spell continued to pour out of his own clawed hand.

The silver flashed again, from inside the cloud - the hilt of a blade, perhaps? The hilt and blade of a sword. Someone was holding a silver sword; his sword. Someone inside the cloud raised the sword high and brought it down on his clawed hand. The blade severed his demonic hand, clean and swift. He felt the cold of the blade, followed by the immense burning as the claw fell to the ground and the channeling ended. More blood poured from the wound, ticking down the moments he had left. Jayecob was far away, still fighting the spell as it ate at every part of him. He ran in panic, covering his eyes as he ran, blindly heading deeper into the Thin Line. Then, it was over. Everything was simply dark. No light. No sound. He finally knew a true death.

CHAPTER TWENTY-TWO

THE MAGPIE SCREECHED, *You are insatiable.*

"Pemazu? Do pray tell how even in death I can't rid myself of you."

Consider my voice a blessing. If you had not heard me, we would both be in a terrible situation.

"Are we dead? We must be. Dead together... This must be my final punishment, to be linked with you forever."

Do not flatter yourself. You are not dead.

"Of course I am. I remember what happened. The Thin Line, Jayecob, the spell. What of the silver-sword and losing a hand? Thankfully it was not the one that matters."

Perhaps you should open your eyes, come to terms with the fact you are, in fact, not dead, so that we can get on with this mindless endeavor. You still have a job to do, Pemazu quipped.

"My job is done. Jayecob is dead, and I will be too. I just need to lay here."

Where is here, Arbiter?

"The Thin Line, where I'm drifting in and out of consciousness. Where I'll soon awaken to find that I'm dead, and my soul will forever be trapped here."

Wrong again. I am at the point that I wish you were dead, just so that you would know the difference between dead and dying. Wake up.

Shaw was ripped out of unconsciousness by a building ache in his gemmed arm. It faded a moment later and he drifted off again. The gems throbbed again; this time they seared like a hot iron was pressed against his skin.

Open your eyes, or the next time I will light us on fire.

"I can't, the Line…"

We are not on the Line, you horse. Wake up! Pemazu screeched.

Weary and sluggish, Shaw opened his eyes to see not the gray of the Thin Line, but the midnight moon, high above, lighting the crumbling remains of the castle courtyard. He saw bodies, strewn about. He could very easily be one of them…he just needed to close his eyes…give in to the pull.

"Wake up, brother." Beggen Ostra said, just as his eyes closed once more. "Wake up and drink this."

He felt a hand on the back of his head and another under his back, lifting him up.

"Shaw, you need to drink this. I have to stop the bleeding and infection." She pressed a cup to his lips; something warm and smelling strongly of spices sloshed inside and against his lips. The liquid was not hot, yet it seared his skin.

"It will only burn for a moment, but it will heal you. Hurry. This elixir won't last long." She pressed the cup against his lips, more forcefully this time.

Reluctant, he drank the liquid, and it burned every part of his throat and tongue until it settled, hot and heavy, in his stomach. From there, the burning faded, and his skin felt as though he'd been caught in an afternoon shower. He felt invigorated, energized, and alert. He opened his eyes fully now and sat up on his own. He checked the gems in his arm first, knowing but not wanting to know what he'd see when he looked at his other arm. Two gems shined bright; the magpie was resting calmly in the center gem once again. It stuck a forked tongue out at him, which it unspooled around itself and attempted to hang itself with it. He smiled at the demon. Somehow, the spell hadn't consumed them both.

He examined his right arm, or lack thereof. Instead of a matching hand, or even a demonic claw, he was left with a cauterized stump just above his forearm. Interestingly, he could wiggle his fingers and still feel them, though they were clearly missing. He looked at his sister, her eyes reflecting what he was about to ask her.

"This was your doing, was it not?"

She glanced down at his severed arm then caught his eye. "You were dying. That spell...I felt it from out here. Something of that magnitude...it doesn't end well. I followed you through the Gateway, to that...place...I saw you, channeling that spell. But you were not you...you were different, changed. And Jayecob, he was not him either. You both appeared more demon than man. He was burning. The flames, that spell, it was consuming you, and him. I had to act."

"How did you know to stop the spell by cutting off my arm?"

"It was your companion's suggestion."

"What? Pemazu?"

She looked at him, apparently curious. "He came back through the Gateway. Told me what to do."

"Impossible. He can't manifest on our plane. He is under my command."

"Not when you are unconscious; I asked him the same thing. He briefed me about the Thin Line, to remove your arm to stop the spell...and how to close the Gateway."

Do not make that face, Arbiter. Even if you have no regard for your own life, I have a vested interest in making sure you live long enough to kill me.

"What of my brother, and the remaining undead?"

"The last I saw of our brother he was saturated by the spell. The soldiers continue to rise as more die of wounds sustained in battle. Second City has retreated to the rear camp. Stone-haven is gathering their remaining forces, at least those willing to fight the undead, near the barracks on the west side of the castle."

"That means Jayecob wasn't the source."

"I'm afraid so. Griss gathered a small cohort of mages of those that survived, they are prepared to cast a summoning spell. Once you've found your wife, they will cast the spell to remove you both from the castle."

"Avana? Has Griss seen her? Where is she now?"

"One of my men reported that, the last he'd seen of Avana, she was locked away in a room just off the main hall where the Argomancy chamber is. He said he ran past it on his way to the battle. It was empty, but he heard whispers that she may be hiding on the landing above."

Shaw looked up at the landing she was talking about. Halfway up the castle itself, the landing served as an overlook by which one could examine the castle and all those living around it. The landing was equipped with massive mirrors and lenses, designed to enhance sight beyond that of ordinary men. From there, Jayecob would have watched in great detail as his army lay ruin to Second City's forces. The landing could be locked from the outside, making it ideal for her to protect herself and hide."

"She'll be there. It's protected by a solid core door. One way in, one way out. I'll go for her. Will you be coming, sister?"

"No; the threat is over. You won't be tested in the castle. I must spread the word of the King's defeat at your hands. They must know you have returned. Only then can we attempt to rally Second City. With Second City at our side, and Stone-haven in ruins without a leader, they'll bow to you. I'll head to the rear guard and prepare the mages; I'll cast the spell with them. I'll also check on the boy and meet with whatever leaders Second City has left."

"Even in the wake of battle you can't get your hand out of the political pot."

"Excuse me, brother, but you will find that it isn't a sword that will win you the Kingdom, but politics."

"We will have to disagree. This war began with a blade, and it ended with one."

She shrugged and pushed herself up by her knee, stifling a groan with a wince instead. She looked up at the castle keep and squinted her eyes against the sun setting behind the castle. "What was his plan?" She asked Shaw without looking at him. "What did he hope to accomplish?"

"It seems to me he didn't have as much control over the undead as he thought. They kill everyone without regard for what uniform they may be wearing. He turned many of Second City's military leaders, and their personal guards into those things. He even turned his own men it seems. The only thing worse than fighting an enemy is fighting an undead enemy."

She sighed deeply. "Then why did some of his own men turn?"

"He must have been testing the process on them. There were many chemicals involved and the process must have needed to be perfected."

"Well, this day didn't go as I had planned, but I'm glad it's over," Beggen Ostra said.

"Indeed. But I was able to defeat Jayecob. I need to go to Avana. Have you heard from your crew of swashbucklers?" he asked, pulling himself up and examining the remains of his arm. She handed him his pack and his sword, and he noticed that she hadn't bothered to wipe his blood off. He wiped it on a pant leg before shoving it into the scabbard, now forced to draw with his left hand.

He spun the belt around to his right side for canted cross-draw and shrugged at her as she raised an eyebrow.

"Hopefully I won't need this; I've yet to learn to fight proficiently with my left hand."

"I pray the same. I won't be here to save you again."

"I do owe a great debt to you, sister."

"Consider it repaid. Just the few moments I was in that place...it explained a lot to me. It's a fitting end for Jayecob."

"The Thin Line is infinite, endless, and timeless. He has been sent to a place beyond that. I'll go now, sister, while I still have the strength. What was in that elixir of yours? Can you make more?" He asked.

"That was a healing elixir I've only been able to make once in my life. Its properties to heal the body and soul are incredible, but costly."

"What kind of cost? No more riddles, sister, tell me what it's made of; what did you have to sacrifice?"

She paused and looked down. "I had a single sugar cube left. Half of what I owe Madrigal."

"If the horse finds you, and you aren't prepared to repay the debt..."

"Yes, I know! The beast will just have to understand that I had to save your life."

Shaw chuckled and shouldered his pack. "If there is anyone more stubborn than you, sister, it's that horse."

"Well, if you could talk to him, try to convince him to let us ride him without a bribe of one of the most elusive substances in existence."

"Like I said, he is stubborn."

The old woman pouted and turned on her heels. She made her way to the makeshift doorway left in the wake of the Leech's attack and disappeared into the outer wall of the courtyard. As she left, he heard her yell out, "Just tell the horse I've died!"

He watched her leave before heading into the outer wall after her, but instead of turning right towards the tower, he turned left, heading deeper into the castle. Upon entering the

hall he was surprised to see that the demon's damage was local-
ized to the courtyard. The long hall connecting the outer wall to
the exterior of the castle was untouched, save for a few torches
and supplies that hadn't been scattered or toppled over in the
attack. No soldiers poured from side doors, nor were there any
signs that they would be travelling this hall. The remaining
undead still called for their attention outside. He followed the
hall until it ended at an iron door. He prepared to cast a spell to
melt the lock, but upon further examination, he noticed that it
was already melted.

"Thank you again, sister," he said to himself, smiling at her
quick wit and thorough planning.

He pulled on the door and entered another hallway, this one
wider and taller, meant for local travel and trade. It was cooler
inside as well, and the light stone walls reflected light in such a
way that even a single torch could light a stretch of hall well
beyond what one would expect. He did not remember this hall.
It had been quite some time since he'd been in Stonehaven, and
the castle had been added to. When he'd first helped raise the
castle, only a single spire, the landing, a tower, and an outer ring
had been built. Over the years, more was added, and it didn't
seem as though that had stopped even in his death.

He took off at a slow jog, each footstep from his heavy boots
echoing along the empty hall. He was near the bottom of the
castle, and he knew he needed to go up several floors to check
the Argomancy chamber, and then up again several more to
check the landing. He found a tight spiral stair of metal leading
to another smaller but well-lit hall. This one seemed more akin
to the parts of the castle he remembered. With a wall to his
right, he exited the stair and ran further into the castle. It got
darker the further inward he went, as if the walls themselves
were consuming the light.

Soon after, no ambient light remained, and he called on
Pemazu to guide the way.

Without a word, the demon complied.

"No retort or snide remark?"

What is there to say, Arbiter?

"Why do you seem unusually drab?"

Surely you cannot be that stupid? To feel excited and without care at a time such as this? Pemazu said.

"Such as this? Jayecob is gone. Once we find Avana, we will destroy any remnant of the chamber and I'll fulfill my end of the bargain. I don't see what you mean," Shaw said.

Of course you do not, because you fail to look at the details. Your sister said the dead continue to rise; that means Jayecob was not the source. Meaning there is another piece on the board, one strong enough to power the Argomancy. If that piece still remains - and it does, because I am never wrong - that means that you still have a debt to the Book, and this time, you won't have your sister's help. And you are one arm short.

His heart gave a violent flutter. The demon was right. He hated admitting it, but he was right. The Book would hold him to his word, and if the Argomancy chamber and the source were not destroyed, the Book would come for him. How could he be so stupid? How could he have overlooked this? His focus on finding his wife had blinded him.

"What does this mean?"

It means our excursion into the belly of the beast itself needs to be short and sweet. Get the broad and get out. We can regroup later, once we are prepared to fight the source. I fear we will not be as lucky as we were with your brother, Pemazu said.

"Even if we find the source now, I'm getting Avana."

Just remember, the Book gave you a warning of what would happen if you disobeyed it.

The hall ended at another stair, this one made of stone and not nearly as narrow. It went in both directions, down to the lower levels and upwards. Shaw followed them upwards, noting again that he appeared to be in one of the castle's many towers.

Interesting, the demon chirped.

"What is?"

The poem, from the boy, or the Book, however you choose to look at it.

"What of it?"

It seems the Book has predicted all of the events of today and those leading up to it. Black spires...black spires...raise the night.

Shaw examined the walls as he took the spiral stair, noting they were just as the hall below: devoid of light. In fact, it seemed as though they were absorbing the glow from the gems in his arm. The staircase opened up to the hall with a stone wall at one end, and great pillars of stone barring the way on the other. A faint light outlined the entryway to the Argomancy room. Beggen Ostra had told him that Pasket had already seen that the room was empty, but the Book had still commanded he destroy the chamber.

He looked at the side room first, noting that it was now open. The inside cover of the coffin didn't yield further information as to who, or what, had been inside. He had at least expected scratch marks or some other signs of struggle. He noted there were no locks, bands or other ways to secure the coffin.

"Whoever was in this, they did so willingly. Even more reason to destroy this place."

For once we agree, Arbiter.

He examined the mass of pipes and hoses fed through the hole in the wall into the larger chamber on the other side of the stone. He examined the various wooden barrels, filled with a thick liquid inside, and covered in runes. The smell was both sour and sweet at the same time. He coughed after getting too close to one.

"What is this chemical? It's very strong."

Acid...strong enough to eat through most anything, except for these barrels which are spelled quite heavily.

"Then it may be worth a shot to think it will burn through stone."

Try not to melt your feet.

Shaw checked behind him to make sure that the pathway was clear before using a foot to slowly tip the barrel over, spilling the liquid out onto the stone floor, where it immediately went to work, devouring everything it touched in a plume of silver gas and smoke. Shaw left the acid to do its work and ran for the stair at the end of the hallway. As he rounded the corner into the stairwell, a large crash and a thump told him the coffin had fallen to the floor below. He imagined the room as it would be now, with it a gaping hole where the coffin had once stood.

He took the stair upwards again, until he could go no further. At the top, he turned, and ended up in a great rotunda adorned with tapestries, a hand-carved wooden table spanning the length of the room and a great golden chair sitting high on a platform. The chair itself was magnificent, but it was a reflection of the King's greed. While he had sat upon a golden throne, his people had starved below, civil war had brewed itself into existence, and the Far East had pummeled their sea-bound Great Barges with flaming arrows or took them for themselves. All while the King sat and filled his table with food, drink, and women. He cared not for the throne, but made a point to remember to melt it down later.

At the other end of the rotunda was a massive wooden door, double his height. It was inset with decorative stones in reds, blues, and blacks, from the bottom of the door to the top. The decorative gems were new and a useless waste of money. The door itself was more important than any gem or any amount of gold he could muster. On the other side of that door, he expected to find his wife.

His feet were heavy as he made his way to the door, expecting to have to yell out to Avana to get her to open it from the other side. He hadn't talked to her in many years; he was unsure of what he should say. He'd have to prove himself to her, as she'd most likely believe it to be a trick of some kind.

Arbiter, I believe these to be minimal worries to have right now.

"What would you know of talking to women?"

Do you remember the Pit? The trail of magic we found? The draft you used the power from to get you out?

"Yes; what of it?"

Whoever, or whatever, is on the other side of that door also has a draft.

"The source of the Argomancy...it has Avana!" he realized.

I believe so, Pemazu said.

Shaw placed his hand on the handle and pulled. Ropes attached to weights helped swing the door aside and revealed the landing. At the end of the landing, near where the retaining walls dropped off and the magnifying glasses ended, stood a woman in a black dress that gently flowed around her. He walked through the doorway and made his way to the end of the landing. Behind him, the door closed and locked with a muffled click.

CHAPTER TWENTY-THREE

THE WALK to the end of the landing felt longer than the one hundred and eighty years of walking the Thin Line. Each step closer sped his heart up and poured fresh sweat down his back. He found he was holding his breath every few steps only to release it heavily to suck in more air again. He strained to make out her face in the late evening, but he knew she was looking back at him. He knew that she was smiling. She must have been waiting for him just as he'd been waiting for her. She must have seen the battle below and recognized him and his sister.

Soon, he'd hold her again. He'd whisk her away from this place until he could return and kill the source. He'd make sure she was far from here when he did so.

Arbiter, there is something in the air. Something is not right.

"Be quiet, demon."

Arbiter, you really need to be careful - something is off.

"I said be quiet."

Shaw! Listen to me, this is not right.

Shaw infused power into his words and gave the demon a command, "Silence, Pemazu!"

The demon clammed up and its muffled squeaks were now

just a minor annoyance in his mind. It continued to push against his commands and communicate with him, but now its squeal of a voice would not be able to break his concentration. He came upon the woman and noted that she was not, in fact, looking at him, but looking out from the landing. He paused within arm's reach of her and tried to slow his breathing enough that he could talk to her. After so many years, he just wanted to call her name, and see her smile back at him.

"Avana. I've come back to take you away from here."

"Hello, Shaw," she said without looking back. Her voice was that of the woman he loved, but there was no emotion in her words, and she did not turn around.

"My love, please turn so I may look upon you after so many years."

She turned in one fluid motion, her feet hidden by the dress giving the appearance that she was gliding on the stone below. In the back of his head, the demon fought to give sound to its voice.

Shaw was now more afraid than nervous. Pemazu was showing an enormous amount of concern and Avana was not as excited and vibrant as he remembered her to be. Perhaps thirty years in captivity had hardened her, made her callous? Perhaps she was in just as much shock as he was?

He was wrong. She faced him, her face not bearing a single wrinkle, and her black hair not revealing a single, graying strand. She was perfect, just as he remembered her. Her eyes sparkled blue and her lips outlined a sincere and genuine smile. A few strands of hair danced across her face as she looked at him. He smiled back, and tears ran down his cheeks. He looked at her through the tears and noticed that there were none in her eyes; just the same, heartfelt smile he remembered.

He reached out and pressed his hand to her cheek. Her skin was cold and clammy, but still as soft as he remembered. He brushed the hairs out of her face and pulled her in, meeting her lips with his. Together, they engaged in a kiss that could have lasted the night if they had let it. He pulled away from the embrace and took her hand in his uninjured hand. She ran her hand up his arms, swirling the gems with her fingers before resting it on his shoulder. With her other hand she gingerly touched the remains of his severed arm and stifled a cry.

"What happened?" she asked,

"Just a small portion of a long story. We've time to talk about everything later. For now, we must leave."

She continued to smile and it worried him.

"I can't leave."

"What do you mean, you can't leave? Jayecob is dead but there is another force here greater than him. You must come with me. We can make it out of the castle right now. I have mages waiting for us to be ready for the spell."

"I can't leave."

"Why? Tell me why. Avana, if there are others who are in danger we can retrieve them later, but for now, you must come."

The gems throbbed, and he ignored them.

He grabbed onto her wrist and held it to his chest, pleading with her, "Please my love, trust me. It's me. You must come with me. There's nothing but death and destruction here now."

The gems increased in temperature from a mild morning heat to that of a pot left too long over the coals of a fire.

"Avana, you must leave with me. There is an evil at work here. It means to continue the war and destroy everything. I won't lose you again. Please, come with me." He tugged on her arm, but she was unmoving like a stout tree, whose only give was from a single branch.

The gems seared his skin now, glowing an angry red.

"What is it?" he yelled aloud at the demon in his arm.

IT IS HER.

Shaw dropped her arm and stepped away from her. Her smile grew until it stretched her skin tight across her cheek bones, becoming unnaturally wide and revealing space that her teeth didn't cover.

"No..." he said, stepping back. His legs shook and his heart pounded firmly in his throat. The landing rattled violently, and he fell, then began scooting backward in a panic. His hasty retreat was delayed by the lack of a second hand to help move him quickly. Avana bore down on him, floating inches from the ground, gliding as she followed him, her inhuman grin sprawled across her face.

"Why?" he cried out. "Why did you take her?"

She stopped floating towards him and rested midair.

"What do you mean take her?" Her soft voice had been replaced by one much deeper. "I have yet to take anyone, though I dare say I am strong enough."

"Who are you?" Shaw demanded.

"*Who* is an interesting question. *What* is far more revealing, and *what* I am is very simple compared to who I am. I know who you are, Arbiter."

"If you know who I am, then you know what I'm capable of."

"Defiant, even in the face of one of the First! I like that about you. Your ignorance gives you strength, even in the end times."

One of the first of my kind, Pemazu said.

"What have you done with Avana?"

"Oh, her? She is still in here, somewhere," the demon said, tapping its head. "She said she loves you by the way, not that it does you much good now. You must know this night does not end with you and Avana running away together."

"I'll pull you from her with my bare hands."

"There it is, the famous Shaw anger! You know, for the last thirty years I have been picking your wife's every memory apart. I know everything about you. I know you mask your fear with anger, and I know you mask revenge with love."

"Quiet!" Shaw pulled himself to his feet and drew his sword awkwardly with his left hand.

"Go ahead, cut your wife, and prove me right as she watches. Show her who you really are."

"What do you want?" he yelled.

She floated towards him and her feet dangled as she loomed over him. Her smile spread across her face and she basked in the near-helplessness of the once confident man.

"I want you to see how insignificant you are. I want you to see how even the Book's great Arbiter is useless against someone such as me. I want you to feel the pain of knowing that I sat in this woman's body as she pined for you for thirty long years. Her ache for you was astounding." She put her hand on her hip in matter-of-factly way.

"I sifted through her memories and showed her the true you. See, I need her soul, willing and broken to finish my work here. For thirty years she held strong, unwavering. No matter how many horrid ways I twisted her own memories against her, and defiled her body, and tore apart her friends for her to eat, she held strong. But when I heard that the Book had chosen you, of all people to be its Arbiter, I knew I had the final piece. So go ahead, strike me down so we may both watch her crumble."

He looked up at the twisted, haunted image of his wife. He looked into her eyes, and beyond the green, something swirled within. Something imprisoned within, tucked away, watching, only to be shoved out of the way by another presence.

"What do we do, Pemazu?"

For once, I do not have an answer. If we die, her will crumbles. If we strike at her, only she feels the pain, and her will crumbles. We are at the end of the line.

"Would you like to talk to her? Perhaps she can give you a recollection of that night, the night in which you fell, and I rose. The night she called to me."

"She'd never."

"Oh, she would! And in the simplest of ways, I answered. Go ahead. Ask her."

CHAPTER TWENTY-FOUR

THE CROOKED SMILE HIDDEN behind the few straggling strands of hair faded. Avana's hair shifted from black to gray. Crow's feet developed in the corners of her eyes and thick wrinkles crossed her forehead. She aged thirty years before his eyes. She plopped down on the stone, no longer floating, fell to her knees, and began crawling towards him.

Shaw backpedaled again. This had to be another trick.

"It's me, it's me." She reached out to him and her voice cracked. It was soft again, but it sounded gritty and forced. "Listen, you mustn't do what it wants. You can't let it break me. You must kill it. Send it back to the void. I know you, no matter how it tries to twist your image." She took his hand in hers. Though aged, they were soft and warm.

"Shaw, listen. The Argomancy. It's only the beginning. It will use my soul to give permanent life to demons. You must kill it. They'll consume everything."

"What, what happened, how did this happen?" he asked softly.

"That night in the Pit. I lost everything. I lost you, your father. I believed your sister dead, and an entire city crumbled around us. I watched you die. Then Jayecob...he dragged me and threw me into the coffin. He left me there, in the dark, forever, it felt. In there, I did not age, nor did I sleep, or eat. I was left alone with my thoughts. I thought the most horrible things. I saw you die over and over again. Until one day, as I plotted to take my own life...something reached out to me. It made promises. It promised to end the pain, the suffering. It promised to give me peace. I was naive. I don't know the things of your world, not as I do now." She closed her eyes and looked down and sniffled. "I was weak. The demon came to me as you. It took your form. It tricked me...and I believed it. Because I needed to believe it. It called to me, and I answered. Like a fool I answered. So, you see my love, you must kill me. At least then it won't have my soul. Please. We will be together in the next life."

"I can't defeat it. It's too strong."

"This creature, it fears you. It has my thoughts, and I have its. It fears you will know its true name. Its name is-"

"Ah, now now, that is not playing nice," Avana's soft voice was once again interrupted by the chesty voice of the demon inside her. "She lies. I fear nothing. I am one of the First, and I have waited eons for my brothers and sisters to once again occupy this plane. I have created for them the perfect hosts, and with you gone, Arbiter, demons will walk unhindered."

Shaw, that is no longer your wife. Look past the face. You cannot allow the Argomancy to continue. If her will breaks, only you will be able to kill the undead, and without you, the undead will decimate everything, leaving it ripe and bare for demons to walk the world. Death brings sorrow. Sorrow thins the line between life and death.

"I can't. I won't," Shaw said.

You must. This is beyond you. You will see your wife again, but my kind must not be allowed to walk free.

"Why do you care so much? What could possibly give a demon the compassion to care for the wellbeing of humans?"

There is evil in this world, Arbiter, some of which I have not only seen, but been a part of. There are things that threaten both my existence and yours. Things so terrible, reality itself will soon become a victim. The demon that now occupies your wife's body is one of those things. It's one of the First, and it must not leave this landing. If you die, your wife's will shall die as well, and that is exactly what this thing wants, Pemazu said.

Avana floated inches off the surface of the landing again, her head half-cocked and the oversized smile stretching from cheek to cheek.

"Arbiter, for one so designed to vanquish demons, you consult with the one you have imprisoned quite a bit. What is it telling you? For its own sake, hopefully to give up, quit, lean in, so I might take your head off cleanly."

You need to fight Arbiter. Fight.

"What of Avana? You'd have me kill her?" Shaw asked.

Only her physical body. Her spirit will move on, and whatever demon is in there with her will be cast back to the Thin Line. If you do not dispel the demon, her spirit will be trapped within the vessel forever; the demon will kill you, and you will never see her again.

"Can we defeat her?"

It, not her. And probably not. I will not lie. We are out of time. Fight it, perhaps it will get complacent. It is old, and confident, but it is constrained to the body it inhabits. Fight.

"Arbiter, your wife, she screams and yells endlessly in here, fighting against me, or trying to, at least. If you heard half of the things she said about me, you wouldn't think so highly of her-"

"Quiet, demon," he said with power behind his voice. She grabbed at her throat and the smile wavered from her face for a moment.

"Oh! Defiant until the end. There was some power behind that, Arbiter. I got a bit choked up and felt a slight tickle. Do it again; I am *highly* amused at the extent of your power."

Throughout this exchange, clouds had rolled in from all sides, smothering the moon, casting the land into deeper darkness. Thunder had followed the clouds, and rain had followed the thunder, now making its presence known on the landing.

Shaw dragged himself to his feet, his silent tears hidden by the downpour that now slicked the landing and threatened to flood the lower rings of the keep. Avana seemed unconcerned; perhaps this storm was her doing. Perhaps the thing inside her really was as strong as it had suggested.

Get those thoughts out of your head, Arbiter. This storm is indeed hers, but it's just a show of force, a ruse.

"I see through you, demon. You may wear my wife's body, but that won't prevent me from sending you back to the Thin Line and beyond the Void, as I have so many of your kind. For one hundred and eighty years I fought on the Thin Line, and countless times your brethren fell. Just as you will. Avana will move on; you won't be so lucky."

"Valiant, Arbiter. Let us see if you can truly put a blade through your own wife."

"Give me the sword," he told Pemazu.

Of course.

"Not just a blade. Perr-da-ra-na!" The familiar demonic fire poured from his mouth and fused with his gemmed arm. He leapt at the thing that was his wife, aiming to slash her across her body. Avana did not move, nor did she flinch or attempt to intercede. The slash came close enough to split her dress across the front, but her skin did not show any signs of being touched by his blade.

He bounded backwards, shocked to see nothing more than her pale skin peeking through the dress. He aimed to strike again; this time, he'd pierce her through the middle. He'd run her through, just as he was run through...Avana continued to smile her wicked smile; the rain stuck her hair to her face and drenched her dress and still she hovered just above the floor of the landing. Again, he closed the distance, thrusting the blade towards her chest. Knowing the blade would not miss this time, he closed his eyes, unable to look upon her face as he ended her life.

He expected the feeling of blade meeting flesh and braced himself for the image of his dying wife, possessed by a demon, and how she'd look with his blade through her chest. He opened his eyes, expecting blood, or some other sign that he had hurt the demon. At first he was confused, and then the remains of his courage were flushed out of him in a single moment. His blade hadn't touched Avana; instead, it was a mere hair from her skin. He had prepared himself to end her life, to end her suffering, and to end his journey, only to find that he had not only failed, but that he had failed by his own accord. Avana hadn't moved - he was sure of it - meaning that even his subconscious would not allow him to strike her down. He withdrew from the strike and backpedaled closer to the door of the landing.

Your heart is not in this, Shaw. You cannot strike your own wife down.

"I have to! Everything says I must. I must...even if it means losing her again," Shaw screamed in his head.

That is the concern, Shaw. I do not think you are ready to lose her. I, on the other hand, do not have such concerns.

"What do you mean? If anyone is responsible, it must be me. I won't let anyone else take her from me."

You have already proven that you do not have what it takes to kill her, which in turn means that we will lose more than your wife to this creature. My kind will decimate the Kingdom, and more, through the undead army, with this demon at the helm.

"There is one other way...What if I release you? You said your kind is confined to the body it occupies and without a body, you will be stronger. We can fight it together," he said.

You would trust to release yet another demon onto this plane?

"You have already said you don't have the power it takes as you are. But together, we may have a shot. I have to trust you, even though my every fiber tells me I shouldn't. I believe you when you say you want to die. I know the feeling. I thought about it a lot on the Thin Line. But then, I was given hope in the form of a new chance to make things right. Will you fight her with me?"

You have made many mistakes in the past, Arbiter. If our little deal is still in effect, then I will try my best to not let this choice be one of them.

"Do we have a plan?"

We will fight it together. You will destroy the demon and the vessel it rides in. It will be forced back to the Thin Line, where you will banish it and send it beyond the Void, Pemazu said.

"And then what will you do? How do I know you won't go on to decimate everything and everyone that remains?" he asked.

You do not know that I will not, but leaving this demon, this strong, to continue to spew forth those broken-souled things onto the land... Without a doubt, all will be dead.

"What will you do? Return to the Thin Line?"

Surely not to wander again. You still have to uphold your end of the bargain. You will banish her, and then me. If there was another way, I would prefer it. I would very much dislike being forced out of you, only to wander the Thin Line for another few millennia.

"Again, we're faced with a horrible decision," he said.

Indeed. There is one other concern I need to address.

"What is that?"

There is a cost for releasing me onto this world.

"There is always a cost."

Yes...and this is one of the heaviest, Pemazu said.

"Cost and risk. There are too many chances here. I must try to do this alone first."

CHAPTER TWENTY-FIVE

AFTER HE FAILED to pierce her with his blade, she smiled wider and cackled at his helplessness. She turned her palms out and rake-like barbs burst from her fingertips. She used them with the speed of a cracking whip, each hand a quick blur of scale and claw. He barely managed to parry and dodge the first flurry of strikes before one of her hands slipped past his guard and tore into his shoulder. In the flash of pain, another follow up claw tore into his leg, forcing him to shift his weight to his good leg to stay upright.

Pouring blood from two wounds, he felt his strength waning, and his courage left his body with his blood, only to settle in his boot or mix with the torrential downpour that threatened to flood the landing. Still, he was determined to stall and racked his brain for any solution other than releasing yet another demon into the world. He decided he needed another option, as the narrow defeat of the Leech weighed heavily on his mind. He was determined not to make the same mistake twice.

"Give in, Shaw, why fight? Avana does not want you to suffer any longer. She cries silently as you bleed onto the terrace."

"Lies. She wants me to defeat you, to send you beyond the hole you crawled out of, beyond where you can return. Avana knows that what I do is for her," he said, catching his breath. He tried to reach out to the well for the power to cast the spell to burn the demon, wrap it in flames, as he had to Jayecob, but the pain from his leg and shoulder interrupted every thought with each heartbeat.

Do you plan to stall her until you pass out?

"Shut-up, I am thinking," Shaw said.

You are obviously not, Arbiter. Every second you lose more blood and become slower. Soon, she will consume your body just to make your wife watch and suffer in silence.

"You aren't helping, Pemazu."

I am trying to help, if you would listen to me! Release me, and I will fight her.

Shaw struggled to match the demon's ferocity enough to counterattack. One claw followed another so quickly, he was forced to backpedal to avoid them, and came close to tripping several times. Avana looked at him between the strikes, staring deeply into his eyes, but not with love. Instead of his wife, it was the demon that looked at him and still it smiled as it attempted to flay him with its claws.

"What of Jayecob? What was his role in all this? If you are so powerful, why not take the throne from Jayecob and destroy the lesser demon, Amekath?" Shaw asked it as they deadlocked, claw against sword.

"Jayecob was a necessary pawn. Avana was not a leader, despite being royalty. Jayecob had a certain Kingly quality about him, and he was more than willing to toss Avana into that coffin if he believed it would secure him the throne," the demon said as it broke the tangle and reset the fight.

"You never needed Jayecob."

"Never."

"What of Third City, and the Book. Was that you at Third City?"

"That was his own doing. He opened a Gateway and released Amekath to do most of the heavy lifting. After he made a deal with her, they worked on releasing me. I soon followed, and more would have come, but that pesky Book has a way of losing itself."

The demon picked at its overly distended smile with a claw, apparently amused with Shaw's surprise and building sense of dread. The demon's words sunk in as its claws would, cutting him away piece by piece, until there was nothing left.

What is it going to be, Arbiter? Trust me, or die? Pemazu interjected.

"The Book would have told me if I was meant to release you. It would have made that clear," Shaw replied to the bird.

Since when has the Book been clear about anything? Do this for retribution, to tip the scales in your kind's favor; do it for your wife. Since the beginning, you have been so reliant on the Book providing you with answers that you failed to seek out any of your own. The answer is before you now: take advantage of my help. Avana is gone, but her soul will live on, as will yours. There are still others who will suffer if you do not do what is necessary.

"They will never follow me, nor will they believe my story. I leave behind a broken land and a broken kingdom in my wake. The people below us come to watch the spectacle, not to help as their city crumbles around them under the heels of war. Do you expect me to believe those are the others you speak of?" Shaw questioned.

No, I speak of the rest of the land; the entire nation that is still loyal to the King, the true King. The King that rose from the dead to avenge his family's death, who came back to set forth a Kingdom that is no longer fearful of the King, but proud of who he is. Leave behind your arrogant pride, Arbiter, and your name will live on, just as you will live on with your wife. Your goal was to find her, and if you do not release me so that I might destroy the demon latched onto her soul, she will be trapped forever, and you will never see her.

"The Book promised I'd find her if I did as it asked," Shaw said.

The Book told you that you would find her, and you have! It never promised anything more, and you should not trust it anyways!

"But I should trust you?"

At least I am clear about my intentions. I am looking after my own self-interest here. Watch out!

Avana transformed yet again, becoming more grotesque, resembling of something from a nightmare. The clouds blocked out the moon, casting the landing in overwhelming darkness. She became a specter of the night, and only two glints of light behind her eyes were visible before the attacks began again.

She dashed through the air, claws extended in front of her, barreling towards him. He raised his blade and knocked away the claws at the last second. She flew off into the dark and every so often, lightning flashed and highlighted the parts of her body not covered by the tattered dress. She was a disappearing and reappearing ghost, and she used the dark to her advantage. Without the lightning, she was near invisible. Between the ambient flashes, she retreated into the darkness, only to hack and slash at him with near-invisible clawed hands as he flailed about madly with his bladed arm.

"Where are you?" he yelled in the dark.

"Over here…" her voice drifted to his ears from behind.

He whirled around and slashed blindly behind him.

"Pemazu, light."

She will begin her attacks beyond the reach of my glow, and it will only burn more energy, which, I should mention, is at critical levels, given how long you have used the sword.

"Then use a Pulse."

If I do, we will walk the Thin Line.

"Do something!" he yelled in his own mind.

It is your turn to do something only you can do, Shaw. Release me.

A screech behind him made his heart jump as he slashed at the air again. Then searing pain shot down his spine as the demon's claws dug into his back, tearing through his leather armor and into his skin, before pulling away violently. He fell to his knees, unable to continue standing, the pain clouding his vision.

Goodbye, Shaw. Eternity on the Thin Line awaits us.

He fell to the ground in slow motion; his vision was only a blur of colors. The dark of night mixed with a flash of lightning. The vague outline of Avana, speeding towards him, like some apparition locked onto its prey. His mind warped her image before him, so instead of the clawed, smiling repulsive creature, it was his wife, with outstretched arms, begging for his embrace.

No. Avana was still trapped. This image was not really her. He saw through the pain for a final moment, at the thing that was once his wife. Mouth agape, teeth gnashing at the air, vicious hooked claws ready to rip his throat out. With his remaining strength, he lifted his bladed arm and angled it towards the oncoming demon.

"Do you always uphold your promises?" he asked Pemazu.

As well as any demon can, I suppose.

"What will happen to me?"

You will die, Pemazu said.

"You can free her from the demon?"

I will try.

"Then do it. I am willing to pay what I must for her, for everyone, even my life."

This began with a spell, end it with a spell.

"I'll see you on the other side."

He pushed himself up with his bladed-arm, and willed himself to stand tall, though he was dizzy and drained. With everything he could muster, he reached out to the well one last time and released the mental dams protecting the flow of energy. He opened it fully, and let the power consume him. With a mighty voice he cried out the spell infusing his words so they echoed throughout the land. He gave his final command to the demon.

"Doret-et-al! I am Prince Shaw Ostra, the Arbiter, the Ender!" Shaw breathed in a chest-full of air. "Pemazu the Black! I have read your name from the Book, and I release you. Hekda-los-du-atra!"

Another screech rang in his ears as the demon inside his wife realized what had happened. A great patch of darkness swirled out of the wounds in Shaw's back as he lay bleeding on the landing. It took shape against the white facade of the castle, like a shadowed pigment upon castle walls. Arms and legs burst from the darkness followed by four leathery wings and mighty legs. As the demon fell towards the landing, the wings beat against the air, flinging particles of dust as it hovered. A resounding boom shook the landing as the demon reached through the fabric of space itself and pulled a blade of crackling fire and twisting energy from a Gateway in midair.

The demon examined Shaw's lifeless body from above, noting that his arm was no longer bladed, and that the gems in his arm were barren and dark. It turned towards the pale figure at the end of the landing and spoke in a voice that was so deep, it rattled the stone itself.

"While I have no interest in the plight of humans, I do take an interest in the status of my own existence. The Arbiter and I have an arrangement, one which only he may fulfill. I speak to the woman holding the demon at bay; Shaw is dead and you need not hold back this demon any longer. Release it, and move on to the afterlife."

The demon spoke through the woman. "Avana won't release me. Argomancy is a peculiar thing, is it not? Her will holds on by a thread and I am unable to be released. It seems you will have to strike her down as well. Is that a problem for you? Do you and the Arbiter have an agreement?" The woman looked up, and white sphere's glowed behind her eyes.

"Your name is Pemazu. You are like me: powerful, one of the First. Together, we can set the course of a new world, a world in which our kind are not restricted to the Thin Line; a world where our existence has substance."

"I care not for our kind. Nor for being constrained to yet another plane of existence. There is not a place for our kind on this plane," Pemazu said.

Pemazu, unbound and released upon the world, gripped a blade as long as his own arms in both hands. Red flame dripped off the blade, dropping to the landing below, where the rain tried in vain to put out the fires. It ceased flapping its four wings, turned the blade downward and plummeted towards the landing. The force of the blade drove through the end of the landing before the flames around it engulfed the area in a single burst of heat so hot that the landing itself began to melt.

Pemazu sensed something behind him and turned towards the door leading back into the castle, which was now scattered about the landing in pieces, leaving the doorway gaping and outlined by torchlight. An old woman ran out onto the landing with four other men and made their way to Shaw's body, where they picked him up between them and ran back into the castle. The demon ignored them and withdrew his blade from the stone. He leapt into the air, with the assistance of its wings, heading towards the highest tower of the castle. It landed on the peak and used its hooked claws to dig into the stone, perching atop the castle like a bird of prey.

CHAPTER TWENTY-SIX

FAR BELOW THE LANDING, beyond the market on the other side of the barracks, a stubborn crowd of curious onlookers had gathered in the wake of the commotion. At first, intrigue kept them in place, but when the skies blackened and a storm came together above the castle in a matter of minutes, intrigue was closely followed by panic. For some, they had seen this type of storm before. They remembered that a storm of this type meant a demon had been released upon the world. They remembered. They remembered the destruction of Third City, and they remembered the events of the Great Betrayal. From the other side of the market, behind the barracks they watched.

When the sky blackened and a booming voice shook the castle, many memories were lifted from the deepest places, where horrors of great magnitude were stored. Many of these people returned to their homes to gather their loved ones. Others remained, prepared to bear witness to the cataclysmic event. One man, confused as to what was happening, took to the roof of his home with his two sons and held them close. He spoke to them softly, comforting them, and telling them to keep their eyes sharp, as he felt history was about to be made. He was right.

A colossal black being with four wings rose above the edge of the landing and drew a sword from a window in space. The sword erupted in flames before the creature tucked in its wings and dropped the full might of its body, the sword pointed down at the landing. The sword sunk through the frontal-half and poked through the rock below. The man and his children gasped as the tip of the blade cut through the edge of the landing and severed it from the castle itself, leaving a jarring nub of mismatched stone jutting out from the castle's once attractive facade. They saw the stone crumble and roll down the face of the castle before crashing onto the homes below. One of the boys noticed something falling amongst the stones. It almost looked like a woman.

As the crowd grew in the aftermath of the cascade of rock, voiced concerns became visible panic. From the pile of rubble, a geyser of red mist spewed into the air and coagulated. It became a shapeless mass, writhing and churning. Only when the mist had ceased coming forth did the mass begin to take shape. First, a torso of fibrous muscle formed in midair, followed by skeletal arms and legs. Tendons and tissue grew out of the creature's back to form a set of wings, which draped to the ground. Finally, a skeletal head formed, with void eyelets and a mouth agape with rows of teeth. Only after this creature had formed did the crowd begin to disperse. Some ran out of fear of the creature; others ran because they knew what it was. A second demon now walked on their plane. To those who knew, this was the end of everything. The creature hovered for a moment after the mist had settled, before unfolding its great wings and darting upwards in a streak of red and black. A hand reached out and gripped the father's shoulder, startling him so much that he released the boy's and wheeled around with his fists up.

"Easy now." A woman stood before him, hunched over and

cloaked. He could tell from her voice she was elderly. Half of her face was hidden in shadow by her cloak, but her wrinkled forehead was clearly visible. "Can you tell me what has happened?" she asked.

The father spoke with a slight waver in his voice as he clutched his two frightened boys. "Something fell from above, with the rock. Then there was a mist and a creature formed out of nothing. It had wings. It flew upwards to the landing. I think there is a demon amongst us once again."

The old woman did not respond. She raised a hand over her head and ground her finger and thumb together. Dark granules fell from her fingers like a pinch of blackened salt, and she was enveloped in a cloud of shadow. She leapt from rooftop to rooftop with incredible speed, eventually landing on the main road in moments, rather than attempting to climb down. She followed the road to the castle, running toward the landing. Several men in robes converged from alleyways and rooftops to follow her towards the castle.

Once they had regrouped inside, she took precious moments to show the mages who followed her how to cloak themselves in shadow and increase their speed tenfold. One by one, each mage carefully cast the spell, after being made aware of the energy that would be required to maintain it. In a single-file line, like a march of speedy ants, five shadows dashed through the castle as quickly as a fleeting thought, and together they arrived at the highest tower. Together they stood before a wooden door, which led to what was left of the landing. Once there, the old woman dropped her shadow, as did the others. As one, they raised their hands to the door which barred their way and cast a spell of destruction. The door was blown outward in a whirlwind of wood and metal. On the landing, the woman noticed a man lying in a pool of blood, which was slowly being washed away by the rain. Without waiting for the others, she rushed onto the landing, where she saw what she believed the villagers were talking about. A creature, with wings and scales, with a blade of pure darkness, stood at the crumbled edge of the landing. It withdrew the blade from the stone before leaping into the air and perching on the highest tower.

Sensing no ill intentions from the creature, she ran out onto the landing, motioning for the others to follow her. Together, they lifted the man amongst them and retreated into the castle. As they made it back inside, they carefully laid him on his back, and the old woman whispered to him.

"Hold on, Shaw, just hold on." She flipped him over onto his stomach to examine the wounds that were still bleeding. Ten deep gouges continued to bleed little ribbons of blood down his back. His tunic was shredded, and she used the remains of it to create makeshift bandages. After tying them off, she rolled him onto his back again to examine the wound on his shoulder. Though it was deeper and more threatening, the blood had already clotted around the skin where something had hooked into it and pulled it away. She listened closely for breathing and checked for a heartbeat. She began to cry silently as one of the mages pulled her away from his body.

"Ma'am, please; we can't stay here. The might of both creatures threatens the castle. Please, we will take his body, but you must come with us."

Sniffling and wiping tears on her sleeve, "No, I'll stay. One of those things killed my brother, and I'll see to its end."

"Ma'am, you can't possibly contend with these creatures."

"Demons...they are demons. I'll stay. Go, if you value your life. Given I have no need for mine anymore, with the King and my brother dead, I'll wait to see what they intend to do."

"Ma'am, we aren't leaving your side. Second City has retreated to the rear encampment, Stonehaven is evacuating, the King's Guard are either dead or worse. Even the soldiers have left to be with their families. Some have seen these creatures...err...demons before and remembered what happened to

Third City. There isn't a lot of hope. Without hope, there is no purpose. Whatever you have planned, we'd like to be a part of it. Many years ago, you trusted us with your knowledge of magic, and today we'd like to trust in you once more."

She was shocked at the courage of the men. She had only just met them on the battlefield, but as other soldiers had run, they had stayed at her side. Why?

"Why did you stay when others fled?"

"You give us hope, Ma'am. We don't know how Prince Shaw has returned from the dead, but we do know he has died, again alone, with no one but that demon on the landing. To us, this means he tried to fight it alone. Without hesitation you rushed towards the demon when others fled. For this, we share your cause."

She teared up, thankful that there were still some who supported the Royal Family and were willing to blindly follow her into the unknown.

"I fear it's too late, though I admire your courage and loyalty. However, Shaw is dead, and the demon..." She trailed off, noticing that Shaw's traveling pack hung off his shoulder by a single strap. She removed the pack and emptied its contents onto the floor. A white cloth bearing the Royal mark fell out first, followed by a flesh-colored metal-bound book. It clattered to the floor and the straps holding it unlatched. She jammed her hand down on its surface, holding it closed.

"Back away! Back away! Nobody look at it. Face the wall."

The mages complied, covering their eyes or looking away.

"What is it, ma'am?" one of them asked.

"A book of evil. Don't look at it. It can taint you from afar."

Unwilling to risk the truth of her statement, she kept her hand on it, but she felt her mind turning toward the possibilities. Perhaps the Book had something, anything, that could help her. Give her guidance or direction. Perhaps it could give her the purpose these mages thought she had. Truthfully, she had run up to the landing without expecting her brother to be alive and she definitely did not expect to find the Book unguarded. She feared the Book and its influence. She remembered what it had almost caused her to do in the past. She shuddered at the memory and refocused. Mustering just enough strength and courage to remove her hand was hard enough. To admit she needed its help was harder still.

She felt incomplete even though the King was dead. After thirty years of plotting to right his wrongs, now he was dead, leaving her without a purpose. The throne was now unoccupied, and no one would know of Shaw's valor in defeating him. From Shaw's sacrifice, the Kingdom would have the opportunity to regrow and unite, instead of being constantly under the thumb of the King's selfish cruelty. The nation could flourish now. It could move on. Though with these demons released and unbound, those visions of grandeur were quickly shattered. Perhaps she could bargain for a solution, just as Shaw did.

She had nothing left to lose. With that final thought empowering her, she removed her hand and flipped the Book open. The words *hello Princess* were already printed on the first page. It was waiting for her. She whispered to it, "Shaw is dead, the King is dead, and I don't care if you put those awful thoughts in my head again. I need answers."

The words smeared and distorted to form the word *ask* in the middle of the page.

How do I defeat the demons?

A moment's pause before the Book presented the words, *they are not your concern.*

"So you will let them destroy everything? This city? Second City? More?"

They are not your concern.

Frustrated she snapped at it. "Then what am I supposed to do?"

Take me to the rear guard.

"What?"

The words did not shift.

"Why?"

Take me to the rear guard. The words appeared a second time, then a third, then so many times the pages filled over and over again.

"Okay, fine. One final question. What happened to Shaw?"

He did as he was told. You cannot help him.

Though she expected her own tears to flow freely, she was surprised by the finality of the words on the page, and had a sense of relief flush over her. She was hoping that she was wrong, and that he was, in fact, not dead, or at least that he was not yet beyond magical reach, but the Book was firm. It had always been right; she felt no need to question it now. A part of her was actually happy to hear that Shaw had found peace. She snapped the Book shut, wrapped it in the protective cloth, and put it into her own pack.

She touched the mages one by one on their shoulders to notify them that it was safe to look and to move about. They gathered around her as she spoke.

"Our work here is done. We can't do anything about these demons. Go. Spread the word of what was done here today. Spread the word of Shaw's attempts to right the wrongs of his brother, the fallen King. Let all know what was done by those who are loyal to the Royal Family, the true Royal Family. Spread these words to all that you can, for I don't know who will survive these demons' onslaught on the Kingdom and elsewhere."

One by one, the mages embraced her or kissed her hand before departing in silence. Once they had all left, she took one final look at Shaw, examining the lifeless jewels in his arm, before casting a simple spell to shield his body from harm, and from view. Should the castle survive the demon's attack, she'd send a proper procession to escort his body to its final resting place. For now, she'd head to the rear guard as the Book had suggested.

With her heart heavier than ever before, she departed the chamber down the staircase and made her way to the outer wall of the castle. Upon exiting the tunnel, she looked up and beyond the walls to see the other demon, blood-red and flapping its wings, hovering above the castle, squaring off with the black one perched on the roof of the highest spire.

CHAPTER TWENTY-SEVEN

PEMAZU TAPPED his flame-bathed blade on the side of the castle a few times before skewering the roof of the tower while he stretched his wings. It had been quite some time since he'd been able to do so. As he did, a sort of shadowy dust traced the veins in the skin between the bones before dripping off and evaporating before they touched the ground. He was as prepared as he could be. Shaw was dead, but he intended to keep his promise to the man because, dead Arbiter or not, Shaw still had some power, as long as his soul hadn't moved on. Of course, none of this would matter if he couldn't destroy the demon that had pulled its way from the woman's body. He tucked his wings in before standing tall and stretching.

At least now Shaw would stop painfully pining for his wife and their souls could meet on the Thin Line. Pemazu had made the choice for the demon that had a stranglehold on the woman's soul. He destroyed her body when he collapsed the landing, releasing the demon to be free. That was enough for Pemazu to consider his end of the bargain complete, even if he did not manage to defeat the demon. He'd try, but if it proved to be too strong, to be more powerful than him, then he doubted if the Arbiter would uphold his end. Should he fail, die, and end up on the Thin Line without defeating the demon, he fully expected the Arbiter to move on, leaving him to wander for eternity. Should he defeat it, he was relying on the Arbiter to banish him, not because he had to, but because he wanted to. Either way, he had put his trust in a human. He had to deal with the consequences, and he had far more to lose as a result.

A gust of wind rattled the wooden slats of the roof and signaled that the demon below was on the move. Pemazu withdrew his sword from the roof and stretched his wings one final time. The sword burst into angry, writhing flames as he held it before him. He was as ready as he could be.

The demon's arrival was quite the spectacle. It rose above the remains of the landing, flapping its wings steadily to maintain its place in the air. The clouds had cleared, leaving the air warm and thick, and the early morning sun would have to work hard to dry up the storm from the night before. The demon looked up at him through the skull of whatever creature it was attempting to resemble. Only small sparks were visible in the pits of the eyes, but the amount of life in them was beyond that of mere sparks. He felt the rage, disdain, and hatred emanating from the demon, and its form reflected its emotions. It was red, like blood, covered in scales on its vital areas, such as its chest and neck, with fur on the rest. Its arms hung limp at its sides, long and thin, and the fur clung to them tightly.

Just as Pemazu had done, the demon reached into a rip in reality and drew one blade, then another. It held a blade in each hand, but unlike his own, they were not flame-ridden, and they were not broadswords. They were scimitars, with runes crawling along both sides of each blade. The runes lit up and then faded as they shifted positions. He read the Demonic runes and discovered the blades were spelled for speed and dexterity. He drew himself up to his full height and leapt from the tower, landing heavily on the remains of the landing, caving it in with his feet.

The titans squared off just as the sun broke the horizon, giving an unnerving amount of attention to creatures one would not expect to see in the daylight. The demons were obscure fixtures upon the landing, and people as far Second City's encampment took notice of the two winged figures. When they collided midair, and unholy blade met unholy blade, the concussions were felt as far as the castle walls. Tainted blades were accompanied by horrific vocalizations as each beast howled, screamed, growled, and grunted in voices deeper and louder than any human. Between the howls, blinding flashes of greens, reds and purples lit the shadowed skies as the demon's cast a variety of destructive spells at each other. The battle took to the sky and the demon's fought with swords, all the while trying to rip whatever body part they could off of their enemy. Whenever their blades collided, glass broke as demonic blade scraped and screeched on demonic blade. It was becoming more dangerous by the minute as neither demon seemed to care what was behind their spells. The city was taking a beating and beginning to crumble.

Those who might have considered waiting out the commotion in the confines of the city were easily dissuaded as stone fell, unnaturally hot fire rained down, and demonic voices flooded the air. The city was clearing out fast. Some vacated through the front gate, while others chose the exterior walls of the city, which contained passageways leading outside the castle walls. The city was being abandoned, just as Third City had been and the sheer concussion of their fists striking one another shook the foundations of the city. Those who remembered what had happened so many years ago warned others, and upon seeing the demons collide, they believed them and followed. Chaos above was inciting chaos below. All of which was, of course, no concern for the demons fighting; the world was their battlefield.

Pemazu gave two sturdy flaps of his wings and summoned a murder of crows to hide his ascent into the sky. He brought himself above the red demon, commanded the crows to attack as a swarm and then brought the entire weight of his broadsword on his foe as it struggled to see beyond the cloud of feathers and beaks. The red demon responded by bursting into violet flames to destroy the birds, then deflecting Pemazu's sword off to the side with its scimitars. It counterattacked with a wide, forward-arcing slash. Another beat of his wings and Pemazu was slung backward out of range of the blade.

He drew his sword back, gave a half spin, slung the blade around him in a whirlwind and let it go. It sung through the air, slinging flames. The red demon ducked under the blade and closed the distance between them before lunging with its scimitars, aiming for Pemazu's torso. He cast another spell, bringing the blade singing through the air again, caught it, and brought the hilt of his blade down on the red demon's arms. Before it could attack, Pemazu leaned back and planted a clawed foot in its chest, kicking with all his might. The red demon was pushed backward, hard, but it used its swords to carve deep grooves into the landing and slow its slide.

Pemazu used the opportunity gained from his attack to follow up with an overhead slash at the red demon's neck and shoulder. The demon pulled out of the slide and deflected the attack. It was quick, but not quick enough to avoid the sword. The blade came down on the demon's shoulder, cracking scales and peeling back flesh. Black blood spewed from the wound and onto the blade as it sunk deep enough to hit bone. The red demon howled in pain, opened its bone-clad mouth impossibly wide, and chomped on the shadow blade, shattering it. The flames died out as the top half of the sword clattered uselessly to the ground. Another boom echoed as the red demon balled its fist around the hilt of one of its blades and punched Pemazu in the face. He was dazed and thrown off balance, causing him to stumble.

The red demon leapt into the sky and hid in the wake of the sun.

Pemazu attempted to look for it, but the sun was blinding. He opened his wings and pumped them three times, sending himself hurtling backwards, but causing him to lose his footing in the process. He landed on his back, and in moments, the red demon was on top of him, and his sword, snapped in half, could no longer deflect both scimitars at once. He deflected one attack, but the second blade sunk through his torso and out of his back. Pemazu howled in agony, writhing, kicking, and lashing out with his broken sword at the red demon, but the flurry of attacks was relentless, as quick, precise strikes from the faster blades connected with every bit of his exposed flesh.

Though he struggled to defend himself, the red demon was too quick for him, and his sword had been broken. If he did not get up quickly, he knew he would die. The red demon lunged at him with its skeletal face, looking to end the fight by biting into him with its bone-clad head and razor teeth. Pemazu dragged his blade from his side and wedged the blade between its top and bottom jaw. The demon was not expecting the blade and it wriggled backward, attempting to pull the blade from its mouth. Pemazu propped himself up before leaping into the sky, his fragile, wounded wings barely able to keep him aloft. With the last feeble pumps of his wings, he managed to put himself above the red demon as it continued to struggle with the blade. He tucked his wings in and dropped the entire weight of his body on it, pummeling it into the landing. Once he was on top of it, it looked up at him with what he believed to be fear.

Pemazu gripped the broken-off end of the blade with one hand and the hilt with the other, twisting with all his might. He roared in anguish as the red demon drove a scimitar through his chest and sent searing pain throughout his body. Pemazu wrenched with all his might and flapped his wings powerfully, ripping the red demon's bony head from its body. With the red demon's head in his hands, Pemazu limped to the landing, drew the scimitar from his chest, roared in triumph, and then drank deeply from its skull before slinging the bleeding, lifeless head of the red demon off the edge.

He returned to the corpse in time to see a wisp of essence float up from its neck. Pemazu opened his mouth wide and sucked the essence in, restoring his energy and healing his wounds. He left the corpse on the landing and headed back towards the castle. As he walked with his wings tucked in behind him, his body began to shrink, and what was left of his sword disappeared into nothing. The twenty-foot tall demon now took the shape of a magpie with too many eyes, casually hopping its way to the entrance of the landing. Near the entryway, a bug tried in vain to burrow its way between the stones. The magpie excitedly hopped over and eyed it for a moment before furiously pecking at it to dislodge it from between the stones. Keeping a note of where it was, he gave up and entered the castle, where he found the lifeless body of a man, hidden from the average eye by a simple illusion spell. He eyed the corpse of the red demon one last time before ripping a hole in reality with his beak and casually hopping through, leaving one black feather on the man's corpse.

CHAPTER-TWENTY-EIGHT

After what seemed like a lifetime, Shaw did not awake, he simply *was*. He had clarity, and his clarity was pure, and untainted. He remembered the battle, releasing the demon Pemazu, and the feeling of his power leaving his body. He paid the cost of releasing the demon, and hoped on the other plane, the demon had kept its promise and defeated the red demon. He felt *different* in comparison to his other excursions to the Thin Line. He felt relieved, almost light-hearted. As if the worries of his life were a long time ago. He supposed they were. He took the moments to explore what he *could* feel. He felt his hand touching something. Something dull, and full. He turned his face and saw something he recognized from his past life. A beautiful woman, and she was holding his hand. He smiled at her, and she smiled at him, and together, there was no pain, only a sense of total completeness. He smiled at the woman, and in an instant the remaining memories came rushing back like a current.

Shaw blinked his eyes, smiled wider than before, and pulled his wife into his arms. They embraced each other and sometime later, finally let go, but they couldn't find themselves able to stay out of arms reach together. Then, they simply talked. They talked, smiled, and laughed together. Like time-lost friends finally coming together. They were so filled with love; the darker memories struggled to surface. But when they did, he held his wife tight, and they still talked. Another wave of memories and feelings hit him like the first waters from a flood; cold.

The Thin Line seemed different to Shaw now that he was here of his own accord. He felt significantly less lonely and more complete than ever, especially since his wife had joined him. She told him that she did not feel that he was responsible for her capture, or her death, or the deal with the demon that was once inside her. She told him that she had always loved him and that together, they would move on.

"The demon that was with you, Pemazu. What sort of deal did you make with him?" she asked.

"We had an arrangement," he clarified. "Though I was certainly not bound by my end. I had control of the demon, I promised him death; a true death that only I could give."

"Why is it only you could give him true death?"

"I am, or was, the Arbiter. The Balancer. The Ender. I was brought back from death by the Book to tip the scales of good and evil back into place. I wanted life, I wanted you, and the Book offered it to me. While I didn't make a deal with Pemazu, I made a deal with the Book."

"What did the Book ask you to do?"

"End the reign of the King, and, in turn, destroy the source of the Argomancy. It said I'd be able to save you in the process. It did not explain exactly *how* I'd save you."

"What do you mean? You were not bound to your deal with the demon? I thought all demon deals were binding agreements."

"My agreement was more out of pity, and it wasn't binding. The creature asked me to help it die, telling me that it was old and tired, and, unfortunately, only I was capable of killing it.

When demons die, they return here, but by my hand as the Arbiter, I can give them a true death. It seems the demon was like every other one of its kind, a liar by nature. I don't know where it is, and I don't know what happened after I released it."

"I didn't lie, it just took me longer than expected," a voice boomed from behind him.

Shaw whirled around, only to see more of the same drab existence of the Thin Line. A continual, endless path of gray, with tiny glowing stones and no ambient sound. The Thin Line was nothingness. Shaw felt something land on his shoulder, and he reached up to grab it before looking. Something sharp jabbed his thumb, and he pulled his hand away, only to have a magpie flutter in front of him, then land on Avana's shoulder.

"Pemazu?"

"Of course," he boomed. It was jarring to hear such a loud noise from such a tiny animal.

"But I'm dead, and if you're here, that means you are too."

"Until you have moved on, you will always be the Arbiter. And no, I am not dead. I have a great deal of power now that you have released me."

"I suppose you are here to torture us? Drive us mad with your undying sarcasm?" he asked.

"I had considered it, but I am here so that you may uphold your end of our little bargain," Pemazu said.

"I half-expected you to join forces with the other demon."

"I think it expected me to as well. But I am here, speaking to you," the bird fluffed up.

"I suppose it will destroy the Kingdom and the rest of the world now."

"Doubtful, considering I removed its head and consumed its essence. It is not alive, nor dead. It is within me. We are one."

"I didn't know you could do that."

"Neither did I, but I am one of the First, and the red demon is a part of me now," he said.

"Why didn't you tell me you were one of the First?"

The bird shrugged and winked one of its extra eyes. "Would it have mattered?"

"Why did you fight it? After all, you could have simply told me it was gone and returned here to collect."

"Indeed; but I am old, Arbiter, and wiser than most, I like to believe. Contrary to what you may believe about us, evil thoughts and deeds are inherent to our kind, but they are a choice."

"That, I don't believe. You expect me to accept your kind *chooses* to be evil?" Shaw asked.

"Believe what you want. It's our nature, but it's still a choice. Like hunger, the feeling is there, but to eat is a choice." The bird shrugged and picked at a string on Avana's dress.

"What now?"

"Well, after you banish me, I fully expect you and this woman to move on."

Shaw was once again startled by something brushing up against him. He saw a mess of black hair from the corner of his eye. A little boy stood next to him. At first, he believed it was Cereal, and was sad to think that the boy hadn't made it. But, to his dismay, the boy looked up at him with deep black pits for eyes and tiny jagged teeth.

"Hello, Arbiter."

Shaw growled. "I have completed your tasks, despite your disbelief and mistrust. Yet here I am, dead."

"Indeed. I promised you that you would return to life, but I never stated you would keep it. Hello, Pemazu."

The bird gagged, hacked and hung upside down by one leg from Avana's dress.

"It worked in his own favor that Pemazu managed to end the other demon's tirade. If he would have failed, I would have left him wander the Thin Line for eternity. A fate worse than death, for those who wish to die."

"What do you want? The red demon is dead. I'm dead. Avana is dead. Pemazu will soon be. Why else would you continue to pester us?"

"Defiance and disrespect are two of your finer qualities, Arbiter. You have a final task. *You* must move on."

"I have time on my side now, and I have an arrangement with Pemazu."

"Not entirely on your side. Stay in this place any longer, and you will soon find creatures such as Pemazu eagerly hunting your essence. Leave Pemazu for me to handle. Look down, Shaw; your task is done."

As if an unseen set of hands were wrapped tightly around his neck and head, Shaw felt his head tilt downward, and he snapped his eyes shut. The hands squeezed tighter, and he felt invisible tendrils groping at his eyelids, attempting to force them open by digging between them.

The bird hopped off the woman's shoulder, attempting to flee but the boy spoke first. "Stay, Pemazu, and let us get a glimpse of what you really look like."

The bird twitched and rolled off of Avana's shoulder. She stepped away as it began to expand from a bird into an amorphous blob. The blob was dark and feathery at first, and then it sprouted multiple tendrils, eyes, and mouths. It smacked its tendrils against the ground of the Thin Line in what she thought was anger, and maybe a little embarrassment.

The fingers continued to pry at Shaw's eyes as he did everything he could to keep them shut. He brought his hands over his face and clamped down on it. Avana cried and screamed, "Please, please let-"

The boy cocked his head. "I have a task for you."

"A what?"

"A task, a deal, if you will. I know you are very fond of deals." The boy smiled mischievously, and a chunk of flesh fell off his cheek.

"Why do you want him to look down? I know of this place, and I know that nothingness awaits him, should he open his eyes."

"You are correct, to a point. But I need to offer you a task, and persuasion is by far the most efficient way to elicit the response I want."

"Just stop. Leave him be. I'll do whatever you want," she said.

"No, Avana, don't listen to it. Argh!" The tendrils pried away Shaw's hands and began to work again on his eyelids.

"Tell me my task."

The boy smiled and looked up at her. "The Argomancy may be in the past, but I have work that still needs to be done. Given that my last Arbiter is indisposed...I need a new one."

"You want me to be your Arbiter? Why me?"

"Because your soul is in one piece, and Shaw's is, well, a bit mangled. Salvageable enough to move on but mangled. It's what happens when you rely on magic as much as he has. Be my Arbiter, return to life, and I'll let his soul move on. Once you have completed my tasks, you will be with him forever."

"And if I say no?"

The boy lifted a hand and Shaw yelled out as his eyes were forced open a hair.

She felt as if she was crying, but no tears ran down her face. "I'll do it! Leave him be!"

The boy looked surprised but satisfied. "Excellent. Stand up, Shaw." The boy looked at him, and he stood up straight, but brought his hands to his eyes, just in case he was forced down again.

"Avana, don't do this. I'll be okay," Shaw said.

"No, my love. I can't be with you in life, but I can be with you for eternity in death." She turned to face the boy again. "I'll be your Arbiter."

"Excellent. You may say goodbye, Shaw." The boy turned

away and examined the squid-like demon as it pounded its tentacles in defiance.

With silent tears streaming down his face from behind his hands, he felt his wife press her body against his. Her soft hands pulled his away from his face, and he looked into her eyes. He longed for her so much, and now that they were finally together, they'd once again be separated.

"I won't forget you," Shaw whispered.

"I surely hope not. I'll see you soon, darling."

"I love you, Avana."

"I love you, Shaw."

Shaw pulled away from her embrace and looked at the boy. He paused for a moment, before the boy raised a hand and pointed upward. Shaw closed his eyes before tilting his head back and looking upward and opening them again to a visage no living person had ever seen. He saw that the bleakness of the Thin Line ended abruptly as it reached toward the sky, though it hadn't been visible when looking forward. The darkness exploded into heavenly stars, wrapped in glorious light. It was so bright, yet the Thin Line was almost void of light. This beautiful place was just a moment's glance upward. He took it all in as he felt the weight of sorrow, sadness, and grief lifted. Without the weight, he felt as though he was flying. He felt his body lift high up off the ground before drifting towards one of the brightest stars in one of the most faraway places.

Shaw vanished before Avana's eyes, and she was left gripping nothing. Unseen tendrils crept up her back and onto her head, locking them in a vice-like grip.

"I do not need you attempting to join him prematurely," the boy said. "You know, only your kind sees anything when they look up. Others, well, they just take a shortcut to the Void."

"I don't care. I expect to be with Shaw soon. I hope the task you have for me is short."

"It can be, but that depends on you," the boy said.

"Whatever. What do you want from me?"

"First things first - every Arbiter must bind a demon. Luckily, we have one readily available, and a powerful one at that."

The boy turned toward the beastly pile of tentacles and teeth, which responded with a rude gesture. The boy smiled, and the demon crossed its tentacles in what Avana would describe as the equivalent of a child sulking.

She sighed. "Pemazu, let's make this quick, shall we? Your bargain with my husband still stands."

Finally, she turned to the boy and met her eyes with the bottomless black holes that were his eyes. She stared into the emptiness and asked, "What do you need?"

"Cereal. Help me find him."

Continue the story with The Queen of Duska - Available from Amazon and on Kindle Unlimited.

THE QUEEN OF DUSKA

THE DEMONIC COMPENDIUM BOOK 2

THE ROYAL FAMILY has felt the pain of death many times over.

Newly appointed Queen Avana struggles to hold the very fabric of her kingdom together.

She yearns for the days of harmony — the days when her husband, the fallen prince, was by her side. The days when demons were but a legend...

But rest is a luxury even the queen can't afford, and her mistakes weight heavily on her heart.

Assassins.

Civil war.

Treachery.

Every day, another troubling matter tugs at her attention, distracting her from the real threat that lurks in the shadows.

Whispers of an ancient evil drift through the castle, melding with the backhanded plans of those who want to see her fail, and the country burn.

The pieces are in place. War is imminent.

Queen Avana is prepared to fight to save her people, but will her greatest efforts be enough?

Continue the story with The Queen of Duska - Available from Amazon and on Kindle Unlimited.

Building a relationship with my readers is the very best thing about writing. I send newsletters with details on new releases, writer-life, deals and other bits of news related to my books. And if you sign up to my mailing list I'll send you something I think you'll like, my terrifying novella, *Peel*.

Tell me where to send the book by visiting www.davidviergutz.com/freebooks

HOW YOU CAN HELP

Did you enjoy this book? You can make a big difference.

Reviews are the most powerful tools I utilize for gathering attention for my books. As much as I wish I could, I can't load the newspaper with massive ads or slam the subway with posters.

At least, not yet.

But I *do* have something more effective than that and it's something major NYC publishers wished they could get their hands on ...

My committed and loyal cohort of readers.

Honest reviews of my books help other readers to know what to expect.

If you enjoyed this book, I would be eternally grateful if you could take a few minutes of your time to leave a review. (It can be as long or as short as you'd like)

Thank you!

DAVID'S CATALOGUE

To see an entire list of my titles, simply head on over to www. davidviergutz.com

I write a lot of books and my catalogue has grown too large to list them all here. I write in many shades of horror from dark fantasy to pure terror. Head to my website to check out the covers, read the blurbs, and start your next fear-filled adventure.

ABOUT DAVID VIERGUTZ

Disabled Army veteran, law enforcement veteran, husband, and proud father, David Viergutz is an author of stories from every flavor of horror.

Take the plunge into David's imagination as he delivers chill-bringing adventures where the good guy doesn't always win. David remembers dragging a backpack full of books to class, beginning in middle school, and leaving his textbooks behind.

David takes his inspiration from the greats and fell in love with complex universes from the desks of Nix, Tolkien, King, Stroud, and Lovecraft, to name a few. David's imagination, combined with his experience in uniform, gives his books an edge when it comes to the spooky and unnerving.

One day, David's wife sat him down and gave him the confidence to start putting his imagination on paper. From then on out, David's creativity has no longer been stifled by self-doubt and he continues to write with a smile on his face in a dark, candlelit room.

"Things can always get worse." - David Viergutz

amazon.com/David-Viergutz/e/B07WNDZGC1
facebook.com/authordavidviergutz
bookbub.com/profile/david-viergutz
goodreads.com/authordavidviergutz

DEDICATION

To my first fans and supporters.

This journey is but one I have taken up and you have been with me on every step of the way. Thank you for being who you are. Thank you for doing what you do. Thank you for loving me how you do.